# STORIES
## of THE
# *wild*
# WEST
# GANG

# JOY COWLEY
# STORIES
## of THE
# *wild*
# WEST
# GANG

*with illustrations by*
TREVOR PYE

GECKO PRESS

*For John and Ruth McIntyre*
*who encourage the love of reading,*
*in kids old and young*
♥

First American edition published in 2012 by Gecko Press USA, an
imprint of Gecko Press Ltd.

A catalog record for this book is available from the US Library of
Congress.

Distributed in the United States and Canada by
Lerner Publishing Group, Inc.
241 First Avenue North
Minneapolis, MN 55401 USA
www.lernerbooks.com

This collection first published in 2011 by Gecko Press
PO Box 9335, Marion Square, Wellington 6141, New Zealand
info@geckopress.com

Designed by Catherine Griffiths, Wellington, New Zealand
with typefaces Dala Floda, Verlag and Feijoa
Printed by Everbest, China

ISBN hardback: 978-1-877579-21-9

For more curiously good books, visit www.geckopress.com

Gecko Press acknowledges the generous support of

ARTS COUNCIL OF NEW ZEALAND TOI AOTEAROA

# The
# Wild West Gang
# *and the Raft*

## 1.

Mom said she nearly died. That wasn't true. But it was a shock for her. She and her sister didn't get along, and here was Auntie Rosie West, Uncle Leo West and the five West children moving in just a street away.

"They'll be around here every minute of the day," she moaned to Dad.

"Hide the goldfish," said Dad. He was remembering last Christmas when the baby tried to wash her dirty diaper in the goldfish bowl.

"They'll want to sit with us in church!" Mom cried. "It's not just those kids. Rose forgets to brush her own hair. She goes to church in old jeans and with safety pins in her jacket. Leo's always got food down his shirt."

Then Mom saw that I was listening. She said quickly to Dad, "I'm not judging them. Rose and Leo are very kind. They'd do anything for anyone. I'm just saying they're not strong on tidiness and good manners." She looked hard at me. "We don't ever say anything to hurt them. We just leave them to get on with their lives. Do you understand, Michael?"

I nodded, but inside I was jumping up and down and laughing. Wow! The Wests were coming! There was my cousin Royce who had orange hair and freckles, could crack his knuckles, invent things, and whistle between his fingers like a shepherd. Then there was Miranda, my age, with more red hair and freckles. She could do a double backward flip and walk on her hands, as well as play the guitar and yodel. The twins, Johnny and Jeannie, were seven. They had brown hair and dark eyes like Auntie Rosie. Johnny danced. He was learning ballet. He had a set of real carpenter's tools. Jeannie could swallow air and do huge belches. She had a mouse farm that took up nearly half her bedroom. I didn't know the baby's real name. Everyone called her Honey. She was two years old and she had red hair but a lighter color than the others. She also had six toes on each foot. Auntie Rosie said that showed she was extra special. All angels have six toes, said Auntie Rosie.

The Wests were moving into a big old house with a backyard full of trees. I couldn't wait! The laugh inside me must have crept out onto my face because Mom was looking at me, her eyes all sharp.

"Michael, I don't want you rushing over there. Auntie Rosie's got enough to look after without you as well."

"I could help her!" I said.

Mom looked at Dad. He straightened the knot on his tie and said, "There will be times when you can visit, son. They are family, after all. But you don't go without your mother's permission. Is that clear?"

I nodded several times. It was always good to nod. It made them happy. "Yes, Dad."

"That's my man," said Dad. "As you get older, you will understand," Dad said. "The Wests are—are—"

"Different," said Mom.

"Yes, different," said Dad. "Different lifestyle, different values."

I kept on nodding. The Wests were different, all right. And more than anything else in the world, I wanted to be like them.

# 2.

I heard Mom and Dad talking in their bedroom.

"He's such a sensible boy," said Mom. "I don't think it would do any harm."

"They're happy to have him," said Dad.

"We don't get many chances to get away for the weekend," Mom added.

I got ready with my smile and my nod, and sure enough, less than a minute and they were at the door of my room.

"Michael," said Mom, "your father and I have a chance to go on a golfing tournament next weekend. We wondered how you'd feel—"

"It won't be like this place," said Dad. "You may find it quite—"

"Different," said Mom. "But it's only for two days."

"We would really appreciate it, old man," Dad said.

"Appreciate what?" I asked.

"Staying with the Wests," said Mom, not looking at me.

My nod got a bit slower. It was important I did this right. I waited a while and said, "How long?"

"From Friday night to Sunday afternoon," said Dad.

I thought about it. "All right, I'll do it." I gave them a small, lost smile. "But I'll miss you."

Dad reached into his back pocket and started counting out dollars. "You might want to get a movie."

"They don't have a TV," said Mom.

"Well, you could go to a movie with—whatshisname?"

"Royce," Mom said. "Michael, you won't forget your allergy medicine, will you? Brush your teeth. Eat your greens. No sugar or butter. Tell Auntie Rosie you have to be asleep by nine o'clock. You'll take your own pillow with you." I nodded until my head was ready to drop off and thanked Dad for the money. Fantasmo! Enough for a bucketful of jelly beans, licorice whips, salt and vinegar chips, chocolate bars, and gumdrops. My cousins' favorites!

When they went downstairs I lay back on my bed and kicked my feet in the air. There were a few good things about being an only child and having my own phone by my bed was one of them. I picked it up and dialed the Wests. Uncle Leo answered. "Hullo, this is the city morgue."

"It's me," I said. "Uncle Leo, it worked!"

"You're coming for the weekend?" he said. "Good sausage! I'll tell the vampires to sharpen their teeth, so I will." He yelled away from the phone. "Rosie? Put on your crash helmet and hide the family jewels. Mickey's on his way!"

# 3.

Uncle Leo and Auntie Rosie were always joking but in different ways. Auntie Rosie had a way of saying terrible things to her children but in a friendly sort of voice. Like the time Miranda let the sink overflow. "May the fleas of a thousand dogs bite your bottom," Auntie Rosie said.

Miranda saw my face. "She doesn't mean it."

"Oh yes, I do," said Auntie Rosie. "You wait and see, young Mickey. Nothing is worse than a Rosie curse."

After that, I waited for her to say something funny and terrible to me, but she never did.

When she saw me standing at the back door, she pulled me in, gave me a fat hug and got flour on my face from her apron. "Mickey, darling, this is a lovely treat for us!"

Uncle Leo was kneeling on the kitchen floor, mending the lawnmower. Johnny was helping him. The other kids were in the front room. I could tell from the noise.

"So we did it, did we?" said Uncle Leo with a grin. His red hair was curly and long round his ears and neck. He really suited his name.

I didn't have to nod. I stood there, grinning.

"You can sleep in my room," said Johnny. "I won't grind my teeth."

"You've got to sleep in everyone's room," said Uncle Leo. "Change every two hours. And that includes the dog kennel. They'll all die of grief if you don't."

Auntie Rosie was back at the counter, stirring in a bowl. She pointed her floury wooden spoon at Uncle Leo. "And you'll die of a bad dose of scheming, Leo West."

"Who me?" said Uncle Leo, his eyes open wide. "All I did was tell the president of the golf club that Mickey's Mom and dad would surely like a personal invitation to the tournament. Now tell me, Mickey, is that scheming or is that simple human kindness?"

"Don't confuse him with your blarney," said Auntie Rosie. "You know it was nothing more than scheming, and it was a wonderful idea. Mickey, you're sleeping with Royce." She put her head back and yelled, "Miranda? Royce? Jeannie?"

The noise went on in the front room.

She bellowed again, "Come here at once, or I'll tie your heads together!"

No one came and the noise did not stop.

Auntie Rosie took a deep breath. "Mickey is here!"

That worked. They came running. Jeannie with her arms outstretched for the first hug, Miranda, Royce, and then Honey, squealing, "Mitty! Mitty! Mitty!"

I couldn't breathe, partly because I was excited and partly because they were all on top of me.

"Take Mickey's bag into Royce's room and come straight back," said Auntie Rosie, tipping a ball of dough out of the bowl. "It's celebration time. We're having pizza, and if you scrub your filthy paws, you can do your own toppings." She looked down at the lawnmower bits spread over the floor. "For Leo and Johnny, I take orders," she added.

At last I had a chance to say something. "Auntie Rosie? Uncle Leo? Thank you for having me. I hope I won't be too much trouble."

"Trouble?" Auntie Rosie put her hands on her hips and stared at me. "Mickey, darling, this family invented trouble. We've got a copyright on the word." Then she put her arms round me for another of her fat hugs. "Bless you, angel boy, I only wish we could have you every weekend."

I kind of liked Auntie Rosie's hugs, but I still wished she would say something terrible and funny to me.

# 4.

They had a black and white terrier called Goof and two cats, Pooh and Frodo. The cats couldn't go in Jeannie's room because of her mice, and Goof couldn't go in Royce's room because there was a dead rabbit in there. Neither Goof nor the cats were allowed in Uncle Leo's and Auntie Rosie's room because Uncle Leo had his home brew at the end of the bed, wrapped in an electric blanket to help it ferment. The cats couldn't go in Miranda's room either. Sometimes they wet on her sheepskin rugs. It was hard to remember which doors had to be kept closed.

Royce's bedroom was directly above the laundry room. In the floor beside his bed, he had cut a hole as big as a basketball. The laundry hole, he called it. If he lay on the floor with his arm through the hole, he could toss his dirty clothes sideways into the basket by the washing machine.

"When you get out of bed, don't step in it," he said.

I looked down the hole and saw the white top of the washing machine. "I'll try not to," I said.

Royce had a huge room with a spare bed in it, a chest of drawers, three cupboards, and plenty of space for his things. There were posters on the walls, the skull of a sheep, some photos of his family, and a formula for making stink bombs. I didn't know why he wanted to make stink bombs. He was doing well with the dead rabbit he'd found on the road. He was going to skin it, he said, just as soon as he found out how. In the meantime, he'd leave the window wide open.

I lay back, my hands under my head, and yawned. I'd forgotten to brush my teeth or take my medicine but it was too late for that. Nearly midnight. We'd played cards all evening. At first it had been a pain because they'd all cheated. Then they showed me how to cheat and I won three games. At eleven o'clock, we ate the rest of the pizza for supper. Now my stomach was so full I couldn't lie on it.

"What'll we do tomorrow?" I asked Royce.

"Can you swim?" He was lying on his back, too. I could see the outline of his curly hair and sharp nose.

"Of course."

"I've been thinking of building a raft," he said. "We'll have to hunt around for gear. You know, bits of wood, rope, a couple of drums to float it. We could go down the river."

I said, "Dad gave me some money. I'll get some chocolate and stuff to take along."

Royce got up on one elbow. "How much?"

"Ten dollars."

"Ten whole dollars!"

"Yes."

"You were going to spend ten whole dollars on chocolate?"

I had forgotten that the Wests didn't have much money. "Or anything else," I said quickly.

"Wowee! That'll get us a couple of old tire tubes from the garage. Better than drums. We can tie the wood to the tubes and put a rudder between them. It'd be brilliant!"

"Fantasmo!" I said, yawning again.

He went on talking, but I must have fallen asleep because when I opened my eyes again, he was silent. The whole house was silent. No, not quite. When I really listened, I could hear soft noises coming through the walls: breathing, little snores, mumbles, rustling sounds and, once, the dog scratching itself. I turned over and saw a round yellow light shining up from the floor. I blinked at it. Why was there a light in the laundry room at this time of night? Then I realized Auntie Rosie had turned it on to stop me putting my foot in the hole.

# 5.

I woke up at about ten o'clock with the washing machine chugging like a train on the other side of the laundry hole. There were other sounds, too—the mower cutting the lawn, someone playing a guitar, the radio gabbling, and lots of voices downstairs.

Auntie Rosie was sitting in the kitchen, her feet up on another chair, reading the newspaper. She was wearing floppy shorts and a big T-shirt with one of the kids' paintings on it. Honey was kneeling on a chair beside her, spreading peanut butter, honey, and jam over half a loaf of bread. Johnny was at the counter making toast and Royce was eating cornflakes. The table and counter were covered with crumbs and puddles of milk, but not the floor. Goof was running round like a vacuum cleaner.

"Help yourself, Mickey darling." Auntie Rosie waved her hand round the kitchen. "If you can't find anything, ask Royce."

Cornflakes seemed easiest. I said to Royce, "There are blowflies in your bedroom."

He shrugged.

"I think they're after the rabbit."

"Yeah, yeah," he said. "I will skin it. Let's do the raft first."

"If you leave it long enough," said Auntie Rosie, "it'll skin itself."

"I'll do it!" said Royce. "Honest! But Mom, we've got to build a raft and get it down to the river. We've got it all planned."

Johnny sat up straight, "I'll help!"

At once, Jeannie came running into the room, yelling, "You're going to make a raft? Wicked, man!"

"Just me and Mickey!" said Royce. "No one else!"

That started a big argument. Miranda walked in, her guitar slung round her neck and said that no raft was going down the river without her. Honey slapped her hand up and down on her sticky bread, screaming, "Me too! Me too!" In a moment, everyone was yelling, no one listening.

"Shut up!" bellowed Auntie Rosie. She put down her paper. "Any more fighting and you will all spend the day digging the garden—with your mouths! Royce, you'd better work this out. If you and Mickey do this by yourselves, you've got a war on your hands. If everyone helps, you might have chaos but it won't be war. Your choice."

"I really don't mind who helps," I said, hoping Royce would take Miranda, too.

Royce had made up his mind. "Me and Mickey are doing this," he said.

"Mickey and I," corrected Auntie Rosie.

"The other kids can do something else," he said. "Hurry up, Mickey."

I gobbled my cornflakes, looking at the others over my plate. Miranda, Johnny and Jeannie were giving us hard looks. There was a dark planning in their faces. I wished that Auntie Rosie hadn't mentioned the word war.

I gave Royce the ten dollars, and we ran to the garage on the corner of Main Street. It was a big place, busy on a Saturday morning, and I hung back to let Royce do the talking.

He walked right up to a man in an orange jacket who was washing the windshield of a car. He said to him, "I can take some of those old tubes off your hands."

"What tubes?" said the man.

"You know, those old patched inner tubes. No good for anything."

"Who says?" growled the man, flicking the wipers out to clean behind them.

"You can't use them in tires. They're dangerous. And you can't burn them. That's environmental pollution."

"Listen, kid," said the man. "Put an egg in your shoe and beat it."

"I'm a customer!" said Royce.

"Oh yeah?" The man looked at him for the first time. "You're one of the West kids, aren't you. I suppose you want something for nothing."

Royce was as cool as a popsicle. He walked round the car, looking at it, kicking its tires. Then he came back to the man. "I told you, I want to buy two old inner tubes."

"How much?" the man said.

"I'll give you a dollar each as long as all the holes are patched."

The man snapped back the windshield wipers. "Don't waste my time."

"What else would you do with them?" Royce pleaded. "Okay, two dollars each."

"I'm busy! Didn't you get the message?" The man turned to walk away.

"Three," said Royce, following him. "That's my final offer."

I reckon the man sold him the tubes to get rid of him.

Royce came out dragging two flat black donuts and grinning from ear to ear. As we filled them from the free air hose, he told me what a bargain we had. "You know, Mickey, the guys who do river tube rafting pay ten bucks each for these. Ten each! We got two for six!"

"What about my change?" I said.

"Change?" The air hissed into a tube and it sprang out fat, shining black, with bumps of patches on it like scabs. "But you expected to pay ten bucks for them, didn't you?"

I didn't answer.

Royce sighed and reached for the back pocket of his jeans. "Okay. We'll go halves in the change."

We rolled the tubes down the edge of the road. Royce was full of plans. "The planks and the rope are stashed away in our woodshed. I'll whizz home and get them. They won't see me. You have to stay with the tubes."

"Where?"

"I've been thinking about that. I was going to build it by the river near our place. But that's where Miranda and the twins think they'll find us. So we'll go where the river loops round by the park. There are lots of trees there. Okay?"

"Okay."

"I reckon we'll be launching the raft before lunch. By this afternoon, we'll be away down the river, halfway between here and the sea."

"How will we get back?" I asked.

He hadn't thought of that. He rubbed the back of his neck. "I'll ask Dad to meet us in the car."

"But how will he know where we'll be?"

"Mickey, you're always worrying about things," he said. "Do you think Thor Heyerdahl would have sailed a balsa wood raft clear across the Pacific if he was a worrier? Come on, race you to the park."

We ran as fast as we could, rolling our tubes. I didn't like to tell him that my tube was getting softer by the minute.

# 6.

We didn't get to the river that afternoon. The big black donuts hissed under their patches, sagged, squished, and collapsed before we could get near the park. We dragged them back to the Wests' house.

Royce reckoned the garage man was an outright crook taking advantage of a couple of kids. Uncle Leo said we got what we paid for. The tubes were laid out on the half-cut lawn while Jeannie filled Honey's swimming pool with the hose, and Uncle Leo hunted through boxes in the garage for his repair kit and the pump.

I thought the other kids would say ha, ha, serves you right, but they were all on Royce's side against the man at the garage.

"He's so mean, I bet he recycles his toilet paper," said Miranda, and they all rolled about laughing.

"So mean he steals bread from bird-feeders," said Jeannie.

"He sends back old Christmas cards," added Johnny.

"He cleans his teeth and his nails and the sink with the same brush!" Royce said.

They went on like this until Uncle Leo came back, then everyone shook off the laughter and got ready to help with fixing the leaks. Even the cats, Pooh and Frodo, and old Goof the dog poked their noses in.

When the tubes were filled with air and held down in

Honey's swimming pool, we could see bubbles rising like silver chains from the edges of some of the patches. Uncle Leo shook his head at Royce. "I don't like the look of this, my little leprechaun. Patching a tube is one thing. Patching a patch is a bird of an entirely different species. But never let it be said that a West gave in with the blow of a feather. We'll see what can be done."

Mending the tubes took all afternoon. Uncle Leo was right. Putting a patch over a patch and making an airtight seal wasn't easy. The edge of the first patch would make a ridge that let the air leak out.

About four o'clock, Auntie Rosie came out with glasses of lemonade and banana cake. She said to Royce, "That rabbit in your room stinks."

"I know, I know." He was helping his father hold down a patch.

"The flies have been at it."

"Mom, I am going to skin it. I told you. As soon as I get time."

She put her hands on her hips. "I'm throwing it out, Royce."

"No!" He looked at her. "Mom, you promised you wouldn't touch anything in my room!"

"Okay, so I break promises," said Auntie Rosie.

"You wouldn't!" he yelled.

"Then do something about it. I warn you. I'll hang it round your neck and you'll have maggots dropping down your shirt." She said it in that light, laughing voice.

Royce laughed back at her.

I looked in my glass. "Auntie Rosie, this lemonade is full of seeds."

She smiled at me. "So what would lemons have? Peapods?"

"My mother always strains out the seeds," I said.

There was a flicker in her eyes and for a moment I thought she was going to say something wonderfully funny and terrible. But she just gave me another smile and said, "Mickey, if you didn't have any seeds in lemonade, what would you spit?"

# 7.

The rabbit lay on the dressing table, its eyes glazed over and little white maggots wriggling in the fur round its mouth.

"It smells like fart," said Royce. "I should do something about it tonight."

But he didn't. And when we had been in the room for a while, we got used to the smell.

Royce was drawing pictures of the raft we were going to build in the morning. I thought the plans were a bit grand, but I didn't say anything. Royce's inventions were interesting but they didn't always work out.

"The tubes are good and strong now," he said. "I reckon they'll be safe enough for the little kids to have a turn." He looked at me. "They really want to come."

"Okay," I said. "Good."

"The tubes will hold us. I don't want you to worry about it."

"I'm not worrying," I said.

"You are. You're frowning."

"I am not. I'm just concentrating."

"You're always worrying," he said.

"Not!"

It was Uncle Leo who stopped the argument. He called up the stairs, "Mickey? It's your mother on the phone. Better rattle your chains. I just told her we put you in slavery and we're working you to death."

I ran down the stairs and grabbed the phone, warm from Uncle Leo's breath. "He didn't, Mom. I mean, they haven't been making me work."

"Michael, what on earth are you talking about?" said Mom.

I looked at Uncle Leo's grinning face and then relaxed. "Oh, nothing. How are you, Mom?"

"Very well, thank you, Michael. Your father had a very pleasant day on the golf course and now we're going out to dinner. Are you all right, Michael? I realize you can't talk, but can you answer yes or no?"

"Yes, Mom."

"Are you managing at Auntie Rose's?"

"Yes, Mom."

"Are you eating well? Lots of fruits and vegetables? Are you taking your medicine and going to bed on time? Not forgetting to brush your teeth?"

"Yes, Mom."

"You're not homesick, are you?"

"No, Mom!" I said it too quickly and there was a funny little silence at the other end. "Well, sort of," I added.

"It's only until tomorrow afternoon," she said. "We'll pick you up about four o'clock. I have to go now, Michael. The car has arrived to take us to dinner. What's that noise?"

"That's our dinner."

"Your dinner?"

"Auntie Rosie bangs a saucepan to let us know it's ready."

"Oh. Well, be good, Michael. It's not for long. Tomorrow

you'll be back home in your own nice room."

I put the phone down. For dinner there was macaroni and cheese and salad. None of us liked macaroni and cheese, but Auntie Rosie had put a face on top of it: curly hair made of spaghetti and tomato sauce, mashed potato nose, olive eyes and sliced red pepper for a mouth. It looked like Uncle Leo.

Auntie Rosie said that she'd also put two dollars of coins in the macaroni and cheese but that wasn't true. When we got sick of looking, we left the stuff on our plates.

"It's gruesome!" said Miranda, who was reading a book at the table.

"Absolutely foul," muttered Johnny.

Honey spat into her bowl.

Auntie Rosie shrugged. Uncle Leo looked at her and then said to the rest of us, "The cook thanks you for your compliments and regrets that the homemade chocolate ice cream is not now available."

Miranda dropped her book. "You didn't tell us you were making ice cream!"

We picked up our forks and ate the macaroni and cheese in record time. Royce ran to the freezer, yanked open the door, and peered into trails of steam. "Where is it?"

Auntie Rosie turned. "I didn't say there was chocolate ice cream."

"I didn't either," said Uncle Leo. "In fact, I recall saying it was not available."

There were howls around the table and Jeannie yelled, "You mean, rotten parents! I'm going to divorce both of you!"

Auntie Rosie laughed. "But there is the rest of the carrot cake," she said. "And carrot cake sits well on top of macaroni and cheese."

After the cake, I helped the others with the dishes. We were all tired from the late night on Friday, and we wanted to go to bed so we could have an early start on the raft. Jeannie was yawning and Honey was already asleep with her smudged face against the table.

"Goodnight, Auntie Rosie," I said.

She grabbed my chin and tilted my head. "Mickey, you haven't been brushing your teeth!"

I didn't say anything.

"Green!" she cried. "Positively green! You grubby little rodent! Find your toothbrush or I'll run the lawnmower over them!"

That was it! I laughed and laughed. I went on laughing until my stomach hurt and I had to cross my arms over it.

Auntie Rosie looked puzzled. "It wasn't that funny," she said.

I hugged her. "Wow! Thanks, Auntie Rosie!" I said, and I ran upstairs.

# 8.

None of Royce's raft ideas worked out until he thought of the door on the old empty chicken shed. He unscrewed the hinges, bored holes at either end for ropes, and then tied it onto the inner tubes.

At last we had something that looked as though it would float on the river.

"We're going, too," said Johnny. "You promised."

"Sure thing," said Royce, really pleased with himself. He looked at his raft from all angles. "We'll all have a turn.

What we need now are some paddles."

But then it was time for church and we had to stop what we were doing to pile in the car with Auntie Rosie and Uncle Leo.

Uncle Leo sang in the choir. That meant we had to get there early.

At other times, I'd sat with Mom and Dad at the back of the church, but Auntie Rosie led us right to the front. She gave us hymn books and a newsletter to look at. Johnny already had a comic tucked up his sweatshirt and Miranda had brought the novel she'd been reading. Honey crawled back under seats to say hello to people. Jeannie folded the newsletter into an origami frog. Royce leaned against me and whispered in my ear about ideas for paddles. Brooms. Bats. Swimming flippers nailed on poles.

The moment church was out, we streaked home. We didn't wait for the others. I reckoned we were in the gate before Uncle Leo and Auntie Rosie had stopped talking in front of the church, and by the time the car came in the drive, Royce had found a pair of ready-made paddles under the house. They were blue plastic and had belonged to an inflatable boat worn out years ago.

Now we had everything. We were ready to go.

The whole West gang helped carry the raft to the river. We got it over the fence at the back of the yard and then across the paddock between the Wests' house and the river. The long grass whipped about our legs. Cows stood still to stare at us as we tripped over the uneven ground. Goof barked behind us. Not at the cows. He couldn't see them. He barked because he kept getting lost in the high weeds and someone had to keep going back to rescue him.

"Have you thought of a name for it?" asked Uncle Leo. "It's dead bad luck to launch a boat without a name."

"*Patches*," said Royce. "Patches is what it mostly is."

Miranda, who carried the paddles for us, shook her long red hair. "That's an awful name. How about *Westward Ho*?"

"Yeah!" said Royce. "That's brilliant! *Westward Ho*!"

"*Westward Ho*! Off we go!" chanted the twins.

The river was a silent dark avenue between willow trees. Not enough current here to make a noise or ripples. We trod through the last of the grass and into the thick, dark mud at the bank. It came over the top of our shoes like thick oil and made a sucking sound as we lifted our feet.

"What's the plan, Skipper?" Uncle Leo asked Royce.

"Give it a heave into the water," Royce said.

We did that. One, two, *three*! The *Westward Ho* lunged through the air and hit the water with a splash. It floated. A shed door on two rubber rings. It actually floated like a real raft on a real river.

"It works!" yelled Royce, thumping me on the back. "I told you it would!"

We all cheered, passing the thumps around.

"Something is lacking," said Uncle Leo.

"Nothing is lacking," said Royce. "It's perfect!"

"Fantasmo!" I agreed.

"Begging your pardon," said Uncle Leo, "the lack is not with the construction."

"What do you mean?" asked Royce.

"Well, there's no one on it and it's sailing off into the wide blue yonder," said Uncle Leo.

It was true. The raft had moved out into the middle of the river where it had caught the gentle current. It was setting off on a journey on its own.

# 9.

I had never seen Royce move so fast. He didn't even take his shoes off. He was in that water and swimming arm over arm before anyone could say a word. We watched him climb onto the raft. It bobbed slightly but didn't tip. He knelt, shaking the water out of his hair, and then stood up. He looked at his feet, jiggled a little. Then he did a small jump. The raft sent out a few ripples but didn't roll over. We all cheered.

Royce was yelling something. "Paddles! I haven't got any paddles!"

Miranda and I took off our socks and shoes, grabbed a paddle each, and waded through the mud and river grass near the bank. I let Miranda go first. She seemed to know what to do. I kept thinking of eels and crawly things in the mud, and I was glad when the water was deep enough to let me kick my feet up off the bottom. The river was cool, smelling of autumn leaves.

When we got out to where Royce had been, we found he was further down the river, and we had to follow with the current. The paddles were hollow and they floated. It was best to hold them out in front of us and kick like crazy. The sun lit up our splashes and ripples. But by the time we had caught up with Royce, we were out of the sun and in a dark space of water shaded by overhanging willows. We could hear the others calling us, but their voices were made smaller by distance.

We held onto the edge of the raft and Royce hauled us up, first Miranda and then me. He made us stay in the middle so we didn't tip anything. With the three of us on it, the shed door sank to water level but was not awash. Our teeth were chattering. We had goose bumps on our arms.

"You two can paddle," Royce said. "I'll tell you where to go."

"Back to the others?" said Miranda, her hair dripping over her nose and mouth.

"Nah!" said Royce. "Waste of time going against the current. Carry on down the river."

"The little kids are waiting for a ride," said Miranda.

"Tough!" said Royce. "Paddle!"

The moment we tried to paddle, the raft stopped acting like a boat and became a chicken shed door. It veered right and left but would not go straight ahead.

"Paddle!" yelled Royce.

It took us a while to get it right. We found that if we dug in our paddles at exactly the same time, and exactly opposite, the raft would move sluggishly forward. But mainly it was the current that carried us along.

"Keep going!" cried Royce. "Past the next bend we come to the park."

We drifted out of the willows to sunshine again. There was neatly cut lawn on either bank, beds of flowers, and garden seats. Ducks quacked in a chorus and swam out of our way. Some panicked and flapped until they were in the air. But there weren't only ducks by the river. People were sitting on the seats and when they saw us, they stared.

I felt a bit embarrassed, kneeling in wet clothes, paddling a door. I hoped I didn't see anyone I knew. Royce stood up, as straight as a flagpole and saluted as we went past. That made me feel good, especially when a man on the bank stood tall and saluted back.

Miranda looked behind us. Her face lost its grin. "Pirates!" she said.

I turned my head and saw what she meant. Bursting into the park were the rest of the family—Johnny and Jeannie, then Auntie Rosie, then Uncle Leo with Honey riding on his shoulders. Goof was running with them, barking his head off.

"Paddle, paddle, paddle!" yelled Royce. "Give it full throttle!"

What kind of speed did he expect with little plastic paddles, a square-edged door and a sluggish river? They caught up with us and we saw Johnny reach down to the river bank. He stood again and raised his arm. Plop! A ball of black mud hit my shoulder and spattered all over me and Miranda. I tried to paddle harder, but the raft turned in a circle. A mud ball splashed in the water. Then plop! A handful of the squishy stuff hit Royce fair and square in the chest.

They were all at it. Uncle Leo, Auntie Rosie with her skirt tucked up, the twins. Even Honey was trying to throw mud. It didn't worry them that people were watching. They were laughing so much that we couldn't hear what they were yelling at us.

"Paddle to the bank!" Royce shouted.

"They'll catch us!" I said.

"That's the idea!" He was grinning, a wild, mud-spattered grin. "Mudfight! We need ammunition!"

We brought the raft into the shallows and I pulled it up on the bank while Royce and Miranda scooped up mud. What a battle! The blobs of mud flew both ways and exploded against us, getting in our hair, our face, our eyes.

Once I was used to the feel of the mud, I was as good as they were. It was squishy stuff, but if we balled it between our hands it got solid enough to throw without breaking up midair. I hit Uncle Leo four times, Auntie Rosie twice, and

Johnny and Jeannie once each. I would have done better, but I was weak with laughter. The mud was wetter than snow and stickier. It hung on our skin and clothes. By the time the fight was finished, we all looked as though we'd been dipped in molasses.

Uncle Leo tied the *Westward Ho* to a willow tree and said he'd come back for it later on with the car and trailer. We all squelched across the park, the mud drying in the sun. There was no difference in color between our clothing, our hair, and our skin. We were like eight columns of earth.

Uncle Leo said loudly, "You know, Rosie girl, the way people are staring you'd think we'd all got up out of our graves."

Auntie Rosie still had the hiccups from laughing. "I haven't had this much fun in years," she said.

"You say that at least once a week," Miranda reminded her.

None of them seemed worried about the people we passed. I wasn't hugely worried, either. With all that mud hanging on me, no one would know who I was.

All the same, I was hoping like crazy that Mom and Dad wouldn't come home early. I thought that if I saw their car, I would hide in someone's hedge.

# 10.

Auntie Rosie remembered Mom and Dad when we got back to the house. "They'll be here in an hour! Saints alive! If they see you like this, they'll never let you darken our door again."

We stood on the lawn and sloshed each other with the garden hose until the worst of the mud was lying in dark, wet patches on the grass. Then we had to put our clothes in the laundry room and have a shower, me first. It was good getting clean again, but I had liked the other feelings on my skin—the river water and then the mud. I'd never been in a real mudfight before.

While the others were having their showers, I went upstairs and began to pack my bag. Mom had made a list and had put in a pencil so that I could check everything off as I packed—socks, shirts, pajamas, shorts.

Royce came in with his face shining with soap and his red hair standing on end. "Come again next weekend!" he said. "I'll make some better paddles and we'll go all the way down to the sea." He stopped by the dead rabbit. "Hey! Did you see these maggots? They're big enough for bait. You know what you're supposed to do with maggots? Put them in the fridge. That slows them down. Then we can take them with us next weekend. I'll bet there are fish right along the river."

"I don't think I'll be allowed to come," I said. "But I'll ask."

I checked down the list—robe, slippers, sandals, best shirt, best pants. I hoped Auntie Rosie had a good washing machine. My best shirt and pants were being chugged around in the suds at that moment. Auntie Rosie said the mud would wash out, but she wasn't always reliable, as I'd found out with the macaroni and cheese. I looked again at my list. Toiletries bag, tissues, allergy medicine. Medicine! I hadn't taken any the entire weekend! Mom would know by the level in the bottle.

I held up the bottle to Royce.

"Chuck it out the window," he said.

"Throw my medicine out the window?" I laughed at the idea.

"Not all of it. Just the amount you should have taken."

I went over to the window and poured the stuff into the medicine glass.

I was trying not to look at the stinking rabbit. One dose. It splashed pink on the hydrangea leaves far below. Two doses. Three.

Then I was aware of a shiny shape that had been sitting at the edge of my vision. I looked up. It was our car! It was parked at the end of the driveway and it was empty!

I think it took me a second or two to work it out. "They're here!" I said to Royce. "They're fifteen minutes early!"

I jammed the cap back on the medicine bottle and wiped out the glass with a tissue. Bottle and glass got stuffed into the bag.

"Michael? Are you there, son?" Dad called. His voice was close. He was coming up the stairs!

"Rabbit!" I said to Royce in a kind of yelled whisper.

He stared at me, not understanding my panic. There wasn't time to explain that my parents didn't cope really well with things like bad smells and maggots. If Dad saw the rabbit, my chances of coming back were pretty slim. But I couldn't say all that, so I just hissed at him. "Get rid of the rabbit!"

"Michael?" Dad was almost outside the door.

Royce must have worked it out because he jumped up as though he had been sitting on a bee. He crossed the room in two leaps and grabbed the rabbit by its hind legs.

I thought he was going to heave it out the window but he dashed across the room in a wave of bad smell, and dropped the horrible thing down the laundry hole.

We didn't hear it land. There was just this scream. It was the kind of scream I'd heard in the movies when a woman saw a corpse or a vampire. Not just one shriek, either. It went on and on.

I didn't breathe. I think my heart stopped beating.

There was a pounding of feet as Dad ran down the stairs. Auntie Rosie was shouting. Everyone was shouting. Up in the bedroom, Royce and I stood dead still, looking at each other in shocked understanding.

My mother had been in the laundry room. She had been taking my clothes out of her sister's washing machine.

# 11.

My mother was not a person to make a scene. I think it worried her that she lost control because she would not talk about it afterwards. I wanted her to mention the rabbit because I had my side of the story ready. She didn't say a word about it. But on the way home in the car, she criticized Auntie Rosie for letting me play in my best clothes. "You'd think someone who has been a schoolteacher would have more sense," she said.

For dinner that night we had chicken, baked potatoes, and salad. There was a fresh blue cloth on the table and a small vase with two flowers in it.

I unfolded my blue napkin. "Mom, Royce had that rabbit because he was going to use the maggots for bait."

She put down her knife and fork. "Michael! If you please!"

"It was my fault. I didn't think Dad would like the smell."

"Not another word! Do you hear? The subject is closed."

"But I have to tell you, Mom. It wasn't Royce. I told him to put the rabbit down the hole."

Actually, I hadn't, and I felt a bit of a hero for taking the blame. It made no difference to Mom. She stood up from her chair, made herself very tall, and then left the table and the room.

Dad gave me a hurt look. "That was not very wise, old man," he said. "A little consideration would have been appreciated. This, after all, is the meal table."

I didn't answer. I had noticed something about my parents. They were careful with laughter just as they were careful with everything. They didn't laugh often and they never, never laughed out loud.

But Mom was all right when it was time for me to go to bed. She tilted her head so I could kiss her on the cheek, and she asked me if I had missed my Saturday night show on TV.

"A bit," I said. Then I said, "Did you really like your golf?"

"Oh yes, Michael. It was a most enjoyable weekend."

"Do you want to go again next weekend?"

She smiled. "Oh no. We couldn't do that to you. But there may be another time. We talked about it, but decided we'd have to see how you felt. Would you mind?"

I tried not to look pleased. "That's fine," I said. "Goodnight, Mom."

"Have you brushed your teeth?" she asked.

"Yes."

"Did you brush them at Auntie Rosie's place?"

I nodded. "Yes, she made sure I did. Mom, do you know what she said to me? If I didn't brush my teeth she'd run the lawnmower over them. The lawnmower!"

Mom almost smiled. She put her hands on her cheeks and shook her head in a wondering way. "Oh, that wild Rose! That wild, wild West gang. Still—" she gave me a look that filled me with hope, "it is only for two days at a time."

"That's right," I said, and I raced off to my room to use the phone.

# The
# Wild West Gang
# Go Camping

## 1.

Dad gave Mom an electric rice cooker, some lavender soap, and a card with kittens on it. I had drawn golf clubs on a card made of pink paper. On the front it said, "Happy Birthday to a Lovely Beautiful Mother." Inside was a gift certificate I had made myself.

Mom read the gift certificate out loud. "Michael's present to his Lovely Beautiful Mother is a Fantastic two days of playing Golf with Dad while Michael goes to stay with Uncle Leo and Auntie Rosie NEXT WEEKEND."

She wiped her nose with a tissue and smiled at Dad. "So much for those people who say that an only child grows up to be self-centered."

"Indeed," said Dad, giving me a funny look.

"Only if you want to," I said quickly. "It's just that you haven't had a vacation for ages and ages and you deserve it."

"And the Wests happen to be going camping next weekend," said Dad.

"Are they?" I put on my amazed expression. "Really and truly?"

Dad gave me another funny look, then he smiled at Mom and said, "We could book a room at the Wairakei Hotel."

But Mom was shaking her head. "He's not going camping with the Wests," she said. "You know what happened the last time they went camping. The baby crawled into someone's camper. She was in the next town before they discovered she was missing. And their gas cooker exploded. And that oldest boy got swept over a waterfall. He could have been drowned. And Rose told me herself that she made soup out of a duck they'd run over in their van. No, definitely not camping."

"It won't do him any harm," replied Dad, getting used to the idea of a weekend at Wairakei.

Mom put her arm around my shoulders and looked at Dad. "Will you say that when Rose tells us he's fallen over a cliff or been buried by an avalanche? I hate to say this about my own sister and brother-in-law, but they are not responsible people."

"You have a point," said Dad.

I shrugged. "Well, if they did go camping—and if I went with them—there'd be no cliffs or waterfalls. None of that stuff. I reckon I'd be looking after the baby so she didn't go into any campers and I'd be helping Auntie Rosie with the cooking and things like that. With all those kids, she'd need some help. And I honestly wouldn't mind because I'd know you two'd be having a great time playing golf at Wairakei."

"Thanks, Michael, but no," said Mom. "We'll consider it some other weekend when the Wests are at home."

I couldn't say any more without overdoing it. But then I realized that I didn't have to say another word. I could tell from their faces that Wairakei was working inside them like yeast in ginger ale. This coming weekend, I'd be camping in the forest with the Wild West Gang for sure.

# 2.

On the back of the van, Jeannie had written in the dust, "GOING WEST." Actually, we were going north-east on the dirt road that went into the hills behind the town, although there was so much stuff in the van we could hardly see out the windows.

Uncle Leo was driving and singing in his big voice, "Who put the overalls in Mrs. Murphy's chowder? Nobody answered so he shouted all the louder."

Honey was in a car seat between him and Auntie Rosie and she was fast asleep, her fingers in her mouth shining with dribble. How could anyone sleep with so much noise? Jeannie was swallowing air and trying to do a Morse code SOS in belches. She had a cage of white mice on her lap because she couldn't leave them at home with the cats. Johnny had brought along Lucy, his bantam hen. She was sitting in another cage on top of the potatoes and tea towels, her feathers ruffled, her eyes half shut as though she was ready to die. Johnny said she was okay, she just got that dopey look when she was happy. Goof the dog was scratching fleas in the back of the van, and Royce and I were trying to play I Spy. Because it was hard to see out the van windows, we used the stuff inside, like, "I spy something beginning with F and L." "Fishing lines." "I spy something beginning with S and K!" "Saucepan and kettle!"

Royce said, "I spy something beginning with S-H-I-T!"

Miranda laughed. I looked at Auntie Rosie and Uncle Leo to see if they had heard.

"S-H-I-T!" Royce yelled.

Uncle Leo stopped singing. He took his foot off the accelerator and pulled over to the side of the road. "Saints alive! Why didn't you go before we left?"

Auntie Rosie reached across Honey to put her hand on Uncle Leo's shoulder. "Don't stop, dear. It's just a game."

"He said he wanted to—"

"They're playing I Spy," said Auntie Rosie. "Royce is using his dictionary of boring words."

"I didn't say a boring word," shouted Royce. "I said S-H-I-T. It means Six Holes in Tent!"

"That's not I Spy," Uncle Leo growled. "That's the game of L-S-C-M."

"What's that?" Royce asked.

"Let's Shock Cousin Mickey," Uncle Leo replied.

Now I could laugh with Miranda. "Who's shocked?" I said.

"Listen!" cried Jeannie. "I can burp backwards and forwards. I can push the air both ways." She did a whole lot of double belches like a saw moving in a bit of wood. We all had a go, but no one could make it sound as good as Jeannie. I could make a loud burp backwards. My forwards burp was just a little squiff.

Then it happened. Johnny had been feeling a bit carsick. When he tried to belch, he threw up all over Jeannie, the mouse cage, me, and one of the tents. Jeannie screamed. Honey woke up and began to cry. Uncle Leo stopped the van.

Royce was laughing so hard it was a wonder he didn't throw up too. "Johnny won!" he cried. "Burp of the year award!"

Even Johnny managed a pale smile.

Uncle Leo got out and went to the back of the van to look for the roll of paper towels.

I sat dead still, not knowing what to do. Johnny had been eating corn. And some pink stuff. Uncle Leo tore off paper towels and threw them my way. "We give our guests a nice warm welcome," he said, winking at me.

I didn't laugh. To tell the absolute truth, I was shocked.

# 3.

Auntie Rosie said it was their favorite campsite. All I could see was some grass on a bank above a river and a whole lot of trees behind it. The grass was so long you didn't know there were cowpats until you trod in them. I put down the box of food I'd been carrying and pulled out some grass to wipe my new white sneakers.

"Wuss, wuss, wuss!" said Royce as though he was calling a cat. I didn't care. I'd had enough of yuck stuff. Auntie Rosie had made me change my pants but I could still smell Johnny's vomit on me and I didn't want cowpat as well. I found a clean, dry place and then sat down to make a good job of wiping my shoes. Green stuff filled the tread on the sole and oozed up each side, thick as mashed spinach.

Miranda and Uncle Leo were putting up the tents nearer the trees. There were three, one big and two little, and Royce had been right about the big one. It did have six holes above the flap for lacing on an awning. The boxes of food and the fold-up table went in the big tent. The sleeping bags went into the others. From the corner of my eye, I noticed that Auntie

Rosie and Uncle Leo were having one small tent and all the kids' sleeping bags were going in the other. Brilliant!

"What's Mickey doing?" bellowed Uncle Leo.

The others answered for me. "He stepped in the Royce word," grinned Auntie Rosie.

"Being a big wuss," said Royce.

"Cowpat," called Johnny, stroking the hen under her wing.

"Poo on shoe," said Jeannie.

Honey, whirling with her arms outstretched, shouted, "Poo, poo, poo, poo, poo!"

I threw away the handful of grass and stood up. "Where can I wash my hands?"

They all stared at me. Then Uncle Leo said, "Mickey lad, I think you'll find a wash basin at the bottom of that bank."

He meant the river. I had forgotten about that. I heard Royce laughing as I climbed down the bank, my face as red as a boiled tomato. It was all right for them. They'd been here heaps of times before.

I squatted at the edge of the river where the water ran thin as paper over small gray stones. I expected it to be warm, but it was icy cold on my hands. Further out there were white ripples where it broke over bigger stones and on the other side there was a pool so deep I couldn't see the bottom. I went on scrubbing at my fingers, wondering what Mom and Dad were doing.

A small shower of dirt came down the bank and next thing I saw bare feet, Miranda's, on the stones beside me. I didn't look up. If she was going to tell me I was dumb or if she was going to feel sorry for me, I didn't want to see her face.

She squatted down beside me and was silent for a while. Then she pointed. "See that pool?"

I nodded again.

"Last year I got an eel in there, thick as my arm. I just had a bit of meat tied on a string. Their teeth curve backwards so when they take a bite the meat won't come out of their mouths. It's easy to haul them out of the water. Thicker than my arm. Big as Dad's arm."

I nodded again.

"I cut the string," she said.

"You let it go?" I looked at her. Her eyes staring out across the river were as green as glass and the sun made her hair look as though it was on fire.

"Yeah. Probably still down there."

I dried my hands on my shirt. "As big as a leg now. As big as a tree trunk. Hey, Miranda—" I glanced at her shoulder, which was not quite touching mine. I could feel it kind of warm and buzzy through my sleeve.

"What?"

"Will you do us a yodel?"

The great thing about Miranda is that she never made a fuss. She just did things. She stood up, her hands on her hips, her head back.

Then she opened her mouth and sang, "yo-de-odly-odly-ay," making the sound jump up and down her throat. I laughed and my spine shivered. She was more brilliant than any country and western singer.

"Odly-odly-odly."

The yodel went across the river and came back through the trees in the different voice of an echo.

Then Uncle Leo was standing on the bank. "I sure as eggs hope the cowgirl isn't calling up more cows," he said. "One tent. One pair of shoes. That's enough cow paint for the day.

Come on up. Miranda, you can undress the Irish while I switch on the stove."

"He means I peel the spuds while he lights the fire," said Miranda. "I hate doing spuds. It's a lousy job."

I raced her up the bank. I was as good at peeling potatoes as she was at yodeling, maybe even better. "It won't take long," I promised. "I'll help you."

The heart of the fire was the exact color of the sunset. We sat on a log watching stuff bubble and ooze under the lids of the blackened pots, one full of potatoes, the other full of beans and peas. We were all starving. Uncle Leo had a metal sheet like an oven tray that he was trying to put on the coals to cook chops and sausages, but he had a can of beer in one hand so wasn't managing all that well. I jumped up to help him.

"Well, thankee, Mickey lad," he said. "It's nice to know that someone in this family hasn't got a backside nailed to the ground."

"Want a pack of butter?" Royce said to me.

Miranda hit him on the arm. "He wasn't greasing, you lazy toad."

Royce hit her arm in return and in a flash she threw a headlock on him. They rolled backwards off the log and fought each other in the trampled grass, arms punching, legs kicking and waving.

No one took any notice so I guessed they were okay, especially now that Auntie Rosie had cleaned up the cowpats. But all the same I couldn't help looking at them and wishing I was Royce.

Auntie Rosie smiled at me. "Relax, Michael. This is their idea of aerobics. If you're going to bite your nails every time someone in this family gets into a fight, by the time you go home you'll have no arms."

But she was wrong. That's not what I was worrying about.

Uncle Leo put the chops and sausages, one by one, onto the metal plate. They sizzled in a loud chorus, sending up a delicious smell that had Miranda and Royce back in no time, grabbing for their tin plates. Auntie Rosie poured the water off the potatoes and beans while Johnny buttered the bread. I tried to remember if I had seen Johnny wash his hands, and I decided that I wouldn't eat any bread, but by the time the meat was cooked, I was so hungry that I forgot. We squeezed tomato sauce over the chops, sausages, bread and each other and ate with sauce and grease dripping down to our elbows, our mouths so bulgy that when we talked, bits of food fell out. Mom and Dad would have had a double king-size fit. Auntie Rosie and Uncle Leo acted like it was normal and pulled off bits of paper towel so we could wipe our hands.

There was hardly any light in the sky now and the trees behind us were dark. The birds had stopped chirping although, as Jeannie said, the sound of the water running on stones was a bit like a bird warble. Uncle Leo went down to the river with a flashlight and all the dirty dishes stacked inside the cooking pots. The rest of us stayed by the fire, eating ginger cookies and telling stories. Honey was asleep again, curled up in Auntie Rosie's lap, so it was all right to talk about ghosts.

Jeannie said, "Mice have ghosts. They do so. After Squeak died he came back. Seriously. In the middle of the night— scratch, scratch, scratch by my ear. The whole of my pillow went icy cold. Honestly. I felt his whiskers on my face but when I opened my eyes he wasn't there!"

"Not true, not true," said Johnny.

"Is so, is so!"

"How could you see in the dark?" he said. "How did you know it was Squeak?"

"Shh," said Auntie Rosie. "We mustn't let a few facts spoil a good story. Were you scared, Jeannie?"

"Not really. Squeak wasn't haunting me. It was Frodo he was after because Frodo had bitten his head off. He jumped on Frodo's back and pulled out his fur, one hair at a time. Poor old Frodo. He meowed and howled. He didn't know what was happening. Then Squeak's ghost chewed Frodo's ears."

Johnny shook his head. "Liar, liar, your pants are on fire."

Jeannie grinned at him. "That's why Frodo meows at night and that's why he's got holes in his ears."

It was Royce's turn. He twisted his fingers, cracking all the knuckles. "There was this guy on a country road and he picks up a hitch-hiker, this woman in a white dress, and she asks him to take her to the next town, so he does and when he gets there he says, 'What address?' and she says, 'The cemetery.' Then he notices when she smiles her mouth is full of maggots and there's wet earth on her dress and he gets such a fright he crashes in to the cemetery gates and gets killed."

We were all quiet. I looked at the dark trees behind us and thought about the maggots. Jeannie said, "How do we know?"

"Know what?" said Royce.

"If he got killed, how do we know what happened?"

"Because it's on a video," said Royce.

"I've got one!" Miranda waved her hands to stop us talking. "There's a ghost in a castle. It walks up the stairs at night. It's got its head under its arm and its lips are moving. It is saying—" Miranda dropped her voice to a whisper.

We leaned closer to hear.

She went on whispering.

"What?" said Johnny.

"Arrgh!" Miranda sprang up with a huge shout and we all jumped, even Honey and Frodo, who had been asleep. Honey began to cry and Auntie Rosie said, "That's enough now."

"Mickey hasn't had his turn yet," said Royce.

"He can save it until tomorrow night," said Auntie Rosie. "It's time for bed. Come on. Last one into their sleeping bag cooks breakfast."

I was last. But that was only because I didn't know where to go to change into my pajamas and I was frightened of treading in another cowpat. In the end, I undressed behind the van. Every time I shone the flashlight up front, I thought I could see a maggoty lady in a white dress in the passenger seat. I was glad to get back to the firelight and the tent.

They had put my sleeping bag between Royce and Miranda. Brilliant! I scrambled in quickly and huffed against my hand to see if my breath was okay. No one had said anything about cleaning teeth. My toothbrush and medicine were down the bottom of my pack and I wasn't going to get either.

"Tell us your ghost story, Mickey," said Royce. "Now!"

There was a click and Miranda's flashlight shone in my face. "Make it as scary as you like," she said.

The truth was, I didn't know a story. Mom and Dad didn't let me read about ghosts or see scary movies. I would have to make something up. "Once upon a time there was a haunted tent."

There was quiet, then Johnny said, "How can a tent be haunted?"

"It was a very, very old tent. It had been in the war and hundreds of soldiers died in it. It was the kind of tent they

41

used for a hospital when there was a battle going on. It had blood stains all over it."

Miranda's flashlight turned off my face and made a circle of light on the wall. As the circle slid down the fabric, I felt a thrill of power. She was believing it! "The bloodstains turned brown like rust but they never washed out. People went camping in the tent and at night they could hear soldiers marching." I turned my head. "What's that?"

"Soldiers' boots," said Royce.

"No. That moaning noise."

"Just an owl," said Miranda. "Go on."

"It isn't!" I grabbed the flashlight from her and shone it towards the flap of the tent. "I know what an owl sounds like."

It came again, a low hooting noise so close it seemed right against the thin skin of the wall. We were all quiet. I turned off the flashlight and slid down into my sleeping bag.

"Hoo-oo-oo-oo-oo!"

Royce said his favorite word. Jeannie whimpered and Miranda whispered, "Shh!" It was certainly not an owl out there.

"Where's Goof?" Royce wanted to know.

The last time I'd seen the old dog he was stretched out in the big tent.

"He'd be barking if there was something wrong," Royce said.

Johnny gave a shrill giggle. "Maybe the soldiers shot him."

"Hoo-oo! Hoo-oo! Hoo-oo!"

"Leo?" Auntie Rosie yelled from the other side of the fire. "Stop that, you big hairy twit, and let them get to sleep."

I laughed and gave Miranda back her flashlight.

"Dad!" muttered Royce in a disgusted voice.

"Hoo-hoo! Good night to you!" sang Uncle Leo, slapping the tent. Then we heard him say, "Coming, lovely cozy Rosie."

"Go on about the soldiers," said Miranda. "So what happened next?"

But I pretended to be too tired. The truth was I had spooked myself with my own story, and even after they were all asleep I could hear boots marching on the gravel of the river bed.

# 4.

I was up before any of them. Auntie Rosie had said that we had to have a morning bath in the river and I wanted to be first so no one would see me undressed. Outside the tent, the grass was cold and wet and everything had a soaked smell, even the dead fire. The sky looked far away and empty, like it hadn't decided yet what kind of day it would be, and the air was full of river noise. I climbed down the bank with my towel and toiletries bag and clothes and was just unbuttoning my PJs when Goof put his nose over the bank. His head was on one side. He barked to ask if I was doing anything interesting.

I didn't want him to wake up everyone so called softly, "Here Goof, here Goof!" and picked up a stick to throw in the river. He came flying down in a skid of gravel, barking even louder. Stupid dog. I heaved the stick and it splashed in Miranda's deep pool on the far side. He took off after it.

"Hope the giant eel eats you," I muttered, but I didn't really mean it. I stood with my feet just in the river, and had a thorough wash in water that was practically ice. It took a while because I had to keep throwing the stick for Goof. I had brushed my teeth and was mostly dressed when Royce came galloping down the bank, stark naked and yelling. He yahooed as he splashed through the shallows and then he leapt, pale and freckled, into the deep pool. Goof dropped his stick and swam to him. They came back together, splashing and grinning over the stones and climbed up the bank. More yelling. More barking. Then Goof shook himself, flap, flap, flap, sending a rain of river drops down on me. I looked at the ripples still moving across the deep pool. Royce's bath had taken no more than fifteen seconds and he hadn't used any soap. Brilliant! I might try that myself tomorrow morning.

Everyone had a job. Mine was to beat sixteen eggs with a wooden spoon while Uncle Leo cooked the bacon and Auntie Rosie dressed Honey. Johnny was feeding his hen, Lucy, and Jeannie was cleaning out the mouse cage. Royce sat on the log, toasting bread on a fork tied to a long stick. Miranda put out mugs for hot chocolate. I was amazed at all the things that could be done with a plain old fire, like boiling a kettle, making toast, cooking eggs and bacon. The breakfast tasted so good I wondered why people bothered with boring old gas and electricity.

Uncle Leo said, "Mickey, tell me, have you been camping before?"

I shook my head.

Royce leaned over his plate of eggs and bacon. "Last night was the first time you ever slept in a tent?"

"Yes."

Uncle Leo and Auntie Rosie gave each other a look and Uncle Leo said, "Well, Mickey, let's see if we can blow your socks off. What do we do today, gang?"

"Go to the swing bridge!" yelled Johnny and Jeannie together.

"Swimming," said Miranda.

"Hunt wild pigs and search for gold," Royce said.

"What's your choice, Mickey?" Uncle Leo asked.

"All of them," I said.

Uncle Leo scratched his head and laughed.

"Well, now, we might leave the wild pigs in peace, but I think we can manage the rest. You coming, Rosie?"

Auntie Rosie stretched her arms above her head. She had egg yolk dripped like candle grease down her T-shirt. "I think Honey and I might stay here and cook something extra delicious for lunch."

"Like what?" I asked her.

She frowned. "Like hedgehogs boiled in slug juice, you greedy little cabbage," she said.

I laughed until I fell back off the log. I loved it when Auntie Rosie said terrible things to me.

# 5.

The narrow track to the old swing bridge didn't always follow the river. Sometimes it looped into the forest and we would be walking over giant tree roots or through patches of mud and ferns. It took a long time because we kept stopping to look at things: a giant fungus growing out of the side of the tree, a brown and white bug that looked like the monster in *Alien*, some rough ground where pigs had been rooting, a dead baby wood pigeon. Royce got a handful of purple tree fuchsia berries and told me to eat them.

"Nah. Not hungry," I said, thinking he was trying to poison me.

He put them in his mouth and chewed, but he dropped one on the path. I picked it up when he wasn't looking. It was delicious!

The track came back to the river at a place where the water flowed deep between two steep banks covered with fern and mosses and little bushes. Between the banks was the swing bridge they'd been talking about. It was made of two thick wires with planks across and a couple of ropes each side to hang on to. It didn't look very safe.

"Me first!" yelled Jeannie, running.

"No! Me, me!" cried Johnny

"One at a time, you spalpeens!" shouted Uncle Leo.

Too late. They were both on the swing bridge, standing like starfish with legs on the planks and hands on the ropes. Then, deliberately, they rocked the bridge. It rippled and began to sway from side to side, increasing its swing until they were leaning over sideways each way. They screamed with laughter and it was a while before they heard Uncle Leo calling, "That's enough now. Quite enough."

"Mickey and me next," said Royce, cracking his knuckles with eagerness.

"Have you all got turnips in your ears?" said Uncle Leo. "I told you one at a time, especially you big lumps!"

"Want to have a go?" Royce said to me.

"Your turn," I said, giving him a bit of a push.

He ran out into the middle of the bridge, grabbed the ropes as the twins had done, and heaved to one side, then the other.

The wires creaked like rusty gates and I wondered what would happen if one of them broke. You saw it in movies all the time, a swing bridge collapsing and someone hanging on to a broken rope above the jaws of hungry crocodiles or pits full of poisonous snakes.

Royce came back grinning. "Fantasmo, man! Go on. Give it heaps."

I scratched the back of my neck. I had been going to suggest that Miranda have her turn next but now everyone was expecting me to go and I couldn't refuse, not with the twins and the olds watching. If they could do it, so could I. I licked my lips and stepped onto the swing bridge.

The first surprise was that the boards weren't together. There were gaps between them that showed the river far below. The second surprise was that the bridge didn't wait for someone to deliberately rock it. The moment I stepped on it, it moved like some living animal. I got such a shock I grabbed at the side. Two hands on the one rope.

I heard them shout a warning from the bank but I was already leaning over the rope and the bridge was tilting up under my feet. I saw the dark water under me and I thought about the movies. I thought about the way people could hang onto a rope and be safe. That didn't happen. My hands came off and I slid head first into the river.

There was an explosion of water in my ears and a blackness filled with silver bubbles. I shot up to the surface, gasping, as three other splashes sounded close by. I trod water and shook my hair out of my eyes. Miranda, Uncle Leo and Royce bobbed up beside me. They'd jumped in with all their clothes on. Did they think I was going to drown? I lay on my back and spat out a thin jet of water. Next thing, Johnny and Jeannie flew through the air and came down almost on top of me, swamping me with their wave. They came up doing dog paddle.

"I can swim!" I shouted at them, my voice cramped with cold. "You know I can swim."

"Sure now," grinned Uncle Leo. "You think we'd let you have all this fun on your own?"

Just to show them, I did my best crawl stroke across the river and back again, but it wasn't all that fast with clothes and shoes on. My feet were as heavy as lead. By now we had floated away from the swing bridge but the river was still deep in parts. I could see a gravel beach further down. I was in no hurry to go there. The cold wasn't so bad once you got used to it. I hit the water with my hand and splashed Uncle Leo and Miranda full on. They squealed and a major water fight started, with Royce and the twins joining in. The idea was that you kicked and smacked up fountains of river in someone's face and then dove before they could get you back. Uncle Leo cheated. He started grabbing our toes. We all ganged up on him and tried to push him under.

We were just about winning when he stopped laughing. His eyes opened up really wide and he gasped. "I've been bitten by an eel!"

That was it. In a few seconds we were out of the river and on the gravel beach, shivering. Uncle Leo limped from the water in squelching shoes.

"Where? Where?" We crowded around him to inspect his legs. The black hairs on his shins were trickling water but there was no blood. Not a drop.

Uncle Leo stopped limping. He stood up straight and grinned like someone who had just won the lottery. "Blessed saints!" he said. "That river heals like a holy miracle!"

We all groaned and Johnny said, "Liar, liar, your pants are on fire."

The sun warmed us past our shivering. We shook and squeezed our clothes, but there wasn't much we could do about our feet. Every step, our shoes made rude noises on the gravel.

"Dead soldiers marching," said Miranda.

"Dead what?" said Uncle Leo.

We looked at each other and didn't tell him.

Up the bank and into the forest, we found the track again. We had to go back to the swing bridge because Royce's camera and Uncle Leo's backpack were there. This time, no one ran out onto the bridge—not even Miranda, who hadn't had a turn.

It was a rotten little bridge. It sat there, pretending to be innocent, waiting for an unsuspecting passerby. The moment someone got out on its back it would try to buck them off like a wild horse at a rodeo. I clenched my fists.

"Wait a minute," I said to the Wests.

They didn't try to talk me out of it. They didn't make a big deal of it either. They just stood kind of quiet while I walked out onto the planks. Stupid bridge. Dumb, stupid, useless trap of a bridge. It started to wobble but I was ready for it. I put my hands out either side and held the ropes. "Do your worst," I muttered.

Out in the middle, I stopped. The water wasn't all that far down. Just an ordinary pool. I spread my legs a bit, anchoring my squishy shoes on the outside planks. "This is it, bridge," I said. Then I gave it heaps. I rocked and rocked, until I was almost lying on one side and then the other, and all the time I yelled the way Royce had yelled when he was having his wash that morning.

# 6.

The sun was so hot you could almost see the steam coming off our shorts and shirts as we walked through the long grass on the river bank. Uncle Leo told us about the history of gold in the river. No big claims, he said, just a few specks here and there, and gold could still be found if you knew where to look.

"Ever been gold-panning before, Mickey?" He knew I hadn't. "Seeing you're family, we'll let you in on the great West Company Gold Mine. Not as rich as Fort Knox but success guaranteed. Dead secret, though, Mickey. Tell another blessed soul and all your hair falls out. Right? It's at this bend in the river."

The river in that place didn't look different from anywhere else but Uncle Leo was taking a trowel and a tin dish out of his pack and the kids were racing ahead yelling stuff about nuggets as big as your head.

We stood around Uncle Leo while he dug in the river and scooped stones and clay into the dish. He swirled it around. It was just a mucky mixture of dirty water and pebbles, sounding like concrete in a mixer. Bit by bit he sloshed the dirty water out and clean water in, picking out the stones until there was just a little bit of gravel left in the crease of the pan. We crowded in closer until our heads were almost touching. I could see something glittering and I pointed at it.

"Nah," said Uncle Leo. "Iron pyrites. Fool's gold. The real stuff doesn't shine. It's clay color." He carefully moved the gravel with his finger. "Nothing there. We'll try again."

"Let Mickey do it," said Royce and they all looked at me.

I stepped backwards. "I don't know how."

"Dad'll help you," said Jeannie.

"You might bring us luck," said Miranda.

"To be sure he will. It's dead easy, Mickey, but tell you what, I'll find you a nice little heap of rich dirt." He walked into the river to where the water swirled around the tops of his shoes and bent over to fill the pan with the trowel. He was careful about it and it took a long time. Then he stood behind me with his arms around mine and showed me how to sloosh the pan around to wash the stones and gravel.

When we got to the last bit of gravel in the pan, I poked through it with my finger as he had done. "Nothing here," I said, and I was going to throw it back in the river when Uncle Leo caught the edge of the pan. "Not too hasty, Mickey lad. Look again!"

I looked again.

He reached past me and pressed his finger into the small spoonful of gravel. Then he showed me his fingertip. Pressed onto the flesh was a speck of yellow stuff no bigger than a flea.

The kids started to cheer and jump up and down.

"That's gold?" I said.

"That's it." Uncle Leo took a little bottle out of his pack, filled it with water and put the yellow speck in it. It went straight to the bottom, really heavy for its size. "I told you success was guaranteed."

I picked up the trowel. "Can I pan again?"

Uncle Leo laughed and scratched the back of his neck. "Oh surely and welcome. But realize you don't get color every time."

I scraped back the stones at the edge of the river and dug up the gravel underneath. Then I tilted the pan into the water and shook it in wide circles to make a thick, dirty gravel soup.

It took a while, easing the dirty water out, getting clean water in, and finally, Royce was the only one watching. Uncle Leo was getting the tube of sunblock from the pack for Miranda. Johnny and Jeannie were skipping stones across the water.

Royce and I saw it at the same time. He leaned over the last bit of gravel in the tin dish and said his favorite word. I couldn't say anything. I just stared at it. It was about as big as a small pea but not round, a flattish lump almost like a triangle. It didn't shine but it didn't look like clay, either. You couldn't mistake it in a million years.

"Mickey's got a nugget!" Royce screamed.

What a fuss they made, so much yelling I realized I'd found something really special. I put it in the bottle of water and held it up to the light to see it from all sides. "How much is it worth?" I asked.

Uncle Leo, who was already digging up gravel from the same place, said, "All of eighty or ninety dollars, I'd say. It's a fine little nugget, Mickey, indeed. Hearty congratulations!"

"Eighty or ninety!" Royce groaned. "And we thought we were making your day with a microscopic dot!"

"Royce!" growled Miranda. "Shut up!"

"Oh, tell him," said Uncle Leo, not looking up from the trowel.

"That microscopic dot," said Miranda, "was something Dad took out of his gold collection. He put it in the pan so you would find something."

"It's called salting," Johnny said.

I didn't mind. I looked at the dot alongside my beautiful nugget. I swished them both around the bottle. I didn't mind at all.

Uncle Leo was busy for ages, dipping the pan in the river

and shaking it for all he was worth, but although he found a couple of specks, there were no more nuggets that morning.

# 7.

Jeannie started it, a kind of marching chant along the path. We all joined in, swinging our arms and yelling, "Hungry. Famished. Dying of starvation. Hungry. Famished. Dying of starvation."

It made me think of ghost soldiers and how I'd be expected to finish the story that night, even though I hadn't the faintest idea what the ending was going to be.

Our voices grew louder as we neared the campsite. I think we were expecting Auntie Rosie to rush out, all smiley, with masses of wonderful food. She didn't. There was no sign of Auntie Rosie or Honey or Goof, and the fire wasn't going. The only movement came from some washing flapping on a rope between two trees. I saw my jeans and shirt there and my stomach sagged with relief. At least I wouldn't be taking them home to Mom with Johnny's puke on them.

Uncle Leo was quiet. I guessed that meant he was worried. He walked around the campfire as though he was looking for some clue in the gray ash, then he peered in each of the tents and the van. Finally he stood in front of the big tent, put his hands around his mouth and bellowed, "Rosee-ee! Rosee-ee!"

We heard an answer, very faint, from the other side of the river and there they were, Auntie Rosie carrying Honey, Goof leaping to clear the tussock grass. As we watched, Rosie waded into the shallows with Honey on her hip. Goof raced ahead, barking a welcome to us.

Miranda called out what we were all thinking. "What's for lunch, Mom?"

It was the wrong thing to ask. Auntie Rosie was fierce and this time she wasn't joking. "Chicken with feather sauce and roast stinking dog to follow. Do you know how I've spent my fantastically peaceful morning? Looking for that blasted hen! Why didn't you take Goof with you?"

Johnny's face went blank. "Lucy!" he cried.

Auntie Rosie came out of the river, put Honey down and then stood looking up at us, her hands on her hips.

"Honey opened the cage. The hen got out. Then that senile fleabag started barking and next moment, Lucy's off flying, heaven knows where. You should have kept her wings clipped." She looked at Johnny and her voice changed. "She'll come back, of course. No two ways about it. It's just that I've spent the whole morning—" She shook her head, grabbed Honey's hand and hauled her up the bank.

"What about my mice?" cried Jeannie. "Did Honey let out my mice?"

"No, worse luck," Auntie Rosie said.

"I'm going to look." Johnny's brown eyes were full to overflowing. "Which way did she go?"

"Have lunch first," Auntie Rosie said. Her hair, normally wild, was sticking out everywhere and caught with bits of twig and leaves. She had cuts on her big arms and her shorts were muddy. She looked at our feet. "You're a daft lot! You've been wading with your shoes on!"

"I'll hunt for her now," said Johnny. "Before she goes too far." He turned to the trees and called, "Lucy? Lucy? Here, hen, hen, hen, hen. Here Lucy."

Uncle Leo stopped him. "Peanut butter sandwiches," he

said. "Then we'll all go." He held an imaginary radio hand-piece. "Calling West Search and Rescue, West Search and Rescue. Do you copy? This is Miss Lucy Cackleberry calling. I've just lost an egg in the river—"

Johnny didn't laugh. He pulled away, folded his arms and put his head against them. He really loved that little brown hen.

As we crowded into the big tent to find stuff to make sand-wiches, the talk was all hen this and Lucy that. It was only much later that someone thought to tell Auntie Rosie about my fantastic nugget and the swing bridge.

# 8.

The trees behind the campsite were part of the forest park, original forest that had never been cut down. There were huge trees growing straight up like the masts of giant sailing ships. In between were smaller trees and tree ferns stretching up to the light and all laced together with vines. Nearer the ground there were so many little bushes and ferns and fallen logs that if you got off the track you wouldn't find it again.

Uncle Leo said, "I'm telling you, once more, you don't go off the track for anything. If you see Lucy, call her. She'll come. Got some bread in your pocket? Oh, that's grand. A few crumbs of bread on the path and she'll fly down to you as tame as a feather duster."

He took Jeannie and Johnny and went in one direction. Royce, Miranda, and I went in the other. We could hear Goof barking back at the camp, complaining about being tied to a tree. Uncle Leo would have shut him in the van except that the mice were in there.

We walked along the track calling, "Lucy, Lucy, here Lucy," into the trees. In the distance we could hear Uncle Leo, Johnny and Jeannie saying the same thing, then their voices faded right out.

We had been on this part of the track twice already that day and Royce didn't think we'd see the hen.

"She normally comes when you call her," Miranda said.

"Hens haven't always been tame," said Royce. "They've got wild instincts. Give her half a chance and she'll be nesting in the top of a tree. I'm going to pick fuchsia berries."

"They don't nest in trees," said Miranda. "They nest on the ground. Here, Lucy! Good girl, Lucy!"

I hit my toe on a tree root and would have fallen forward except that Miranda grabbed my arm. My face went into her long red hair and I pulled back so hard that I nearly fell the other way. I hated myself for pulling away like that. I walked on ahead, my stomach all grinched up, wondering why I was always so stupid around Miranda. She would think I didn't like her.

"Lucy!" I called. "Lucy! Lucy!"

Royce came up behind me. "What are you going to do with that gold nugget?"

"I dunno. Keep it. Why?"

"I can sell it for you. I know a place. Good bucks."

"Oh yeah? What would you get out of it?"

"Nothing." He looked innocent. "Honestly, nothing. Just a bit of commission. That's all. It's worth at least eighty bucks."

I knew how much Royce loved money. "What kind of commission?"

"The usual. Nothing much. Think of what you could buy."

I laughed. "I'm going to keep it. Lucee-ee-ee! Hen, hen, hen!"

"You'll lose it," Royce argued.

"No, I won't."

"Yes, you will. You'll put it down somewhere and—"

"Oh, shut up, Royce," said Miranda. "Of course he wants to keep it. He found it himself. It's special. Right, Mickey?"

So she wasn't mad at me! "Yeah! Right!" I turned towards her and saw something move in the ferns. "What's that?"

Then we all saw it, brown feathers, a scaly leg scratching under an outstretched wing. Lucy!

"Lucy, Lucy, Lucy, Lucy!" We rushed toward her, calling and spilling breadcrumbs from our pockets. It was a bit much for her. She squawked with fright and bolted through the ferns. We could see fronds rustling as she went and we followed, calling, "Here, Lucy! Good girl. Cluck, cluck, cluck. Come and get some bread." The movement in the undergrowth stopped. Then Royce pointed. "Over there!"

She was behind a moss-covered log. We could see her tail feathers jerking up and down.

"Lucy! Lucy!"

But as soon as we came near, she took off again with another squawk.

"I told you she'd go wild," said Royce. "She doesn't even remember her name."

We tracked her through the undergrowth. We glimpsed a foot, some feathers, some quivering fern stalks, and then, suddenly, the bird darted across a small clearing.

It wasn't Lucy.

"A woodhen!" cried Miranda.

I laughed. "No wonder she didn't remember her name!"

"Lucy, Lucy, Lucy!" Royce mimicked.

The bird disappeared into the forest and we turned back,

making jokes about catching a wild woodhen for Johnny. Our laughter didn't last long. Where was the path? It had disappeared as though someone had rolled it up and carried it away.

Royce said to me, "Don't throw away the rest of your bread. You might need it."

"Why?"

Miranda leaned against a tree trunk. "We're lost," she said.

# 9.

"Don't get in a sweat," Royce said to me. "We get lost on a regular basis. That's why Dad was raving on about us keeping to the path."

"And we didn't," I said.

"The path can't be far away," Miranda scratched her back against the tree. "We didn't chase the bird for long. I think the important thing is to stay here."

Royce looked at his watch. "It's ten past two. They'll get back at three and we won't be there. They'll give us some extra time and then they'll come to look for us. We'll yell. They'll hear us."

"I'll yodel," said Miranda, trying to comfort me. She put her head back and sang, "Ye-odle, ye-odle, ye-odle, ee-ay." Here, there was no echo. The sounds were squashed up small, muffled by trees.

After a while we sat on the mossy log. It was surprisingly wet and squishy and our pants were instantly soaked, but we stayed there. We had a long wait.

"Tell us the ghost story," Royce said, pushing me with his elbow.

"Not now." I didn't want him to know that really there was no story. "I'm not in the mood."

"Mickey, you mustn't worry so much," said Miranda. "Dad will find us. It's just like Royce said. These things happen all the time and they always turn out okay."

I didn't answer. I was thinking of what Mom and Dad would say when they found out that all their worst fears had come true. Leo sent them out into the forest to look for a bantam hen and they were never seen again.

I looked up at the roof of trees that blocked out most of the sun. Birds flitted across, small birds. It would be neat to be able to fly out of here.

Then I wondered how Auntie Rosie and Mom got on together when they were kids. They didn't even look alike. I bet they fought. Bet they argued something fierce. Now they just shocked each other. Mom was shocked that Auntie Rosie washed her hair with laundry soap. Auntie Rosie was shocked that Mom ironed my T-shirts with spray starch.

"Come on, tell us the story," said Royce. "You can tell it again tonight."

"Dead soldiers," said Miranda.

I shrugged. "It was like the sound of the river," I said. "Dead soldiers walking on a gravel road at midnight."

"What happened about the tent?" Miranda asked.

Then I sat up straight. "We can hear the river now," I said. "It's loud."

"So?" Miranda shrugged.

"Go on with the story!" Royce insisted.

"Listen! If we follow the noise of water, we'll come out at the river and then all we have to do is walk down it to the campsite."

59

They were quiet for a moment. Royce jumped off the log. "Yeah. Okay. I was going to suggest that, but I didn't think you'd want to get your feet wet again."

Miranda gave him a shove. "Just as well your seat is wet," she said. "It puts out the flames."

Just in case he didn't get it, I danced in front of him, yelling, "Liar, liar, your pants are on fire."

Then we took off, the three of us stumbling through the ferns, laughing, pushing each other, heading towards the river that would take us home.

It didn't take long to get back, no more than twenty minutes, but the others were already at the camp. Uncle Leo was chopping wood, and Johnny had Lucy in her cage. She had flown out of a tree and down to his shoulder no more than five minutes after they had left us.

Uncle Leo wanted to know why we had come back by the river.

"We thought Lucy might be by the river bank," I said, and that had been partly true. We had called her on the way back to camp.

"We got lost," said Miranda.

She and Royce told it like it happened, about chasing the woodhen, losing the path, and me suggesting we follow the river.

Uncle Leo didn't say a word about us going off the path. He laughed about the woodhen and slapped me on the back. "Very sensible, Mickey, I think we'll keep you on board." Then he put the matches in my hand. "Would you be wanting to light the fire now?"

I couldn't believe that he wasn't mad at us. "Yeah! Thanks, Uncle Leo."

"Look out for your pants," said Royce.

Uncle Leo didn't know why the three of us couldn't stop laughing.

# 10.

Royce didn't let up about selling the gold nugget. I put the glass bottle in my toiletries bag then put the toiletries bag in the bottom of the sleeping bag. There was room enough for it.

"You'll pollute your toothbrush." Royce was in a bad mood. "In the morning your mouth'll taste like stinky feet."

Miranda put her pillow over Royce's head and Jeannie, shining her flashlight around the tent, said, "What about Mickey's story?"

Miranda snatched back her pillow, Royce lay with his hands behind his head, and the twins turned towards me, half-sitting, propped up on their elbows.

I still didn't know what to say. There was a wind blowing around the tent, rustling leaves and cracking the door flap and puffing in drifts of smoke from the fire. Auntie Rosie and Uncle Leo were still putting away the dishes. I could hear them talking in the other tent.

"Well, go on," said Royce.

I made my voice sound ghostly like the wind. "The tent had all this blood on it from dead soldiers. It had dried on the canvas like rust marks and it never went away."

"You already told us that," Royce hissed.

"Shut up, Royce," said Miranda.

"After the war, the tent was in a junk shop. For years and

years it lay in the back of the shop and then a family came in. Mom and Dad and six kids. They wanted a big tent for the vacations. Well, the man from the shop dragged out this big old canvas tent. 'It was in the war,' he said. 'What are those marks?' said the father. 'Just rust,' said the man in the shop. 'It's had machines on it.'"

"What machines?" Johnny asked.

"In the shop. Tools and farm stuff. You know. Well anyway, they bought it and they took it to the beach. But when they put it up, the tent groaned and moaned something terrible and they thought it was just the wind." I stopped and there was silence. I knew they were feeling the wind on the walls of our tent. I went on in a spooky voice. "All that night the tent moaned and moaned. Then they heard this other noise. Like feet marching. They looked out in the moonlight. There was no one there. The feet went on, marching and marching all night. And then something else happened, something so terrible you're not going to believe it." I stopped again. No one said a word. "The rust stains," I said. "They became blood again. The blood dripped down the tent and onto the people. It covered their faces and their pillows and their sleeping bags—"

There was a shrill cry from Jeannie and next thing she was out of her sleeping bag, treading over the rest of us and diving out of the tent door. We heard her crying, "Mom, Mom—"

"Go on, go on!" Royce shook me.

I didn't want to go on. I could see my made-up story as though it was actually happening, and my heart was going like crazy.

"What happened to them?" said Royce.

"In—in the morning, the tent—well, the blood had turned to rust stains again. But guess what? The family had rust stains on their sleeping bags and pillows. And rust stains on their faces! They never got rid of them. It didn't matter how much they washed—"

"Holy moo-cow!" said Royce.

"You morbid lot!" It was Auntie Rosie at the tent flap. "Filling your heads up with a lot of hoogly piggly. Give me Jeannie's sleeping bag. She's coming in with us."

"Can I come too?" Johnny asked.

"I suppose so," said Auntie Rosie. "We'll leave the three musketeers to their tales of terror."

But we didn't tell any more ghost stories that night. We got down in our sleeping bags, only our faces showing, while the wind moaned around us and the moonlight through the trees made patterns on the wall of the tent.

# 11.

Dad was impressed with the gold nugget. He held it up to the light and swirled the bottle.

"Found it all by himself, he did," said Uncle Leo.

"He has obviously enjoyed himself," said Dad. "I do hope that he wasn't too much trouble."

"Oh no, no. We were the trouble," said Uncle Leo, putting his arm around my shoulders. "He got puked on, near drowned and lost in the forest, but bless him, he still came up smelling of roses."

Dad's smile fluttered a bit. He never knew when Uncle Leo was joking. "It's very good of you, Leo. Thank you."

"Dad," I said. "Why don't we go camping?"

He gave me back the nugget. "I'd love to, Michael, but you know what grass does to my hay fever."

"The golf went well, then?" said Uncle Leo.

"Terrible!" Dad laughed. "My putting was way off form. But we did have a very pleasant weekend. Come on, Michael, say thank you to Uncle Leo and we'll be on our way. Your mother will have tea on the table at six o'clock sharp and I believe it is something special."

I sat in the front next to Dad. I had to admit that it felt good to get into a car that didn't smell of mice, dog, hen, Johnny puke, spilled yogurt and old tuna sandwiches. Dad smiled at me. "We missed you, Michael. Your mother and I certainly missed you."

I knew what to say. "Me too, Dad."

Something in the back of my mind whispered, Liar, liar, your pants—I stopped the words. In a way I truly had missed him and Mom but it had been no big problem. In fact, I thought I was the luckiest kid in the world to have two families.

Dad turned the wheel and we drove slowly up our driveway. The tires on the gravel sounded just like dead soldiers marching.

"Holy moo-cow," I said to myself. "Holy beautiful fantastic moo-cow."

"What's that, son?" said Dad.

"Nothing," I replied.

# The
# Wild West Gang
# at the School Fair

## 1.

It was the third time that Mom had taken over the school fair cake stall. At both other fairs, she'd won the silver cup for the most successful fundraiser. She reckoned she'd get it again. The *Edmonds Cookery Book*, a writing pad, and a long list of school mothers were beside her and the phone.

"Two dozen date squares, my dear. With lemon icing, please. Can you manage a batch of oatmeal cookies as well? Oh. How very kind of you! It's for a good cause, you know. New computers for the school."

She put down the phone, had a sip of peppermint tea and started again. "Good morning? Is that Mrs. Judith Flynn?"

Dad was waiting to use the phone and so was I. I needed to call my cousin Royce West to find out his secret recipe for putting the taste back in old chewing gum. But Mom had been on the phone so long, I reckoned it would be quicker if

I went around to Royce's place.

"I am running the cake stall at the school fair," said Mom, flicking through the cookbook. "I am wondering if you would be so kind as to do some baking. You would? Oh, you are so very generous. A chocolate cake? A small batch of almond cookies?"

Dad was getting impatient. He muttered at me, "Take cover, Michael. The great cake invasion has begun."

"It will be, by far, the best stall in the entire fair," said Mom into the phone.

I remembered Mom's other cake stalls, when I was five and when I was eight. Our house was filled with cakes and cookies and I wasn't allowed to touch a crumb because of the sugar. It was agony.

A week earlier, I'd said to her, "Mom, if sugar's so bad, why do you sell cakes for other people's kids?"

She'd got her hurt look. "Michael, dear, there are three things I want to say. First of all, the word *kids* is vulgar. You should say *children*. The second is that not everyone has your sugar allergy. The third concerns your tone, Michael. You have been seeing far too much of your cousins. You're getting sassy. You are beginning to sound like a West."

When she said that last bit, I was so pleased, I hugged her. Then I remembered to say, "Sorry, Mom."

She patted me on the cheek. "Good manners are important, Michael. Your father and I want you to grow up to be a gentleman."

But now she prodded another set of numbers on the phone. "Good morning, Mary. It's Eileen here. I'm calling about the school fair. Yes, yes, I'm doing the cake stall again this year."

Dad groaned. "I'll use my cell phone," he said.

"And I'm going to the Wests'," I said.

Dad lifted his eyebrows, making ridges in his forehead. "You were there last night."

"That was the twins' birthday party. Today I need to see Royce."

"What about?" he asked.

"Homework—and other things."

"Well, don't be long," said Dad. "You know how your mother—"

"Royce is brilliant at math," I told him.

Mom had the phone tucked into her neck. She smiled. "Oh, Mary! You are so very kind!"

Outside, I said to Dad, "You know this school fair? Well, Auntie Rosie's got a stall, too. She told me."

Dad stopped in a crunch of gravel. "What kind of stall?"

"I don't know, but she said it'd be a hoot."

"We can assume she's not selling owls," said Dad.

"No, not that kind of hoot. The whole family's doing it. Auntie Rosie wouldn't tell me because she wanted it to be a surprise."

"In other words," said Dad, "she doesn't want your mother to know."

I shrugged, thinking he'd probably hit the nail on the head.

Dad stopped outside the garage, and scratched the back of his neck. "Michael, I have a bad feeling about this school fair. When the day comes, I might just be playing golf."

"Why?" I asked.

"Cakes and hoots," he groaned, and I knew exactly what he was thinking.

# 2.

There was a lot of noise in the Wests' family room. The twins, Johnny and Jeannie, were standing on the couch, singing pop songs and waggling their hips until their jeans fell down. It was their way of telling Auntie Rosie that their birthday jeans were too big.

"You'll grow into them," said Auntie Rosie, who was eating peanuts and reading a book. "They have to last a year."

Johnny pulled his jeans back up and started singing again, moving his hips around as though he was whirling a hula hoop. He held a wooden spoon for a microphone, shut his eyes and yelled, "Baby, baby, I love you so much. Oo-oo-oo! I need your touch!" The new jeans, stiff as cardboard, slid down to his knees. He was wearing his birthday underpants, red with black penguins on them.

Jeannie was a bit fatter so her jeans didn't come down so easily. She jumped up and down on the couch to get them moving and the bouncing made Johnny lose his balance. He tried to take a step but his jeans were around his ankles and he fell flat on the floor. Goof the dog jumped on top of him, barking like mad.

"See?" said Jeannie. "Big jeans are dangerous!"

"Tough toenails," said Auntie Rosie, not looking up from her book.

"If that happened on the road, I could get run over by a car and killed," said Johnny, trying to stop Goof from licking his face.

"Think of the news headline," said Auntie Rosie. "Boy killed by big birthday jeans."

Johnny sat up in his penguin underpants and kicked his feet out of the jeans. "You're a terrible mother," he sighed.

"I know," said Auntie Rosie, eating more peanuts.

Jeannie said, "I bet Auntie Eileen doesn't make Mickey wear jeans too big for him."

Auntie Rosie got this really wide smile. "Mickey's mother is perfect," she said. "Isn't that right, Mickey?"

"I—I've come to see Royce," I told her.

"Absolutely perfect," Auntie Rosie said. "Never does a thing wrong."

Johnny put his jeans on his head so that the legs stood out like bent rabbit's ears. Goof barked and barked, and his breath smelled awful.

"What's happening with my sister's plans for the cake stall?" said Auntie Rosie.

But I didn't want to discuss Mom. "Royce!" I shouted above the noise. "I want to talk to Royce!"

Honey, the baby, came in, walking wide in soaking pants. Her mouth was smeared dark brown and she was clutching crumbs of chocolate cake in her fists. She sat down with a wet plop and stuffed her hands in her mouth.

"Where did you leave the rest of your birthday cake?" Auntie Rosie asked Jeannie and Johnny.

They both squealed like smoke alarms and rushed out of the room in their underpants, leaving the birthday jeans on the floor. Goof went to Honey and tried to lick the chocolate off her fingers.

"Where's Royce?" I asked for about the millionth time.

Auntie Rosie picked up Honey, wet pants and all, and sat her on her lap. Then she wiped Honey's hands with her T-shirt. "Garden shed," she said. "He's been doing the trash again. Like a rat up a sewer, that kid."

I knew what she meant. Royce was crazy about junk. On Saturday mornings, he rode his bike around town looking in the big dumpsters outside shops or building sites. He came home with all kinds of stuff tied to his bike—cardboard boxes, sheets of polystirene, bits of timber and glass. Once he had a store mannequin on the back of his bike, a bald figure with bumps on its chest and one arm missing. Now it sat in a bean bag in his bedroom. He called it Venus and he said that one day, when it's an antique, it would be just as valuable as the real Venus statue.

I found him in the shed at the back of the garage, counting stacks of cardboard. They were an odd shape and I realized they were boxes squashed thin. Tuck in the flaps at the bottom and the top and you had a small carton with a picture of a red dragon and *Hong Kong Cafe Takeaway* printed on the top.

Royce yelled at me, "Check out this! Hundreds of them! Thousands! Brand new! I was just going to bring them down to your place."

"What for?"

"Your mother." He tried to give me an armful of cardboard. "She's doing the cake stall, isn't she? Take a good look! Perfect for one dozen cookies. Cut them in half for a cake. All her packaging problems solved in one go."

I folded my arms. "Chinese takeout."

"She can put another label on top."

"From a dumpster dive," I said. "Filthy. Probably got thrown out because rats peed on them."

"Don't be stupid! The Hong Kong Cafe's changed to plastic containers. That's the only reason. These are totally hygienic, not a mark on them. See? Clean as a hospital." He was leaning over me with his wild look, his eyes big, his freckles dark in his flushed face. "Not a single germ in the whole lot! But all right, if you're going to be fussy, I'll give them a squirt of fly spray just to make sure."

I backed off. "You're trying to sell these to my mother?"

"They're exactly what she needs!"

"You want money for them?"

"No, no!" Then he stopped. "Well, they're worth something. I went up there and got them, didn't I? At my own expense?"

"What expense?"

"My time is worth something. Wear-and-tear on my bike. Shipping and handling costs."

"Come off it, Royce."

He waved a box at me. "All right, Mickey, you're a tough guy, but you win. I was going to ask for twenty cents a box. But because you're my best friend, and because your mother is my aunt, she can have them for five cents. That's five cents each. And that's providing she takes the lot. Five measly cents. You couldn't get better than that."

I shook my head. "Sorry, Royce. I know Mom. She wouldn't touch them with gloves on."

"You don't have to tell her where I found them. She'll be rapt. Perfect for cookies, muffins, cakes, scones. I'll even help her to fold them."

I looked at the stacks of cardboard taking up every bit of spare space in the shed. He must have had hundreds of them. "She's already got containers. You know, ice cream cartons, trays, plastic bags."

"She needs more!"

"No, she doesn't, and she wouldn't take them. Not even if they were free."

Royce lost his selling fever. He threw a box on the floor and kicked it into the corner beside a rake and shovel. He said his favorite word as he wiped his hands on his shorts. "What am I going to do with them?"

"You'll think of something," I told him. "What about your mother's stall?"

"Nah. It's not that kind of stall. Are you really sure Auntie Eileen—"

"I'm really sure."

He started to whine. "But I got them especially for her."

"Sorry, Royce."

"Oh, shut up! You're always saying you're sorry. I get sick of it."

"Sorry," I said.

We went back to the house. He was in a bad mood. I would be, too, if I had hundreds of useless boxes to get rid of. He didn't want to talk about our math homework. He wasn't even interested when I showed him my matchbox full of old chewing gum. Goof was, though. The stupid dog snapped at the box and I pulled it away just in time.

"You told me you had a secret recipe," I reminded Royce.

"What if I did?"

"You said it made old gum taste like new."

"So what?"

"Well, are you going to tell me or aren't you?"

He scratched his head. His hair was long and looked like ginger sheep's wool. "Maybe I will and maybe I won't." Then he punched me on the arm. "It's no big deal, you stupid nerd. You just chew it up soft, then you roll it in sugar and leave it

74

all night. Brings back the flavor."

"Oh, is that all? I knew that ages ago." I didn't really know, but I was wild because he called me a nerd. I pushed Goof away with my foot. "You should do something about that dog's breath. It absolutely stinks."

Royce sniffed in front of Goof's face. "Just like when you fart," he said.

I felt my face getting hot. "I don't!"

"Yes, you do! Every morning at school." He cupped his hand against his armpit and wagged his arm up and down, making disgusting noises.

"I do not!"

"I should know," he said. "I sit behind you, and it's far worse than Goof's breath, I can tell you."

Actually, it was true. I pushed Goof away again. "It's because I'm allergic."

"So am I," said Royce. "Allergic to your stinkbombs."

"It's my sugar allergy."

"Nah!" Royce laughed. "It's that muesli stuff your mother gives you for breakfast. Too much fiber. It makes wind in your stomach. The wind goes down your innards in little bubbles, gathering up stink along the way. I know. I saw a movie about it. By the time it gets to your backside, it's so bad—"

"What is?" said Miranda.

She was standing in the doorway, her long ginger hair brushed out like a halo. She had on a pink shirt and brown shorts with paint on them. She looked really beautiful and I didn't want Royce to tell her what we'd been talking about. "Muesli," I said quickly. "We're discussing muesli and sugar allergy and—and dogs."

"And Mickey's rotten farts," said Royce.

"That's not true!" I had to tell a lie. "You're making that up!"

Royce laughed. He put his hand under his arm and made that hideous noise again.

"Cool it, Royce," Miranda said.

My face was as hot as a boiled potato. "I don't!" I shouted at Royce, my voice all shaky. "I don't, I don't, I don't—" I couldn't say any more because I was just about crying.

Royce was cackling like a hen. "Muesli farts! Muesli farts!" he shrieked.

Miranda put her arm across my back. Her hair was nearly touching my face and it smelled like lemons. "Ignore him," she said. "He's in a vile mood because Mrs. Killeen wouldn't buy his silly old cardboard boxes."

I blinked. "Who?"

Royce stopped making horrible noises. He looked out the window and shrugged.

"Mrs. Killeen," said Miranda. "She's doing the sweets for the school fair. Old moneybags here thought he'd make a fortune. He tried to sell her boxes for her fudge and coconut ice. You know where he got them?"

"Yeah, yeah, yeah," said Royce. "I'm hungry. Let's see if there's any party stuff left over—"

"From a dumpster!" said Miranda.

The thick feeling in my throat had gone. My eyes were dry and as hard as stones. I gave Royce the kind of smile that detectives give crooks in the movies. "Was this before or after you tried to sell me those boxes for my mother?" I asked.

"He tried what?" said Miranda.

Royce smiled back, a big cheesy grin, then put his thumbs in his ears and waggled his fingers at me. There wasn't much else he could do. I didn't laugh. I was still mad at him for talking about my farts in front of Miranda. Mom was right. Royce had horrible manners.

# 3.

I'd lost my chewing gum. It was a bit of a worry because I wasn't supposed to have gum in the first place. I'd saved it for ages, bits given to me by my cousins or kids at school. The box was full.

I did what Royce said. I shoved the whole lot in my mouth and nearly choked, chewing it up soft. Then I got a bowl of sugar, pushed the lump of gum into it and hid the bowl at the back of the kitchen cupboard. At least, I think that's what I did. I forgot about it for a couple of days and when I looked, it was gone.

I did a big search along the shelves. No bowl of sugar. No gum. If Mom had found it, I'd have known all about it by then, so I figured it must have got thrown out. What a waste! Six months of gum, and I still didn't know if Royce's recipe worked.

The school fair was next week and the house was filling up with the smell of cookies. There were big cartons stacked along the hall with names on them—coconut cookies, ginger snaps, shortbread, raspberry bars. The smell was driving me mad. Chocolate chip and macadamia nut cookies sat right outside my bedroom door. I even dreamed about them.

I knew how easy it was for the wicked witch to trap Hansel and Gretel with her cookie cottage. She'd have got me for sure. But Mom was a different kind of witch. She'd got all these cookies plastic-wrapped in trays and bags, all named and priced and counted. If I tried to snitch just one, she'd have known. I reckoned I'd just get tortured to death by the smell.

I watched her wrap and pack some caramel shortcake.

"From Mrs. Fa'alo," said Mom. "She's going to make a mango cake, as well, and five dozen sausage rolls. Michael, this stall will be the biggest fundraiser the school has ever seen. People always make jokes about cake stalls. Just you see how fast these little trays of cookies turn into computers."

"You'll get the cup again," I told her. "You'll be best."

She smiled. "Well, I don't know—"

"Mom, you're sure to win."

"It's not a game of chance, Michael," she said. "Not like winning a raffle or the lottery. Fundraising requires hard work." She put a price sticker on some caramel shortcake and then looked at me. "I wonder what Rose is selling? Old clothing? Crafts? Plants?"

I shrugged.

"You really don't know?" said Mom.

"No. Honest. Auntie Rosie and Uncle Leo are telling everyone it's going to be a surprise."

Mom made a noise that was almost a laugh. "No one could ever accuse Leo and Rose of being addicted to hard work," she said. "I find it very strange that anyone could organize a stall for the school fair and keep it a secret. In fact, I'm beginning to believe there is no stall."

"There is," I told her. "Miranda was painting a sign for it."

"What sign?"

"She wouldn't let me see."

"How very curious," said Mom. "Well, Michael, all will

be revealed on Saturday. Maybe the Wests' fundraising effort will buy the school a computer mouse-pad." She put packages of brownies into a cardboard box. "I'm only joking," she said.

I looked at her face. She was laughing but she was not joking.

"You will definitely get the silver cup," I told her. Then I asked, "Are those brownies sugar-free?"

She patted me on the head. "Have an orange," she said.

# 4.

The school fair day was fine. No wind. No clouds. Before seven o'clock, my teacher Mr. Fromish had his van in our driveway, helping Mom and Dad to load the cartons of cakes for the stall. Mr. Fromish liked cakes. At school, he had icing sugar on his mouth while he talked to us about healthy eating. Donuts were his absolute favorite and he often wore a pink or white moustache. My cousin Jeannie reckoned that Mrs. Fromish must have liked kissing Mr. Fromish.

Mr. Fromish also liked apple pies. Mom had made twenty apple pies and stored them in the freezer. As Mr. Fromish helped Dad stack them in a box, he told Mom she made the best apple pies in town.

"You must have one," said Dad.

"Yes, you must," said Mom. "A small thank-you to the van driver."

"What a pleasant surprise!" said Mr. Fromish, and he put the pie on the seat of the van. "Eileen, what would the school do without your support? You'll win the cup again, for sure."

Mom smiled and wiped her hand on her apron. "Are you doing the book stall again this year?" she asked.

"I am, I am. Not as popular as cakes, though." Mr. Fromish put the last carton in the van. "Is that the lot?"

"I understand the West family has a stall," said Mom.

"No one knows what it is," said Mr. Fromish. "They haven't been collecting but they did ask to borrow six school chairs. Oh well, I'm sure we'll all know in about three hours." He opened his van door and jumped in. There was a crackling sound and Mr. Fromish got a look of pain. He pulled the frozen pie from underneath him. It hadn't squished, but the crust had broken like glass.

"Oh dear!" said Mom. "You must have another. Take two. Open the carton and help yourself."

Mr. Fromish gave her the broken pie. "What would the school do without you?" he sighed.

# 5.

Face painting and fake tattoos. That's what the Wests were doing. The sign over their stall said BODY ART and all of them, from Uncle Leo down to Honey, had their faces, arms and legs painted in bright colors. They'd even done the dog. There were pink stripes down Goof's back and the fur on his head had been gelled bright purple.

"Mickey!" my cousins yelled, waving at me to come over.

Mom made a funny sound and I thought she'd stopped breathing. She stopped moving, too.

"Mickey! Mickey! Auntie Eileen!" they shouted.

"Oh no!" Mom murmured. "Oh no, please no!"

Their stall was like everyone else's, a long table with a sign over the top, but on the table were boxes of body paint, brushes, sponges and bowls, towels, sheets of tattoo transfers. In front were six plastic chairs, ready for customers.

One half of Royce's face was black, the other blue. His legs and arms were ringed in black and blue as though his skin had turned into striped socks. I hardly recognized him without his freckles. Miranda had her hair tied up in two ginger ears and her face painted like a cat. Uncle Leo had a green and white face like Count Dracula, blood dripping down his chin. Auntie Rosie was a baby.

"Hello, Eileen!" she called. "Good to see you!"

"I don't believe it!" Mom moaned.

Auntie Rosie's hair was done in tiny braids that stuck out all over her head. Her face was pink with huge brown freckles painted on it. Long painted eyelashes made her eyes look like daisies. She was dressed in a bulgy stretch-and-grow suit with a big baby pacifier on a cord around her neck.

She strode across the grass. "Need some help to set up your cakes?"

Mom grabbed my hand. "No, thank you, Rose. I've got Michael and Arthur. We'll manage."

"Does Mickey want his face painted?" said Auntie Rosie.

"No," said Mom. "He doesn't like that sort of thing."

Auntie Rosie smiled. "Don't you think he should answer for himself?"

Mom closed her mouth and held my hand tight.

"Want to be our first customer?" Auntie Rosie asked me.

"For free," said Johnny. He was like a bumble bee, his face zig-zagged brown and yellow.

Yes, I wanted my face painted, but not like a baby or a

bumble bee or a vampire. I wanted to be like Miranda, a cat with a pink nose and whiskers. I wanted to be Miranda's twin.

Mom tugged my hand.

"I'm sorry," I said to Auntie Rosie. "I'm helping Mom with the stall. Thanks, all the same."

The cake stall was on the other side of the school playground, which was just as well for Mom. She was so upset, her hands were shaking.

"Rose deliberately does it," she said to Dad. "Don't tell me otherwise. I've known her all my life. She takes delight in showing me up."

"Look at it this way." Dad was helping to unpack the cookies. "If someone else was doing a face painting stall, wouldn't you think it was a good idea?"

"Certainly not!" said Mom.

"What's wrong with it?" said Dad.

Mom stacked some trays of ginger snaps on her table. "You're taking her side," she said.

"I'm not taking anyone's side," said Dad. "I think it's a bit of harmless fun and I don't know why you're so upset."

They couldn't say any more because people had stopped to look at the cakes. The fair wasn't open yet but already the parking lot was full and crowds were gathering around the stalls. There was an old-fashioned band tune playing over the public address system and the flags above our cake table were fluttering in time to the music. Mom had made the flags red and white to match the tablecloth and her apron.

On one side of us was the craft stall, with homemade candles, soaps, pottery mugs and dolls with skirts to hide toilet paper rolls. On the other side was the stall with the raffles.

Neither of them looked as good as the cake stall and I felt proud when the people told Mom she'd done a great job. Mom smiled at them and said, "Why, thank you. I do appreciate your kindness." Then, as they moved on, she turned to me. "Michael, I absolutely forbid you to have your face painted. Do you hear? You are not to go near the Wests' stall and that is final."

I couldn't believe she meant that. It wasn't right. It was definitely unfair.

"Promise me!" she said.

I mumbled something.

"What was that?"

"All right," I told her. "I promise."

I turned to Dad for support but all he did was shake his head as he stowed some boxes under the table. "Cakes and hoots," he muttered.

# 6.

The principal, Mr. Anderson, had the school choir open the fair with a song. After that came his speech about parent support and school computers and how this was going to be another fantastic year. By the time he had finished, the people were four deep around the cake stall, grabbing at packages of cookies and shortcakes. Mom, Dad, and I were all so busy that I forgot all about face painting.

Dad kept a locked money box chained to the leg of the table. He and I wore bags around our waists. As our bags got fat with bills, Dad transferred the money to the tin. Within an hour, that money box was half full and I was sure that Mom's stall would win again this year. Shortbread, muffins, sponge cakes, chocolate walnut cookies. As fast as I unpacked them from the boxes under the table, they sold. To tell the truth, I no longer wanted any of them. Handling so much cake had zapped my appetite for it. Right then, I'd have happily demolished some pepperoni pizza or a big chicken and lettuce sandwich.

Mrs. Huirama wanted three apple pies. I found one in a box but it was the pie squashed by Mr. Fromish.

"Mom? Where are the apple pies?"

Mom crawled under the table and dragged out a carton. She put three pies in a plastic shopping bag and told Mrs. Huirama that the apples were off her own tree and the recipe once belonged to her great-grandmother. "Actually," she said, "I thought I was going to run out of sugar. Michael has a sugar allergy and we don't use much, except for a little baking. But as it turned out, I did have some extra. Exactly the right amount, in fact. The pies should be perfect."

"Wonderful," said Mrs. Huirama, giving Mom the money.

"I hope you like them," Mom said.

I put the rest of the apple pies on the table. "You ran out of sugar?" I asked in a very careful voice.

"No. I found an extra bowlful on the shelf behind the baking powder," Mom said. "I don't remember putting it there, but I've been so busy—" She turned to a customer. "Yes, may I help you? Some almond cookies? Certainly."

I counted the apple pies on the table. Fourteen. Mr. Fromish had two. Mrs. Huirama had three. Somewhere, there was an apple pie which had in it a lump of chewing gum as big as a matchbox.

My stomach filled up with jitters. What would Mrs.

Huirama say when she cut the apple pies for her family? Suppose it was Mr. Fromish? That would be worse. He was my teacher. I would have to face him all year. A lump of gum in a pie? That's as bad as a cigarette butt or a Band-Aid. People get put in jail for things like that.

The bad feeling in my insides got worse. No way could I have eaten even a tiny chicken sandwich or a small sliver of pizza.

Dad was going off for a ten minute break. I told Mom she should go, too. I thought if she did then maybe I could have done something with the rest of the pies. "You look tired," I told her.

"Thank you, Michael, but I am not tired," she said, "and we are far too busy for you to manage on your own."

She sold two more apple pies to a family with painted faces. She pretended not to notice that the woman was a tiger, her husband a monster, and that their children were all clowns. Again, I heard all about Mom's apples and her great-grandmother's recipe. I wondered if people would think it was her great-grandmother's idea to add chewing gum.

When Dad came back, he had a cup of camomile tea for Mom and something for me. It was a small carton with a red dragon on the top.

"It's not a Chinese takeaway," said Dad. "It's a mystery package. They're being sold at Mr. Armour's jumble stall, five dollars each. Yours is quite heavy. Open it."

I didn't want to open it. My jittery stomach got worse, as the bad feelings from my argument with Royce got mixed with my chewing gum cramp.

Dad took the carton from me. "They've sealed it with tape. There. That's it. Now it will open."

Inside there was a small wrench, an old pocket knife, a plastic spinning top, a keyring with a skull on it, and a package of rubber bands. "Thanks, Dad," I said.

"It's nothing but junk!" said Mom.

"Yes, but what an interesting way to sell junk!" Dad said. "Combine the human love of mystery with the human love of a bargain, and you have a sure-fire recipe for financial success. I think Fred Armour will do well. He's got four tubs full of these. Man, woman, boy, girl."

"You don't know where those things have been!" said Mom, holding out a plastic bag. "Drop it in there, Michael, and go wash your hands. You can't handle junk and then sell cakes. It's unhygienic."

I nearly asked why it's okay to handle money and cakes, but I thought better of it and went off to the bathrooms, walking all the way around the school grounds so I could see what was going on.

The noise of the crowd was so loud, I could hardly hear the music from the overhead speakers. Children with balloons and cotton candy held onto parents who carried overstuffed shopping bags. A lot of the children and some adults wore face paint, and everywhere I saw Chinese takeaway boxes. I wondered why Royce never told me he'd got rid of those boxes to Mr. Armour for his jumble stall. Then I remembered that I hadn't talked to Royce for a week because I'd been mad at him. I wondered if I should talk to him. I really wanted to know how much he'd got for that useless stack of cardboard.

I promised Mom that I wouldn't go near the West's stall, so I stood about four yards away from it until Count Dracula saw me.

"Mickey, my lad, you've come to the beauty parlor?"

I shook my head.

Uncle Leo put down his brush, said, "Excuse me," to the boy who was having his face painted red, and came over. "Is there something wrong?"

"No. Not really." I looked towards Royce and Miranda who were busy doing faces. "I—I just wanted to talk to Royce."

"Go on over," said Uncle Leo.

"I can't." I looked into the spooky Dracula face and saw Uncle Leo's kind eyes. "Mom made me promise."

"Promise what, Mickey?"

"That I wouldn't go near your stall and I wouldn't have my face painted."

Uncle Leo scratched under his black wig. "All I can say is, it's common for parents to get promises from their kids, but it's a mighty rare thing for kids to keep promises. Good on you, Mickey lad. You're a hero. Wait there and soon as Royce is finished—"

But I'd run out of time. "I'm sorry," I told him, "I have to go," and before he could say anything, I ran back through the crowd.

I arrived back at the cake stall just in time to see Dad selling the last apple pie to Mr. Anderson's teenage daughter, Carol. As she paid for it, I realized that she had a fake tattoo rose on each cheek. Did she know how long it takes to get rid of those things?

"Thank you," Carol said. "My father adores apple pie."

Oh great! The chewing gum would be in the last apple pie, which would be served up to our principal Mr. Anderson. One mouthful and I'd be suspended.

"You've been a long time." Mom gave me her detective look. "I suppose you couldn't wait to see the face painting side-show."

"I haven't been near the Wests' stall," I told her.

She gave me another long look and then started tidying the table, putting banana cakes in the gaps left by the apple pies. "They went quickly," she said. "Most people like apple pies."

"Were they all well wrapped?"

"Of course," she said. "Why do you ask?"

"Oh, I don't know. I thought the plastic looked a bit loose."

"Michael, what are you talking about?"

"Nothing really, Mom. Just a couple of the pies. You can't be too careful. There are crazy people who go around deliberately putting things in food."

"What things?" she asked.

"Horrible. Like cigarette butts or—Band-Aids—or—"

She looked concerned. "Go on."

But I couldn't say it. "You read it in the papers all the time," I told her.

She smiled and ruffled my hair, "Oh Michael! What a funny one you are! I assure you, every pie was wrapped and sealed. The only things in them are the high-quality ingredients that I put there. Satisfied?"

No, I was not satisfied. My stomach groaned in misery. It was lunch time and people were sitting in the big tent or under trees, sharing picnics. Any moment, someone could have come over with the remains of an apple pie and the police.

Mom said, "Are you hungry, Michael?"

"No."

"Everything's quiet," she said. "Can you manage here while your dad and I have a cup of tea?"

"Yes."

"You're sure?"

"Yes, I'm sure."

"We won't be long," she said.

I watched them walk towards the big tent. By the time they got back, I would probably be arrested.

# 7.

The moment Mom and Dad entered the tent, two figures arrived at the cake stall, one a ginger cat carrying a white bucket, the other a blue and black creature with striped arms and legs.

"We were watching," said Royce. "Waiting for them to go."

I grabbed him by the shirt. "Royce West! My dad just bought me a mystery carton."

His grin was half blue, half black, white teeth. "Choice idea, eh?"

"You didn't tell me you sold those boxes to Mr. Armour."

"You weren't interested," he said.

"He didn't exactly sell them," said Miranda. "He did a swap for some other junk."

"Junk?" squealed Royce. "You call an antique clockwork Hornby locomotive in one hundred percent perfect condition, junk? It's worth thousands. Hundreds, at least." He stretched his skinny striped arms towards me and spread his hands. "It's wicked, man! Made in the 1920s. Mr. Armour did a straight trade."

"After Royce sold him the mystery package idea," said Miranda.

"I didn't sell it. I gave the idea away for nothing. Make up mystery packages, I told him. People will buy all sorts of stuff when they don't know what they're getting. Mickey, you've got to come and see my engine. It's the real thing."

"I don't know, Royce. I'd like to. I really would." I turned away to sell a package of peanut butter brownies.

"Yeah, yeah, you're busy. You got to help your mother. But when you've done that. Come this evening." He was looking over the table. "Shoot, these cakes are expensive! Don't you have any broken cookies going cheap?"

"No, and don't you break any, either!" I gave the man his change and put his cookies in a plastic bag.

Royce lifted the tablecloth and looked through the cardboard cartons, most of them empty. "What's this?" he said, dragging out a box filled with bits of paper and plastic.

"Just trash," I told him.

"Leave it, Royce," said Miranda. "Mickey, we actually came here to ask if you'd like an arm or leg painting."

"Arm or leg?"

"Sure," said Miranda and she took some face paints from her bucket. "You can't come to our stall and you can't get your face painted. So what about right here? Snakes and ladders on your legs?"

I thought about it. The stall was quiet with nearly everyone at lunch. "Can you do that?" I asked her.

The ginger cat nodded. "I'm good at snakes and ladders."

I didn't know what to say. I wanted Miranda to paint my legs, yes, but suppose an angry customer came back with an apple pie? In the end, I decided to risk it. "Snakes and ladders will be fine."

Miranda turned her plastic bucket upside down behind the table and told me to sit on it. She set her paints, sponges and brushes on an empty cardboard carton, and rolled down my socks. Her fingers on my ankles made my back shiver and I worried that my shoes might smell.

"Royce can look after any customers," she said, "can't you, Royce?"

He didn't answer.

We looked up and saw that he had gone.

# 8.

By four o'clock, all that was left on the stall was a bundle of shortbread, three packages of ginger snaps, and a banana bread. Dad counted the money.

"You've done it, my dear!" he said to Mom. "Over four-teen hundred dollars. That's three hundred up on the last cake stall."

Mom nodded, too tired to get excited. Besides, she was still wild at me for getting my legs painted. The snakes were beautiful, green and yellow, dark blue and white, orange and black, big and small. They had glitter stuck on for eyes, and long forked tongues. In the spaces between them were brown ladders. When I wiggled my knees, the heads of the big snakes moved up and down.

"Deception, Michael," she said. "Plain and simple decep-tion. I suppose you thought you were being clever."

Dad tried not to smile. "Not so much deception as fine definition," he said. "He'll make a good lawyer."

"Don't encourage him, Arthur," snapped Mom. "He knew full well that he was disobeying me, and he looks quite ridiculous."

"It's only a bit of fun," said Dad.

"Deception," said Mom again.

The stalls were supposed to close at four, all money in by four-thirty. At five o'clock, the winning fundraiser would be announced. One hour was a long time to wait. Mom leaned against the nearly empty table and kicked her shoes off. She closed her eyes.

No one had returned an apple pie.

My stomach was still jittery, but there was a tiny little hope. Maybe the pie was going home to someone's freezer. In six months, when they defrosted it, maybe they wouldn't remember where they bought it. Then again, maybe they'd eat it tonight. We'd just get home and a police car with sirens would come down the street. I stretched out my legs. My thoughts went up and down like snakes and ladders. At the end of my thinking there was a thundering voice. Silence in the court. The next case concerns a boy who deliberately put a disgusting substance into an apple pie sold at a school fair. How do you find him? Guilty, Your Honor! Down the tail of the snake to jail!

"Eileen! Mickey!"

I looked up and saw them all coming towards us: Auntie Rosie, the huge baby, dragging a white plastic chair, Count Dracula, the cat, the black and blue thing, two bumble bees, a small butterfly and a pink and purple dog with its tongue hanging out.

Mom was too tired to do anything but groan.

"Where's Arthur?" said Count Dracula, waving a six pack. "I've got a little drop of the brown stuff."

"He's taking in the money," said Mom, not opening her eyes.

"You did well then?" Uncle Leo popped the top off a can

of beer and took off his fangs to drink. "Got the silver cup in the bag?"

"Shut up, Leo!" said Auntie Rosie. "Eileen, you look exhausted. I'll bet you've been going since dawn."

"I'm all right, Rose," said Mom. "It's just my feet."

Auntie Rosie plopped a plastic chair in front of Mom. "Sit down and I'll give you a foot massage. No, come on, now. I insist. Royce, get me that other chair. Miranda? Towel and hand cream."

"No, really!" said Mom but she sat down and let Auntie Rosie lift her foot and put it on a towel draped over her big knees. Auntie Rosie spread cream over her hands, then pressed her thumbs into the sole of Mom's foot. Mom gave a sigh and closed her eyes again.

Uncle Leo picked up Mom's limp hand, and closed her fingers around a can of beer. Mom never drinks beer. She never drinks from a can. Uncle Leo knew that. "Doctor's orders," he said.

She held the can in her lap.

"We had a hoot of a day," said Auntie Rosie. "But I'm glad it's over."

"How much did you make?" Mom asked.

"Three or four hundred. Not much." She put more cream on Mom's foot. "But you can't put a price on the fun. That's what it's all about, Eileen. Having a good time."

"Computers for the school," Mom murmured.

"We only charged a dollar," said Auntie Rosie. "One dollar a face or an arm or a leg, five dollars the whole lot. We just wanted to create an atmosphere, you know. Make people look as though they were at a fair."

"And sure, most people take themselves far too seriously."

Uncle Leo's green and white cheeks puffed out in a small belch. "Beg your pardon. Folks need to kick up their heels."

"I think there is something to be said for a little dignity," said Mom, without opening her eyes.

"Perish the thought!" cried Uncle Leo. "The saints preserve us from all dignity, both little and large."

We all sat up, thinking there would be an argument, but Auntie Rosie told Uncle Leo to close his mouth before a jumbo jet flew into it, and then Dad came back to take the can of beer from Mom's hand. Within five minutes, everyone was smiling and talking—even Mom.

Most people were leaving. Royce sat next to me on the grass, and we watched the cars moving bumper to bumper out of the parking lot. We tried to work out who belonged to which vehicle and most times we were right. "That's Mr. Fromish's van," I said. "Boy, you should have seen him this morning. Mom gave him an apple pie and he sat right on it—squish!"

Royce leaned forward. "What apple pie?"

"Mom threw it out. He put it on the van seat, then he jumped in without looking—"

"Threw it out where?" said Royce.

"I don't know. Well, yes, I do. It's in the trash box under—" I stopped and looked at the blue and black face with the round staring eyes. "You didn't!"

"I'm going to throw up!" he said.

"I told you it was trash. Didn't you see it was squashed?"

"I don't believe it!" Royce held his stomach and rocked back and forth. "I ate an apple pie that was under Fromish's big fat backside!"

"It was wrapped. I mean, it had plastic on it." I grabbed

Royce's arm. "You ate it all?"

"Yeah."

"The whole lot?"

"No one told me, did they!" he moaned.

"You didn't find anything inside the pie?"

"Like what?"

"Like gum?"

"Why would there be gum in an apple pie?"

So I told him all about it, his famous fantastic recipe and the bowl of sugar, and how Mom found it on the shelf.

Royce let go of his stomach. "That horrible great lump of old gum you showed me?"

"What am I going to do?"

He shook his head. "Oh man, you are really in it! I mean really! No way out!"

I was so scared, I was shivering. I said to him, "Putting stuff in food is a criminal offence, isn't it?"

"Yeah, but wait a minute." He smiled. "It was your mother who put it in the pies. Technically speaking, you're in the clear."

That didn't make me feel any better. I looked at my legs. Big snakes, small ladders. "I don't know what's going to happen. I mean, if you found a huge lump of old chewing gum in your food, wouldn't you raise a stink?"

Royce shrugged. "I dunno. Look at it this way. Old gum is a lot better than eating a pie that's had Fromish's butt on it."

We couldn't say any more because Miranda and Jeannie sat down beside us. "Time to leave," said Miranda, "we're all going to our place for tea. Dad and Uncle Arthur are getting pizzas on the way."

I looked back and saw that the four adults were packing

up the stall. Mom was taking down the sign. Auntie Rosie was folding the tablecloth. Dad and Uncle Leo were flattening cartons and putting them in the trunk of our car.

"What about the fundraising results?" I asked.

"You missed it?" said Miranda, her cat's eyes wide. "It came over the public address speakers."

"I didn't hear anything," said Royce.

"You've been talking so hard you made yourself deaf," said Miranda. She leaned towards him and with her hands close to his face gave him a message in rapid sign language.

Royce's mouth and eyes fell wide open. Miranda laughed, her whiskers stretching on either side of her cat nose. Then she said to me, "The cup went to Mr. Armour for his jumble stall."

# 9.

Uncle Leo said there had been a small problem. Mr. Lim of the Hong Kong Cafe had made an official complaint because his restaurant's name had been used in connection with a jumble stall.

"Quite right, too," said Uncle Leo. "He won't take any action because he's a nice man. But I'm thinking, now it'd be good if Royce went around to the Hong Kong Cafe and apologized to Mr. Lim."

"Apologize!" said Royce, spitting out bits of pizza. "Never!"

We were all sitting around the Wests' kitchen table and Mom was holding her pizza carefully on a paper napkin. She hadn't eaten much. I think she was disappointed about not winning the cup, but she didn't mention it. She was trying to push Goof away with her knee. That stupid Goof didn't know there are people who don't like dogs.

Auntie Rosie said to Royce, "You'll apologize if I have to march you down there and nail your tongue to the counter."

"What for?" said Royce. "It was the best idea in the whole fair. I made money for dozens of computers. I went to all that trouble—"

"And you told me Mr. Lim *gave* you the boxes," said Auntie Rosie.

"He threw them out in the trash! Same thing!" said Royce.

"No, it's not the same thing," Auntie Rosie insisted. "It's just as well for the school, and for you, that he didn't go to the police."

I put my pizza down on the table. If they were making such a fuss about Royce's boxes, what would happen about my gum? When the meal was over, I followed Royce up the stairs to his room. He was moaning about adults being un-grateful. I said to him, "Just wait till they get to the apple pie business. They'll forget all about the Hong Kong Cafe."

I sat on the spare bed in his room and stared past my snakes and ladders legs at the laundry hole in his floor. I could see the washing machine and heaps of clothes in the room below.

"I should have got that silver cup," said Royce. "It was my idea that won it."

I tried to say something about the chewing gum, but he wasn't interested.

"Those mystery boxes were the biggest fundraising success of the whole fair!" he complained.

"I bet my mother doesn't think so," I told him.

He walked around, throwing out his arms like an actor.

"I make all that money for them and what thanks do I get? 'Congratulations, Royce?' 'Cool job, Royce?' 'Hit the big one this time, Royce?' No way! I've got to apologize to the man who threw those stupid boxes away!" He turned to me. "You think that's justice?"

I didn't answer because from where I was sitting, it seemed he was making a fuss about nothing. A simple apology didn't line up alongside a food poisoning charge. I looked down my snakes and ladders to the laundry hole. Someone had opened a door, and noise from the kitchen was drifting through. Johnny and Jeannie were telling Mom about their birthday jeans, two sizes too big. Dad and Uncle Leo were talking computers.

"Mr. Armour got the cup," said Royce. "He should apologize."

"He probably has," I said. "I don't know what you're worrying about. I reckon chewing gum's going to need a lot more than an apology."

Royce dropped his striped arms. "Oh, shut up, will you?" he said. "I'm sick of hearing about your stupid gum." Then he remembered why we were there. "I'll get the engine."

The locomotive made us both feel better. This time, Royce hadn't exaggerated. It was nearly perfect—a real Hornby antique, painted green and gold with numbers on the side, and a place in the smokestack to put solid fuel so that it would smoke as it went along. One wheel was missing and the clockwork mechanism was broken. That was all.

"No problem getting a wheel," said Royce. "We need a mainspring out of an old clock."

In the distance, I could hear Mom talking and Auntie Rosie laughing.

"Dad's got an old alarm clock," I said. "He never uses it. I know he'll give it to me, if I ask."

"You're sure it's not digital?" Royce said.

"You think I don't know the difference between clockwork and digital? What kind of an idiot do you think—" I stopped because his hand was on my arm and he was hushing me.

Auntie Rosie's voice came up loud and clear through the laundry hole. "We got into a heap of trouble," she said. "Who told us to do that? Was it Uncle Joe? Or Uncle Davie? I still remember Mother's face when she realized it had come out of her crystal sugar bowl."

Mom was laughing. Really laughing. I couldn't believe what I was hearing. My mother smiled. Sometimes she went ha-ha in a polite way. But she'd never laughed like this, squeaking and gasping for air. "Oh Rose, I don't know where he got the idea. I never—I never said anything."

"It could have been any of my kids," said Auntie Rosie. "I told them. Now they all do it."

I looked straight at Royce and he looked at me. He flicked his hand over the wheels of the engine and they spun, making silver light.

Mom's voice came up, high-pitched and shaking. "You should have seen him, Rose. He—he—said—wrapping loose. People could—put—things in food. Oh dear, it—it was so hard to keep a straight face!"

"You didn't tell him?" said Auntie Rosie.

"No, I didn't. He's not supposed to have—he's not. I've warned him over and over. As soon as I saw that bowl of sugar, I knew. Did I tell you how—how big it was? Like a golf ball! I thought it would block the garbage disposal."

"When are you going to put him out of his misery?" said Auntie Rosie.

"Tonight or tomorrow," said Mom. "It won't do him any harm, Rose. He has to learn a lesson."

"Eileen, you sound just like Mother," said Auntie Rosie, and they both laughed again. Their voices got fainter, then a door closed, shutting them off.

Royce spun the wheels again on the engine and whistled under his breath. All I could think of was the word deception. I wasn't jittery, just angry. Plain and simple deception. How could my own mother let me suffer like that?

Royce wiped his nose with his arm, leaving a smear of freckled white in the black and blue. "It's true what Mom said. When she and your mother were little, they put their chewing gum in Grandma's crystal sugar bowl. Grandma had visitors. A lady got stringy chewing gum in her tea and our mothers got walloped."

I looked at him for a while, and then smiled. "I needed to know that. Thanks, Royce, you're a pal. I owe you one."

"You can apologize to Mr. Lim for me, if you like," he said.

"No way." I stood up. "Just the clock spring."

"Okay," he said. "Clock spring."

I was feeling good, so light and strong I reckoned I could fly down the stairs in one go. But I stopped at the door and looked back at Royce. "I've got some news for you. I've started having toast for breakfast."

He fell back on his bed, waving his striped arms and legs like an upturned beetle. "Thank goodness for that," he said. "But promise me! Whatever you do, don't switch to baked beans!"

# The Wild West Gang and Stink Castle

## 1.

Drawing house plans was Mr. Fromish's idea of a math project.

He said to our class, "Start with yourself, your interests, your needs. Design the kind of home that suits you. First, draw a rough plan and when you think you've got it right, you can draw it to scale."

"Fish scale or music scale?" said my cousin Royce, trying to be smart.

Fromish got his tired look. "Act your age, West, not your shoe size."

Royce grinned. He was feeling good. He had seventy dollars fattening his pocket. He'd shown it to us. Seventy whole dollars, as much as I earned in seven weeks of cutting Mom's lawn, and he'd got it from selling a bag of old junk to Mr. Vivek's second hand shop. The kids who saw the money didn't know whether to be mad at him or extra nice. I figured that Royce was so stingy he wouldn't part with a cent, so I just got mad.

"What kind of junk?" I wanted to know.

"Old stuff, Mickey," he said. "Thrown out."

"Thrown out where?"

"Just junk." He looked a bit squinty and I knew he was trying one of his dodgy answers.

"Some old doorknobs and coat hooks. Funny old bolts, hinges, you know, useless stuff."

"You don't get seventy dollars for useless stuff!" said Linda Bryant.

"Supply and demand," said Royce. "That's what business is all about."

There was no way of getting a straight answer out of him and anyway, he knew we were all rotten with envy. The wilder we got, the smarter he acted, flicking bits of paper around the classroom and acting up like crazy. What a pain!

But I guess old Fromish got his own back when he checked the rough designs for our houses. "Very interesting plan, West," he said, leaning over Royce's desk. "Kitchen, living room, two small bedrooms, a large room labeled *Collections* and another sizeable room labeled *Museum*."

"For my stuff," Royce said, smiling at the rest of us as though he was some comedian.

Mr. Fromish nodded. "I understand. What I don't see is how you're going to manage without a bathroom."

Royce took a quick look at his drawing and then tried to pretend the mistake was deliberate. "Who needs a bath?" he said.

"Who needs to go to the toilet?" said Mr. Fromish.

Everybody laughed. Royce went red under his freckles and put his hand over his drawing, but Mr. Fromish had moved on to my desk.

"Another interesting design," he said. "A house shaped like the letter C."

I quickly explained. "It's actually two houses, Mr. Fromish, one for my parents and one for me, with a long hallway in between."

"That's nice," said Mr. Fromish. "So, even on wet days, your mother will be able to look after you."

I started to nod, but all the kids burst out laughing and I realized that old Fromish was being sarcastic. Roger Bennet from the other side of the room called, "Mommy's little boy!" and the laughing got louder. I felt my face glow like a neon sign.

"Choice!" yelled Royce. "Mickey's mother's an absolutely awesome cook. Way better than any restaurant."

With that the noise got huge, everyone switching to talk about mothers and food and Mr. Fromish completely lost it. The more he called for order, the louder grew the yelling. Royce grinned at me. I grinned back. I'd stopped being mad with him. That was the thing about Royce and all his family— you could never be wild with them for long because they suddenly did nice things.

Slowly, like he thought he was on stage, Royce stood up and walked to the front of the room where Mr. Fromish was waving his hands uselessly for silence. My crazy cousin put his thumb and forefinger in his mouth, breathed deep and gave a whistle as loud as a car alarm. That did it. Everyone shut up and he strolled cheerfully back to his desk, pausing to look at my drawing. "Nice one, Mickey," he said in a loud voice.

After school, I reconsidered my design and decided that instead of a hallway between the two houses, I'd have a path and a rose garden because my mother was dead keen on roses. I figured that if it was raining, I could order a pizza or have jam on toast.

"Suppose you learn to cook like your mother?" Royce said.

"Fat chance," I said.

"I'll tell you something for nothing," he said. "The best cooks and dressmakers in the world are men. Didn't you know that?"

"I mean fat chance Mom would teach me. She never lets anyone mess up her kitchen."

Royce patted me kindly on the back. "You'll probably get married. Your wife'll show you how to cook. Look at my parents. They take turns. I grant you sometimes they fall down on communication and we get either two dinners one night or none at all. Want some advice? Marry a woman who runs a fancy restaurant."

I didn't tell him that I'd already thought about the woman part of my house design and the picture I kept getting was of his sister Miranda, who could do a zillion amazing things, not one of them being cooking.

"You could save a lot of money by not building that extra house," said Royce.

"Heck, man, it's not real!" I reminded him. "It's only a math project." I looked at my drawing, which was now a bit messy and crumpled. "I'll keep the second house and if my mother and father don't live there, I'll rent it out. The money I get in rent will pay for the cost of building it."

Royce smiled. "Cool!" he said, and there was real admiration in his voice. "If you tried you could be a really good businessman, Mickey. We could set up a partnership."

"Yeah?" I smiled back. "Then tell me this, partner. Where

did you find that useless junk you got seventy bucks for?"

"Where does anyone find junk? In a junk heap, of course."

"What junk heap?"

His eyes got very careful. "Your parents wouldn't want you to know."

"Royce! I'm your cousin. I'm your best friend!"

"Good," he said. "You can take me home and give me some of your mother's baking."

# 2.

Royce had a big slice of raisin cake with orange icing. I had a bran biscuit.

"Michael is allergic to sugar," Mom said to Royce, as though she'd never mentioned it before.

Royce looked at the dry old bran biscuit and didn't say a thing about me eating a whole bag of chocolate peanuts at his house last night. Actually the bran biscuit didn't taste all that bad. It was just hard watching Royce gobble up all that icing, especially when he was nearly finished and hinting for another slice. The way he slobbered and smacked his lips was disgusting.

"Auntie Eileen, I reckon this has to be the most delicious, scrumptious, fantastic cake I've ever eaten. Of all the mothers I know, you'd be the best cake baker, no kidding, and of all the cakes you make that's the all-time winner."

I kicked him under the table. "Want some butter to go with it?" I said. "Grease, grease?"

It was even too much for Mom. She laughed and said, "Oh Royce! That West blarney is in your genes. You, your father, your grandfather, you all have so much Irish charm you could talk wishes out of a leprechaun. Why don't you just say you would like another slice?"

"Please, Auntie Eileen?" said Royce with a smile so sweet that it almost set my allergy going.

"What about you, Michael? Another bran biscuit?" Mom looked sad for me. "Some cheese on toast?"

I decided to look sad back. "No thanks." I sighed and turned my head away from the second slice of raisin cake she was putting in front of my cousin. This, I thought, was how the starving people in famine countries felt when they saw tourists stuffing their fat gobs with luxury food. Their stomachs writhed in agony. They fell on their knees and held out arms as thin as pencils. Just a crumb! They begged. Please! Just a small taste!

But I discovered that being a martyr only worked if some-one was looking, which they weren't. Royce was stuffing him-self with cake and Mom was talking about his ears.

"I always get a lot of wax," he said through soggy crumbs.

"A little soap and water wouldn't go amiss," Mom said. "You've got a fine crop of potatoes growing in those ears."

He swallowed, his skinny neck jumping up and down. "Potatoes were last year's crop, Auntie. These are cabbages."

But he couldn't charm his way out of this one. Dirt was something Mom really hated and she was always going on about her sister Rose, her brother-in-law Leo, the five chil-dren, and their lack of hygiene. She stared at Royce's grubby ears and the dust in his curly red hair. "You're old enough to keep yourself clean," she said, her face all pinched as though the words tasted bad. "Your mother's got enough to do, look-ing after the little ones."

Royce gave me a quick look and took another bite of cake. He knew all about Mom's lectures, but I reckon he thought the cake was worth it.

"Cleanliness is next to godliness," Mom continued. "That's what my mother always told me—and my sister Rose. Now, you look at Michael's ears. See how clean they are?"

"I get wax!" Royce protested.

Mom had hold of one of my ears and had turned my head around so Royce could see right in my ear. "I never have to remind Michael to have a shower. I've taught him how important it is to keep himself clean."

She was going too far. I said, "Royce has a shower every morning, too. Don't you, Royce?"

He grinned. "Nope," he said. "Miranda's always in it."

"Royce works," I added. "He works really hard to help Uncle Leo and some of that doesn't wash off. You know, paint and grease and stuff?"

Mom let me go and I saw she had the same tired look that Mr. Fromish sometimes got. "Hurry and finish," she said. "I've got things to do."

I reckoned Royce wouldn't be begging for a third slice of cake and I was right. The last mouthful and he was through the back door, saying thank you Auntie this, and thank you Auntie that, keen to make a getaway before she pushed him into our shower. But as he went out the porch, she called him back, and it wasn't about his dirty ears.

"Royce, dear, I understand your parents are painting the kitchen on Saturday," she said.

"That's right," said Royce.

"Rose phoned me this morning," said Mom. "She asked if all you children could come here for the day."

"Here?" I cried. "Wow! That'll be terrific!"

But Royce didn't look pleased. His eyes got big, his mouth opened, and for once, he didn't have anything to say.

"I'm always at your place," I told him. "I never get a chance to have your family down here. Tell Miranda to bring her guitar. I've got my own TV now. You can use my computer. I'll get out some of my old toys like my tricycle and pedal car for Honey. That'll be all right, won't it, Mom?"

"I'm sorry," said Mom. She put her hand on her chest. "Royce, will you please tell your mother how sorry I am? I've just discovered that Michael's dad and I are playing golf on Saturday."

"Oh, no!" I yelled. "You can't be playing golf!"

The shocked look cleared from Royce's face and he smiled. "That's okay, Auntie Eileen."

"I feel I'm letting your mother down," said Mom, her hand still on her heart.

"We'll think of something," Royce said, waving goodbye.

I was so disappointed, I didn't trust myself to talk to Mom. I reckon if I had been a few years younger I'd have kicked my feet and screamed like Royce's baby sister Honey.

Since when had Mom and Dad arranged to play golf on Saturday? Since this morning! That was for sure.

The thought of having five West kids here had been too much for Mom. She'd been worried about mess, worried about noise, worried that her newly covered couch and chairs might get dirty. So she'd phoned Dad and they'd set up a game of golf. I knew sure as anything that's what had happened.

No one had even thought how I felt about it. For months I'd been visiting the Wests, staying with them on weekends,

THE WILD WEST GANG AND PONG CASTLE

visiting after school and always they were really happy to see me. Now Auntie Rosie had asked Mom to look after her children for one little day and Mom couldn't do it.

I think Mom knew I felt rotten. She put her hand on my shoulder and murmured, "Some other time."

I said in a really grumpy voice, "If you and Dad are playing golf, what happens to me?"

She hugged me and her tired look got some wrinkles in it. "Oh Michael! I don't know! Rose and Leo will be painting—" she shut her eyes for a moment. "Maybe you could all go for a picnic or something."

"Where?"

"I don't know—the park, perhaps."

I said, "Maybe we could all have a picnic right here while you and Dad play golf."

Mom made herself laugh. "Very funny, Michael," she said.

# 3.

Auntie Rosie saw through it, quick as a blink. "Wonders will never cease," she said, as she folded laundry on the kitchen table. "What's the difference between a game of golf and a package of instant pudding? Both can be whipped up in a few seconds."

"You mean," said Miranda, "why is a game of golf like a package of instant pudding."

"That's what I said." Auntie Rosie shook out a small pair of jeans, folded them in half, then quarters.

Miranda shook her long red hair. "No, you said, what's the difference between—"

"Oh, bite your butt!" said Auntie Rosie. "Here, give me a hand with these, will you?"

Miranda went to the laundry basket and I followed. As she leaned forward, pushing back her hair, I had a quick look at her ear. It was as clean as clean with a row of freckles on the outside rim, and a small gold stud on the lobe. Cool, I thought. But then everything about Miranda was cool. She picked up a T-shirt. I grabbed the baby's overalls. We folded together in perfect timing like it was some kind of drill. Mom never folded clothes like this. She ironed everything, even the tea towels and sheets, and she never let me get close because she reckoned I'd burn myself. I decided that when I built my house, I probably wouldn't even have an iron in it. Miranda and I would just fold clothes straight off the clothes line, while they were still smelling of sunshine and fresh air.

But about then, the air became not so fresh. Honey was in the doorway, walking very slowly, staring at her mother with wide gray eyes. She put her finger in her mouth and said, "Poos!"

"Poos is right, you darling little stinker," said Auntie Rosie. "Why didn't you tell me?"

"Honey done poos." She smiled at us as though her diaper was full of diamonds.

Auntie Rosie dropped Uncle Leo's shirt back in the basket and grabbed a clean diaper and the overalls I'd just folded. "You went on the potty yesterday. Why not today?"

Honey giggled, and Auntie Rosie gave a big sigh. "I do hope we can get you out of diapers before your twenty-first birthday. Come on, before you pollute the entire kitchen!" She grabbed Honey's hand and took her and the smell down the hall to the bathroom.

That left just me with Miranda, who was standing so close I got a whiff of the lemony scent of her skin and hair, which was much better, I might add, than Honey's effort. As we folded towels, she talked about the paint for their kitchen and that reminded me of my house drawings which I'd just finished, and the small concern I had about neither her nor I being able to cook. I didn't tell her that, of course. I just said, "What are we going to do tomorrow?"

"Keep out of the kitchen," she replied.

"My mother suggested we go for a picnic, maybe to the park."

"Hey! That's an idea! Honey loves the park."

I got brave. "I could come around really early and you and me could make the picnic lunch for us all. How about it?"

"I suppose so." She looked a bit vague. "What'll we make?"

"Oh, sandwiches and cakes and that sort of stuff. You know, like people always have at picnics."

"Cakes?" She looked at me. "I don't bake cakes. Can you do that, Mickey?"

I tried to think of something to say apart from no, but just then Royce and the twins came in and there was a lot of noise because Jeannie's brown and white mouse had given birth to seven babies, and Johnny still couldn't find some screwdrivers and a wrench missing from his tool kit. I knew Mom would make us a cake. It'd be the least she could do.

"I'll come around at seven," I told Miranda.

# 4.

It was just as well I arrived at the Wests' house at seven the next morning because at half-past seven Uncle Leo was up and clearing stuff out of the kitchen cupboards to get ready for the painting. Miranda and I had buttered all the bread by then, but when we looked for the jam and peanut butter, it had gone. It was all right, though. Miranda found a dish of meat and some lettuce and tomatoes in the fridge, so we made thick, healthy sandwiches and grabbed a bag of apples before they disappeared into one of Uncle Leo's boxes.

Mom had made us a carrot cake. It didn't have any icing on it. Maybe Mom ran out of time, or maybe she thought she was saving me from temptation. Anyway, it still looked pretty good. Miranda filled some bottles with water and there it was, a whole picnic lunch for six kids.

No one seemed to notice our great work. About eight, Auntie Rosie and the others came storming out and we all had cornflakes with cold milk. By that time, Uncle Leo had cleared all the saucepans and pulled the fridge out from the wall.

There was a bit of an argument about who was going to carry the picnic box to the park. It was amazingly heavy.

Uncle Leo suggested we put it in Honey's stroller. "Sure, and she can walk. Those little legs can go a mile on a full tank of cornflakes. She'll be tired on the way home, but by then your box'll be light as a balloon, and Honey can have a ride."

Auntie Rosie was full of instructions about what to do and not to do at the park. She actually sounded a bit like Mom. Stay together. Watch Honey. Don't talk to strangers.

Don't go near the river. Take your coats in case it rains. Be careful with the swings and slides. Don't take your eyes off Honey. No one's to wander off by themselves. Don't pull out any plants. Don't make too much noise or do anything that'll get up the nose of the caretaker. All hold hands crossing the street. Don't let go of Honey.

"What if it rains hard?" said Johnny. "Are we supposed to stay there and die of pneumonia?"

"If that's what you want, my boy," said Uncle Leo, rubbing a cupboard door with sandpaper.

Jeannie looked hopeful. "You could give us some money and we could go to the video arcade."

"Don't be silly," said Auntie Rosie. "If it pours, you'll all come back here and have a picnic upstairs in Royce's bedroom."

Royce got very upset at that and yelled his favorite word, adding it to "No!" I was afraid that one day he'd use his "sh" word in front of my mother and that'd be the end of the cake hunting season, for sure. Mom hated swearing. All Auntie Rosie said was, "Close those lips, Royce, before I staple them shut."

"I'm not having everyone in my room!" he cried. "I've got a lot of valuable gear up there."

"Then pray it won't rain," said Uncle Leo.

We had the picnic box and our raincoats in the stroller and were ready to leave when Auntie Rosie came out holding Honey's green plastic potty.

"Have you got room for this?"

"Mom!" said Miranda.

"She's so close to being potty-trained," said Auntie Rosie. "I don't want to break her routine."

"I'll take her to the toilet in the park," said Miranda.

"It's too big. She's afraid she'll fall in."

"I'll hold her," Miranda said.

"She's used to her potty," pleaded Auntie Rosie. "I'll wrap it in a plastic bag."

"If that potty goes, I stay home," Miranda said, folding her arms. As if it was a signal, Royce, Jeannie, and Johnny folded their arms, too. Honey looked up at them then did the same.

"I think you're all a little potty!" said Auntie Rosie, laughing at her own joke. She put down the green plastic thing and instead gave Miranda a package with a clean diaper and pants in it. "Enjoy yourselves," she said.

To tell the truth, the only person who wanted to go to the park was Honey. Royce, Johnny, and Jeannie grumbled, kicked stones and reckoned they were being pushed out of the house.

"We might as well be orphans," said Johnny.

"The thing is," said Jeannie, taking her turn to push the stroller, "we could have helped them paint the kitchen. They'd have got it done in record time."

"They're remembering the disaster with the living room," said Miranda.

"But we were younger then," said Jeannie.

Royce grinned, enjoying the memory. He said to me, "Johnny rode his tricycle into the can of yellow paint and it tipped all over the wallpaper rolls. Mom got such a shock she fell off the ladder, and then Miranda—"

"It wasn't my fault," said Miranda.

"Miranda dropped her paint tray on Dad's head."

"Because Royce bumped me!" said Miranda.

"It was like one of those funny old black and white movies," said Royce.

"But we're older now," Jeannie insisted.

We were all walking very slowly, partly because of Honey and partly because we weren't keen to get there. We'd done the park dozens of times.

Although she was only little, Honey knew we were in a gloomy mood, and she tried to cheer us up, picking dandelions for us and pretending to do somersaults on the pavement. She patted herself on the seat of her pants. "No poos! No wees!" she said cheerfully.

There weren't many people in the park, just a couple of joggers and a woman walking her dog. The paths and grass were still wet from last night's rain and from the look of the gray clouds heaped up like dirty soap suds, it would rain again before long. I felt really bad about Mom and Dad and their golf game and I said so to Royce.

"We should be at my place. Stupid golf! I'm sorry. We could be playing computer games. I would've set up my train—"

"Stop apologizing!" said Royce. "I thought you'd got out of that habit."

"All the times I've been to your place—"

"Forget it," Royce growled, looking at the sky.

At least Honey was happy, squealing with pleasure as Miranda pushed her on the baby swing. Johnny and Jeannie went on the merry-go-round, I stayed by the stroller with all our gear, and Royce walked over to one of the big swings. He worked it so hard and high that it squealed, its chains shivered, and the supporting posts swayed in the ground. Sure enough, the caretaker appeared from nowhere and started telling him off.

"Do you know how much this equipment costs?" the man bellowed.

Royce dragged his feet to slow the swing and a bit of turf flew up off his toe. The caretaker yelled even louder.

"That's right! Dig up the grass! I only planted it last spring. It's little devils like you—" The man stopped. "You're that West kid."

"Yeah," said Royce. "What about it?"

The man was breathing hard and his bald head was as red as his face. "The last time you were here, you were trying to kill my ducks."

"Dream on," muttered Royce.

"What'd you say?"

"I said I wasn't killing ducks," Royce replied. "I was skipping stones on the water."

"Don't lie to me!" the caretaker yelled. He grabbed Royce by the jacket and pulled him out of the swing. "You were throwing stones at my ducks. I saw you."

Miranda stepped over, holding Honey in her arms. "He's not lying. Leave him alone."

"And you're his sister. Right?"

"I'm his sister too," called Jeannie.

"I'm his brother," said Johnny. They had left the merry-go-round and were walking towards the caretaker, who was holding Royce by the front of his jacket.

In a few seconds the whole West gang was standing together. I didn't know what to do. I ran towards them, pushing the stroller, the picnic stuff jiggling up and down, the apples falling out on the grass. I shouted, "I'm their cousin!" My voice came out kind of squeaky and I felt embarrassed, but no one laughed.

"Take your hands off my brother or we'll go to the police," Miranda said.

The man let Royce go, but he was very angry. "Okay! You do that and I'll charge him with vandalism. I'll tell the cops how he tried to kill the park's ducks." His face was now crimson and he was wheezing so hard I thought he might fall down with a heart attack or something.

Royce straightened his jacket and dusted the front as though he was getting rid of the man's fingerprints. "You're the one telling lies," he said calmly.

Actually, his voice was more than calm. He was enjoying himself. The two joggers had stopped to listen and now the woman with the dog was approaching to see what the fuss was about.

"Get the hell out of here!" the man said, pointing to the gate.

Slowly, Royce shook his head. "We can't. Our parents told us to play in the park and we always obey our parents. If you want us to leave, you'll have to go around to number twenty-three Silverman Street and ask Mr. and Mrs. West—"

"Get out!" the caretaker bellowed.

"Come on, Royce," said Miranda. "Enough's enough."

She was right. We didn't want to play in the stupid park anyway, and at any moment it was going to pour with rain.

Royce grinned and waggled his fingers at the caretaker. "See you later, alligator," he said, and then we all trundled back over the wet grass, Miranda carrying Honey and me pushing the stroller.

"What a mean man!" I said. "He shouldn't be allowed to work in a park where he has to deal with people."

"It's not much of a job," said Jeannie.

"He's having a bad day," Johnny said.

I turned to look at them. Sometimes, I didn't understand

my cousins. Here was I, all churned up about the caretaker, and they were acting as though nothing had happened.

Miranda was actually laughing. "Did you try to kill his ducks?" she asked Royce.

"Nope. I really was skimming stones. He knew that."

"You sure?" Miranda asked.

"Oh yeah. He would have remembered, all right."

"Then why was he so mad?"

"I got the stones from his path."

"That all?" asked Miranda.

"So he tried to chase me," said Royce, "and he fell flat on his face in the mud. You should have seen him. He looked like the creature from the black lagoon."

Now they were all laughing, but my stomach still felt as though it was full of jumping frogs. I decided I would never go in that park again. I pushed the stroller out the gate and wondered which way to turn. "Your place?" I said.

"Nah," said Royce, who was now full of enthusiasm. "I know where we can have our picnic. In Stink Castle!"

# 5.

It was a bit of a letdown to discover that Stink Castle was the West gang's name for the old Ledbetter place. It wasn't a castle at all but a dilapidated farmhouse at the end of town. Dad reckoned the farm had once been huge, but now the town had swallowed up most of it. The rotting old house stood in the middle of the last field, but you couldn't see the building from the road because of the trees that grew thickly around it.

"You can't get into that house," I said. "It's all boarded up."

"The back door's okay," said Johnny. "We unboarded it."

"We used to play hide and seek after school."

"And ghosts," added Johnny. "We pretend it's haunted."

"Why do you call it Stink Castle?" I asked.

"Because it stinks," said Miranda. "Cats' pee. Old Mrs. Ledbetter had dozens of cats and you can still smell it."

I stopped pushing the stroller. "I'm not having lunch in cats'—in—in a horrible smell. You can forget that."

"It's only downstairs in the old carpet," said Royce, who was having his turn at carrying Honey. "Upstairs is as clean as a whistle. Nothing on the windows upstairs. You look out on the trees. Like sitting in a bird's nest."

I was not convinced. "It'll be old and moldy. We'll get hepatitis or boils or something."

"No, Mickey. Royce is right," said Miranda. "Upstairs really is okay. It's a big room and it's sort of clean. It's even got a table built against the wall."

"Only thing is there's a bit of glass on the floor," said Jeannie.

"What?" I stopped again.

"Not much," said Jeannie. "It won't bother us because we pushed it all into a corner."

I shook my head. "Broken glass means broken windows means rain coming in means rotten and moldy. Count me out."

"It's not that bad," said Miranda.

Normally I would do anything for Miranda, but the thought of eating our special picnic lunch in a place called Stink Castle made me feel sick. "I'm not going," I said.

"You could make up your mind after you've looked," Miranda suggested.

It was the rain that decided us. We put on our coats as the spitty drops began. A dark gray sky was promising a big downpour within seconds and we had to find shelter quickly. We ran as fast as we could along the footpath and down the overgrown drive. Once we were under the trees we were all right. The dark leaves and branches hid our view of the sky, but we could hear the hiss of rain overhead. There wasn't much light under those trees. I pushed the stroller over uneven ground littered with paper, plastic, and old beer cans until we got to the dismal farmhouse, then I stopped again. It was not as bad as I remembered. It was worse!

Most of the verandah boards had rotted away and small trees were growing through the gaps. There were planks nailed across the downstairs door and windows, so the house looked blind as well as sick. The walls were gray cracked boards, some of them edged with moss and green slime, and the upstairs windows had no glass in them.

"Forget it," I said. "I'm not going in there."

"It really is okay upstairs," said Miranda, taking the stroller from me.

"No!" I told her.

"Then you'll have to stand out here on your own," said Royce. "We'll throw your lunch down to you."

I realized that they were all going in whether I wanted to or not. I shrugged and thought, what the heck! Mom and Dad would go crazy if they knew I was going into this filthy, dangerous old place. But then it was their fault we were here, wasn't it? Serve them right if I did get leprosy or the plague.

We ran through the rain around the back of the building and sure enough, there was a door that didn't have boards on it.

"Hey!" said Johnny. "The doorknob's gone!"

"Give it a push," said Royce.

I let them go first. It was like walking from twilight into midnight, the place was so dark. After a while I could make out bars of gray light at the windows and I guessed the room we were in was once a kitchen, but it seemed empty, and yes, it stank like a dirty toilet. I lifted the edge of my jacket and held it over my nose.

This, I thought, was what my parents had forced me to endure.

The Wests knew where they were going. Johnny led the way and we went in single file down some kind of hallway. We stopped and Johnny's voice came through the darkness. "All the doorknobs are missing!"

"Just open it!" Jeannie said.

There was a creaking noise and a wedge of light came into the darkened hallway. I saw peeling wallpaper and the straw of old birds' nests, and then I was through the door and in a room with a fireplace and a spiral staircase. This room was much brighter than the kitchen or hallway. The windows were covered with boards, but light came from above the staircase and at the front wall, up near the ceiling, there was a big hole. I could see dark green trees outside and a glint of wetness.

The bad smell in this room was even stronger. It came through the cloth of my jacket and made me think of dead things. I remembered the time Mom and Dad had gone out and the babysitter had let me watch a horror movie. It had been set in an old house like this and I'd watched it with my hands over my eyes, peeping through my fingers. Seeing was scary enough, but if horror movies had smells to match, I reckon people would faint right away with fright.

The room was a mess. The fireplace was packed with

the straw of birds' nests and the carpet was so dirty it could have been the ground outside. There were bits of junk lying around, a broken saucer, an old flowerpot, more beer cans. Miranda pushed the stroller to the bottom of the spiral staircase, which was made of iron padded with dust. She lifted out the picnic box and said to Royce, "You all go up and I'll pass the food to you."

Royce put his hand on the banister and the stairs swayed like a rope ladder. "Let's go up one at a time."

Miranda frowned at the wobbly steps. "What happened to it?"

"It's come away from the wall," said Johnny.

"Yeah, but it's perfectly safe," said Royce. "It moves like a swing bridge. If we go up one at a time, it won't sway so much. I'll go first with Honey." He set her down and took her hand. "Okay, Honey Bunny? One step at a time."

"It wasn't like that last time we were here," Jeannie said, as the staircase creaked and wobbled.

"It's old," said Royce. "Everything's old. Soon they're going to run a bulldozer through this house." He was going slowly, one step at a time, pulling Honey up after him. "This time next year, no Stink Castle. Even the trees'll be gone. They're building a retirement village on the land."

When Royce got to the top, Johnny went up. The stairs clanked and squeaked and rocked back and forth. Then it was Jeannie's turn. I took a deep breath and thought I couldn't really refuse to go up that wonky staircase if two-year-old Honey had managed it.

Now it was just me and Miranda.

"I'll go halfway up, then you can pass the box to me," she said.

"Okay."

As she stepped on the bottom rung, the staircase lurched sideways. She said, "It used to have some fancy iron bits shaped like cherubs, to hold it against the wall. They've gone. That'll be why it's so wobbly." She climbed seven more steps and then reached down. "Give me the box, Mickey."

When I passed up the picnic box, I bumped the side of the staircase and it swayed so much, it nearly knocked her off. She held tight until it stopped, then took the box and carefully passed it over her head to Royce at the top.

Now it was my turn. I held on to each side as I went up, expecting the staircase to fall to pieces at any moment like in some bad dream.

It not only swung about and creaked, there was also a squealing noise, like nails being pulled out of timber. I didn't like that one little bit. But I did get to the top and I had to admit that they were right about the top room. It had two broken windows, but it was light and not too dirty. It was painted pink, the color of a new scar, and I guessed it had once been a bedroom. There were floorboards clean enough for us to see the grain in the wood, a built-in wardrobe along one wall, a small pink table near the door, and, as Jeannie had described, there was a small heap of dirt and broken glass in the comer where someone had swept it. Across the landing was a small room that looked as though it had been a bathroom, but the bathtub and sink were gone. There were just some pipes sticking out of the wall and a broken toilet with some bricks in it.

Miranda put the picnic box on the table. The rest of us went to the windows. The trees were taller than the house and so close that I could put my hand out in the rain and touch branches. I saw what Royce meant about the room being like a bird's nest.

"Okay?" he asked.

"I suppose so," I said.

Honey, who had been stamping up and down the room to hear the echo of her footsteps, halted in front of Miranda. "Potty," she said.

Miranda frowned. "Oh Honey!"

"Potty!" Honey grabbed the seat of her pants. "Honey do wees."

"Can't you wait?" Miranda asked.

"Potty! Potty!" Honey started to cry.

"Your responsibility," said Royce, who was rummaging through the picnic box. "You refused to bring her little green potty."

"There's a toilet in the bathroom," said Johnny pointing to the room across the landing.

"It's broken," said Miranda. "Honey, do you have to go right now?"

In answer, Honey's howling got louder. She rubbed her eyes with her fists and her mouth went into the square shape of serious crying.

"All right, Honey Bunny," said Miranda. "I'll take you downstairs and you can go outside under the trees." But as she lifted Honey she rolled her eyes.

"Uh-oh, too late," she said.

Sure enough, there was a big wet patch on Honey's overalls.

Miranda set Honey down again. "It's all right, Honey. Don't cry. It's not your fault. It's me. Naughty Miranda didn't bring Honey's potty."

Miranda hopped around in a circle, smacking herself on the seat of her jeans. She pretended to cry and Honey laughed. Then Miranda hugged her. "Don't worry, we've got clean, dry pants for you." She looked over her shoulder. "Royce? Will you get that package of dry clothes out of the stroller?"

Royce stopped picking bits off the carrot cake and went out to the landing. We heard the loud squeaking and groaning that accompanied every step of his descent. It sounded worse than before.

I went out too, and had a close look at the stairs.

At each side of the top step there were big empty holes where there should have been bolts to anchor the stairs to the landing. In the middle, in smaller holes, were four screws, and they were pulled so far out of the wood that there was a five or six inch gap between the iron and the edge of the landing floor.

"This isn't safe," I called down to Royce, who was getting the plastic package out of the stroller.

"These circular stairs always make a lot of noise," he said, coming back and grasping the rail. "Perfectly safe. Look." He jumped up and down on the bottom step.

Not only did the entire staircase sway like a hooded cobra, the screws at the top came out an extra inch.

"Stop!" I yelled. "It's coming loose."

"Nah!" he said, and he came up the steps, deliberately bouncing and swinging.

"They're going to fall!" I couldn't make him believe me. "Royce, don't do that!"

Then I heard Johnny's voice behind me. "No kidding, Royce! The screws are coming out!"

As Royce got to the top, three screws came right out of the wood and the top step slid sideways. If Johnny and I hadn't been there, Royce would have fallen. He lurched, put out his hands, and we grabbed him, plastic bag and all. As we pulled him onto the landing, the other screw gave way and there was the biggest noise I have ever heard. The spiral staircase went down like a major traffic accident, squeal, creak, rattle, smash, crash, crash! Then there was a long silence of settling dust.

The others rushed out to the landing and we all looked down into the room below.

We were marooned!

"Holy moo-cow!" said Royce. Then he gave us his usual sassy grin, "Just as well it didn't hit the stroller," he said.

# 6.

I said to Royce, "I told you! You wouldn't listen!"

"Yeah, yeah! But you're always going on about things. You're scared of your own shadow."

That wasn't fair and the others knew it. Miranda said, "Royce, you're forever in the middle of trouble and every time you find someone to blame. Give me that bag."

He handed her the bag with Honey's pants in it. "I'm not blaming Mickey," he said. "But you have to admit, he's got this big streak of caution in him and he does go on—"

"Shut up, Royce!" Miranda took Honey by the hand and led her towards the bathroom. "If you're so clever, you can think of a way to get us out of here."

Royce put his tongue out at her and then leaned out of a window. "No problem," he said, spreading his hands to the rain. "We'll climb down these trees!"

I was going to tell him that the branches against the house were very skinny but I shut my mouth.

Jeannie said it for me. "They'd never hold our weight."

"It's like rappelling," said Royce. "You grab the branch and it bends right down to the next branch and the next until you're on the ground!"

"What if a branch breaks?" said Johnny.

"Honey can't rappel," Jeannie said.

I had another idea. "If we had a rope we could tie it to the table leg and go down from the landing. We could lower Honey on the rope and the rest of us could slide down."

"No rope," said Royce.

I looked around the room. There had to be something we could use. I opened the cupboard doors.

"Nothing in there," said Jeannie.

"Yes, there is!" I said. But it wasn't a rope I saw. It was a blue plastic tool holder lying on the bottom shelf of the cupboard. The holder contained two screwdrivers and a crescent wrench. "Look at this!"

Royce tried to grab them but Johnny got there first. "My tools!" he yelled. "My missing tools!"

"I just borrowed them," Royce said.

"I asked you!" shrieked Johnny. "I asked you if you had them and you said no."

"It was true," Royce said. "I didn't have them. I didn't know where they were. I thought I might have put them back."

"You didn't say you borrowed them, did you? So how did they get here, huh? What did you—" A sudden look of knowing came over Johnny's face.

Jeannie looked at me, and the three of us yelled, "Royce!"

"The missing door handles!" said Johnny.

"The cherubs that held the staircase against the wall!" cried Miranda, who was coming in with Honey.

"Seventy dollars for old junk." I poked Royce in the chest with my finger. "Old junk?"

"Yeah, yeah, yeah!" He shrugged. "So what? I couldn't let them go under the bulldozer. You know—conservation, recycling. They were too good to waste."

"They didn't belong to you," Miranda said.

"They didn't belong to anyone," Royce protested. "The new owner had taken out what he wanted, the bath, the stove, things like that. The rest would be destroyed."

"You didn't even ask me!" said Johnny, who was checking his screwdrivers and wrench. "When I borrowed your bike, you charged me three dollars an hour. Three bucks, for one measly hour! You've had my tools for over a week!"

"Not working with them," said Royce quickly. "I used them less than an hour. Only a few minutes. And tools are a lot smaller than a bike."

"Stop!" cried Miranda. "Both of you, stop it!" She turned on Royce. "We can't go down the trees and it's about a four yard drop to the living room. You created this problem, brother Scrooge. You solve it."

"Doomed, doomed," said Jeannie in a dramatic voice. "Prisoners forever in Stink Castle."

"I told you, it's not a problem," said Royce. "When we've had lunch, I'll climb down the tree and get you a ladder."

"From where?" asked Miranda.

"I'll find one," said Royce. "Okay? Okay! It's near enough to lunch time. Let's eat."

This really was the stuff of horror movies. There we were in a room the color of flesh surrounded by dark trees, and no way out, no one to hear calls for help. The only trouble with this horror movie—it was real.

I didn't feel like eating. I wanted out, like now, or even sooner. But my cousins? They wanted lunch.

Miranda closed the door so Honey wouldn't go out on the landing and fall over the edge. Royce and Jeannie unpacked the picnic box, draping the tablecloth over the table, setting out the bottles of water, opening the cake tin, unwrapping the sandwiches.

"There's only one apple," said Jeannie.

I remembered. "Sorry. They fell out at the park. When that man was yelling at you and I was running with the stroller. I'm really sorry."

"Stop apologizing," Royce growled. He grabbed a sandwich and shoved almost half of it into his mouth.

Jeannie separated the layers of bread and looked at the filling. "What's that?" she asked, sniffing at it.

"Lettuce and tomato," said Miranda.

"I know, I know," said Jeannie, "but what's the meat?"

"Mince."

"Where'd you get it?"

"Out of the fridge."

"Was it on a blue and white plate?"

Miranda looked at me before she said, "Yes."

Jeannie dropped the sandwich. "Cat meat!" she yelled. "You used Frodo's jellymeat!"

"What?" Royce had almost finished his sandwich.

"It was on a plate in the fridge," Miranda said.

"Because I put it there!" said Jeannie. "I took it out of the tin and scraped it onto the dish—"

Royce said his favorite word and stared in horror at the sandwich crust in his hand. Then he got mad. "I ate it!" he yelled, throwing the crust out the window. "You know what

131

they put in cat meat? Dead calves! Sheep's guts and chicken heads!"

The rest of us hadn't started eating, and we really cracked up. We couldn't help it. The more Royce raged, the more we laughed. Even Honey, who didn't understand what was going on, lay on her back, kicked her legs in the air and squealed.

I held on to my stomach. "Ghosts," I gasped. "Revenge of the cat ghosts of Stink Castle."

"Oh, shut your face!" said Royce, now in a big sulk.

"That's what happens when you let Miranda make the lunch," said Jeannie, throwing the rest of the sandwiches back in the box. "Never, never trust Miranda to prepare a meal."

"I made it, too," I said. "Sorry but it wasn't just Miranda—"

"Double disaster!" said Jeannie. "But all is not lost. We have one of Mickey's mother's famous cakes!" She held up the carrot cake as though it were a silver cup she had won in a race.

We hadn't packed a knife to cut the carrot cake but that didn't bother the wild West gang. They tore it apart like hungry wolves.

I was hungry too, but I wouldn't eat it. I was still wild with Mom and her stupid golf.

# 7.

It was Miranda who worked out how to get us down, although she was actually borrowing my idea. The rope was made of one tablecloth, two nylon jackets and four raincoats, tied end to end with square knots. By the time we had fastened it to the table leg, the other end was about two yards short but that didn't matter. Hanging off the end of it, we'd be only a yard at the most from the living room floor.

The plan was that Royce would stay upstairs until we were all down. Then he'd untie the tablecloth from the table leg and throw the rope down to us. While we were undoing the knots and putting our coats back on, he would slide down the tree branches. It sounded easy the way Miranda said it.

Actually it *was* easy. For the first time that day we did something that didn't go wrong. Miranda went first, the rest of us holding the tablecloth just in case the table leg came off. When she was down, we tied Honey to the end of the last coat, wrapping the sleeves around her and under the straps of her overalls so she couldn't fall. I thought she'd be scared when she went over the edge but she acted as though it was a big joke. I guess that in the West family, a baby gets used to all sorts of dangers.

I went next. Lowering myself over the landing was ultra-scary, because after the tablecloth my hands slipped on the smooth nylon of Royce's jacket. But then I came to the knot at the end of the sleeve and I hung there for a while before sliding down the next bit. Nothing ripped. No sleeve came out. It truly was okay. Miranda held me around the knees to stop me swinging, then I let go and dropped to the floor.

Johnny came next, and after him, Jeannie. Royce untied the knot from the table leg and threw our rope down to us. "See you outside," he said in a cheerful voice and I guessed he'd already forgotten about the cat meat sandwiches.

With all that weight and swinging, most of the knots had become tight and difficult to undo. Honey played with the fallen staircase, crawling in and out of the curves, while

Johnny, Miranda, Jeannie and I worked on those rock hard lumps of cloth. It was taking such a long time that finally Royce came in to see where we were. Apart from being as wet as a trout, he looked fine after his climb down the tree.

"Use the screwdrivers," he said.

"Screwdrivers?" said Johnny.

"As levers. Push them in to loosen the knots."

That worked like magic, but we made a couple of holes: one in the tablecloth and the other in the sleeve of my raincoat. I didn't know how I would explain that to Mom and Dad.

"Better put your coats on," said Royce. "It's pouring out there."

Miranda sat Honey in the stroller and pulled down the plastic rain canopy. No one said anything about the box of cat meat sandwiches that had been left in the pink room. By this time next week, they'd smell really awful, but then Stink Castle specialized in evil smells.

Royce tried to lift the end of the wrought iron staircase. He couldn't move it. He said to me, "Has your father still got his trailer?"

I knew what he was thinking. "No!" I said. "No way!" Then I asked, "What's wrong with your father's van?"

Royce got his squinty look and didn't answer. He kicked the staircase, making it clank and clang throughout its length. "It's worth hundreds," he said mournfully.

I was sick of Royce and his wheeling and dealing. I sniffed. "I expect you'll find some way of taking the steps apart and removing them one by one."

My sarcasm missed the mark. He looked at me with an amazed grin and said, "Mickey, you're a genius!"

"Are you two coming?" called Miranda, who was pushing the stroller towards the hall door.

"Absolute genius!" said Royce.

"Where are we going?" Jeannie asked.

I looked at my watch. It was only half past eleven. I took a deep breath. "My place," I said.

# 8.

I had to change my mind about my parents. When they set their mind to it, they could be really kind. I mean really, really kind.

Mom was shocked at first. "What are you doing here?"

"We had nowhere else to go," I said.

Her expression changed and I thought she was going to cry. "You're all so wet!" she said.

Dad came to the door behind her and I noticed that they were both wearing their house clothes and slippers.

"I thought you were playing golf," I said.

"It was raining." Mom looked at Dad.

Dad gave a smile that lasted about half a second. "The forecast was bad," he said.

The Wests were all behind me and even Royce was silent. I could hear water drip-dripping off our raincoats onto the floor of the porch. "So you didn't go," I said.

Mom didn't answer me. She shook her head in a sorrowful way. "You poor, poor children, soaked to the skin!"

It wasn't quite true. Only Royce was as wet as that.

"Take off your coats. Leave them on the porch. I'll get you some towels." She turned, and as she brushed past Dad I heard her say, "Rose has done it this time, Arthur."

Whatever Mom thought of her sister, she couldn't have been nicer to her nieces and nephews. When we had dried our hair and Royce had on some of my clothes, we went into my bedroom to play.

I have to hand it to the West gang, they were not wild or messy or even noisy. In fact, they were very quiet and polite. Honey, too tired to play, fell asleep on my bed. Miranda and the twins turned on my TV and started watching an old pirate movie. I showed Royce how I had done the scale plans for my houses on the computer.

"It looks like a real blueprint," said Royce, very impressed.

"We can do your plans this way too," I said. "I'll show you how. It's quite easy."

Mom came in with some popcorn in case we needed a snack before lunch. This, I might add, was the mother who never let me eat as much as a sandwich in my bedroom because she thought I'd get crumbs on the carpet. Not only was it a huge amount of popcorn but it was in her best porcelain bowl, pale green and painted with roses.

I couldn't believe it. "Thanks, Mom," I said.

She gave me a funny little smile. "I hope you're enjoying yourselves," she said.

That's when I realized that there had never been a golf game. My parents, who always insisted that I should tell the truth about everything, had made up the game to avoid looking after the Wests. Mom had told an outright whopper. Which was why she was acting so guilty.

I thought about this for a while and then decided it was all right because it meant I wouldn't have to explain how I got a hole in my coat sleeve.

The popcorn was warm and buttery and although it did spill over the desk and floor, we were careful to pick up most of the bits.

"I wish we'd come here in the first place," said Johnny. "This is awesome, man."

About one o'clock, Mom called us for lunch. We left Honey asleep on the bed and went into the dining room, where the table was set with a red and white cloth and napkins to match. The Wests stared, thinking it was some kind of party, and I couldn't tell them the table was always set like this even if it was just Mom and me at home. My mother likes to do things properly.

"I know you've already had lunch," said Mom, "but I thought a little pumpkin soup—"

We looked at each other and no one said a word about cat meat sandwiches.

"—and some cheese scones. I do believe there is some raisin cake left." Mom smiled. "I know Royce is very partial to raisin cake."

My cousins were the quietest I had known them. No one put their elbows on the table. No one reached and grabbed and no one slurped.

"Fantastic as usual, Auntie Eileen," said Royce. "Delishimo!"

"Lovely, thank you," said Miranda.

Mom shook her head. "My dear silly children, you could have got pneumonia! I can't believe you were in the park in the pouring rain all that time."

We looked at each other again. We all knew that my mother suffered from her nerves and the story of Stink Castle would only upset her.

"Didn't you have anywhere else to go?" she said.

I said, "Mom, it was your idea for us to have a picnic in the park."

She got a bit snippy at that. "Use your common sense Michael. Nobody in their right mind has a picnic in torrential rain." She placed on the table a large plate with half of the raisin cake with orange icing. "Who's for dessert?" she said.

I was allowed one small slice of cake without the icing, and I had to admit it was as good as Royce had said, juicy raisins, lemon peel, rich yellow cake. It calmed my stomach and made the park and that horrible house seem far, far away. I decided that as much as I liked my cousins, it was nice to live in a clean, tidy house with a mother who could cook like a TV chef.

Then it all changed.

Mom was giving Dad and Royce second helpings of cake when the room suddenly filled with the most awful smell. It was as bad as Stink Castle. Worse! I turned in my chair. The dining room door was open and there stood Honey with her pants around her ankles.

Dad jumped up and said something I couldn't believe. Not my father. He never swore. But he did. He said it. He used Royce's favorite word and then he put his napkin over his mouth to hide his embarrassment.

Mom didn't say anything. She just made this high-pitched noise through her nose.

The smell was really, really bad.

Honey was holding Mom's green porcelain bowl with the roses on it between her hands. She smiled proudly as she held it out to us. "Honey done poos," she said.

# The Wild West Gang and the Wonky Fence

## 1.

My mother was eating her Saturday morning poached egg. "I hear Rose and Leo are having problems with their new neighbor," she said. "It's a shame. It always happens. I told Rose. I said, with five children and your lifestyle you should have a house in the country where there are no neighbors."

I crouched over my breakfast and didn't say a word. How could Mom suggest that her sister move away? If my cousins left town, I'd die. Especially right now when Miranda was going to teach me to play the guitar.

"What is it this time?" said Dad, reading the paper beside his plate of toast.

"She doesn't like dogs," said Mom.

"Rose?" Dad said, without looking up.

"No! Mrs. Gollanti, the new neighbor."

"You don't like dogs," said Dad.

Mom poured more tea in his cup. "That's not correct, Arthur. I don't mind dogs in their right place, but the Wests have that smelly old animal practically in bed with them."

"That shouldn't worry their neighbor," said Dad.

"Leo hasn't got round to repairing the fence," said Mom. "You know what he's like about these things. Rose has to keep the animal on a chain when it's outside and that makes it bark. Mrs. Gollanti has complained to the council and Leo has been sent an official letter. He's got one month to make his fence dog-proof or the dog has to go. What a lot of fuss! It would be easier for everyone if they just had the disgusting old thing put down."

That was too much. I slammed my spoon on the table. "His name is Goof, and he is not disgusting. He's kind and friendly and everybody loves him and—and—"

"Michael," said Mom, "if you want to take part in this conversation, please mind your manners."

"Sorry, Mom." But actually, I wasn't sorry. Goof was like a part of the West family and I didn't know how anyone could talk about him like that.

Dad lifted his head from the paper. "Your mother's got a point, Michael, old son. The dog's so old he's not going to live more than a couple of years. It might be the kindest thing for him and the best thing for the Wests if they took him along to the vet."

"Never!" I said. "They wouldn't do that to Goof!"

"They might have to think about it," said Dad. "I doubt if Leo's got the money for a dog-proof fence."

I was so upset, I went to my room and phoned my cousins' house. Auntie Rosie answered. Royce was out on his bike, Miranda had gone to the store for some provisions, Jeannie was in the middle of cleaning out her mouse cages and did I want to talk to Johnny?

I said I did. As soon as he came to the phone, I asked if Goof was all right.

"Goof?" Johnny sounded vague. "What about him?"

"Your mom and dad got a letter from the council," I said.

"Oh yeah. That." I could hear him thinking. "It's got something to do with the lady next door, Mrs. Gollanti."

"How can anyone not like Goof?" I said. "He's so friendly."

"She's got little animals," said Johnny. "She reckons Goof chases them. She says he poops on her vegetable garden. Are you coming to my ballet rehearsal tonight?"

I had forgotten about Johnny's ballet. "I'll have to ask Mom and Dad."

"You can come with us," he said.

"Thanks. Uncle Leo isn't going to take Goof to the vet, is he?"

"What for?"

"You know—euthanasia."

There was a short silence, then Johnny asked, "Who's in Asia?"

"Injection," I said. "Put down. Killed."

"Oh. You mean are we going to get rid of him? No way! Did Mom tell you I was Jack Frost? That's the lead role in *Winter Serenade*."

"Yes, I think she did. Johnny, what about the letter from the council?"

"She's still working on my tunic and tights," he said. "They're silver. I've got a hat with spiky icicles on it and a whole jar of white body paint. Want to come over and see?"

I wasn't all that interested in Johnny's ballet costume but I did have a strong desire to pat Goof and hear the flap, flap of his big waggy tail. "I'll be right over," I said, and put down the phone.

# 2.

There was no one in the kitchen of the Wests' house but I could hear a rattling sound coming from the living room. Auntie Rosie was at her sewing machine and bits of silver thread and cloth were on the floor. Her machine was old and when she put her foot on the pedal, I could feel the noise vibrating up through the floorboards.

"Typical!" Auntie Rosie moaned. "Started planning two months ago then left everything to the last minute."

"Who?" I asked.

"Me," she said. "It's the rehearsal tonight and the costume's not finished. Dang and blast! Pass me one of those donuts, Mickey. I need some comfort."

I looked around and saw on top of the piano a plate of sugary donuts. I held the plate in front of her. "Have one," she said. "Leo made them."

"No thanks, Auntie Rosie."

"Sugar allergy?" she asked.

"It's not that. I've just had breakfast."

"You're a sensible lad, Mickey." She bit into a donut and scattered sugar over the silver cloth. "But we're trying to knock that out of you," she said.

Johnny must have heard us talking because he came running in and did a leap with a scissor kick. "Da-dah!" he said, throwing out his arms. He was in a shirt and jeans but he had on his head something that looked like a silver bathing cap with spikes.

Honey came in behind him, trying to imitate his steps. Her hands were spread out and on her head was a bit of the silver cloth. She jumped about an inch off the floor as she said, "Dadda!"

"Bravo!" cheered Johnny. When he picked her up, she reached for the spikes on his hat and I saw that they were soft and bendy and made of plastic or rubber.

"Jack Frost, that's me," said Johnny "What do you think?"

"Cool," I said, and he laughed.

Auntie Rosie was making a real mess of the donut. She brushed her hands together and more sugar fell on the costume. "Royce and Miranda are out," she said.

"I know," I replied. "Actually, I came to see Johnny and— and because I was worried about Goof."

"Goof?" Auntie Rosie laughed. "Oh, so you've heard. Poor old Goof just adores those little animals next door. Mrs. Gollanti's got bantam hens, an aviary full of canaries, two Burmese cats, and an old white rabbit. Goof wants to play, that's all."

"He'd never hurt a fly," said Johnny.

"He's particularly in love with the rabbit," said Auntie Rosie. "He's been going over there with his nose against the rabbit hutch. You know what a big softy he is. Mrs. Gollanti, though, she thinks he's up to no good. She is certain he's planning a rabbit dinner." Auntie Rosie sighed. "It's all got a bit out of hand, I'm afraid. We have to keep Goof inside until the fence is fixed."

"Where is he?" I asked

"Asleep on the—" Auntie Rosie looked at the couch. "He was there," she said. "Mickey, did you shut the back door when you came in?"

"I don't know." I had a funny feeling. "Well, no, I don't think—"

"May a thousand fleas infest your armpits!" said Auntie Rosie, getting up from the machine. "May your fingers grow eyeballs! May your head turn into a potato!"

"Mickey didn't know we had to keep the door shut," said Johnny.

"That won't stop a Rosie curse," said Auntie Rosie, bustling towards the kitchen. "Goof! Goof!" she called. "Goof! Wretched dog's getting so deaf. Here, Goof!"

There was no Goof in the house or in the backyard. I ran across the grass and looked through one of the gaps in the fence.

"Yes," I said. "That's where he is."

The new neighbor had changed the next-door yard so that it was now full of toys and wire cages. Plastic sunflowers on stalks marked the rows of lettuces and tomatoes. A painted duck and a seagull spun their wings like propellers in the wind. By the flower gardens, there was a fountain with two gnomes beside it, a small windmill, and a concrete statue of a fairy reading a book. I saw little birds in one of the cages and some white fluffy chickens in the other, but by far the easiest thing to see was Goof who was standing by the rabbit hutch, his tail wagging like a flag. No sign of the rabbit behind the wire. I guessed it was hiding.

Auntie Rosie was beside me. "Goof!" she called softly. "Goof!"

He didn't hear, or didn't want to hear. I looked at the house, thinking the lady might come running out. There was no one at the back windows.

Auntie Rosie groaned. "I can't go through this again," she said. "Johnny?"

"Not me," Johnny said. "She screams at us."

"She could still be in bed," said Auntie Rosie. "She doesn't get up early."

I looked again at the neighbor's back windows. "I'll go," I said.

"Oh. Would you, Mickey?" Auntie Rosie looked relieved.

"I was the one who left the door open," I said, feeling brave. I put my foot through the fence and tried not to stand on any plants.

Goof was close, only the width of a swimming pool away, and I was sure I could get him back before the neighbor no-ticed. I squeezed my shoulders through the gap in the fence and then walked very carefully between some flowers, past the small windmill, past the fairy statue, and over the path. My plan was to grab Goof by the collar and lead him back. It was only when I got to him that I realized he didn't have a collar.

I patted him and he was pleased to see me, but not as pleased as he was with the rabbit. He was leaning towards the cage, sniffing against the wire. I tried to turn his head away but he turned it right back again.

"Goof!" I whispered. "Come on, Goof!"

I could see the rabbit in the corner of the hutch, backed up against a heap of straw. It wasn't anything special. In fact it looked really old and miserable, sunken pink eyes, scraggly fur. I didn't know why Goof was so excited about it.

"Come back home!" I tried to push him towards the fence, but no luck. He came straight back to the rabbit hutch.

Auntie Rosie must have been watching because the next instant something came whizzing through the air to land with a clunk against the fairy statue. It was Goof's collar and leash wrapped up in a ball. I picked it up. Now we could get somewhere.

I fastened the collar around Goof's neck and pulled on the leash. He made a coughing noise but wouldn't leave the cage. I pulled harder. He walked a couple of steps and then tried to turn back. I leaned back on the leash with all my strength. We made another few steps but Goof fought every one of them. I had never seen him so stubborn. The collar was half choking him, yet he still pulled against me. It took ages to get him across the garden, halfway to the fence.

I thought we were going to get there when the back door of the house flew open and out came this small woman with fuzzy gray hair. "Boy!" she screeched. "You! Boy!"

I stopped and immediately that stupid Goof tried to pull me back to the rabbit hutch.

The woman had on a pink robe and fluffy slippers that made her look a bit like a bunny herself. Not her face, though. Her face was pure, furious, madder-than-mad human. "Did you hear me, boy?"

I didn't say anything. I wasn't good at quick answers when people yelled.

"I've warned you!" she shrieked. "I'm sick of that foul dog and I'm tired of talking to you and your parents. I'm calling the dog control officer, you hear? This time, the animal's going to the pound!"

I wanted to say this wasn't my family, or my dog, but no words came out. I looked towards the fence, wondering where Auntie Rosie was.

"Look at my poor petunias!" The woman came down the path. "Just look! Your family would try the patience of an angel! I ask you!"

"Sorry," I mumbled, walking backwards and pulling on the leash. "Sorry. I was just trying—"

"Mrs. Gollanti!" At last, Auntie Rosie's head appeared over the fence. "This is not Michael's problem. He's my nephew. He's here on a visit."

"I suppose it's not your dog, either!" Mrs. Gollanti yelled.

"My apologies," said Auntie Rosie. "The door was left open and Goof got out. We'll try to make sure it doesn't happen again."

"You said that last time!" screamed the woman. "It has happened again! When are you going to do something about that fence?" Her fluffy pink slippers came down the path towards us.

Goof may have been deaf but there was nothing wrong with his sight. He turned his head, saw Mrs. Gollanti, and immediately forgot about the rabbit. His eyes rolled backwards, he tucked his tail between his legs, and then he leaped for the hole in the fence, dragging the leash right out of my hand. I followed as quickly as I could.

"I'm calling the pound!" Mrs. Gollanti yelled after me.

As I came through the fence, Auntie Rosie put her arm around me and gave me a squashy hug. "Poor Mickey! You certainly got an earful."

"See why I wouldn't go?" said Johnny, who was holding Goof by the collar.

"Leo's starting the fence tomorrow." Auntie Rosie led us back to the house. "Thank goodness for that. He's bought some demolition timber from Mr. Vivek's second hand shop."

"Demolition timber?" I asked, and then I saw Johnny's quick silencing look. We took Goof inside and closed the back door firmly behind us.

"Demolition timber?" I whispered close to Johnny's ear.

He shrugged. But later, when Auntie Rosie and Goof had

gone back to the front room, Johnny said, "Royce is hiring my crowbar and saw for a dollar an hour."

I knew then that the fence was coming from Stink Castle.

# 3.

Johnny's ballet rehearsal was in the church hall. It was more like a show than a rehearsal. They had costumes and a stage set and makeup, just like a real performance. Johnny's ballet teacher explained to the audience that her ballet school was taking the dance *Winter Serenade* to the national competitions in Wellington next weekend, and this was an opportunity for family and friends to see it first.

There was a big crowd in the hall, more than anyone had expected. All the Wests were there, and Honey had to sit on Uncle Leo's knee because I didn't have a seat.

"Put it this way, Mickey," said Uncle Leo. "I'd rather have Honey on my knee than you. No offence meant."

Sitting next to Uncle Leo, I didn't have a chance to quiz Royce about the timber for the fence and why he was selling it through Mr. Vivek. He probably wouldn't have told me, anyway. He was sitting down the other end next to Jeannie, and he looked totally clean. His hair was still wet and combed flat, his face had a soap shine, and I thought his ears were probably clean, too. My mother would have approved, except she had been too tired to come to the ballet.

The ballet teacher pressed the button for the music and the dance started. First, the little kids came on dressed as the last fruits of summer. Some weren't much older than Honey and they didn't really dance, just skipped in a circle pretending to be apples and berries and mushrooms and things. Honey got off Uncle Leo's knee and jumped up and down, waving her hands. Uncle Leo whispered to me, "I can see another lot of ballet lessons coming up."

The little ones ran off and some bigger kids came on as autumn leaves. They wore red and yellow and orange leaf costumes and leaves, whirling and fluttering in an imaginary wind. I quite liked that, but it went on too long. At last some of the leaves danced off stage and Jack Frost came on.

He was good. He was really good. When he danced doing those high scissor kicks, everyone applauded. The Wests did more than clap. They stood up yelling, "Johnny! Johnny!" and Miranda gave him one of her sheep dog whistles with her fingers in her mouth.

I didn't stand. To tell the truth I was a bit embarrassed, and I was worrying about the people sitting behind the Wests, who wouldn't be able to see the stage. But I did clap. I clapped as hard as could. I saw Johnny look at us and smile.

Behind him, the snowflakes came on, a whole lot of kids in white dresses with big snowflakes in front. They swayed at the back of the stage while Johnny whirled round and round, faster and faster.

Then the music stopped. A little kid had come out from behind the curtains and tripped on the stereo cord.

For a while, the dancers went on dancing, but they no longer seemed as light as feathers. Without music to hide the noise, their shoes squeaked and thumped on the wooden stage and you could hear their fast breathing. One by one, they stopped and looked helpless.

Meanwhile, the little kid was out front trying to turn in circles like Jack Frost.

The audience roared and some of them started clapping. It was chaotic. I glanced at Uncle Leo and Auntie Rosie. They were laughing so hard, I thought they might fall backwards off the seat. I didn't even smile. I folded my arms and refused to be embarrassed. This was nothing to do with me.

Jack Frost looked fed up. He put his hands on his hips, walked to the edge of the stage and shouted over the noise, "Dad! Will you come and get Honey?"

# 4.

At school on Monday, Royce told me that the whole family was going to Wellington the next weekend to see Johnny dance in the competition.

"I guess the fence won't get finished," he said.

"But your dad's got another two weeks, hasn't he?"

"It's not that," said Royce. "The problem is having to take Goof for a walk each morning and night. He's not used to a leash. Yesterday I had the bright idea of tying him to my bike. Look!" He held up his arm and I saw a red graze on his elbow.

"At least the fence is making you rich," I said.

"Are you kidding? Dad will only pay two dollars a board for the timber and Mr. Vivek takes fifty per cent of that because he picks it up from the site. By the time I pay Johnny for his tools, I don't get enough to cover my labor. Spitting camels, Mickey! You know how much work is involved? I have to pry the boards off the walls. Half of them split. Then I've got to cut the good ones into two-yard lengths and get the nails out. It's lousy work."

"Did you find a way to get the iron staircase to bits?"

He immediately got a faraway look and said, "Why don't you come to Wellington with us?"

I wouldn't let him change the subject. "Bet you made a mint out of that staircase."

"It's perfectly legal," he replied.

"Oh yeah?"

"It is," he insisted. "I went to see Mr. Chen. He said I could take anything I wanted."

"Who's he? The bulldozer driver?"

Royce looked me straight in the eye. "Mr. Chen's the new owner of Stink Castle. He's the one who's going to build the retirement village. He said when he was my age, he started out the same as me."

"Did you tell him you'd already stripped the house?"

Royce gave me a ha-ha smile. "I'll tell you something for nothing. Mr. Chen congratulated me on my business ventures. He did. He said it was good to see a kid being useful."

I said, "Come on, Royce! You can't fool me. If it's all so legal, why aren't you selling the timber direct to your father?"

"Because he'd want it for nothing." Royce's grin faded. "He would. Or else he'd go and get it himself for nothing. I wish now I'd just told him where he could help himself. I'm not making anything, and it's stinking hard work. You should see the rats' nests in those walls! I tell you, I'm losing money! I wish I'd never started."

I didn't believe him. Royce always made money. Miranda told me he had over three thousand dollars in his bank account.

The bell rang the end of break and we walked into class. "What about Wellington?" he asked. "Are you coming or not?"

"I'll ask Mom and Dad," I replied.

By Friday though, things had changed. Miranda had a bad cold. She'd missed two days of school and she couldn't go to Wellington to see Johnny dance.

Mom said, "Rose was going to stay home to look after her, but I told Rose to go. Miranda's the most sensible one of the bunch. She'll be all right. I'll keep an eye on her."

"Are you going there? Or is she coming here?" said Dad. "I merely ask because I'm not interested in catching her cold."

"She's over the contagious stage," said Mom. "But she's probably better off on her own. I'll phone every hour or so to make sure she's all right."

"I'll stay with her," I said.

"No, Michael," said Mom firmly. "That won't be necessary."

"She might need someone," I said. "I can get her orange juice."

Mom and Dad looked at each other and smiled. I hated it when they did that.

Dad said, "She'll be just fine getting her own orange juice. You go with the others to Wellington."

"The forecast's bad," I said. "You told me yourself, it's going to rain and rain all weekend."

Dad smiled at Mom again. "They don't hold the competitions outside. I expect you'll be dry enough."

Mom said, "Don't worry, Michael dear. I'll take care of Miranda."

They could say what they liked. I had already decided to cancel my trip to Wellington.

# 5.

It was funny how things turned out. I actually did wake up on Saturday morning with a cold—or at least, the beginning of one. My throat was scratchy and I had a runny nose.

At first, Mom didn't believe me. "I'm disappointed in you, Michael," she said, thinking I was telling a whopper. But she changed her tune after she'd taken my temperature. "You'd better stay in bed," she said, fluffing up my pillows. "I'll tell Rose you're not going."

Bed was not exactly what I'd had in mind. It was a miserable day with gray sky and gray rain, and there wasn't much on TV. I read half a book, ate half my lunch, then put on my robe and said, "I'm sick of bed."

Mom came up behind me and put her hand on my forehead. "You are sick, no question," she said, steering me out of the room. "You've still got a temperature. Get into bed and I'll read you a story."

"Mom! I can read my own stories! Please, I want to get up. I'm not dying or anything."

But she marched me down the hall to my room. "Now Michael, tell me where your father is going next week."

"I don't know."

"Yes, you do. You've heard us talk about it."

I thought hard. "A conference?"

"A conference on the other side of the country," said Mom. "I don't need to tell you how delicate your father's ears are. If he gets a cold it goes straight to his ears and he can't fly."

"Why not?"

"Pressure," said Mom. "The eardrums can burst."

I tried to imagine Dad's eardrums bursting all over the plane, but all I could picture in my mind were Royce's ears full of wax.

"So," said Mom, "it's very, very important that you stay away from your father while you have this cold. We'd both appreciate your cooperation."

"Can I go and see Miranda?"

For a moment I thought Mom would say yes but her face got that firm look and she pushed me through the door. "A weekend in bed won't do you any harm," she said.

Boredom was making my cold worse. I phoned Miranda.

"What are you doing?" she asked, her voice still croaky.

"Nothing. What are you doing?"

"Making masks and talking to your mother," she said. "She's been really sweet, calling me every hour."

"How do you make masks?" I asked.

"Some with papier mâché," she said. "Some with brown paper bags. Why don't you come over?"

"I can't. Mom says I have to stay in bed."

"You must be really sick," she said.

"No, I'm not. Only a sore throat and runny nose. But I'm not allowed to get up. Mom doesn't want Dad to catch it because of his ears." I didn't go on because I thought Miranda might not be fascinated by my father's bursting eardrums.

"Would you like to come over and make masks?" she asked.

"Yes, I really would, but it's no use. Mom won't let me."

Miranda said, "I'll phone your mother and see if I can work something out. I'm sure she'll say yes."

"Don't count on it," I said.

But I should have known that Miranda would be able to

get around Mom as easy as pie. Before I knew it, Mom was in the room asking me if I felt any worse.

"No, just the same."

"Do you feel like visiting Miranda?" she asked.

"Yes!" I jumped up in bed. "Yes, yes, yes!"

"I think she's feeling a bit lonely in that house by herself," said Mom. "Put warm clothes on. Undershirt, jeans, wool socks, wooly cap with the ear flaps."

"I won't get wet," I said. "Promise. I'll wear my raincoat and take an umbrella."

"You're not walking," said Mom. "Goodness me, it's pouring down. What kind of a mother do you think I am? I'll take you in the car and pick you up again about eight."

I ran into the Wests' house yelling through my scratchy throat, "I'm here! I'm here!"

"And I'm up here!" came a croaky reply from the stairs.

I galloped up those steps two at a time. "You did it! Mom even brought me in the car."

Miranda came to the door of her room. She had paste and bits of wet newspaper stuck to her fingers. "You don't look sick," she said.

I liked the way the cold had made her voice all husky like a movie star's. I tried to make my voice sound deep, too. "Just a head cold."

"Come and see the masks," she said.

On the table under her window was a heap of paper, a bowl of paste, paints, glitter. She picked up a balloon covered with small pieces of wet newspaper. "It's not drying fast. The air's too damp. When all the layers are properly dry, I'll prick the balloon, then I'll cut the paper ball in half. That'll give me two masks. I'll cut out eyes and a mouth and make a nose."

She put the balloon down and showed me some brown goggles. "These are easy. Cut them out from brown paper bags and then paint them. What would you like to make?"

I looked at all the things on the table. Not just the table. The entire room was full of Miranda's art: paper sculpture, painting, potato prints, little trolls made of clay, a needlepoint picture. Miranda could do just about anything.

"How did you change Mom's mind?" I asked.

She looked at me sideways, and it was a real Royce look. "I said I was feeling lonely and could I come over to your place."

"You said that?" I was impressed.

Miranda laughed. "It was your mother who thought it would be a good idea if you came here."

I made a brown paper mask: three layers of heavy brown paper pasted and then dried over the heater in the hall. Miranda painted it for me with gold and black enamel. She showed me to how to glue on some feathers and glittery stuff. It was a Venetian mask, she said.

I went along with her suggestions, although I would rather have made a mask of Frankenstein or Dracula. Still, if the gold paint and feathers turned out all right I thought maybe I could give it to Mom.

Miranda put the mask to one side. "It won't take long to clean up. Then I can give you that guitar lesson, if you like."

"Would you? Cool!"

As I watched her put away the paper and paint, I couldn't help noticing how quiet the house was. It was weird. Other times the walls rocked with noise, doors banging, kids crying, shouting, laughing, singing, arguing, Auntie Rosie and Uncle Leo yelling, the dog barking...

I put down the mask. A sick feeling came into my stomach.

"Has—has your dad finished the fence?" I asked.

"No. Why?"

"Miranda, I'm sorry." I looked around her room. Goof wasn't there. I ran out into the hall. He wasn't in Royce's room, either. "I'm sorry! I'm really sorry!"

"What's wrong?" she croaked.

"I—I think I left the back door open!"

# 6.

We stood in the back porch, staring through the gap in the backyard. Deaf as Goof was, he seemed to have an extra sense that told him when the back door had been left open.

I noticed the newly sawn boards that covered about half the wet fence. They were from Stink Castle, all right. Some still had bits of moss on them. Further down the fence there was a huge gap where Uncle Leo had taken down the broken posts. Goof could have gone through anywhere.

My stomach felt as though it had a tight rubber band round it. I'd left the door open again, and I would have to get Goof back from next door. Facing Mrs. Gollanti's screams was more than I could cope with right then. I stood in the porch and did nothing.

"We could always leave him," said Miranda, trying to be helpful. "Mrs. Gollanti will send him to the pound and Dad can pick him up in the morning."

"It costs money to get a dog out of the pound," I said.

Miranda shrugged. "If Dad had fixed the fence this wouldn't have happened."

But I couldn't let Goof go to the pound just because I'd

been stupid. "I'll go and get him," I said.

At that moment, the phone rang in the kitchen. We both jumped.

"That'll be Mrs. Gollanti," Miranda said. "If she screams at me, I'll scream right back."

I knew Miranda wouldn't be able to scream back. She didn't have a voice for yelling. I stood looking at the backyard, wondering how something small like a broken fence could get to be so big and scary.

It wasn't Mrs. Gollanti on the phone. It was Mom doing her hourly check and when she had finished with Miranda, she wanted to talk to me.

"Are you keeping warm, Michael? How is your temperature? Is your throat any better? Do you have plenty of tissues? What about oranges? Does Rose have any oranges in that house?"

I didn't tell Mom that my cold was getting worse. My throat was hot and sore and I had a bit of a headache, but that was nothing compared with the tightness in my stomach.

Then, with my other ear, I heard Miranda croaking, "Goof! Goof!"

"Got to go, Mom," I said and put the phone down.

Miranda was in the porch, pointing. "Goof came through the gap in the fence! He's behind our shed! He's got something in his mouth!"

We didn't wait to put on coats. We ran together through the rain, over the wet lawn, down to the shed behind the garage. Goof was there, soaking wet and covered in mud. He was playing with something that looked like an old sock. When we got closer, we saw that it was the rabbit.

"No, Goof! No! How could you?" rasped Miranda.

I bent down and snatched the thing away from the dog. Yuck! It was wet and brown with mud. Its sunken eyes had a film over them and its mouth was half open, showing two muddy front teeth. It was very dead.

"Is it Mrs. Gollanti's rabbit?" Miranda asked.

"Looks like it," I said.

The rain came down harder and we ran back to the porch, me carrying the rabbit, Miranda holding Goof's collar. It wasn't difficult to get the dog inside. He followed the rabbit with huge enthusiasm. Auntie Rosie had said he loved that thing. Love? Oh sure! The way I loved Hawaiian pizza!

"Goof can't come in the house," said Miranda. "Not with all that mud on him. I'll tie him up here."

She clipped the leash onto his collar and then found a bit of rope to go between the leash and a coat hook. Goof just sat there panting, his tongue out, looking immensely pleased with himself.

"What'll I do with this?" I held out the rabbit. It was wet, dirty, and it felt gross.

"Kitchen counter," said Miranda.

We left Goof fussing and whining in the porch and went into the kitchen. I dropped the rabbit on the counter and washed the mud off my hands. Miranda told me to leave the cold water turned on. She held the dead rabbit under it. We watched the streams of brown water running off its fur. When she put it back on the counter it was mostly clean with just a bit of mud in its ears and mouth.

"He's been tossing it around the garden," Miranda said. "Rotten dog! I could kill him!"

"Mrs. Gollanti probably will kill him when she finds out," I said.

Miranda ran her fingers over the rabbit, lifting the fur away from the gray mottled skin. "I can't see any tooth marks. Can you?"

I looked without touching it. "No."

"It looks skinny and bony. Would you say it was old?"

"Definitely," I told her. "I saw it in the hutch last week and it looked ancient."

"Do you know what I think?" Miranda smiled. "Goof just wanted to play with it but it got frightened and died of a heart attack."

"Maybe." I looked closely at the eyes to see if there was any look of terror in them. There wasn't.

"It has to be that," said Miranda. "There isn't one tooth mark on its skin."

The rabbit was long and skinny, not enough meat to attract a sensible dog. Not that Goof was a sensible dog. But maybe the family was right and Goof had wanted to play. Didn't make any difference. Mrs. Gollanti's precious rabbit was dead and Goof was the killer either way.

"What are we going to do?" I asked.

Miranda was examining the rabbit from all angles. "I don't know."

"We could put it in one of those brown paper bags," I said. "Then we could go down the road and throw it in a trash can."

"Won't work," said Miranda. "When Mrs. Gollanti finds the hutch empty, Goof'll still get the blame. She'll think he's eaten it."

We stood there in silence for a while, and then I made another suggestion. "Why don't you leave it until your parents get home?"

But now Miranda was smiling. "I've got an idea. We don't

have to tell Mom and Dad," she said. "We don't have to say anything to anyone, and Mrs. Gollanti won't think its Goof. Listen!"

Then Miranda told me her plan, which was nothing short of brilliant, as I would expect of Miranda who can do a zillion brilliant things. The only problem was that I was the one who was volunteered for the doing.

# 7.

Miranda brought me her hair shampoo from the bathroom, and filled the sink with warm water.

"There mustn't be any trace of mud," she said.

"Is that hygienic?" I asked.

"What? Shampoo?"

"A dead rabbit in the sink where you wash your dishes."

"Why not?" she said. "We wash dead potatoes in there."

I couldn't argue. I would have thought that anyone could see the difference between potatoes and a disgusting dead rabbit.

She washed it all over with bubbles that smelled like lemons and got the mud out of the ears and mouth and the paws. I didn't get too close. The white fur was almost transparent against the gray skin and the whole thing looked like meat gone bad.

After the shampoo, she rinsed it and laid it on a towel.

I said, "Why would anyone want a miserable old rabbit for a pet?"

"Did you read *Watership Down*?" she asked.

"I saw the movie."

"It made us think about rabbits the way *Bambi* made us think about deer. You realize that rabbits are very intelligent creatures. They have opinions. They have feelings."

"How do you know?" I asked.

"You said you saw the movie."

"Yes, but that was some person trying to make rabbits like humans. Those were people's opinions and feelings. How do we know what rabbits think?"

"Oh honestly, Mickey." Miranda was wiping the body with the towel. "You don't have much imagination."

Normally, I never get mad with Miranda but that upset me. "I've got plenty of imagination," I said, "but I don't like pretending made-up things are the truth. How can you say that *Watership Down* and *Bambi* are about animals' real feelings? It's people inventing—"

"Okay, okay, don't lay an egg," Miranda said. "I'm going to run upstairs and get my hair dryer."

When she had finished blowing warm air on that rabbit, it looked more like a soft toy than a corpse. The fur came up white and fluffy and we couldn't see any of that blotchy gray skin. In fact, it would have looked cuddly except for the blank milky stare of its dead eyes.

She switched off the hair dryer. "That'll do," she said.

I looked at the sky. It was too dark to see the clouds or the backyard. The rain against the window was silver and the drops that ran down the glass held miniature reflections of the kitchen lights.

"Shall I do it now?" I asked.

"We should wait another half hour," she said. "Then it'll be really dark and she'll be watching TV. How about something to eat?"

I shook my head. It wasn't the sore throat or headache or even my scrunched-up stomach that put me off. It was the thought of eating with a dead rabbit beside us.

That didn't worry Miranda, though. She made herself a huge peanut butter sandwich which she had with a glass of ginger ale. "You must be hungry," she said.

"No," I lied. "Not in the least."

Before the half hour had passed, I had on my raincoat and my wooly cap, and Miranda was putting the rabbit into a large plastic bag. She twisted a tie around the top. "Put it under your coat."

"Under my coat?" I stepped back.

"It can't get any rain on it," she said. "Don't you see? If it's one hundred percent dry, then Goof is innocent."

"Do I have to?"

"Yes. We must make absolutely sure," she said, and she unbuttoned my coat.

I hated the feeling of the rabbit next to me. Even though it was in a bag, it felt cold and hard and I could imagine its dead eyes against my sweater, its dead ears listening to the thumping of my heart. Did rabbits have ghosts?

"You can't go through the fence," said Miranda. "She'll see your footprints in the garden. You'll have to go in through the front gate and down the path by the side of the house. But be careful. The path's covered with gravel."

"I don't suppose I can take a flashlight?" I said.

"No, she might see it."

"How will I find my way?"

"There should be enough light from the house."

We went onto the back porch where Goof was lying asleep on the mat, his coat matted with dry mud. When he saw us he woke up, thumped his tail, and gave us a doggy grin.

"Don't!" Miranda told him. "You caused this catastrophe. Just put your head down and look ashamed."

I had one hand over the rabbit under my coat. With the other, I pulled down the wooly cap until it was almost over my eyes. "Wish me luck," I said.

"You'll do it, Mickey," said Miranda, and she leaned forward to kiss me on the cheek.

I turned away because I felt embarrassed, but actually I felt great. Of course I could do it. I knew I could. It was no big deal.

"Just watch your footsteps on the gravel," she said.

The rain was now as fine as mist and it hung in pale rainbows around the street lights, dimming their glow. As I approached Mrs. Gollanti's front gate, I felt like a spy, secret agent Michael Bond with a dead rabbit tucked up his coat. The gate didn't squeak. There were no lights on in the front rooms. So far, so good. I bent double, my arms folded over the rabbit, and crept up the path.

Miranda was right. There was gravel under my feet and it crunched like popcorn. But she was also right about the TV. I could hear the weather forecast through the wall even before I got to the lighted windows along the side of the house. Mrs. Gollanti had the volume turned up really loud.

I kept my head down and walked close to the house, slowly, slowly. Michael Bond enters the den of Madame Gollanti, who plans to take over the world. He has no weapons save his imagination and a bomb disguised as a dead rabbit.

At the back corner of the house, the path turned and disappeared into the garden. The back lights weren't on, which meant I couldn't see a step in front of me. It was all rain and darkness and gravel crunching under my shoes. I bumped into something, put out my right hand, and felt the wet stone of the fairy statue. That meant the rabbit hutch was a few steps ahead to the right.

I found it. I ran my hand down the wire and discovered that the door was open. So that's what had happened! Goof had found a way to pull back the latch!

With my left hand against the rabbit, I unbuttoned my coat. All the time, I kept glancing towards the back of the house to see if any light went on.

I took out the plastic bag and placed it in the house part of the hutch. Then I undid the twisty tie and eased the rabbit out of the bag, nestling it into the straw to make it look as though it had died comfortably in bed. Next thing? Don't leave any clues, I told myself. I put the bag and the tie in my pocket. Next? A quick glance at the house, and I closed the hutch door, pulling over the latch. Mission accomplished. Goof was off the hook.

My impulse then was to run across the garden to the gap in the fence, but as Miranda had said, that would have left footprints. I had to go back the way I came, creeping very slowly along the crunchy gravel.

The lights along the side of the house still shone around the edges of the blinds. The TV still blasted through the wall. No one's face appeared at the window and no front light went on. I got through the front gate, took a couple of casual steps and then ran as fast as I could back to Miranda.

Michael Bond had solved his most difficult case.

# 8.

The next day my cold was much worse and I had to stay in bed. I didn't mind. My head ached, my eyes hurt, my nose was running like a faucet, and I was coughing.

Dad didn't come in to see me because he was afraid of getting sick, but he sent a get better note in with Mom. I know you'll understand, he had written, and he'd tucked ten dollars in the envelope, which was very nice of him.

I didn't want to read or watch TV. I didn't even phone the Wests because my throat hurt when I tried to talk. The night before, Mom had come to collect me before the Wests got home, so I didn't know how the ballet competition had gone. The trip to Wellington couldn't have been more exciting than the drama about the rabbit. Miranda had been so pleased with me. She'd acted as though I really had saved their lives, and not once did she remind me that I had been stupid enough to leave the back door open a second time.

For lunch, Mom brought me in a tray with some chicken soup and a dish of pineapple jelly. I had almost finished it when there was a big rumpus at the front door and a lot of familiar voices shouting over each other. The Wests had come to visit!

Instantly I felt much better.

Mom showed them all into my bedroom. I guessed she didn't want them in the living room dropping cold germs where Dad could pick them up.

I was so pleased to see them. Auntie Rosie and Uncle Leo hugged me in spite of my cold and gave me a bag of sugar-free sweets they'd got in a Wellington shop. Miranda brought the red and gold mask I'd made. Jeannie had a shoe box with an old bird's nest she'd found, and Royce gave me a copy of the ballet program.

"*Winter Serenade* was lovely," said Auntie Rosie. "Everyone tried hard and danced well, and this time Honey stayed out of it."

"I won the solo performance," said Johnny. "Jack Frost got the cup."

"That's right," Auntie Rosie hushed him. "Johnny did dance beautifully, but as you know, I have mixed feelings about children's competitions. For every winner there are a lot of people who think they are losers."

"That's what a competition is about," said Johnny.

"Still," said Auntie Rosie. "I'm sure the winner can't feel comfortable knowing that he or she has caused people to feel defeat."

I could tell from Johnny's shining face that he wasn't at all worried about winning.

"Where's the cup?" I asked, and my voice was as croaky as Miranda's had been.

"Getting my name on it," he said. "They'll mail it to me when it's ready."

I looked at Miranda and carefully chose my words. "How's Goof?"

She shook her head slightly to let me know that she hadn't told anyone about the rabbit. "He's okay," she said.

Uncle Leo sat on the end of my bed. "I might get the fence finished this afternoon and that'll solve the problems once and for all." He smiled at us all. "I must say it's a blessing to have such cheap timber. Less than a quarter of the price I'd pay in a lumber merchant's yard." He gave me a big wink.

"I'm very happy, Mr. Vivek's happy. Royce is happy and Johnny is happy. Isn't it nice now that the fence has made so many people happy?"

Royce's mouth dropped open. "What do you mean, I'm happy?" He swallowed and said, "You knew?"

"Of course I knew," said Uncle Leo. "Do you think I've got a head like a turnip?"

"Why didn't you tell me?" said Royce.

"What? And spoil a good thing?" Uncle Leo laughed. "Blessed saints, I know a bargain when I see one. If I had to spend time prying old timber off the Ledbetter house, it'd be costing me more than two dollars a plank."

Royce went red under his freckles, and he closed his mouth to a thin line. I reckoned it would take him a while to think of something to say.

Uncle Leo was enjoying himself. "So everyone's happy except poor old Mrs. Gollanti," he said.

"All right, Leo. That's enough," said Auntie Rosie, trying not to laugh.

I glanced at Miranda, who was looking at her father.

"After church I was talking to Des Kerrigan," said Uncle Leo. "Des's wife is Mrs. Gollanti's cousin. Did I tell you that? Well bless my soul, if Des's wife didn't get a phone call this morning. Poor Mrs. Gollanti was near hysterical. She'd just found a lovely white rabbit dead in its little house."

Miranda was now examining her fingernails. I cleared my croaky throat. "It was an old rabbit. I saw it. It probably died of old age."

"Indeed it did," said Uncle Leo, smiling hugely at me and then at Miranda.

I saw Miranda relax and put her hands behind her back.

"Poor Mrs. Gollanti," she said.

"Poor Mrs. Gollanti," agreed Uncle Leo.

"Leo!" said Auntie Rosie. "I think we'll talk about something else."

"The funny thing is," Uncle Leo said, "the thing that got her so upset was this. The rabbit died of natural causes on Friday morning and she had buried it in her garden."

There was silence in the room, except for a snorting sound from Auntie Rosie.

I couldn't look at Miranda. I slid down my pillows and pulled the sheet up to my chin.

I would never touch another rabbit, as long as I lived.

# The
# Wild West Gang
# and the Grumpy Guest

## 1.

Mom helped herself to more salad. "What a dreadful thing!" she said. "Suppose he never walks again?"

Dad chuckled. "More than likely he'll die of thirst and all the bars will go broke." He saw me watching and quickly wiped off the smile with his napkin.

"Who?" I asked.

"Don't talk with your mouth full, Michael," said Mom.

I swallowed. "Who? Who?"

Mom reached across and tapped me on the nose. She had just had her nails done for the Golf Club dinner. I went cross-eyed looking at the long pink claw. She said, "It was an adult conversation, Michael. Now we will talk about something that interests you."

"I was interested in the old man who'll die of thirst," I replied.

"Sorry," said Dad. "Subject closed."

It was my cousin Royce who told me. I didn't even ask.

He grabbed me by the collar as I walked into school. "Guess what? Grandadda's had his leg chopped off."

"Your dad's father?"

"Who else? They cut it clean off. It was getting gangrene."

Other kids stopped to listen. Paul Jasicki said, "What's that?"

"Gangrene? It's when a bit of your body dies before you do. It goes black and rotten." Royce's eyes went narrow with imaginary pain. "It can start with your fingers or toes. They just go numb and turn this funny color. Then they stink something awful."

We all looked at our hands and I saw Paul Jasicki sniff the tips of his fingers.

"Grandadda got it because he's a diabetic," explained Royce. "He's really fat. He's got this big stomach and he couldn't see his toes when they started rotting. By the time they got him to hospital, it was too late. They had to bring out the saw."

One of the kids said, "Oo-oo-oo-ooh! A saw!"

"I think they used a knife to cut through the meat part," said Royce. "The saw was for the bone. The doctor tied up the artery and stuff so blood didn't squirt everywhere, and then he sewed the skin over the stump and bandaged it."

"What do they do with the bit they cut off?" I asked.

Royce's eyebrows wriggled like ginger caterpillars. "I dunno. Dad didn't tell me that. Maybe the doctor's got a dog."

"Oo-ooh!" we all yelled. "Yuck! That's the grossest—" Then we saw Paul sliding down with his face as white as milk. We forgot about Royce's Grandadda and rushed towards the door shouting, "Mr. Fromish! Mr. Fromish! Paul Jasicki's fainted."

After school, just about the whole class was around Royce,

wanting to know about his grandadda's operation. Each time he told the story, he gave more details. You'd think he was there when the doctor cut off the leg. "The blood squirted right across the room," he said. "Nearly got the doctor in the eye. They had to tie up the artery real quick."

"What does it look like now?" someone asked.

Royce scratched his head. He always scratches his head when he doesn't know. Then his eyes got their sharp look. "Disgusting!" he said. "Absolutely hideous! Want to see? No, I was not joking. Next week Grandadda's coming out of the hospital to our place. You can come round after school. One dollar. That's all. Each of you give me a dollar and I'll get Grandadda to show you his leg."

"No bandages?" said Russ Huirama.

"Just horrible bare skin and scars," promised Royce.

"Yeah," they said. "Okay. Yeah, yeah. It's a deal."

But on the way home from school, I told Royce that I wasn't paying.

"What's wrong?" he said. "You poor all of a sudden?"

"I'm family. I can see it for free."

"Why bother?" he snarled. "You've got a sugar allergy. That'll be diabetes before you know it. Just sit around and wait for your own leg to go rotten."

I laughed because he was good and mad.

"Your toes'll go blue and then black," he said. "You'll smell like a dead sheep."

"What if your grandadda won't show them his leg?"

"He will."

"How do you know?"

"I'll ask him," said Royce.

"He might tell you to get lost."

"Then I'll bet him five bucks he's too scared to show his leg to my friends."

"And what if that doesn't work?"

"It will." Royce punched me on the arm and laughed. He's like that, Royce. He gets into bad moods and then good moods with equal speed. "Grandadda thinks the same about money as I do," he said.

# 2.

"Why wouldn't you tell me?" I asked Mom.

She was poking flowers into a green glass bowl. "Michael dear, it's not any big secret. It was the wrong time to tell you. Your father is a polite man. But at that moment he was making a joke about poor old Mr. West and he was a little embarrassed."

"Why did Dad say he'd die of thirst?"

She looked a long time at a red flower and then cut the stalk with a snip that made me wonder if plants feel their legs getting cut off. "You know, Michael, some people don't look after themselves. They ruin their health by drinking and eating too much. They smoke cigarettes. Then they complain when they get ill and they expect the public health system to look after them. We don't live like that, Michael. We take good care—"

"Did Uncle Leo's father do all those things?"

Mom snipped some more flower stalks. "I was not saying it's entirely his fault. Part of it's the Irish problem. He's inherited it. But all the same, he could have done more—"

"What's the Irish problem?"

Mom looked at me and put some fern stuff in with the flowers. "It's just something people say, Michael. It's not important. The one I feel for is my poor sister Rose. He's getting out of the hospital tomorrow and she'll be looking after him. My heart goes out to her. Old Mr. West has been a difficult man at the best of times and now he'll be in a wheelchair. As if she didn't have enough to do with five children and that horrible old house—"

I wasn't interested in the West's old house. I wanted to know what the Irish problem was and I reckoned the best person to ask was Royce. I called him from the phone in my bedroom.

"Spuds," he said. "It was a huge problem last century. All the Irish potatoes got blight and shrivelled up and the people were starving. They had to go to America and New Zealand and Australia to get a decent feed of spuds."

"How does anyone get blight from potatoes?" I asked.

"What are you on about?"

"Mom said your Grandadda inherited the Irish problem."

"Your mother talks funny," said Royce.

"She does not!"

"Yes, she does."

"No, she doesn't!"

Royce started shouting in my ear, "Does, does, does, does, does—"

I put the phone down. Stupid Royce!

Whoever heard of someone getting their leg cut off because they ate a shrivelled-up potato?

# 3.

After lunch, Mom gave me a tin full of ginger snaps and short-bread she had baked for her poor sister Rose. On the way, I opened the lid a couple of times to breathe in the good smells, but I didn't eat any. In my head there is a voice that said, sugar allergy plus ginger snaps equals diabetes, equals gangrene minus one leg. I gave the whole tinful to Auntie Rosie who was getting everyone to help her to clean out Jeannie's bedroom. That's where old Mr. West was going to sleep.

"It used to be a dining room," said Auntie Rosie. "That's why it's got double doors. Good for a wheelchair. It's next to the kitchen. Close to the bathroom, too."

"What about my mice?" cried Jeannie, who had to share her twin brother's room. She was worried because the cats Pooh and Frodo slept on Johnny's bed, and her mouse houses were not very strong.

"The mice have to go with you," said Auntie Rosie.

"But Grandadda might like having mice in his room," she said.

"Well, now, I wouldn't count on that," said Uncle Leo, picking up one of the mouse cages. "You and Johnny take care of these and the cats can go in Miranda's room."

"Maybe Grandadda can have the cats," said Miranda.

"I told you," said Uncle Leo. "Grandadda's not a well man. Just don't count on a single thing, okay?"

At least Uncle Leo knew what the Irish problem was. "Faith, Mickey, your mother'll be talking about the drinking. It's not unknown for some people to like a little drop. Only those who do, don't exactly see it as a problem, you understand."

I nodded.

"My dadda always had two great comforts," said Uncle Leo. "His tin of baccy and his drop of whisky. That and a flutter on the horses from time to time was the stuff of life for a hard working man. But he can't smoke. The baccy is killing him. And he's not allowed to drink. With a foot missing, there's not much he can do about getting his little comforts. No wonder he's like a bear with a sore head."

"Just his foot missing?" I was disappointed. "Royce said it was his whole leg."

"Ah!" said Uncle Leo. "Royce always makes a good story, Mickey. You should know that."

"Have you got the Irish problem, Uncle Leo?"

He put his head back and laughed and laughed, his wooly curls jiggling like springs. "I should be so lucky!" He gave a big hiccup and wiped his eyes. "No, I don't think so, Mickey. A man can't afford those little comforts when he's got five children and a mortgage."

"And a wife who likes diamonds and champagne," said Auntie Rosie, tickling him under the arms.

I was a bit puzzled. I didn't know Auntie Rosie liked diamonds. She never wore jewelry and I hadn't ever seen her drinking champagne. I also felt a little embarrassed at the way they were carrying on, screaming and tickling each other. They fell onto the bedroom floor and lay there in the dust, laughing until they were red in the face. It was stupid behavior for grown-ups. My parents would never have done that.

Jeannie and Johnny took no notice. They just stepped over them to get the other two mouse houses.

Uncle Leo stood up, then pulled Auntie Rosie to her feet. "You know the nicest thing about this world, Mickey?" he said. "It's the way people are different. If we were all the same, now, wouldn't it be a dull old place?"

I thought about that. "Absolutely boring," I said. "I'll help you to clean the room."

Uncle Leo put his big hairy hand on my shoulder. "Mickey, there is no such thing as an Irish problem or an English problem or any other nation's problem. Prejudice is a nasty disease. Worse than diabetes. It's invisible, is prejudice. We never see it in ourselves. But when we catch ourselves thinking we might be better than someone else, that's when we know we've got it." He squeezed my shoulder. "How would you like to come to tea tomorrow night? Meet my dadda?"

"I'd love to!" I told him. "Is he like you?"

"They're two peas in a pod," said Auntie Rosie, laughing and hitting Uncle Leo with a pillow.

He hooted like a train engine, grabbed the other pillow and hit her back.

They were at it again.

# 4.

They brought him up the drive in his wheelchair, through the front door, down the hall, to Jeannie's bedroom, which had been scrubbed clean of every bit of mouse smell. I knew, because I did the scrubbing.

Old Mr. West was very grumpy. He wasn't anything like his son except his talk had the same kind of accent. If he had stood up, he'd have been much taller than Uncle Leo, and much fatter. He had bulgy gray eyes in a red face and a nose like a parrot's beak. What was left of his hair was gray and stringy. Uncle Leo was right about the leg and Royce was wrong. Only the foot was missing. The ankle had a thick bandage that looked like a sock. The foot on the other leg was skinny and white with lumpy blue veins, and it was wearing a brown leather slipper.

I wondered how Mr. West was going to buy shoes now. Would he just order one? Could you do that?

"You!" he said. "You're staring!"

I jumped. He'd turned in his wheelchair and he was pointing a finger at me, but the finger wouldn't stay still and was shaking between me and Royce and Miranda.

"You'll not be denying it!" he growled as his false teeth clicked up and down. "I caught you! Stare, stare, at the freak in the chair. Would you be seeing anything worth looking at?" He lifted the ankle without a foot.

I licked my lips. "I'm sorry, Mr. West. I—I was just wondering how you're going to buy your shoes?"

"What's this Mr. West business? Who are you?"

"Mickey's our cousin, Grandadda," said Miranda.

"The son of Rosie's sister Eileen," said Uncle Leo. "You remember Eileen, Dadda."

"I do and all. Good looking lass, even if she did have a toffee apple up her nose. Eileen's boy, huh? You got the same toffee apple up your snout?"

I felt my face get red. "I'm sorry. I am really sorry. I was just—"

"Wondering about shoes? Listen, lad! I'll buy them just like you. The hospital's making me a foot, a plastic tootsie to strap on my leg, same as the other. It'll be coming in the mail any day." He glared at Uncle Leo. "When I get that, there'll be no stopping me!"

"Mickey helped us to get your room ready, Dadda," said Auntie Rosie.

He took no notice of that. He looked at her and clicked his false teeth. Then he said, "Are you all paralyzed? Can no one around here make a pot of tea?"

Uncle Leo steered the wheelchair into the kitchen and pushed it up to the table where Auntie Rosie had set out cups and a plate of Mom's ginger snaps and shortbread. The plate was close to Mr. West but Royce picked it up and shoved it right under his Grandadda's nose, saying in his nothing kind of voice, "Hey Grandadda, you know there are kids at school reckon you didn't have your foot cut off? I told them they should come and see for themselves."

Before Mr. West could say a word, Auntie Rosie slapped the teapot on the table. "Dadda, there's something you should know. Most of the kids in Royce's class are coming here tomorrow afternoon to look at your leg. He's charging them a dollar each."

Mr. West had a piece of shortbread almost to his mouth. He turned to Royce who had gone all edgy.

Royce glared at me. It's not my fault, I wanted to say. I didn't tell your mother. I just mentioned to Miranda that you—well, you know what. It must have been Miranda who squeaked on you. I mean, squealed.

But Royce was looking at me with fierce eyes and I knew I was in trouble.

"One dollar each?" said old Mr. West.

Royce shrugged.

"And how many would be coming?"

Royce shrugged again. "I dunno. It's nothing, really. Just a joke."

"How many did you say?"

Royce's shoulders dropped. "About twenty."

"And you'll be expecting me to unwrap the bandages and show them the stitch marks?" He glared at Royce who looked over his shoulder and far away, as though there was no one else in the room. Then the old man thumped his fist on the table, making the lid jump in the teapot. "Fifty per cent!" he said. "Ten bucks for me. Ten for you! That's it."

Royce's mouth opened and shut. He didn't say a word.

Mr. West took a big bite of shortbread. "Blessed saints! We can go into business, lad!" he said, blowing crumbs over the table. "You bring a thousand kids round here and I'll take out me glass eye."

Everyone laughed and Jeannie said, "Grandadda! You don't have a glass eye!"

"Isn't that the truth! But for a thousand dollars I'd get one." He made a wheezing noise like he was trying to cough, but actually he was laughing. His top teeth, coated with shortbread, fell down. He took them out and put them on the table by his plate. Then he took out the bottom teeth, put them down too, and closed his mouth. He pushed out his lips so they almost touched his nose. I tried not to look.

"For another fifty shents they can shee theesh and all," he said.

They all laughed as though it was a fantastic joke, but I didn't think it was very funny. To tell the truth, I felt a bit sick. What's more, I was sure the old man knew it. He looked right at me, grinned, and then, with his teeth still on the table, he had another bite of Mom's shortbread.

# 5.

In the end, I paid Royce the dollar, although I hated doing it. I told him it was a matter of principle. He said it was a matter of principle for him, too, and when we put our principles together, we had only two choices—either I stayed away, or I paid up. I paid because I was sick of arguing and anyway, I didn't want to be left out. Even Paul Jasicki said he was coming although there was a good chance he'd faint again.

Mr. West was on the front verandah in his wheelchair, reading a newspaper. When he saw us, he folded the paper, put it down, and then counted us with a shaking finger.

Royce said, "Grandadda, these are some of the kids in my class. This is Jason and Paul and Suzanne and Russ—"

"Twelve!" growled Mr. West.

"—and Andrew and Fio and you already know Mickey and—"

"You said there'd be twenty and there's twelve. You think I don't know me numbers?" His face got even redder and he hit his fist on the arm of the wheelchair. "Me own grandson wouldn't be trying to rob a crippled old man blind, would he?"

We all looked at Royce but he just scratched his head as though he kept a stack of answers in his hair. Russ Huirama took a step backwards. So did Paul Jasicki. I reckoned that in another few seconds, they'd all turn like a flock of sheep and rattle off down the road.

Mr. West held out his right hand and rubbed his thumb and forefinger together. "My share is still ten bucks," he said.

Royce didn't argue. He took out the bunch of bills and

coins, counted ten dollars, and took it up the verandah steps. Mr. West counted it again and put it in his pocket, all except a couple of quarters which he flicked between his fingers. His hand moved as though he was playing the piano and the coins seemed to jump in a flash of silver over the gaps between his fingers. Then he tossed the coins in the air and they vanished. We looked up. We looked down. We listened to hear them land. Nothing.

"But it's me foot you've come to see, isn't it? The one that isn't there?" He suddenly grinned and his top teeth dropped down. He clicked them up again. "Well, first up, I'll show you the other one. This is what it used to look like before they cut it off." He reached down, grunting, and pulled off his leather slipper. We saw a long bony foot, very white, with clumps of blue veins, and gray hairs growing from the big toe. But that wasn't all. In the gaps between his toes were the missing silver coins. Everyone went, "Ooh!" and came close for a better look. Some kids trod on the flower garden but that didn't matter because it was mostly full of weeds. Yes, they were the same quarters.

Mr. West picked up the coins and put them in his shirt pocket with the rest of the money. He held his foot in the air, wriggling his toes. "It was just like this, perfectly good, until the rot set in. Well, I can't complain. I got me a good mileage out of it, so I did. No blowouts, no retreads. Although I did get a puncture once from a rusty nail. Any of you ever trod on a rusty nail?"

I put up my hand. So did Suzanne and Russ.

Mr. West pointed to me. "Eileen's son! You'll do! I'll be needing some help."

I walked up the verandah steps very slowly, thinking he

would ask me to unwrap his bandage, but he just wanted me to help him put his slipper back on. I knelt down by the wheelchair and pushed the slipper over his hairy white toes.

His foot wriggled. "Saints alive!" he bellowed. "Are you trying to destroy me one and only good tootsie?"

Quickly, I pulled the slipper away. Two coins slid from the toes down to the heel and lay against the worn lining, like two silver moons. They were the same quarters! How did they get there? I looked up at Mr. West.

"Ah!" he said. "I thought as much! You'll be doing me a favor, lad, if you put that pesky money in your own pocket." He gave a slow wink with one red watery eye.

I didn't dare look back at Royce. I just grabbed the coins, stuffed them in my jacket, and then put Mr. West's slipper back on.

The other kids had climbed onto the verandah for a really close look and Mr. West was like an actor on a stage. He deliberately clicked his teeth at them as he lifted up his bandaged ankle. "First of all, are you having any questions?"

No one said anything.

"Spit it out or you'll die wondering," he growled.

Suzanne said in a small squeaky voice, "Does it still hurt?"

"To be sure, the ankle doesn't hurt but I got Arthur in me absent foot. You know Mr. Itis?"

Royce said to us, "Grandadda means arthritis."

Mr. West poked his finger towards Royce. "Are you telling your friends they haven't got the brains they were born with? Course they know who Arthur is. It happens, you see. A part of your body goes but its ghost remains to haunt you. The foot bones that aren't there ache when it's raining. I get itchy toes that I can't scratch. Any other questions?"

"How long did the operation take?" asked Paul.

"Oh, about as long as a piece of string." Mr. West bent over, grunting over his big stomach. "Well, here's where you get what you paid for," he said as he peeled off the thick white sock over the stump of his ankle. We held our breath to watch. There was a bandage underneath and more gauze stuff folded over the end. Layer by layer, he took it off and we got ready for the horror of the last unwrapping.

Oh! Was that all?

It was just a plain old leg. Not a dollar's worth, that's for sure, although I couldn't complain because I got some money back. At the end of the leg there were a couple of red lines and some red dots where the stitches had been. No ankle bones. They must have been cut off, too. Above the knobbly end, the skin was white with a few gray hairs and more veins like blue worms. But really, it didn't look like a leg with the foot chopped off. It was more like a normal leg not finished.

"Do you want to know how it feels?" said Mr. West. "Touch it if you like."

All the kids backed off.

The old man laughed. "There's not many your age can say they touched the ghost of a foot. It's good luck, I tell you. The ghost'll be with you and you'll always run like the wind. Now isn't that the truth!"

Royce was first. He put one finger on the red rope scar. Russ did the same. Then one by one, we all touched Mr. West's leg.

Paul asked, "Are you going to get a peg-leg like a pirate?"

Mr. West stared at him and made the wheezing sound that was his laugh. "Saints preserve us, the lad is a genius. Can't you just see me dancing the night away in a peg-leg? Shuffle, thud, shuffle, thud. Oh, but I'd be a right old hit with the ladies." He stopped wheezing. "No, lad. Me pirate days are over. I'll just be getting a plastic tootsie from the hospital, normal shape to wear a normal sock and shoe, so I will."

We watched as he put the bandage back on. We all felt special because we'd touched the leg, like we'd done something very brave, and we didn't want it to be over. Maybe Mr. West would do more tricks for us. We waited as his sock was pulled over the bandage, while he rolled down the leg of his trousers. But the show was over. He didn't say or do anything else for us. He just reached down and picked up his newspaper.

It was Miranda who announced the next bit of entertainment. She came out and told us to go into the kitchen where we could all have lemonade and shortbread and ginger snaps. We walked through the front door and down the hall, pretending we were pirates limping with peg-legs. Shuffle, thud, shuffle, thud, shuffle, thud.

# 6.

Most of the time, Mr. West was really grumpy. He complained about the house, the food, the animals, the noise his grandchildren made, and the people at the hospital who hadn't mailed his plastic foot. Every day he sent someone out to the mailbox to look for a parcel the size of a shoebox.

"It won't come in the mail, Dadda," said Uncle Leo. "You'll get an appointment to go to the hospital and have it fitted."

"And you would be knowing all that, would you?" growled Mr. West. "How many feet have you had chopped off? Five? Six?"

Uncle Leo was really amazing. He never grumped back, just laughed and changed the subject. But I could tell that all the complaining was getting to Auntie Rosie. When Auntie Rosie was happy, she said terrible things to her family. One time Jeannie was sulking with her bottom lip poked out and Auntie Rosie said Jeannie's face was like the back door of an egg factory. And when Royce was really slow setting the table, Auntie Rosie told him his butt needed a rocket. She was like that when things were fine. But when she was unhappy, she got very polite to people. Her round face had this tiny tight smile and she said please and thank you a lot. Most days, she was very polite to her father-in-law.

Mr. West was angry because he spilled pumpkin soup down himself. It lay thick and yellow on his big stomach. "You call this soup?" he bellowed. "It's pig food!"

Royce puts his head down and whispered, "Oink! Oink! Have some more!"

But Auntie Rosie said, "It's all right, Dadda. Don't worry. I'll fix it." And she got up at once to fetch a cloth. As she went past Royce she flicked the cloth across the back of his neck to shut him up. We all knew it was really Mr. West she was mad at.

Mom worried about Auntie Rosie, but she wouldn't go down to see her because she was allergic to flea bites. "Poor Rose," she said. "All those animals, five unruly kids, a middle-aged hippy for a husband and now that—that—" She looked at me. "That disabled man!" she said.

Dad looked at her over the top of his glasses. "If you want to give Rose a break, we could have the old man down here for a few days."

Mom stopped dead still. She stared at Dad, her mouth open.

"I was only joking," said Dad.

Mom said, "That was a very poor joke, Arthur."

"Guess what?" I told them. "Mr. West calls the pain in his joints, Arthur. Mr. Itis. Get it? Arthritis!"

"Yes, yes," said Mom. "And that's another poor joke. Hurry, Michael, or you'll be late for school."

I jumped up and put my lunch and books in my backpack. "Can I go around there again today?"

"Where?" said Dad.

"He's been helping Rose after school," said Mom.

Dad looked at her, "Are you sure—"

"He's a very sensible boy," said Mom. She turned to me. "Isn't that right, Michael? You are sensible and you do remember your manners?"

"Oh yes, Mom."

Mom smiled at Dad, "Rose said he's a great help. Always reliable, she said. Goodness only knows, poor Rose needs someone reliable about that place."

"Oh, come on, Eileen," said Dad. "That's going a bit too far."

Mom put her hand on my head and said to Dad, "I told Rose that Michael could go for an hour, three afternoons a week. Rose said the old man thinks the world of him."

That also was going a bit too far. Mr. West didn't like me any more than the other kids. He called me stupid and useless and said I don't know my arse from breakfast time. But when he was not being grumpy, he did amazing things like playing fast tunes on a tin whistle and making all kinds of animal noises. He could howl like a wolf, roar like a stag, hoot like an owl, and quack to fool any duck. He showed Royce and me how to do cat's cradle string games. He also did heaps of tricks. Once he took all the matches out of a matchbox then told me he would give me a prize if I could squash the empty matchbox with one blow of my fist. Oh boy, did I squash it! Thud! I burst that matchbox into little bits.

"Congratulations!" said Mr. West. "Here is your prize." And he gave me the handful of matches.

But he didn't like being called Mr. West.

I asked him. "Do you want me to call you Grandadda, like Royce and Miranda?"

"I'm not your flaming grandadda, boy. I'm your great-uncle. Call me Great Uncle Tom."

"Great Uncle Tom." I was surprised. I didn't know his name was Tom. I felt kind of special saying his name when no one in the house could do that. "Great Uncle Tom," I said again.

"Never forget it," he said with his wheezing laugh. "I like hearing I'm Great Uncle Tom." But the next second he was in a bad mood again, looking for his newspaper and yelling at me because I couldn't find it for him. "You're about as useful as feathers on a fish!" he complained. "Isn't that the truth?"

"Yes, Great Uncle Tom," I said.

# 7·

On Wednesdays after school, Miranda played hockey, Johnny had his ballet class. and Royce was on his paper route. That left Jeannie, Honey, and me with Auntie Rosie and old Mr. West—my Great Uncle Tom. Auntie Rosie called Wednesday afternoon her quiet time. She usually ate peanuts and read a book with her feet up on the coffee table while Honey played in the sandbox and Jeannie did her homework. I sat with Great Uncle Tom in his favorite place, the front porch, listening to his stories about the war and making him cups of tea. The trouble was, he drank so many cups of tea he was always going to the bathroom. I had to push his wheelchair all the way down the hall and give him his crutches. He locked the bathroom door behind him. Then, because he had to hold onto his crutches, he splashed all over the toilet and the floor and guess who had to clean up afterwards?

"Mickey dear," called Auntie Rosie, "do be a sweetie and mop the seatie."

I reckon Mom would be furious if she knew.

One cold and gray Wednesday afternoon, Jeannie was cleaning out her mouse houses and Honey was in the front room with Auntie Rosie while I was doing the old mop and disinfectant trick in the bathroom. Suddenly, there was a screech from Auntie Rosie. "Honey!" A second later, Honey started to cry really loud.

I ran down the hall, slap bang into Jeannie.

"Oh no! Honey! How could you!" Auntie Rosie yelled while the baby bawled and bawled.

Great Uncle Tom pushed the wheels of his chair through the front door. "What's up?" he growled.

Auntie Rosie held Honey close and patted her on the back, trying to calm her. "She put peanuts up her nose!" she said. "One up each nostril."

"Flaming silly thing to do," growled Great Uncle Tom.

We tried talking to Honey. "Take a deep breath. Blow hard through your nose." But she was too upset to listen. She shook her head and tried to hide her face in her mother's neck.

"The peanuts are right up her nose!" said Auntie Rosie.

"If she inhales hard, they could go into her lungs. That'll mean surgery. Oh! I have to get her to the doctor."

The doctor word made Honey yell all the louder. Auntie Rosie kissed her on the forehead and told her everything was going to be fine. "Jeannie, you come with me! Mickey! Stay and look after Grandadda. I won't be long."

"I am not his grandadda," the old man said. "Where are you going?"

"The ER!" said Auntie Rosie, squeezing past his wheelchair.

Seconds later, their van was backing down the drive and I was wheeling Great Uncle Tom onto the front porch. "They'll be hours," he said. "You'll have to be cooking me tea."

"Auntie Rosie said she wouldn't be—"

"Hours, I tell you! You think I don't know what those places are like? Blessed saints! You sit all day in the waiting room before they even notice you."

"I don't think so, Great Uncle Tom. A doctor will see her straight away. Peanuts up a nose is an emergency. I read somewhere if they go into your lungs they grow into plants and you die."

"Not roasted peanuts, you idjit!" he said. His bulgy red-veined eyes slid around, and he smiled, clicking his teeth. "You think you could get this chair down those steps?"

I shook my head.

"You could do just the chair by itself. I'll slide down the steps on me backside and get on board at the bottom. Then you could be pushing me into town like a good lad, so you could."

"Push you into town?"

"You got peanuts in your ears?" he said.

"I'm sorry. I can't. Not to town, Great Uncle Tom. There's a steep hill."

"I know there's a hill, you stupid lad. But I'd be helping you with the wheels."

In my mind I saw the chair out of control on the Tanika Street hill and Great Uncle Tom with his bandaged leg in the air, racing towards the traffic.

"I couldn't do it," I told him.

He grumbled and growled and said when he was my age he had muscles like tea kettles from making hay with a scythe and pitchfork. Then he went on and on about the hospital not sending him his foot. "If I had my plastic tootsie, I'd not be asking you. I'd be hauling myself out of here so fast, you'd not see me for dust, and isn't that the truth? Well, don't stand there, Eileen's boy. Go and make a pot of tea."

But when I brought back his tea, he didn't want it. He had another idea. "Get me Leo's rain boot. By the back door. Just the one, mind."

"Right or left?"

"Which one do you think?"

I knew where the rain boots were on the back porch. By the time I found Uncle Leo's, black with a red band on the top, I knew what Great Uncle Tom wanted to do. I just didn't know how he'd do it.

"I'll be needing some stuffing," he said. "Something soft."

"Feathers?" I suggested. "Polystirene beads? Old socks?"

"And I'll be needing something strong to make a suspender and something to bore holes in the top of the boot. You know what a suspender is, Eileen's boy? You do? So why are you standing there with your mouth open? We haven't got all day."

The boot worked. Sort of. It was stuffed full of plastic supermarket bags. Great Uncle Tom had put an extra sock with

cotton balls in it on the stump of his ankle. He'd strapped
Goof's dog collar above the knee. From the collar hung
lengths of string that he tied through holes on the top of the
gumboot. He rolled the leg of his trousers down over it all.
Then he stood up with his crutches, put the gumboot on the
verandah, and took a step. The gumboot folded up. He wobbled. His balance had gone, he said. But he could walk. "You'll
need to help me down the steps," he said.

"Are you really going to town?" I asked.

"Maybe." he said. "It'll all be depending on the quality of
Leo's boot."

"What will I tell Auntie Rosie when she comes back?"

He clicked his teeth. "You'll not be telling a single word on
account of you being with me. Don't look surprised, Eileen's
boy. You're supposed to be looking after me, aren't you? So
let's be going!"

# 8.

The Tanika Street hill was very slow because we had to make
stops all along the way. Sometimes Great Uncle Tom rested
on his crutches. Other times, I held a crutch while he leaned
on my shoulder and looked down at the houses. "You'd think
there'd be a better view," he wheezed. It was a real wheeze, too.
Not a laugh.

I didn't say anything. I looked at the people going past
and wondered what they would think about the old man who
wore one brown slipper and one squashy black gumboot.

At the top of the hill, we had to sit for a while on the seat
outside the post office. He was breathing really hard and I

didn't think he could go any further. We had to get home. But I knew that going down the hill would be just as bad as coming up or maybe even worse. I started to panic. I was supposed to be looking after him. I'd promised Auntie Rosie. How would I get him back to the house?

Great Uncle Tom didn't want to go home. As soon as he got his breath, he heaved himself up on his crutches. Shuffle, flop, shuffle, flop. I thought I'd done a good job of stuffing the gumboot but with every step it folded up and slid around. One time it pointed backwards.

"Useless rotten contraption!" growled Great Uncle Tom.

"I'm sorry."

"Not your fault, Eileen's boy. The hospital. Too lazy to get off their backsides and mail me my tootsie. Here. Take the crutch. Let me lean on your shoulder again. It's not far now."

"What's not far?" I asked.

"The lovely old White Heron. What else?"

"The White Heron?" I stopped. "That's a bar!"

His hand grabbed my shoulder hard and gave me a bit of a push. "Why so it is! And here's me thinking it sold magazines and comic books. Get going, Eileen's boy. I just got me second wind."

The White Heron was the bar on the corner. It had frosted windows and green double doors with brass handles. I tried to give Great Uncle Tom his crutch. "I'll wait out here."

"You'll be doing no such thing," he said, leaning harder on my shoulder. "Are you looking after me or are you not?"

There was no choice. I had to go into the bar.

It was dark inside and everything smelled of beer and old cigarette smoke. There were two men at a pool table in the middle of the room and another two sitting on high stools at the counter. They all stopped talking to look at us.

"Take me over to the bar," said Great Uncle Tom.

The man who was wiping the counter with a white towel said, "Sorry. No kids."

"He's fine," said Great Uncle Tom. "I'm a cripple and he's looking after me. Now, isn't that the truth? Hold the barstool, lad. Help me up."

"No kids and that's the law," said the man.

Great Uncle Tom wriggled onto the stool, dropped his other crutch and gave a big sigh. He looked around the room and put his hand on my head. "I told you, he's okay. He's Eileen's boy. Eileen, now, is my daughter-in-law's sister. Pretty as a picture, she is, but she's got a toffee apple up her nose. Stuck up, you see. Not the lad, though." He turned back to the man behind the counter. "I'll have a single malt. Give him a lemonade."

The man didn't move. "He goes or you both go," he said. "Now!"

Great Uncle Tom shrugged at me with his hands. "You'll have to wait outside, Eileen's boy. I'm real sorry about that."

But I was not the least bit sorry. I couldn't wait to get out of there.

# 9.

I was sitting on the edge of the pavement when Uncle Leo and Auntie Rosie drove up in their van. It was getting dark and I was freezing. I must have looked cold because Auntie Rosie grabbed Goof's dog blanket out of the back and wrapped it around my shoulders. I'd probably get fleas but I didn't mind. I liked the warm smell of dog.

"How did you know we'd be here?" I asked.

"It was a good guess," said Uncle Leo, looking at the green doors. He put his head on one side. "Faith, but I can hear him singing from here."

"He's been singing for ages," I told him.

Uncle Leo laughed. "That's my dadda. A glass of whisky to oil his vocal chords and another to wind up his music box. Sounds well and truly wound up now, wouldn't you say, Rosie? I hope we get him out without a fight." He laughed again, hitched up his trousers and went into the White Heron.

Auntie Rosie hugged me as she led me to the van. "My poor, poor Mickey! I didn't know we'd be so long at the clinic."

"How's Honey?"

"She's sleeping. Miranda's keeping an eye on her. It took ages. The peanuts were pushed right up against the septum. Do you know what that is?"

"Her brain?" I ask.

"Not quite. The top part of her nose. She was so scared, she couldn't sit still. In the end they gave her a sedative. Such a long time, and I knew our wicked old Dadda would be up to his tricks. Dear loyal Mickey. Anyone else would have gone home long ago."

I liked Auntie Rosie's fat hugs so I didn't tell her I wasn't being loyal. The only reason I didn't go home was I thought I'd get into trouble for not looking after him. That was the truth. But I had to say, "Auntie Rosie, I don't think he's wicked."

"You'd better believe it," she said. "He's been told a hundred times that alcohol will kill him."

"But it's his—his comfort."

"Comfort?" Auntie Rosie snorted. "Now don't you quote Leo to me, Mickey my boy, or I'll sew your mouth up with a shoelace. That husband of mine is as soft as a jelly in a heat wave. He knows full well his dadda's not supposed to smoke or drink. He just makes excuses for—Uh-oh! Here they come."

The green doors opened. The bartender and Uncle Leo came out, hauling Great Uncle Tom between them. Neither of the old man's legs were working. The slipper and gumboot were dragging on the ground with the gumboot twisted back to front. But Great Uncle Tom was very happy, smoking a cigar and singing at the top of his voice, "In Dublin's fair city, where the girls are so pretty, that's where I first met sweet Molly Malone—"

Auntie Rosie jumped out of the van and held the front passenger door open.

Supporting him under the arms, the man and Uncle Leo dragged Great Uncle Tom across the pavement. As they tried to get him into the van, he waved his arms, conducting his own song. The smoke from his cigar drifted in, making me cough.

He sang, "In streets broad and narrow, a-wheeling her wheelbarrow, singing, 'Cockles and mussels alive, alive-oh!'" He stopped and blinked at Auntie Rosie. Then he smiled. "Good evening, toffee apple's sister," he said in a happy voice as he fell onto the seat.

Uncle Leo drove the van towards my house. He said he would explain everything to Mom and Dad. "You deserve a gold medal, Mickey," he told me. He wasn't angry about his dadda going to the White Heron but he was definitely not pleased about his gumboot. "Dadda, those were new! You put holes in it."

Great Uncle Tom puffed on the cigar and wheezed. "It's

an awful lot of noise you're making, Leo."

"I bought them just last week!" said Uncle Leo. "I've only worn them once. Couldn't you be choosing someone else's boot to mutilate? An old one belonging to one of the kids?"

"Wrong size."

"What do you mean wrong size? You don't have a size! You don't have a foot!"

"Had to match me slipper." Great Uncle Tom grinned at Uncle Leo. "Come on, lad. A face like that'll turn the milk sour. Don't worry. Be happy. The night is yet young." He started singing again. "Oh Shenandoah, I long to see you—"

Auntie Rosie squeezed my hand. "I suppose you're right, Mickey. When a man gets into his eighties he has a right to his comforts. Goodness knows, when I'm eighty, I intend to do exactly as I like."

"Why Rosie girl," Uncle Leo called out over the steering wheel. "I thought you did that now."

Great Uncle Tom stopped singing. "What'd you say?"

"I was just talking to Mickey, Dadda," said Auntie Rosie.

"He's still there, is he? Fine lad, Eileen's boy." He turned around and blew smoke over the back seats. "You can call me Grandadda if you like."

I thought about that. "Thanks," I told him. "But if it's all right, I'd rather call you Great Uncle Tom."

"Me name's not Tom," he said.

I didn't know what he was talking about.

"It's Seamus," Uncle Leo said to me. "That's his name. Seamus Liam. We've all been wondering why you've been calling him Great Uncle Tom."

"But he—" I looked at the old man. "You—you told me to call you—"

"Oh, but I didn't say it was me name now, did I?" He gave me a slow wink. "I just liked hearing it. Now I think I like Grandadda better and even if you're not me grandson then you're as good as." He blew more smoke over the seat. "Although, if you're sensitive about Grandadda, you can always be calling me Great Uncle Seamus."

But now I didn't feel like calling him anything. I pulled the dog blanket tight around my shoulders.

Next to me, Auntie Rosie was shaking with laughter. "I told you he was a wicked old man," she whispered.

# 10.

Mom and Dad said I was not allowed to go near the Wests' house. "Not while he's there," said Dad. "He's definitely not a suitable role model for a young boy."

"That's not fair!" I cried. "I didn't do anything wrong!"

Mom put her arm around me. "Michael, dear, we know you didn't do anything wrong. That's not what it's about. Rose is my sister. I am fond of her. But she's a trained schoolteacher, for goodness sake! She's supposed to be intelligent!"

"She is, Mom. She's really clever."

"So it's clever for her to sit reading books while her children try to kill each other or themselves," snapped Mom. "Well, she can do that, as far as I'm concerned. But to leave you with that wretched old alcoholic is utterly unforgivable!"

"Mom, Auntie Rosie didn't know he would—"

"That's enough, Michael," said Dad. "Do not argue with your mother." He shook his head. "I can't imagine how many people saw my son in that bar. It will be all over town. I'll

201

never hear the end of it."

I looked down at my feet. My face felt hot and my eyes were stinging. I didn't mind not seeing old Mr. West because I was still angry about the name trick. But I felt a big hole inside me when I realized I couldn't visit Auntie Rosie, Uncle Leo, and my cousins. It wasn't fair.

Mom said, "He won't be there forever, Michael. When he's fitted with his artificial limb, he'll be going back to his own home."

"That might be weeks and weeks!"

"I'm sorry, son," said Dad. "We have to be firm about this. While he's with Leo and Rose, you stay away from their house."

A whole week went by and all my cousins felt sad for me. After school, Miranda said, "We really miss you, Mickey," and she gave me a hug that made the other kids stare. The boys in my class thought Miranda was really cool and a hug from her was practically better than winning the cross-country race. Still, it didn't mend the big hole inside me.

Royce told me, "Grandadda goes to the hospital to get his new foot tomorrow."

"So what?"

"Why don't you just come and see it? You can always tell your mother you went somewhere else."

I shook my head. I felt bad about not being able to go to the Wests but I'd feel worse about lying to Mom and Dad.

Once more, they canceled their weekend golf game to stay home with me. That meant we were all unhappy. On Saturday afternoon, Dad went to the office to do some tax returns. Mom put on her leather gloves and mixed spray for the roses. I started making the model airplane Dad bought me, but it was a really boring model and I kept wondering what my cousins were doing. I was just thinking about phoning Royce when the doorbell rang.

Mom was washing her hands in the laundry room. "Will you see who that is, Michael?"

I went to the front door, hoping it was Royce but it wasn't. I stood in the doorway, blinking at old Mr. West.

"Well now, it's Eileen's boy," he said. "How are you doing?" He was wearing a sharp gray suit with a white shirt and a red and blue striped tie. There was a red flower in his buttonhole. His hair had been cut and he had on gold-rimmed glasses. But the biggest surprise was his feet. He had on matching black shoes, new and shiny, and there were no crutches. Instead, he leaned on a silver and black walking stick. He was smiling, waiting for me to say something.

I couldn't find any word except a faint, "Hullo."

He put his right foot on the step. "My new tootsie. See? Not plastic. It's fiberglass. No toes though. Just a plain old foot. I asked my youngest granddaughter to lend me a couple of her toes seeing as how she's got six on each foot, but she's keeping them as spares." He winked at me. "I've come to see your lovely mother, so I have."

I looked over my shoulder, not knowing what to say.

"Well? Is she in?"

I nodded.

"Then kindly do the courtesy of announcing the visit. I am not standing here waiting for Santa Claus."

Slowly, I walked a few steps backwards. Then I turned and called, "Mom? Mom? Someone here to see you."

Mom came through, taking off her apron and tucking it behind a cushion on one of the hall chairs. She patted the back of her hair and put on her front door smile. It disappeared when she saw Mr. West on the steps. Like me, she just stared. I waited for her to get angry but instead she looked nervous, as though she wanted to run back into the house. "Oh!" she said, almost in a whisper, wiping her hands on her dress.

Don't be scared, I wanted to tell her. He plays tricks but he's not dangerous.

"Eileen, mavourneen!" said Mr. West, coming up the rest of the steps. He leaned on his silver walking stick and reached for her hand, but instead of shaking it, he held it up in the air and kissed it. He truly did! On the back of the knuckles! A real smacker! "Lovely as ever!" he said, bowing low. "My, but you make an old man's heart young, so you do!"

Mom tried to smile but she was too jittery. She said to me. "Michael? I've left the rose sprayer on the back lawn. Please, wash it out and put it back in the garden shed." She gave me a hard look. "Do it now!" she said.

I knew what that meant. She wanted me out of the way while she gave him a good telling-off. But he'd argue back. It'd be a real showdown. I just hoped no one would say anything about alcoholics or toffee apples.

I did a thorough job of cleaning the sprayer, taking the brass nozzle to bits and washing all the parts. I figured if it took a long time, he'd be gone when I went back in the house.

I was wrong. He was still there. Not at the front door, either, but in the living room, sitting in the leather chair. I couldn't believe it. He was having a cup of tea with his teeth in, as polite as anything, talking to Mom about pruning roses. When he saw me, he put down his cup and saucer and said, "There you are, boy. I was just telling your lovely mother that there isn't a rose on this earth to match her beauty. You know she was my choice for a daughter-in-law?"

Mom's face was pink and she was laughing. "Oh what blarney!" she said. "Michael, go into the kitchen and get yourself a glass of cranberry juice."

"It's true," said Mr. West. "When Leo brought her home, I told everyone this was the girl for me son. Now isn't that the truth? But then the lovely Eileen met her young accountant and poor Leo—"

"Michael, did you hear me?" Mom said.

"Poor Leo consoled himself with her sister. And isn't that the truth too? But sure and all, boy, I came within a whisker of being your real Grandadda."

"Michael!" said Mom. "Cranberry juice!"

I went away, feeling all muddled up. I didn't know Mom went out with Uncle Leo. No one had ever told me that. I opened the fridge and closed it again. I hate cranberry juice!

When I went back to the living room, Mom was pouring more tea. She said in her light-as-air voice, "Michael, Mr. West is moving back to his own house next week. Tomorrow night, he's taking all his grandchildren out to dinner and he would like to include you in the invitation."

I stared at her. "What about—"

"Would you like to go?"

"Yes, but—but—"

Mr. West stood up and leaned on his cane. "That's grand then," he said, winking at me. "We'll have a fine old time." He took a cigar from his pocket. "Eileen, my dear, if you don't mind, I'll just step outside for a smoke."

"No, no, Seamus!" said Mom. "You don't have to go out. Sit down and smoke in comfort. Michael, will you please get Mr. West an ashtray."

I was more muddled than ever. No one smoked in our house. No one! We didn't have any ashtrays. What would I get? A saucer? A butter dish? And she called him Seamus! I heard her! He was acting so proper and polite, not wheezing or clicking his teeth. He was like someone out of a movie. The Godfather. Or the Prime Minister of England.

The surprise of it all fizzed into laughter inside me. I didn't know why because it wasn't all that funny. Just strange. I went into the kitchen, whistling the old Shenandoah song. We sang it at school, but my whistling was better than my singing. I mean, my whistling was really good, better than Royce's and nearly as good as Miranda's. Another thing, the hole in my stomach had completely disappeared. Gone, just like that. I wondered, how could a hole disappear without leaving a bigger hole? Technically, if you take out a hole, wouldn't a bigger hole remain? But then, I told myself, technically, there wasn't a hole in the first place, it just felt like it, and I supposed the best thing for an ashtray was the glass dish Mom used for old tea bags.

Later, I phoned Royce to tell him that everything was okay again. I could go with them to the restaurant.

He already knew.

So then I told him my other big news, how Mom was once his father's girlfriend.

He knew that too. "Spit a brick!" he said. "Don't your parents tell you anything? That's why Grandadda said your mother is stuck up. She dumped Dad when she met Uncle Arthur. You know what Grandadda calls your father?"

I thought I knew, but Royce told me just the same. "Arthur Itis. Mr. Itis! Ha-ha-ha!"

"That's a very sick joke," I told him.

"Not sick," said Royce. "Just stupid."

He was right. I shifted the phone to the other hand. "You know something, Royce? I'll never, never understand adults, not even when I am one myself."

"Me too," said Royce. "Tell you what. Let's bike down to the gravel pit and do some wheelies."

# The
# Wild West Gang
# and the Haunted Fridge

## 1.

Mom and Dad were spending a week of the school vacation in Australia with their golf clubs while I stayed with my cousins the Wests. Being with the West gang would normally have been great. Terrific. But compared with Australia? The Sydney Harbor Bridge, the zoo with kangaroos and snakes and koalas in gum trees? I wanted to go, too.

"What would you do while we were golfing?" Dad asked.

"Learn to play the didgeridoo," I told them.

"Very funny Michael," said Mom.

"I mean it. I've always wanted to play a didgeridoo. I could go to the zoo. Go surfing. Hunt for opals. I bet there are heaps of things to do in Sydney."

"The only opals are in expensive shops," sniffed Dad. "Ask your mother. She knows all about opal hunting."

I remembered my cousin Royce's advice. If all else fails, he reckoned, try throwing a sickie. I scrunched up my face in agony. "What about my tooth?"

"There's nothing wrong with your tooth, Michael," said Mom. "It isn't even loose."

"It hurts!" I cried.

"Be that as it may," said my mother, who could be very cold-hearted when it suited her. "You'll forget about it when you're with your cousins."

Dad smiled. "Nice try, old chap."

So there I was, stuck, which meant I arrived at the West's house in a really bad mood. As I took off my shoes on their back porch, all I could think was how messy my cousins were. Their porch was full of junk: the wheel of a tricycle, a baby's stroller full of firewood, a stinky blanket covered with dog hair, some old raincoats with cobwebs on the sleeves, buckets of paint gone hard, a shovel, a dead plant, but no shoes apart from mine. They didn't bother to take their shoes off outside the door. They just walked over the floors with mud and chicken poo. I'd seen Royce lying on his bed with his shoes on, the bottoms covered in something horrible. Auntie Rosie didn't even notice. Mom always said her sister was terrible at housework. Not that Mom could talk, with her and Dad off on a plane, leaving me tiptoeing around the Wests' kitchen in my socks. My cousins were finishing lunch and the floor was a minefield with crusts, lettuce, grated cheese, and splodges of butter and jam. I don't know why they didn't let that old vacuum cleaner dog in. There were breadcrumbs stuck on my socks like hard little seeds.

"What's the matter, Mickey boy?" asked Uncle Leo. "You look as though you lost a dollar and found twenty cents."

The twins, Johnny and Jeannie, stopped stacking dishes and looked at me. Royce paused with a chunk of bread and jam halfway to his mouth. Miranda put down her cup. Only

Honey in her high chair went on eating.

My face was hot and I knew that if I tried to say anything I would start to bawl.

Good old Royce said it for me. "He wanted to go to Sydney."

Johnny put his hands on his hips. "Auntie Eileen and Uncle Arthur should have taken him. It isn't fair."

Auntie Rosie was wiping Honey's face with the end of her T-shirt. "Look at it this way, if Mickey was in Sydney he wouldn't be here, and that would be a howling tragedy for us."

"He can come here any time," said Royce.

"My brown mouse is having babies," said Jeannie. "That doesn't happen any time."

"How can you compare mice with Australia?" Miranda wanted to know.

"Easy," said Johnny. "Mice squeak. Australia doesn't."

That started a typical West argument with everybody shouting and no one listening. Even Honey, who didn't know what it was about, yelled and waved a bit of chewed apple. I was wondering why they were getting so wound up about something that didn't concern them when Uncle Leo jumped off his chair and landed in a crouch by the kitchen bench. He put his arms over his head and began hopping around the kitchen like a frog. "I want to go to Sydney too!" he bellowed. "Nobody ever takes me anywhere! Wah-wah-wah!"

That phoney crying made us laugh, even if we didn't want to. Auntie Rosie pushed Uncle Leo with her foot and he rolled over on his back, waving his arms and legs in the air. "Put me in a box and mail me! I want to go to Australia!"

I went to him, grabbed his hands, and tried to drag him to his feet, but he was too fat and heavy.

"Oh, but what a fine and caring lad you are, Mickey," he

said, sitting up. "Will you wrap me up in brown paper? To be sure not surface mail, at all. I'd get cramp in me legs."

"Leo, look! You're in a puddle!" said Auntie Rosie. "So are you, Mickey!"

She was right. My gray socks were wet from a puddle that went all the way across the floor to Uncle Leo's feet and bottom. I arched my feet, shuddering. Even Uncle Leo made a face. "Saints preserve us!" he said. "A three-point landing in Honey's piddle."

"Not Honey!" The baby slapped the tray of her high chair. "Not Honey piddle. Goof dog!"

Uncle Leo grabbed his right leg by the ankle and lifted it until his foot was close enough for him to sniff the wetness. "No, it's not Honey and it's not old Goof. I get a whiff of sour cream and broccoli and the odd splash of ale—"

"The fridge!" cried Auntie Rosie.

Sure enough, the puddle stretched from the fridge almost to the stove.

"The electrician warned us it wouldn't last," Auntie Rosie said, putting her head in her hands.

"It's finally died, so it has," said Uncle Leo. "Defrosted itself all over our socks and my jeans."

The four big West kids stood around the puddle, looking down at it as though there was a body lying there. I backed away and took off my wet socks while Uncle Leo opened the fridge door. More water sloshed about on the bottom shelf around wilted lettuce and bits of blue cheese. At least the light was still working.

Auntie Rosie sighed. "We can't afford a new one!"

No one said anything. Then Honey slapped her tray. "Fridge piddle!" she said, sounding very pleased with herself.

# 2.

When something broke down at home, Mom and Dad would either get it fixed or buy a new one, but the Wests never seemed to have money for repairs or replacements. Mom said it was because the Wests never saved money for a rainy day but when I mentioned that to Auntie Rosie, she snorted and said she wanted to know how dollar bills would keep you dry when it was raining. "The idea, Mickey, is to enjoy your money while the sun shines. All you need for rain is an umbrella."

That made sense to me, but when I told Mom she jumped like a pop-up toaster. "Just what you'd expect from Rose! They're hopelessly irresponsible, the lot of them!"

But Dad, looking at Mom over the top of his glasses, had said, "Not all of them, dear. That young Royce has a head for finance, although I must say some of his money-making schemes are a bit dubious. If he stays on the right side of the law—ha ha—he might do well for himself one day."

Now, at the beginning of summer, the Wests' old fridge was definitely and finally broken. Auntie Rosie was moaning about not having a fridge in the hottest part of the year, and everyone was looking at Royce because he was the only one with money in the bank.

Royce finished eating an orange. He wiped his hands on his frizzy red hair. "No way," he said. "You won't pay it back."

"Be reasonable," said Auntie Rosie. "We can't go through months of runny butter and sour milk. If you won't think of us, think of your own bottomless stomach. No jelly, no ice cream, and no cold drinks."

I couldn't imagine living without a fridge, so I said, "Auntie Rosie, I've got sixty dollars you can have."

"Bless the boy," said Uncle Leo. "Now there's a generous spirit for you. But I'm thinking we'll find a way of getting a new fridge without robbing our favorite relative."

Royce grinned at his father. "Take Mickey's money as a down payment on a new fridge and then pay it off over a year."

"You horrible little miser!" cried Auntie Rosie. "I hope the fleas of a thousand sheepdogs infest your pillow!"

Royce's grin got bigger and he ruffled his mother's hair.

"Forget it, Mom!" said Johnny. "No one can get money out of Royce. He's as tight as a duck's rear end—and that's watertight!"

"Yeah, yeah, yeah!" Royce made a face at Johnny and then turned back to his mother. "Never fear, Mother dear, your amazing eldest son is here to bring you cheer. I can get you a fridge."

"From the garbage dump," said Miranda.

"Nope. From a restaurant."

"Which one?" said Uncle Leo, looking interested.

"That's for me to know and you to find out," said Royce. "But if I get it, a big fridge working a treat, it'll cost you eighty bucks."

"Eighty," repeated Uncle Leo. "Ah!"

"A new fridge'd cost twenty times that," Royce said.

"Eighty dollars sounds very reasonable," said Auntie Rosie. "What's wrong with it?"

"Nothing," said Royce. "Perfect. Big freezer. Bins for vegetables."

"There has to be something wrong," said Uncle Leo, "or they wouldn't be getting rid of it."

"Just the color," Royce said. "It doesn't go with the restaurant décor."

"Color?"

"Yeah, it's purple."

# 3.

"There's something about this fridge I didn't mention," said Royce as we put on our cycle helmets.

"I knew it!" I replied. "You and your broken-down bargains. Why don't you just lend your mother the money and be done with it?"

"But it's a good fridge! True as fish have feet! Motor runs perfectly. The old owners painted it this funny purple color to match the walls."

"Pete's Pizza Parlor!" I said, remembering purple walls and yellow curtains.

"Shh!" Royce looked back at the house, then he clipped a cardboard box onto the rack of his bike. "It's being made into a gourmet restaurant with white tablecloths and velvet chairs. They're calling it Vivaldi after the tennis player."

"Composer," I said. "Vivaldi was an Italian who wrote music."

Royce shrugged. "Who cares?"

"Some people do."

"Sure," said Royce. "Snooty people who can't live with a perfectly good purple fridge, so it has to be chucked out."

"Chucked?" I said. "Like—given away?"

Royce got all shifty. "I have to have my commission."

"Eighty dollars! They're throwing the fridge out and

you're charging your parents eighty bucks?"

"Ten of it's yours if you help me fix it up before Dad comes with the van."

I gave him my hard-eyed detective stare. "Don't tell me. The little thing you forgot to mention is that this wonderful, perfect fridge needs fixing."

Royce returned a silly cross-eyed look. "Worry, worry, worry! Moan, moan, moan!" He pushed his bike through the gateway. "Cool it, man! I've told you a million times, worry can kill you. The fridge is in good working order. All we have to do is clean it up a bit before Dad takes it home!" Then he punched himself on the forehead. "Buckets! We need buckets. Will you get a couple from the garage?"

"Wait a minute," I said. "You're giving me ten dollars just to help you wash down a fridge?"

"It's been lying in their yard for a couple of months."

"You did say ten dollars?"

"I'm feeling generous," he grinned.

The restaurant that used to be Pete's Pizza Parlor was on the main road north of the town. It had closed about four months back, and according to my mother, decorators had moved in six weeks ago to change it to a real Italian restaurant. Mom knew about it from Dad who was the new owner's accountant, and she was very pleased. Vivaldi would have classic gourmet food, she said. None of that horrible greasy pizza.

I rode behind Royce, feeling a real idiot with a plastic bucket over each of my handlebars. It was dangerous. The buckets, one red and one yellow, could have caused an accident. But I didn't have a rack like Royce and I didn't want to say anything or he'd call me a moaner. I could see in the cardboard box behind him, and yes, there were several kinds of soap and sponges. There were also a couple of bits of colored cloth that looked like Auntie Rosie's scarves, but that wasn't possible. Not even Royce would wash down a fridge with a scarf.

We rode through Main Street. There weren't many shops open on Sunday afternoon, but there were enough people around to stare at my knees hitting plastic buckets that danced about, banging like bongo drums. Out of town, past the auto shop, past the racecourse, and now I had the dog from the auto shop, a thing that looked like a barking mop, trying to attack the buckets.

"Go away!" I said. "Go back home!"

The dog's noise increased by several decibels and it showed all its teeth just a bite distance from my leg.

Royce yelled, "Scram, mutt, or I'll use you to scrub out that stinking fridge!"

The animal understood Royce talk. Its eyes rolled, its ears went down and next second, it was running down the road.

I said, "Stinking?"

"Not too bad," Royce replied. "Just needs a bit of water and soap."

We braked in front of the restaurant. There was a black BMW parked outside but no work trucks. The inside looked empty. We could see cream-colored walls painted with pictures of women pouring water out of clay pots and men stamping on grapes to make wine. There was dark red carpet on the floor and wires hanging from the ceiling. I remembered Mom saying they were going to have real chandeliers imported from Venice.

"Around the back," said Royce, pushing his bike towards

the driveway between the restaurant and the fence. I followed. Behind the building we saw a man in jeans and a red checked shirt looking at a piece of timber. "That's the new owner," Royce muttered.

The yard behind the restaurant was such a mess you'd think something had exploded there. Heaps of old wood, new wood, paint cans, a concrete mixer, building paper and insulation, old rusting ovens, a broken counter, and an iron magazine rack that looked as though it had been run over by a truck. I remembered finding a boat magazine in that rack while I was waiting for a pizza.

At the back of the yard, against the fence, stood the big purple two-doored fridge tied up with yellow nylon rope.

The man dropped the piece of wood and brushed his hands together. "You took your time." He looked at Royce and me and then past us. "You said your father was bringing his van."

"He is, he is!" Royce had on his greasiest smile. "In a few minutes. We're going to clean it up first."

"Oh no!" The man put his hands up. "I said you take it as is, where is. Those ropes don't come off it until it's at your place. That's where you clean it."

Royce's smile didn't even flicker. "I'm sorry. Mom won't take it unless it's clean."

"We had an agreement," the man insisted. "You don't open it anywhere on this property, and that's it."

"I know." Royce shrugged. "But it's my mother, she's very fussy."

Auntie Rosie fussy? I think my mouth fell open. I nearly said, no, she isn't—she licks the jam off the front of her shirt and she hardly ever sweeps the floor.

But I didn't have a chance.

"Sorry," said Royce, smiling sweetly. "The fridge can't go home in this condition. I guess you'll have to take it to the dump after all."

The man wasn't smiling. He glared at Royce and then looked towards the back fence where the fridge stood slightly lopsided, a bit muddy but not all that dirty on the outside. How dirty could the inside of a pizza fridge get? The smell of moldy cheese? A bit of tomato paste?

Now the man was scratching the back of his neck. "This isn't my decision to make," he said. "Health regulations. There's no way a Sanitary Inspector will allow you to clean that thing on restaurant grounds. Sorry." He smiled and folded his arms.

"Okay," said Royce. "I understand." He turned his bike around. "Seems a waste to send it to the dump, but I suppose that's the way it has to be. Come on, Mickey."

# 4.

I just stood there. I knew Royce. He was playing one of his sneaky games but I didn't have the faintest idea what it was. The man knew, though. His smile had hardened to a look of pain, as though he was having a heart attack and was being very brave about it. "Wait!" he said, looking hard at Royce, then me. I felt that for the first time he was really noticing me and the stupid buckets on my bike. "What did you intend to do?"

"Oh," I said. "Just wipe it down—"

Royce interrupted. "I thought we'd start by digging a hole."

The man took a deep breath and blew it out in a noisy sigh. "There's a shovel by the concrete mixer. And a hose. But I'm telling you this, young West, if I come back and get one whiff of bad food where that old fridge is, you're in deep trouble. Understand?"

"Absolutely!" Royce said with that cross-my-heart-and-hope-to-die look.

When the man went stomping down the drive, my crazy cousin punched me on the arm and whispered, "I knew it'd be okay. He can't take it to the dump. He's already tried. They told him he had to empty it first."

My bad feeling about the fridge was getting worse. "Why didn't he empty it?" I demanded.

"Doesn't want to get his hands dirty. Like I told you, he's snooty. He isn't even Italian. He comes from Hamilton."

We unloaded our bikes and parked them against the back wall of the restaurant. As we carried the buckets and box of gear towards the back fence, I realized that a noise like a distant lawn mower came from a cloud of black flies that buzzed around the big purple fridge.

"You've seen inside?" I asked Royce.

"I just heard about it."

"Is it really bad?"

"Nah, a piece of cake. Grab that shovel, will you? When Pete's Pizza closed down, they thought the fridge and freezer had been emptied. They shut off the power."

"Pizzas, right?" I said.

Royce balanced the box to grab one end of a green plastic hose. "I don't know about pizzas. Mainly stuff to go on them, you know, seafood and pepperoni. We'll dig the hole before we open it."

I stopped. "Seafood."

"Yeah. Bags of shrimps and mussels and squid. Oh, and—er—some chickens."

"Oh heck!" I said.

"Ten bucks," Royce reminded me.

We were still the width of a tennis court away from the fridge when the smell hit us. I dropped the buckets and shovel and put my hand over my face. It was horrible. I looked at the big black flies that zoomed around, electric and urgent, trying to find a way past the yellow ropes and purple doors.

With my hand still over my mouth and nose, I yelled at Royce, "What is it with you and your smells? That dead rabbit you had in your room! The rotten old house you called Stink Castle! Every one of your great ideas has a big stink attached!"

Royce laughed. "Not as bad as your muesli farts."

That was really unfair. It wasn't my fault my mother made me eat muesli. "I can't do this, Royce," I said. "You know I've got a weak stomach."

"No worries!" He put down the cardboard box and like a conjurer, pulled out two pieces of silk. I was right. They were Auntie Rosie's scarves. Royce gave me the red scarf with white dots on it and kept the orange one for himself. He got out an aerosol can of air freshener for bathrooms and sprayed both squares. "Fold it in half," he said. "It's a mask. Tie it over your nose. Oh, go on! Who cares what you look like?"

I pulled the ends of the scarf behind my head and knotted them. Now I could smell air freshener mixed with rotten fridge, but I had to admit there was more of the first than the last.

Royce, looking like a bandit with his wild orange hair and matching mask, rubbed his hands together and picked up the workman's shovel. "Now just you take it easy, Mickey, while I dig the hole."

# 5.

Royce did the digging because he wanted me to take the rotten food out of the fridge. I worked that one out before we untied the ropes. What I didn't realize was that it was no longer food. It had become green and gray slime, some of it thick and lumpy, some runny, all mixed up with plastic bags. When I opened the door, a wave of it glurped out over my shoes. I jumped back and turned away retching, my arms over my stomach. I couldn't be sick into Auntie Rosie's scarf. I just couldn't. I struggled to control my throat.

"I've got rubber gloves," Royce said cheerfully. "You don't have to touch it."

For a while I just stood there, bent over. The flies were going crazy. There were now zillions of them like a plague. I took the gloves from Royce and slowly put them on. I was going to do this if it killed me, not for a stupid ten dollars but to show Royce that I could even if he couldn't. The trouble was, I didn't know how I could manage without being sick.

While I stretched the yellow rubber gloves up over my wrists, I considered my different techniques for coping with bad situations. Sometimes I pretended I wasn't really me and it was happening to someone else. Sometimes I said to myself, in five years time I'll have forgotten all about this. Other times, I thought, well, this isn't bad compared with floods in India or a plane crash in Russia. But for the fridge I was sure none of those techniques would work. There was only one thing for it. I'd have to:

1. Take a deep breath.
2. Go through the cloud of flies.
3. Reach into the fridge with yellow gloves.
4. Pull out slimy lumps of stuff and plastic bags and drop them in the bucket.
5. Retreat. Turn away. Let out breath and breathe deeply several times.
6. Take another deep breath.
7. Turn and go back to fridge.

Royce was standing well behind the hole when I tipped in a bucket of slime. "We can bury the plastic bags," he said. "They're biodegradable."

I stepped away and let my breath out warm behind Auntie Rosie's scarf. A quick refill of air stinking with slime and perfume, and I said, "Maybe they're not. Maybe you'd better pick them out."

"What?" Royce leaned his head towards me. "I can't hear through the mask!"

I was getting really wild with him. I yelled, "Do you want to recycle them?"

"What?"

I went around the hole and leaned close to his ear. "Plastic isn't biodegradable!"

Royce yelled back his favorite word and jumped away from me. "You stink! It's on your clothes! What've you been doing?"

I pulled the mask down so he could hear me. "Getting my hands dirty," I said in a cold voice.

Royce looked at my hands and my wet shoes. "At least it proves you're not snooty like Mr. Gourmet Vivaldi," he said.

"His name's Peter Nardini, he comes from Hamilton and his father's Italian," I said. "I know because he's Dad's client."

"No way!" Royce stared at me. "Why didn't you tell me?"

"You didn't ask."

"You should have said! If I'd told him my Uncle Arthur was his accountant, he'd have got his men to clean out the fridge for us and deliver it."

I sighed and pulled up my mask. "Royce, you are impossible."

"What's that?"

"I said you're impossible."

"What?"

"Forget it." I turned to the fridge which was no longer purple but black inside and out with celebrating flies. Another bucket of rotting chickens, slimy squid, and plastic bags and I'd be able to clean the rest out with the hose.

Royce said I'd have to hose myself as well. That wasn't such a bad idea. The water was freezing but it had no smell and I wished that I could breathe in it like a fish. I washed the gloves and my shoes thoroughly and poked the hose in all the corners of the fridge and freezer compartments. It looked clean. I hosed down the grass. By the time I'd finished, the hole in the ground was full of water and slime. The flies which had been on the fridge were now focusing on a putrid well of rotting stuff that had once been nice, clean, super-market food.

"It'll soak down," Royce said. "When the soil absorbs all the liquid, we'll just fill the space with dirt."

"I think I'll be a vegetarian," I said.

The slime level didn't go down, so Royce put a few boards over the hole, mounded the dirt on top and then covered it all with old timber. I washed the scarves and cloths and buckets, put the hose and shovel away, closed the fridge doors and retied them with the yellow rope. There were hardly any flies now, and I thought the place was smelling pretty good when the old West van arrived. But Uncle Leo, Miranda, and the twins got out shrieking and holding their noses. "Oooh!" "What's that stink?" "Yuck!" "Saints alive, it's full of rotten meat!"

I had to undo the ropes and open the fridge doors to show them that it was empty and clean, even shining in places. Hardly a trace of slime.

Uncle Leo put his head in, sniffed, and jumped back, his head knocking out two shelves. "Oh, but that's terrible, that is! What was in it?"

Royce didn't mention the hole in the ground. "Nothing much. It's just a shut-in smell. It was closed up for a long time."

"I'd hate to smell like that if I got shut in," said Jeannie.

"No worse than your mice," said Royce. "We'll take it home and put it on the back lawn. A good scrub with hot water, that's all it needs. It'll come up fresh as anything, I kid you not."

Uncle Leo sniffed again, this time from a distance. "We'll see," he said. "Smell, no money. Money, no smell. That's the deal!"

"How is your mouse?" I asked Jeannie.

She knew I meant the fat one who was going to have babies. "She's made a little nest. I think she'll have them today."

"That's nice," I said.

"Have you seen baby mice, Mickey?"

"Ah—no."

Jeannie's eyes were shining. "They are so cool! So awesomely beautiful! Like little squirmy pink peanuts."

I held my arms over my stomach and for a moment shut my eyes. After this morning, a nest full of squirmy pink peanuts would be all I'd need.

"You all right?" Royce was beside me.

"Yes," I said quickly. "Why?"

"You look a bit pale. Not going to do a technicolor yawn, are you?"

"Certainly not!" I said.

"Good. You can help us get the fridge into the van—" He stepped back and said his stupid poo word. "You still stink! Hey, Dad! It's not the fridge that's stinking. It's Mickey." Royce grinned at me. "He's been eating muesli again!"

# 6.

A hot shower got the smell off me but it didn't work for the fridge. It was now in the kitchen in the same place as the old one which had been dumped. Auntie Rosie scrubbed for the rest of the morning with all sorts of stuff: powder cleanser, detergent, bleach, water and baking soda, but the horrible smell remained. She said only time would remove it but didn't say how much time.

"The odour gets into the cracks," she said vaguely.

Everyone agreed that the purple fridge looked better than the old rusted white one. The color gave it a party look which suggested it was full of cakes and ice cream, jellies and fizzy drinks. Miranda said she thought they should paint the tables and chairs purple to match.

I agreed that the fridge was easy on the eyes but not on the nose. The moment someone opened a purple door, the kitchen filled with stink and Goof the dog got excited. He adored rotten smells. If he found a dead sheep, he'd roll in it and scratch his back on the maggots. He could be a disgusting dog when he got the chance.

Uncle Leo had the theory that if the fridge was switched on, the smell would freeze and go away. It didn't. It just became cold stink instead of warm stink. Auntie Rosie thought maybe the fridge could be used as long as every bit of food was packed in airtight tins and glass containers. I decided then and there that I wasn't eating anything that came out of that fridge, no matter how it had been packed.

I didn't have any lunch. That was partly because of the smell and partly because my tooth was hurting. It was the pointy tooth near the front, a canine tooth according to my mother. It proved people were meant to eat meat, she said. Several times I'd looked in the bathroom mirror. The tooth wasn't wobbly. It wasn't even a little bit loose. I decided not to tell my cousins about it. Their way of getting rid of a first tooth was to loop a length of nylon fishing line around it and tie the other end to a door knob. One big slam and either the tooth flew out or the nylon broke and they tried again. I wasn't having that, thank you very much.

Uncle Leo, Royce, Miranda and I were playing volleyball in the backyard when Jeannie came running out yelling, "They're here!" We dropped the ball and stampeded into the house, straight through to Jeannie's room which she shared with dozens of mice—brown, gray, white, and spotted. Her fat mother mouse was mostly brown with a white face. She was peering at us from a nest of shredded paper in the old glass aquarium which was the baby house. Her pink nose was twitching. Her eyes were like dark red beads as she watched four human heads jammed together over the glass.

"Stand back!" Jeannie ordered.

Even Uncle Leo took a step backwards. Jeannie put her hand in and let the mouse sniff it, then, very slowly and gently, she pulled back the torn paper. There were nine tiny, hairless mice nestled against the mother's stomach. They did look like squirmy pink peanuts, but they were interesting peanuts, not nearly as yuck as I'd imagined.

Miranda put her arm over my shoulders and leaned across the glass. I could smell the lemony scent of her long red hair. "Aren't they lovely, Mickey?" she said.

"Beautiful!" I replied, aware that my face was going as red as a beet. "Just fantasmo!"

# 7.

That night everyone gathered in Royce's room to tell ghost stories. It was still light outside but Royce pulled down the blinds and Miranda turned on a flashlight to give the right atmosphere. The only other light was a faint glow from the hole in the floor between Royce's bed and mine. It was the laundry hole that Royce had cut in the floorboards so he could throw his dirty clothes straight into the washing machine below. I had to keep reminding myself not to step in it.

Miranda, Honey, and the dog were on the end of Royce's bed. The twins sat on mine with the duvet pulled up over their legs. They were all looking at me.

They reckoned I was the best teller of spooky stories and

they always got me to begin.

"Listen," I said. "What can you hear?"

"You talking," said Royce.

"Shut up, Royce," said Johnny.

Everyone was quiet for a moment.

"Cars outside," said Miranda. "Goof snoring."

"What else?" I asked.

"Dad putting the saucepans away," said Jeannie. "I can hear the lids banging. I can hear the cupboard door."

"The fridge is going," said Royce.

"Going where?" asked Johnny and he and Jeannie giggled.

"That's not the fridge motor," I said. "Those are ghosts. There's something Royce and I didn't tell you. The purple fridge is haunted."

I heard Jeannie suck in her breath.

"Not human ghosts," I reminded them. "Chickens. Little brown and white feathered hens who thought they were going on vacation to a beautiful farm full of golden wheat. What happened? They were sent to a cruel butcher. Chop, chop, chop! Off came their heads. Off came their feathers. Cold dead chickens got packed in plastic and sent to the terrible purple fridge."

The twins pulled the duvet up to their necks.

"Then there were the squids," I said. "Squids are very gentle intelligent creatures—"

"Squid," said Royce.

"That's what I said."

"You said squids with an s. That's like saying sheeps. Even I know it's the same for one squid or a million squid." Royce looked bored.

I ignored him. "They were swimming in the sea as happy

as anything and this great net comes along and scoops them up. 'Yay!' they all cried. 'An adventure!' But where did they end up?"

"Purple fridge!" laughed Honey. "Stinky poo purple fridge."

"Cut up in squid rings and packed in boxes," I said. "Likewise the innocent little shrimps that never hurt anyone in their entire lives. And the shoals of cod and snapper and herrings. Where did they go?"

Honey put her fingers in her mouth as though she was feeling the words. "Purple fridge."

"It didn't end there," I told them. "There were hundreds of murders. Thousands. A black and white cow with eyelashes called Daisy. A little lamb—"

"Why were her eyelashes called Daisy?" asked Royce.

"I said the cow was called Daisy."

"No. You said it was a cow with eyelashes called Daisy."

"Shut up, Royce!" said Johnny.

"This lamb was having her first birthday party and along came the farmer on his tractor. She thought he was bringing a present. But what was he bringing across the paddocks?"

"Purple fridge," said Honey.

"A death sentence!" I told them. "The little lamb's coat was made into a golfing jacket. Her innards got made into sausages. The rest was cut up and put in the cold morgue with the purple doors. And so the slaughter went on for years and years and years."

Royce yawned and scratched his wooly hair. "Hey man, that is definitely not one of your best stories."

"I haven't finished yet," I said. "Well anyway, all the innocent victims came back to haunt the purple fridge. It was in a restaurant, out back in the kitchen. But even in the dining room, people could hear ghostly clucking and quacking and mooing and splashing. And ghosts have this really disgusting smell. It put people off their food. So the owners didn't have any choice. They had to put the purple fridge out in the backyard and get a new fridge."

I paused and looked at them. Yes, even Royce was interested. I lowered my voice. "But that wasn't the end of the haunting. If you walked around the back of the restaurant at night, you could see the ghosts of cows and sheep and ducks and hens drifting about in the moonlight. People got scared. So the owners tied up the door of the fridge with yellow rope. But that didn't stop the ghostly goings on. Ghosts can glide right through the thickest fridge door. Sometimes they wandered back into the restaurant. How would you like to be eating pizza with a transparent cow looking over your shoulder? Not to mention the terrible smell!"

"So they had to get rid of the fridge," interrupted Royce, stealing the next bit of my story.

I gave him my cold detective look. "They couldn't get rid of it. No one would have it. Who in their right mind would take a stinking, haunted fridge?"

"Royce would," said Johnny.

"Oh, very funny," said Royce. "I'll die laughing."

"If you do," said Jeannie. "Guess where you can go?"

"Purple fridge!" said Honey, clapping her hands.

# 8.

The next morning, when Auntie Rosie opened the purple fridge, we all sniffed the air and screamed, falling out of our chairs and clutching our throats.

"Drama class," said Auntie Rosie as she brought milk and margarine to the table. The milk had been put in glass jars with screw-on lids and the margarine was stored in a biscuit tin.

"It's not contaminated," she said as she poured milk on her cereal.

"I think I'll have fruit this morning," said Miranda.

"I'll just have jam and bread," said Johnny

"I'm opening a can of spaghetti," Royce said. "Anyone else for spaghetti on toast?"

"I told you, there is nothing wrong with the milk or margarine," insisted Auntie Rosie. "They were in airtight containers."

"But I feel like spaghetti," Royce said, grabbing a can from the cupboard.

Jeannie leaned towards me and whispered, "If ghosts can go through fridge doors, what's the bet they can float through milk and margarine?"

"What about you, Mickey?" Auntie Rosie pushed the milk and cornflakes towards me.

I shook my head. "No thank you, Auntie Rosie. I don't think I'll have anything cold like—like out of the fridge. It's my tooth, you see. It's really sore."

I hadn't intended to mention my tooth. It just happened and immediately I regretted it. In a flash, they were all out of their chairs and around me, wanting to look in my mouth, trying to give me advice.

"Door knob trick," said Johnny.

"It isn't even loose," I told him.

"Don't let Royce put his pliers near it," said Miranda. "When he tried to take out Jeannie's tooth, he broke it off and she had to go to the dentist."

Auntie Rosie put a finger in my mouth. "The second tooth is growing and the first tooth isn't moving," she said.

"I'll be all right until Mom and Dad get home."

She sat down again. "You can't have toothache for a week."

"It's not that bad. True, Auntie Rosie. Just every now and then."

"I'll call the dentist this morning," she replied through a spoonful of cornflakes and milk.

"Yay!" shouted Jeannie. "Can we go and watch?"

"Don't waste money on a dentist," said Royce. "If it's loose, try the door knob. If it isn't, the pliers. The only reason Jeannie's tooth broke was she wriggled like an eel. I'll do it for two bucks."

I closed my mouth tight. "Mmm-mmm!" I said, shaking my head.

"He's teasing," said Auntie Rosie. "We'll try to get you an appointment this morning."

I shook my head again. "Mmm-mmm!"

But Auntie Rosie was already up again, looking for the phone book.

"I've been thinking," said Jeannie, "if fridges can get haunted by chickens and cows and fish and stuff, can stomachs get haunted too? I mean, do we have animal ghosts inside us?"

I shrugged. I didn't want to think about that.

"You bet!" Royce cried. "Stomach ghosts!" He tucked his hands in his armpits, waggled his elbows, and started squawking like a chicken. Miranda jumped up and joined him and in a moment four of my cousins were dancing around the table, clucking and pretending to peck each other, while the fifth cousin laughed at them from her highchair.

Auntie Rosie had the phone on the table and was pressing out a number. "Good morning. Is that Dr. Abraham's clinic?"

Johnny, his head bent and arms flapping, was trying to peck the toast off his plate. He got strawberry jam on his nose.

"What did you say?" Auntie Rosie held the phone close to one ear and put her hand over the other.

"Cluck, cluck, cluck!" cried Royce behind her back.

"I'm sorry," said Auntie Rosie. "I can't hear you for the noise. What's that? Oh, it's my children. They're trying to lay eggs."

# 9.

Dr. Abraham came from Kenya and he talked with an English accent like the British royal family. "Good morning, Michael. Isn't it the most pleasant weather?" He had a very white smile which made me realize I hadn't used a toothbrush all day. I sometimes forgot to do things like that when I stayed with the Wests. I gave my teeth a quick wipe with my tongue and whispered to Auntie Rosie, "I didn't brush my teeth."

"It's all right," Auntie Rosie said. "He'll just run the hedge clippers over them."

My aunt and five cousins came into the exam room and

watched me get into the chair. I was hoping that Dr. Abraham would send them out to the waiting room, but he didn't. He talked to them as he fastened a towel around my neck and he seemed to know a lot about Miranda's guitar, Johnny's ballet, and Jeannie's mice. He looked at Royce. "I trust you have not attempted any further extractions," he said.

Royce was looking around the exam room. "I've been too busy."

"In the Middle Ages," said Dr. Abraham, "toothache was treated by driving a sharp spike down the root canal of the tooth. It killed the nerve but it did not cure infection. Sometimes people died of blood poisoning. Open your mouth, please, Michael. Ah! Yes! I see the problem."

I tried to talk. "Ish—ish—all—right."

"You understand that this tooth must be removed to create space for the new one?" said Dr. Abraham, peering into my mouth and prodding with a little silver hook. "If it isn't, the new tooth will grow in the wrong position."

I grunted. I didn't want my tooth out. I didn't even want to be there. But with everyone standing around watching, there was nothing I could do. I held on to the arms of the chair to stop my hands from shaking.

"Look out the window," said Dr. Abraham. "Can you see the street?"

I tried to nod.

"Excellent. You will notice a green car parked directly opposite this building. Can you tell me if the parking meter has expired?"

I could see the green car against the pavement and the meter in front of it but I couldn't tell if the window on the meter was black or red. I half shut my eyes to block out the sun and I stared as hard as I could. I still couldn't read the meter. I shook my head.

Dr. Abraham took his hands away from my mouth.

"It's too far away," I said.

"It doesn't matter," he smiled. "It's not my car. Sometimes I pretend to be an eye doctor so that I can test my patients' sight." He pointed to a glass of pink stuff. "Rinse your mouth, please, Michael."

That was when my tongue touched the gap and I tasted blood. "It's gone!" I cried.

Dr. Abraham held out a little tooth in the jaws of his forceps and the Wests gasped.

"I didn't see it come out!" Miranda said.

"Sometimes I also pretend to be a magician," replied Dr. Abraham, wrapping the tooth in a piece of gauze.

I rinsed and spat into the bowl. In the gap I could feel the sharp edge of the new tooth. "It didn't even hurt!" I said.

Dr. Abraham laughed. "This is not the Middle Ages," he said, offering me the tooth. "We are less barbaric in dental care now."

I didn't want the tooth but Royce told me to take it. "Tooth fairy!" he said.

"Oh, come on!" I leaned forward to let Dr. Abraham unclip the towel from around my neck. "I gave up the tooth fairy four years ago."

Royce shook his head. "The tooth fairy means a dollar a tooth. With your parents, you'd probably get at least five bucks. Man, you should never give up the tooth fairy!"

"Ah," said Dr. Abraham. "Thus speaks the great business tycoon. Tell me, Royce, what is your latest project?"

Auntie Rosie said, "Don't ask, Dr. Abraham! You really

don't want to know about the bargain refrigerator that cost eighty dollars and has a serious problem."

"It smells terrible," said Jeannie.

"Not the purple fridge from Pete's Pizza!" Dr. Abraham almost dropped the towel.

"The very one," said Auntie Rosie. "How did you hear about it?"

"Oh, but everyone knows about the purple fridge," Dr. Abraham said. "My goodness! Did you manage to clean the inside?"

"There was nothing wrong," Royce said quickly. "Just a bit of stale air—"

"Nothing wrong?" Dr. Abraham laughed. "It was full of rotten meat and fish. The garbage dump wouldn't take it. Nobody would touch it. The new owner didn't know what to do. My last information was that he intended hiring a digger to make a deep pit behind the restaurant. The entire fridge was to be buried."

"But there wasn't any rotten—" Auntie Rosie turned to Royce. "Was there?"

Dr. Abraham smiled and frowned at the same time. "This is very bewildering. I cannot understand why the man charged you eighty dollars when all this time he's been offering fifty dollars for someone to take the fridge away."

None of the Wests said anything but they all turned to look at Royce. He gave them his light-as-air smile, drew his shoulders up around his ears and sauntered out the office door.

# 10.

Uncle Leo said that seeing Royce already had fifty dollars from Mr. Nardini for removing the fridge, and seeing the purple monster still stank to high heaven, the deal was off.

"That fridge is going out in the garage for my bottles of home brew," Uncle Leo said. "As a beer fridge, I reckon it's worth about twenty bucks."

"What?" shrieked Royce. "A miserable twenty?"

"That's my offer."

"You promised eighty! Come on Dad! Don't you have some kind of a conscience?"

"None whatsoever," said Uncle Leo.

"A promise is a promise!" cried Royce.

"Just as a scam is a scam," replied Uncle Leo, pulling some bills and coins out of his pocket. "I said twenty but you don't get the full amount. Half goes to Mickey. There you are—ten dollars each."

Royce grabbed the ten dollar bill and glared at his father. "I don't care what you say. You promised eighty. You still owe me sixty bucks!"

"Can't afford it," Uncle Leo said cheerfully. "I have to save all my pennies to get a new fridge for your mother."

"What's that?" Auntie Rosie came in, eating a raspberry cream bun.

"He's just cheated his own son!" roared Royce. "That's what happens when you do business with family. You get robbed blind and stabbed in the back."

"Sounds very violent," said Auntie Rosie, biting the bun and squishing cream onto her face.

"That's what it is—a form of violence," Royce cried. "It's slavery! It's child abuse!"

"Tragedy!" murmured Auntie Rosie. "Murder, mayhem, chaos, disaster!"

"You think it's funny?" Royce yelled at her.

"Sorry," said Auntie Rosie. "I was only trying to help."

The Wests often had terrible rows but they never lasted long. By evening, Royce was joking with his father as though they had never argued in their entire lives, and all the yelling was between the twins. Jeannie reckoned Johnny had left her door open. Frodo the cat had been in. They'd found him by the glass mouse house. The mother mouse and the little pink peanuts had vanished.

Jeannie was lying on her bed, sobbing, Johnny was upset, and Frodo was hiding under the sofa, swishing his tail. Compared with all that, the purple fridge seemed unimportant.

"Poor little mice!" I said to Auntie Rosie.

She didn't look up from her book. "Lucky old Frodo," she said.

But at bedtime, Jeannie found the mice hiding at the bottom of their paper nest. They were all there. The cat hadn't eaten so much as one little peanut, so everyone had to cuddle him and apologize for calling him names.

Jeannie was extra cheerful. "Tell us another ghost story, Mickey."

"It's someone else's turn," I said.

"No. You tell the best ghost stories." Jeannie hugged her knees. "Make up something about haunted stomachs."

"Stomachs?"

"All that meat we eat," Johnny said eagerly.

I shook my head.

"Go on," said Royce. "The ghosts of chicken burgers."

That was the trouble with my cousins. They never realized that some subjects were okay and others weren't. Stories had power. If I started talking about stomach ghosts, we'd all finish up vegetarians.

"No," I said. "This is a story about a vampire who haunted the streets at night. If you were driving along and you had your car window down, he'd stick his head through and bite you on the neck." I put my head back and showed them exactly where the vampire would bite. I saw Johnny shiver and I went on. "When people stopped at traffic lights, that's when he pounced. Bite, bite, suck, suck. But there was this dentist watching out his office window and he had an idea. He left the window wide open and he called to the vampire, 'Hey, Mr. Vampire! I've got lots of blood in here. Bags of it.'"

"Dentists don't have bags of blood," said Royce.

"Yes, they do—for blood transfusions."

"What blood transfusions?"

"For patients," I said. "Suppose a patient needs blood. They have to have lots of bags to make sure it's the right type."

"You're making that up," snorted Royce.

"I'm making it all up," I said. "It's a story, remember?"

"I know, I know. But it has to be logical," Royce insisted. "Dentists don't need bags of blood."

"Shut up, Royce," said Miranda. "Go on, Mickey."

"All right," I said. "This dentist didn't have bags of blood. He just said that to get the vampire interested. As soon as the vampire was in the clinic, the dentist told him to get in the chair. He said he'd sharpen his teeth for free. Now next to blood, the vampire liked money. He thought, wow! Teeth sharpened for nothing! So he sat in the chair."

"He bit the dentist!" cried Jeannie.

"No, he didn't. The dentist was too smart for him. He told the vampire to look at the street to see how many cars had their windows open, and while the vampire was counting the cars—"

"Count Dracula!" said Johnny.

"While he was counting the cars, the dentist took out all his teeth, and that was that."

"What happened?" asked Jeannie.

"Nothing happened," I said. "The vampire couldn't bite people. He starved to death."

"Vampires can't starve to death," said Royce. "They're already dead."

"If they don't get blood they fade away to nothing," I said. "I know. I saw it in a movie."

Royce grinned. "Bet your mother and father don't know you watch horror movies."

There could have been another argument, but right then Auntie Rosie and Uncle Leo came up the stairs calling, "Tooth fairies! Tooth fairies!"

We sat up, watching the door.

"Here come your friendly neighborhood tooth fairies," Auntie Rosie said as they came in.

We just about burst ourselves laughing. Auntie Rosie was wearing red tights that made her legs look extra bulgy and angel wings from Jeannie's Christmas play. She'd put silver glitter on face and hair and she was carrying a wooden spoon decorated to look like a wand and a cardboard box. Uncle Leo had on Auntie Rosie's sunhat with flowers, the ribbons tied under his chin. He had silver glitter on his face too. "Where's that boy's food chopper?" he cried.

"I'm sorry, Uncle Leo. I forgot to leave my tooth in a glass."

Auntie Rosie waved the wooden spoon. "We've got our own teeth. We don't need other people's. But we do have something for you, Mickey, a small souvenir of your visit." She put the box on the end of my bed and pulled out a white T-shirt which had writing and drawings all over it. "Now's as good a time as any to give it to you."

I smoothed the T-shirt over the quilt and looked at the rainbow colors. Jeannie had drawn some mice. Miranda had made a picture of someone looking down a drainpipe, only I think it was supposed to be me playing a didgeridoo. Next to Johnny's name was a graveyard and some ghosts and skeletons. Auntie Rosie had done stick figures of me and Dr. Abraham and a huge tooth coming out of my mouth, and Uncle Leo had drawn Goof and Frodo sitting at the table with me in-between.

"Cool!" I said, loving the shirt and at the same time wondering what Mom and Dad would say when I showed it to them.

"Turn it over," said Royce.

I flipped it and saw Royce's picture on the back. Two figures with masks and buckets were standing next to a huge purple fridge surrounded by black dots of flies.

"I realize it's a very poor substitute for a holiday in Australia," Uncle Leo said, pretending to cry. "Wah, wah, wah!" He rubbed his knuckles in his eyes and silver glitter floated down on the bed.

I pulled the T-shirt on over my pajama jacket and laughed, "Who cares about Sydney?"

# The
# Wild West Gang
# at the Wedding

## 1.

The wedding invitation was written with silver ink on black paper. In the envelope were tiny silver stars that floated out onto Mom's clean carpet.

"That says it all," Mom remarked to Dad.

Dad was at his computer. "Says what?"

"Dogs are invited," Mom replied. "Dogs, for goodness sake! If I want fleas all I have to do is visit Rose and Leo. I don't have to go to Danny West's wedding."

I tried to explain the dog part of the invitation to Mom. Uncle Leo's brother Danny was marrying a woman called Ruby who had boarding kennels. The K9 Motel, she called it. My cousins told me she was absolutely crazy about three things in life: Daniel West and dogs of all shapes and sizes.

"That's two," said Mom.

"The other thing is clowning," I said.

That made Dad look up from his computer. "I beg your pardon?"

"She's a clown," I told him.

"All the Wests are clowns," Mom said, with a little laugh. "Why do they need one more?"

"A real clown," I replied. "When Uncle Danny was at drama school, he did a clowning course. That's how he met Auntie Ruby. Do you know what they do in their spare time? They dress up and go to kids' parties and street shows."

Mom closed her eyes and looked as though she was in pain. "Street shows!"

"They're getting married in their clown costumes," I told her.

Her eyes went wide open at that. So did Dad's.

"What? Clowns in Saint Teresa's?" Dad cried. "What's the church coming to?"

"It's not a church wedding," I told him. "Look at the invitation. They're getting married in a tent at the K9 Motel."

Dad glanced at the black and silver card, then looked at Mom. "It's a shame we can't go," he said. "Office barbecue the same day."

"Such a pity," Mom murmured.

I bent down and picked the silver stars from the carpet. "But I can go, can't I?"

They didn't answer.

I stood up and tipped the stars back into the envelope. "They asked 'specially. Uncle Danny and Auntie Ruby want me to help with the guests."

Dad took a deep breath and let it out slowly as though he were blowing up a balloon. "Michael, he's not your uncle and she's not your aunt. These people are not related to you."

"They are! Sort of!"

Dad's nostrils flickered. "Leo West is your uncle-in-law and may rightly be called uncle since he is married to your mother's sister. His brother Daniel is Mr. West. When his lady friend Ruby becomes his wife, you will call her Mrs. West. Do I make myself clear?"

"Yes, Dad. Can I go to the wedding?"

They looked at each other again. I knew what this was about. They were still in a bad mood over my involvement with that horrible purple fridge. I'd pointed out that Uncle Leo and Auntie Rosie had bought a brand new fridge and the stinky one had gone to the shed for Uncle Leo's beer. Dad said that was beside the point. Everyone was talking about the purple fridge. Royce West was a scavenger and his cousin Michael was his accomplice. The unforgivable thing was, Michael knew that the owner of the fridge was his father's client. What on earth would Mr. Nardini think? My father was always worried about what other people thought.

"Clowns," Mom said. "Dogs. A tent."

"They want Miranda and me to be ushers," I said.

Still, neither of them said anything. Mom looked at Dad and Dad looked at his computer screen.

"Can I go? Please?"

"We'll have to think about it, son," Dad replied.

# 2.

"What do you mean you don't know!" yelped Johnny. "The wedding's only a week away!"

"They'll let me go," I said. "I know they will. But they don't want to give in too easily. Will this wire mesh be all right?" I was helping Johnny to make a new cage for Lucy, his bantam hen.

"It'll have to be. It's the only netting we've got. I don't understand your parents."

"I do." I bent the wire mesh around the frame. "They'll say yes the day before the wedding, believe me."

"Why?" Johnny was genuinely puzzled.

I couldn't tell him that Mom and Dad didn't approve of a clown wedding. That would have got too complicated. I said, "I'll be going. Dad's firm's having its annual barbecue next Saturday afternoon. Kids are never invited to that. What'll they do with me?"

Johnny's smile came back. "You can't come here because we'll be at the wedding."

"You said it."

"And your mother doesn't like babysitters."

"Right." I held the wire mesh against the frame while he hammered in some small staples. Johnny's bantam hen was such a pet that for most of its life it had lived in the house and laid eggs in the towel shelf in the downstairs bathroom. But then it changed its nest to Auntie Rosie's closet and made such a mess on the new dress she was going to wear to the wedding that she really blew a fuse. "I've had it with useless animals!" she screamed. "If that idiot hen comes inside again, it'll be soup."

Everyone knew Auntie Rosie would change her mind in a day or two, but in the meantime Johnny had to make a cage from a wooden box with some wire netting shaped around a frame for a run.

"How long will you be?" Jeannie called from the back porch.

"As long as a piece of string," Johnny replied.

"Dad's waiting," said Jeannie. "We're going around to

Auntie Ruby's to cut the grass and weed the gardens for the wedding. Dad wants us all—"

"I know, I know." Johnny hammered in another staple. "Any holes on your side, Mickey?"

I took the hammer from him, folded a loose corner of wire over some wood and fastened it with a staple. "We're going to the K9 Motel?"

"Work," said Johnny. "Dad volunteered us."

"Can I come too?" I asked.

"You bet! There's a heap to be done." Johnny put his head on one side to look at the bantam's house. "I hope Lucy won't be lonely out here. She likes company. Sometimes she roosts on top of the radio to hear voices."

"I prefer dogs," I said. "Dogs are much better than hens."

Johnny wasn't offended. "You'll be cool with Auntie Ruby. Miranda reckons she's marrying Uncle Danny because he looks like a dog—all that hair on his face. Why don't you get a dog?"

I shrugged. "One day."

Johnny's dark eyes filled with knowing and he nodded. "Oh sure. The parents. No dogs allowed."

I said, "It's a health matter. Mom's allergic to animals."

"And kids," said Johnny.

"That's not true." I was going to add that Mom just didn't like children who were untidy and had bad manners, but that would have started an argument and I was allergic to shouting. "When I get a house of my own I'm going to have two dogs," I said, "and they won't be dribbly and stinky like your dog Goof."

"Yeah, he is a bit smelly," said Johnny. "Even people can get dribbly and stinky when they're old. Maybe me, one day.

That's okay. Will you go and get Lucy? She's locked in the shed."

I hesitated because Johnny's bantam could be fierce, all beak and claws and flying feathers. "What if she pecks me?"

"You won't die," he said. "You definitely will not die."

# 3.

I'd already met Auntie Ruby. She was tall and skinny like Uncle Danny and her yellow hair was almost as short as her yellow eyebrows. Her face was covered with light brown freckles, her eyes were sea-colored, and she had a twisty mouth. I couldn't imagine her in all the white frilly stuff that Mom reckoned brides should wear. She looked more like a clown or a woman that worked with dogs.

I could hear the dogs before Uncle Leo stopped the van. The sounds ranged from the deep woof-woofs of big dogs to the shrill yap-yaps from little terriers. The air was full of noise and it wasn't just from the dogs in the boarding kennels. Auntie Ruby had five of her own that she'd rescued from the SPCA and they were all mongrels, all different. There were two big dogs, one black and wooly with a red tongue and a ginger one with hairy paws and a waggy tail. A fat old dog called Butch had half an ear missing. A black and white cattle dog, also very old, walked stiffly, its face covered in gray hairs. The other dog was small and yappy with wiry hair and a straight tail. Her name was Toilet Brush which I thought was a mean name for a nice dog. She was extra friendly. As soon as Royce opened the van door, she jumped right onto my lap, licking my face.

"She likes you, Michael," said Auntie Ruby.

I patted the dog's bristly coat and tried to turn away but the tongue followed, slopping across my cheek like a wet towel.

"That's enough, Toilet Brush!" cried Auntie Ruby. "Sorry, Michael. She can't resist kissing handsome men. Come into the house. There's lemonade and pancakes before we make a start on the grounds."

There was no doubt about it, Auntie Ruby's house smelled of dog, but it was a good smell, like hay and earth and old leaves. There wasn't much space in the living room with pots of house plants and dog baskets on the floor, so we stood around the table in the kitchen eating pancakes with jam and cream while the dogs nudged us for crumbs. I gave Toilet Brush half of my pancake because she was a nice dog and she did seem to like me better than the others. Every time I moved she was right beside me, looking up through the hair that hung over her eyes.

Auntie Ruby was talking to Miranda about the wedding. "I don't believe in dressing animals in clothes," she said. "But some people are putting fancy collars on their dogs. Or a bandana or a scarf."

"Will all your dogs be there?" Jeannie asked.

"If you mean the kennels, they'll be empty," said Auntie Ruby. "I haven't taken any bookings for next weekend. These guys," she said, patting the big wooly black dog, "will be our attendants."

"Weird!" said Royce. "Dogs for attendants!"

"Awesome!" said Miranda.

"How can you have a dog for a best man?" I asked.

Auntie Ruby laughed. "Leo's the best man. The dogs will

be ring bearers and flower girls. And why not? They're more than pets. They're like my children."

I reminded myself not to repeat this latest information to Mom and Dad who thought a bride and groom dressed as clowns was the worst thing they'd ever heard.

Uncle Leo took charge of the rider mower and the rest of us, protected with sun hats and sunblock, followed Auntie Ruby to the garden shed and the tools she called her weapons. "We advance to make war on foul weeds," she cried, holding a hoe up in the air. "I'll be your general. If you don't recognize the enemy, consult me. Right troops?"

"Right!" we all yelled.

"Remember, no civilian casualties," she said. "We don't destroy flowers, only weeds. Right again?"

"Right again!" we cried.

"Fine and dandy. Forks and trowels, everyone. Present arms! Quick march. You, soldier!" She pointed to Royce and then the wheelbarrow. "You can drive the tank."

Royce shrugged, looking embarrassed. I knew he was thinking he was way too old for this game, but he picked up the wheelbarrow handles and we walked in single file, the dogs close behind, to the gardens in front of the house. Auntie Ruby showed us which were flower plants, which were weeds, and how she wanted the soil loosened until it was like breadcrumbs. I didn't see Uncle Danny anywhere. I guessed he was with the dogs in the kennels, but Royce said he was down in the city with the trailer, collecting some of the rented stuff for the wedding like dishes, glasses, and trestle tables. "It'll cost them a fortune," Royce said, the pain of it showing on his face.

I didn't know how big Auntie Ruby's property was. The kennels were built a long way from the house, rows of wire cages with concrete floors and wooden shelters with a large exercise yard at the back. Between the kennels and the house was a paddock holding three brown sheep and a donkey, then there were some fruit trees and a vegetable garden with peas and wrinkly cabbages in it. The house was quite small but the lawn in front was huge, bigger than a football field. There were fully grown trees here and there and flower beds at the edges. This was the lawn that'd have the wedding tent and further over, under some oak trees, there'd be portable bathrooms for the guests.

Toilet Brush was a terrible name for a dog. I patted the wiry little terrier who stayed beside me while I was pulling weeds. She thought I was on my hands and knees to have a game with her and she kept jumping at my trowel. When I put weeds in a bucket, she grabbed them in her mouth and shook her head, growling.

I wished Mom and Dad didn't hate dogs so much. I said to Royce, who was working on the same flowerbed, "Why don't you get a dog like—like this one."

"We've already got a dog," said Royce.

"But Goof is old. You said yourself he might die soon."

"All the more reason for not getting another dog," said Royce.

I scratched Toilet Brush behind the ears. "If you did get another one, it would be easier for you when Goof popped off. A little dog wouldn't eat very much. I could come around to take it for walks."

Royce stabbed his garden fork into the ground. "What about Goof's feelings? Eh? What about that?"

"His feelings?"

"Yeah." Royce glared at me. "Suppose you were dying of cancer and your parents adopted a young healthy kid so they could replace you when you fell off your perch. How would you feel?"

"That's ridiculous!" I replied. "It's got nothing to do with it."

"Only because you think animals don't have feelings," Royce shouted.

I didn't know what I'd said that could have made him so mad. Then I saw that his face was red, his forehead dotted with drops of sweat, and there was a wet patch on the back of his T-shirt. I shrugged. "You don't care about Goof's feelings. You're just wild because you hate gardening, and you're not getting paid for it."

For a moment, Royce looked as though he was going to burst with rage. But then, surprisingly, he smiled. "Go and bite your butt," he said.

# 4.

Of course, my parents said yes to the wedding. The decision came Friday night, exactly as I'd predicted, along with a lecture about remembering my manners and washing my hands before eating.

"Especially if you've been touching dogs," Mom said. "You could get hydatids or tapeworms."

"They'll be clean dogs," I explained. "Auntie Ruby and her friends—"

"She's not your aunt!" interrupted Dad.

"I can't believe they'll be serving food with dogs

present," said Mom. "Don't wedding receptions have health inspectors?"

"We'll collect you about nine, when the barbecue's finished," said Dad.

I knew that nine o'clock was when the dancing started. "Can't I stay?" I pleaded.

"No, son."

"But it's not going to finish until midnight!" I cried.

Mom looked at Dad and gave a huge sigh.

Dad said, "Michael, which part of the word *no* do you not understand?"

So that was it. But at least they let me go to my cousins' house early the next morning. Mom put my wedding clothes in my backpack with the wedding present on top. She'd bought them a silver butter dish and butter knife, a gift, she said, that was always in good taste.

I was racing through the Wests' gate, thinking what a neat day it was for a wedding, when I heard a rumble of angry voices. The noise grew as I neared the house and by the time I was on the back porch, the sound of morning birdsong and traffic was completely drowned by argument. Not kids' voices, either. These were big bellowing noises—Grandadda West shouting at his sons, Leo and Danny, and those two yelling back at him.

Miranda opened the door. "Mickey! You made it! Come in!" She was all smiles as though nothing was going on.

Grandadda West was sitting in his pajamas on the kitchen couch. He looked exactly as I'd remembered him, bushy eyebrows, blue veins on his nose, and teeth that clicked when he talked. One skinny white foot was stamping on the floor. The other pajama leg flapped empty beside it. He had his artificial foot in his right hand and was beating it on the couch. "The devil take the lot of you! What kind of wedding is it that hasn't been blessed by the Church? A flaming circus tent, is it? A couple of clowns? Is that any way to start married life?"

Uncle Leo waved his hand, "Oh, shut your mouth, Da. You're causing a draft!"

But Grandadda West took no notice. He went on at Uncle Danny. "Who do you and that—that woman think you are to be throwing centuries of beautiful tradition on the muck heap? I brought you up to know better than that."

"Times have changed, you silly old rooster!" yelled Uncle Danny, who was in his underpants and T-shirt and holding a cup of coffee. His ginger beard was quivering with anger. "This is our wedding. We do it our way."

Grandadda West swung his plastic foot at his younger son. "You're needing a good kick up the backside!" he roared.

"Shut your gobs, the both of you!" yelled Uncle Leo, his hands over his ears. "This is my house. If you want to fight, do it in the street!"

At that, Grandadda West and Uncle Danny turned on Uncle Leo and a whole new argument started up. None of them had noticed that I'd come into the room.

Miranda took me down the hall and into the family room where Auntie Rosie was at her sewing machine doing some last minute stitching to some overalls that Jeannie would be wearing. "Noisy, isn't it?" said Auntie Rosie. "They drank whiskey last night and they've all got headaches."

I didn't know how anyone could bear to shout when his head was aching. I tried to be helpful. "My father doesn't drink whiskey but he does get headaches. Mom gives him aspirin tablets. Do you have any aspirin? If you haven't, I can run home and—"

"Bless you, Mickey!" Auntie Rosie laughed. "Of course I've got aspirin, but they'd rather argue."

It didn't make sense. "Why?" I asked.

"Because they enjoy it," said Miranda, and she and her mother giggled as though a family fight was a funny thing.

Auntie Rosie looked at me over her sewing machine and saw that I was feeling uncomfortable. "Give them half an hour and some breakfast, and they'll be the best of buddies," she said.

She was right. When I next went to the kitchen, they were sitting at the table and Grandadda West was telling a story about the time he lost his glasses and ate a tin of cat's meat instead of corned beef. Uncle Danny and Uncle Leo were laughing so much that they were spraying milk and corn-flakes across the table.

Grandadda West noticed me. "Ah! It's Eileen's boy, me lovely Michael. How would you be, lad? How's that beauti-ful mother of yours and her husband—what's he called? Mr. Arthur-itis."

I didn't like him saying things about Dad. I stood up straight. "His name's Arthur," I said.

"Will you listen to that now?" Grandadda West pointed at me but he looked at Uncle Leo and Uncle Danny. "There's a son who's having some respect for his father. What a lovely lad! 'Tis sure, he doesn't call his Da a rooster and a silly old git."

I saw a gleam in Uncle Danny's eye and said quickly, "My parents are very well, thank you. They send their regards."

Grandadda West turned around to face me. "Will your

darlin' mother be coming to the wedding?"

I shook my head.

"The shame! The shame!" He turned back to his breakfast. "I'll be dancing with a chair, so I will. Can someone be telling me what that flaming bird's doing?"

He meant Johnny's bantam hen which was on the kitchen counter pecking at a cereal bowl for leftover cornflakes and milk. I waved my arms at her and she flew down squawking, heading straight for Johnny's room. So much for the prison cage on the back lawn. I knew it wouldn't last. That, I thought, was one of the big differences between my parents and the Wests. When Mom and Dad were unhappy with someone they didn't make a big noise about it. Often they didn't make a noise at all. Their silence would set as heavy as concrete and last practically forever. I didn't know which was worse— long, heavy quiet or short, ear-splitting fights.

I learned later that Goof was to go in the empty bantam cage but only for a couple of hours. He had to be shampooed, which he really hated.

"If he's not locked up, he'll run off and find something horrible to roll in," said Miranda.

I felt sorry for Goof. He wasn't a brilliant dog. He had the brain of an average garden snail. But he knew that his greatest fear in life was about to become real. He struggled and whimpered as we lifted him into the tin tub on the lawn. Miranda and I held him while Jeannie turned on the hose.

"Can't you just tie him up afterwards?" I said.

"He'll slip his collar," said Miranda. "He always does that. Hold on tight."

For a dog who loved to jump into the ocean or rivers, he was the biggest wimp when it came to a bath. We got soaking wet holding him, which was kind of fun with Miranda's arms and mine all in a tangle with dog and shampoo getting in our faces. By the time we'd rinsed him off, we were more washed than he was.

"It's a special shampoo," laughed Jeannie. "You won't get fleas or canine eczema."

We lifted Goof from the tub, rubbed him dry with an old towel, and put him in the chicken run. He was too big for the bantam's house. In fact, he could barely turn around in the run. He was beaten and he knew it. He lay on the grass, whined, and rolled his eyes at us.

Jeannie, Miranda and I were so wet, we were the first to change into our wedding clothes. The invitation had said, *Dress: fun/casual*, and I'd told Mom I wanted my cargo pants and jungle T-shirt. When I opened my backpack I couldn't help yelping like poor old Goof. There, in folds of tissue paper, was my horrible dark gray suit, my ghastly white shirt, and the black bow tie. How could my own mother do that to me?

Royce looked, nodded, and patted me on the back. "No worries, friend," he said, and he found me a pair of old jeans and a T-shirt that had the Spice Girls on it.

I was relieved, but I hesitated. "How much?" I asked.

"What?"

"How much for the rental?"

He looked hurt. "Nothing, Mickey! Big fat zero! This is a family wedding, right? Why should I charge you?" Then he smiled. "Of course, if you want to give me a couple of bucks—"

I laughed and grabbed the T-shirt and jeans. "Bite your butt," I said.

I took the wedding present in to Uncle Danny who was getting into his clown costume with the help of Uncle Leo and two fat pillows which had to be sewed inside a shiny red and yellow shirt. "This is from Mom and Dad," I said. "Where do I put it?"

Uncle Danny took the package from me, looked at the card, and then carefully unwrapped the paper with little white birds and bells on it. Inside was a box and in the box, the silver butter dish and butter knife. "Well look at this," he cried with delight. "Isn't it the nicest little doggy bowl you ever saw, Leo? There's even a knife to cut the meat. It's a bit blunt but we can soon get an edge on it."

I didn't like to tell him it was for butter. "It—it'd be all right for Toi—you know, the little dog."

"She'll think she's a princess, eating from this, so she will," said Uncle Danny.

"Don't tease the lad," said Uncle Leo, winking at me, and I realized Uncle Danny was joking.

"That's all right," I said. "I knew he was joking."

Uncle Danny pulled orange suspenders over his shoulders and looked in the mirror. "Poor little Toilet Brush won't be coming to the wedding. Ruby's keeping her under house arrest."

I think my mouth fell open. I said, "Why?"

Uncle Danny sat down to put on his white face paint. "Ruby doesn't want her mixing with the other dogs."

"But I'd look after her," I said

"Sorry Michael," said Uncle Danny. "It's just one of those things."

I felt as though the sun had gone behind a cloud. Ever since last Saturday, I had been looking forward to seeing that little dog again. She liked me. She really liked me. I'd imagined her staying beside me all through the wedding and the guests thinking she was my dog. I'd even worked out what I'd say when people asked me what her name was. Toya, I'd tell them.

"Can't she come for a little time?" I asked.

"Not a snowball's chance in hell," said Uncle Danny.

I watched him put on his makeup. He did it quickly with a practiced touch, white face down to his beard, black and red on his eyes, a huge red mouth that curved up from his own. I'd never seen another clown with a beard. Uncle Danny's was ginger and curly and he clipped butterfly hair clips into it. Every time he moved his jaw, the butterflies' wings fluttered as though they were going to take off. He put on his curly purple wig, and on top, a small yellow hat with a feather. "Pass me my shoes, Michael," he said.

I didn't see them at first because I was looking for something the size of his feet. The clown shoes were huge. They'd been made from flippers covered with foam plastic. I laughed because I couldn't imagine anyone walking in them, much less getting married.

"How are you going to dance?" I said.

"I'll take them off," he said. "It's not the shoes that are the problem, Michael. It's the talking. You know that clowns are silent. They have to mime everything. So how do we say 'I do' in the marriage service?"

"Can't you use sign language?"

"Not unless we're deaf. They don't have separate marriage laws for clowns."

"You'll just have to talk, Danny boy," said Uncle Leo, putting away the face paint.

"We'll think of something," Uncle Danny said.

"It'd better be a quick think," said Uncle Leo. "It's time to be going."

I looked at Uncle Leo's old paint-splattered overalls with the torn knees. "You have to get dressed, Uncle Leo."

"Saints alive, Mickey, I am dressed. Do you think I wear this sort of gear every day?"

"I'm sorry. I just thought—" I didn't know what I thought. Maybe Mom was right about the Wests being far too sloppy for their own good.

The clown shook his head so that the butterflies on his beard flapped their wings. He put a fat, white-gloved finger against his brother's mouth. Then he unclipped Uncle Leo's overalls and Uncle Leo stepped out. Underneath he was wearing black trousers and a bright purple ruffled shirt like some fat rock star.

"What he's saying," grinned Uncle Leo, "is, don't tease the lad." He rubbed his hands together. "Right. Let's be off. There's a wedding to go to."

# 5.

Miranda wore an ordinary dress and a sun hat with fresh flowers around the brim. The flowers kept falling off but she still looked beautiful. I felt really good, standing at the tent door with her, waiting for the guests to arrive.

Grandadda West was right. The tent did look like a circus with streamers around the walls and hundreds of helium-filled balloons tied to the chairs. Everything else was jumping with color. Even the flowers weren't usual—they were huge paper blooms, purple and orange, blue and yellow.

Some of the guests had come early and were sitting near the front listening to Grandadda West. He'd rolled up his trouser leg to show them his plastic foot and was telling them all about his operation. Whatever Grandadda West said was interesting. That was because he made up exciting details to replace the boring parts of a story.

I noticed that one of the men had shorts and bare feet and the others were in the sort of gear they'd wear for a picnic. I was very glad Royce had lent me his old jeans and T-shirt. In the gray suit, I'd have died from heat and embarrassment.

The early guests had brought two dogs, one a spaniel and the other a tall thin dog with silky red hair. Goof, looking amazingly clean, had joined them and after a bit of circling and sniffing, they all settled down by the chairs, better be-haved than a couple of little kids who were screaming and trying to untie the balloons.

At about quarter to four, the guests poured in and there were so many kids and dogs running around that Miranda and I got really mixed up about who was sitting where. Obviously, it didn't matter too much. I tried to tell Miranda that, but there was so much noise, she couldn't hear me until I put my mouth right against her ear. I wished I knew what kind of shampoo she used. I'd buy some for myself.

Now Uncle Leo and Auntie Rosie came in. Auntie Rosie's new dress was like a sundress, black with a pattern of red roses. The stain where Johnny's hen had pooed on it was covered with a little bunch of red roses and some ferns. It was a nice dress but a bit tight. Auntie Rosie looked like a Christmas stocking full of bulgy presents. She sat near the front with Uncle Leo beside her. The noise in the tent was deafening but it was an exciting noise, people talking and laughing, kids shouting, dogs barking. Most people had their pets on leashes. There were so many pooches, it was like a dog show.

Miranda and I were still at the door of the tent when Uncle Danny the clown came over from the parking lot, his canoe-shaped shoes tucked under his arm. He dropped the shoes, bent over to ease his feet into them, and then nodded at us. It was the signal for us to bring Uncle Leo, the best man, to the door. I nodded a yes but then discovered there was no way I could reach the front of the tent. The aisle was jammed with people and dogs. Nor did I have a hope of shouting above the noise.

Miranda knew what to do. She put two fingers in her mouth and blew her famous shrill dog whistle. The noise stopped just like that. Even the dogs were silent for about two seconds. The guests saw Uncle Danny and they cleared the aisle to allow Uncle Leo through. Good old Uncle Leo. His grin was as wide as a clown's even though he didn't have any face paint. He patted his brother on the back and they walked together to the front of the tent with everyone watching. I was impressed with the way Uncle Danny could march in those shoes. He kept his heels down, toes up and waddled a bit like a duck.

A woman who'd been sitting on the other side of Auntie Rosie stood up to meet them. She looked like somebody's grandmother and she was wearing the kind of dress that older women usually wore to weddings.

"That's Mrs. Harris," said Miranda. "She's the marriage celebrant. She's a Justice of the Peace and she—oh look! Here comes Auntie Ruby and Viv."

I turned and saw another clown coming down the front

steps of the house. She didn't have floppy shoes, just ordinary sneakers painted in stripes. Her wig was made of springy orange pigtails that bounced when she walked, and she had a huge flower in the buttonhole of her red velvet jacket. Like Uncle Danny she had a smiling red mouth that took up half her face, and a round red nose. Beside her was a woman in black pants and a ruffled purple shirt, the same kind of outfit that Uncle Leo was wearing.

"Viv's a vet," said Miranda. "She's the bridesmaid."

With Auntie Ruby and Viv were four dogs with clown ruffles around their necks. I counted again, just to make sure. Toilet Brush wasn't there.

Miranda blew another of her fierce whistles. People turned. Dogs sat up straight, their ears twitching. Someone switched on the music. It was a very old-fashioned recording of *The Teddy Bears' Picnic*, played loud.

"The wedding march," Miranda explained.

# 6.

In my entire life up till that afternoon, I'd been to three weddings and they'd all been boring. This wasn't like a wedding. Well, it was, but it was also a clown show and so funny that everyone was screaming with laughter. Even the marriage celebrant was wiping her eyes and gasping to get her words out.

The clowning started as soon as Auntie Ruby came down the aisle. Uncle Danny bent to kiss her white-gloved hand and as his lips made contact, a fire alarm went off. He tried again. This time, when the alarm sounded, puffs of smoke came out of Uncle Danny's hat. Quick as a blink, Auntie

Ruby squirted his hat with water from her flower buttonhole.

The guests laughed and some of the dogs barked but Auntie Ruby's five attendants took no notice. The fat one sat down and scratched behind its chewed ear. I supposed those dogs were used to clowning.

The marriage celebrant must have known they were going to do a joke routine because she didn't seem surprised when Uncle Danny started sneezing. Auntie Ruby pulled dozens of big silk handkerchiefs from her pocket. She used the last handkerchief to wipe his red nose and the nose came off on her hand. She put it on again with a huge pair of plastic pliers, and while she was doing that, she stepped on his foot. Uncle Danny rolled onto the ground, his foot in the air, shaking, pretending he was in great pain. In the middle of laughing, I let out a breath of thanks that my parents weren't here. I could imagine them sitting beside me with faces tight with shock. Then I got around to wondering how the clowns would cope with the "I do" bit. Would they have to talk?

The celebrant wiped her eyes and said, "Ruby Alison Davenport, do you take Daniel Seamus West to be your lawfully wedded partner?"

There was silence in the tent. Even the dogs and babies were quiet. Auntie Ruby reached under her jacket and brought out a little triangle. She struck it close to her ear. A clear silvery sound shivered in the air. She struck it again and then sang, "I do, I do, I sincerely and dearly and gladly and madly and soundly and clownly do."

The celebrant turned to Uncle Danny. "Do you, Daniel Seamus West, take Ruby Alison Davenport to be your lawfully wedded partner?"

Uncle Danny took off his hat and bowed. There was a roll

of drums from the sound system, and then some music. He pretended to tap dance in his outsize green shoes, then he sang, "I do-de-do-do. I do-de-do-do. Roses are red. Violets are blue. Ruby's my darling and I do-de-do-do."

The music stopped and the celebrant said, "I now pronounce you legally wed." She looked at them and went into another fit of laughter. "It is customary for the groom to kiss the bride," she chuckled.

Uncle Danny and Auntie Ruby spread their arms and rushed at each other. But they both had hugely padded stomachs and they bounced off each other like a couple of beach balls. They tried again and this time bounced so hard that they fell over with their feet in the air. Everyone screamed and clapped and some people stood on their chairs to see better.

Eventually they tried to kiss by standing side to side and leaning across but now their red noses were in the way. Every time their noses touched there was a noise like an air-horn.

I put my hands against my ribs. I'd laughed so much that my sides were hurting.

Miranda, who was clapping, turned, smiling. Then she leaned across and before I realized what was happening, she hugged me.

I smiled back at her, my face getting hot.

The day was almost perfect.

# 7.

After the wedding ceremony, the caterers drove their vans to the front of the tent to set up the tables while we played games on the lawn. Auntie Ruby had put some bats and a laundry basket full of balls under the big tree and it wasn't only the kids who played. Adults played ball games, too. Some threw balls for the dogs to fetch. Others lay on the grass, talking and drinking wine.

Goof, looking dusty and happy, was lying under a tree next to Auntie Rosie. He hadn't been able to find anything stinky to replace the smell of dog shampoo, so he had rolled in one of the flower gardens. I guessed he'd probably wiped out half the plants.

Uncle Danny kicked off his huge green shoes. He and Auntie Ruby put their red noses in their pockets. That meant they were off clown duty and could talk. They greeted everyone and then went to the field by the vegetable garden to join in a ball game. No one seemed to bother with photographs although one of Uncle Danny's friends ran here and there with a video camera.

Royce and I hung about the tent, watching rainbow-colored paper being unrolled over tables which had been arranged in a horseshoe shape. Plates and glasses were coming out of the vans, bowls of salad, seafood, chicken, ham, salmon, curries, kebabs, and mountains of asparagus with yellow sauce.

"Wait here," said Royce and then he sauntered towards one of the van drivers. I don't know what he said, but he returned a minute later looking very pleased with himself and carrying a dish of cream-filled meringues. We took them to the back of Auntie Ruby's house and sat on the doorstep to eat them.

I licked cream off my fingers. "This is by far the best wedding I've ever been to. Most weddings are so—so awful."

"That's what Uncle Danny said. He and Auntie Ruby

wanted people to enjoy themselves."

"Well, I'm certainly enjoying myself." I stuffed another meringue into my mouth.

"I thought you weren't supposed to eat sugar."

"That's right," I said calmly, "and I'm not supposed to put my fingers near my mouth when I've been touching dogs."

"You'll probably die," said Royce.

"Yep." I licked my fingers again. "What a way to go!"

Before I could reach for another meringue, I heard a scratching and whimpering behind me. I turned, looking up, and saw a small whiskery face at the kitchen window. When she saw me looking at her, her crying got louder and her paws scratched flat out on the glass.

"Look, Royce!"

"Leave her," he said.

"But she's lonely!"

"She has to stay in the house." Royce put the last meringue in his mouth and gave me the empty dish. "Time to get back," he said. "They're all going into the tent."

# 8.

Outside the tent, there were bowls of water for thirsty dogs. On the tables, among the hot and cold dishes, there were baskets of little brown cookies labeled dog biscuits. I couldn't figure it out. How could Auntie Ruby be so kind to all these dogs but keep the nicest one, her own Toilet Brush, locked in the house? Why was she punishing her?

I thought of Johnny's bantam hen in the cage on the lawn. What a waste of time that was. Three days and the hen was back inside. Mom and Dad were right about the Wests. They were all a bit extreme.

I sat between Royce and Auntie Rosie who ate as though they were starving. The food was good but I couldn't eat much. I was worried about poor Toilet Brush. I told Royce I was full because of the meringues.

"Nah! Can't be," he said through a mouth full of curry. "Meringues are made of air. One good burp and your stomach's empty again."

Auntie Rosie laughed. "Royce, you talk enough junk to fill the city dump," she said as she speared another steak.

"Anyway," Royce said to me, "you've always got a second stomach for dessert. Didn't you know that?"

Most weddings had speeches. This wedding had jokes. Uncle Danny explained that anyone could tell jokes as long as they were clean and didn't put anyone down. He started off with a string of stories that began with how many elephants can you fit in a mini. Most people had heard them before but they still laughed because everyone was in a laughing mood. The late afternoon sun came through the doors of the tent like gold dust and the caterers hurried out through it bearing empty dishes. They returned with the desserts, more meringues, chocolate cakes, trifles, pies and cheesecakes, fruit salad and cream. The noise of talk filled the tent like the buzzing of a saw and people had to tap their glasses with their spoons when they wanted to tell a joke. Viv, the bridesmaid, stood up. "There was a guy who was selling intelligence pills for a dollar each. Another guy bought five but he came back the next day. 'Hey,' he said. 'I don't think these are intelligence pills. They taste like sheep's droppings.' 'See?' said the salesman. 'You're getting smarter already.'"

I didn't tell any jokes because I wasn't the joke-telling type, but the other Wests joined in. Royce jumped up and bellowed, "What do you get when you cross a kangaroo with an elephant? Big holes all over Australia."

Honey, who was sitting next to Miranda, wanted to tell her joke. She stood on a chair with Miranda holding her. "What's big and—and—" Honey waved her hands in the air, "and got some tails?"

"We don't know," said Auntie Ruby. "What's big and got some tails?"

"Doggies!" said Honey, going into giggles.

A woman on the other side of the tent stood up. I knew that her name was Marcia and she was an actor like Uncle Danny. She had a fox terrier called Jacko. Marcia tapped for attention on a wine bottle.

"All doggies have big hearts, darling," she called to Honey, "but some doggies come in little packages, like my lovely Jacko. Jacko has only one tail and he looks small, doesn't he? But he has a huge heart and huge talent. Would you like to hear him tell you a joke? Come, Jacko."

At once, the fox terrier jumped onto her chair and stood on his hind legs.

"Tell them your joke, Jacko," said Marcia.

Jacko put his head back and gave a long howl that went up and down like a siren. Other dogs leapt to their feet and barked.

"Thank you, Jacko," said Marcia. "Of course, Jacko only speaks in dog language but as you can tell from the applause, it was an excellent joke."

People laughed and clapped, and Marcia gave Jacko one of the dog biscuits. I didn't clap. If I had a nice little dog I wouldn't make it do tricks. I'd look after it and it'd be my best friend, but I wouldn't turn it into a performer to please people. No way!

Uncle Leo stood up. "Sure, and you know about the woman who took her son to the doctor. 'Doctor, Doctor, my boy thinks he's a pack of cards,' she says. 'Big deal!' says the doctor."

"Oh Leo," cried Auntie Rosie. "That's terrible."

The dogs settled down, most of them sprawling under the tables at their owners' feet, their leashes fastened to table or chair legs. Goof, who had been fed heaps of food as well as dog biscuits, was fast asleep with his head on Miranda's hat. I thought he was having a dream because his paws and lips kept twitching.

Auntie Ruby told a joke. "It was a lovely spring day. A little worm popped its head above the ground to say good morning to the sun. What did it see? Close by was another little worm. It looked as though it, too, had popped its head up to greet the sun. The first worm called out, 'Hullo, little worm. Will you be my friend?' Back came the reply. 'Don't be silly. I'm your other end.'"

It was almost dark outside when the coffee was served. Most of the balloons which had been tied to the chairs were bobbing against the tent roof above the strings of colored lights that now lit the tables. As the caterers poured refills of coffee, the Irish band arrived and set up their sound system. There were two men and two women, all in green shirts and with several instruments. I could make out an accordion, a fiddle, a kind of drum, and a guitar. I hoped they weren't going to have real Irish dancing because I couldn't do that. I wanted ordinary pop stuff so I could ask Miranda to dance with me. My mouth went dry just thinking about it.

In spite of the noise, most of the young children and dogs were sleeping. Some babies were in parents' laps or strollers but one little kid, I think she belonged to Viv, was lying with her head on Auntie Ruby's big wooly dog. Both were fast asleep.

I thought, just as well Mom wasn't here to see it. She'd be frantic about germs. But then the weirdest thing happened. Just as I was thinking about Mom and dogs, Auntie Rosie nudged me.

"Look who's arrived," she said.

I turned my head to the tent door and felt sick. Mom and Dad were there to take me home.

# 9.

Royce said it was because my mother had downed a few.

"A few what?" I said.

"Beers. Wine. You should know what your mother drinks. It's made her relax."

"Oh," I said, but I was convinced that Royce was wrong. My parents didn't drink much. I knew they decided to stay for the wedding dance because everyone gave them such a huge welcome. Grandadda West was first to the door, hobbling flat out with his stick, calling, "Eileen, me beauty!" He didn't call Dad Mr. Arthur-itis, either. It was Arthur. "How's the big world of commerce, Arthur?" "Hear you're doing mighty wonders, Arthur." Stuff like that.

Mom's gaze swept over my borrowed T-shirt and jeans but before she could say anything, she and Dad were surrounded.

Auntie Rosie and Uncle Leo were with them, Uncle Danny and Auntie Ruby, the woman called Marcia, other people who knew them from the Golf Club. I was amazed. I didn't know my mom and dad were so popular. I tugged at Mom's hand. "The dancing hasn't started yet," I said. "Can we stay?"

I didn't think she'd heard me above the noise. She and Dad were talking a lot, laughing, really different from the way they were at home. They fitted right in. Even their clothes were okay because they'd dressed for a barbecue. Somebody put glasses of wine into their hands and they were led away to a table on the other side of the tent.

They didn't look at me again, they were so busy with other people. I couldn't decide whether I was pleased or insulted, but I guess that the pleased feeling won.

The band went into some really wild music and it seemed that in two seconds practically everyone was dancing on the grass between the tables. I couldn't see Dad, but Mom was dancing with old Grandadda West who lurched a bit but still whirled her around like a spinning top. I looked for Miranda in the crowd. She was dancing with her brother Johnny. That was all right. I'd ask her for the next dance. In the meantime, there was something I absolutely had to do.

I walked out of the tent, the light and music at my back, dark trees and cars in front of me. At first it was hard to see. I stumbled against the edge of a garden and fell over, hands down in some flowers. But when my eyes got used to the darkness, I could make out the gravel path to the back of the house.

The door wasn't locked. As soon as I touched the handle, I heard the whimpering and then a sad little bark. "Shh, girl," I said. "I'm coming to get you."

I hadn't found out why the little dog was being punished but I decided she'd been locked in the house long enough. No one would notice if I took her to the tent, and if they did, well, I was sure they wouldn't mind. Not now that the wedding was half over.

I pushed the door open and the little dog hurled herself at me. She stood on her hind legs, pawing frantically at me, and her sad whimper changed to high-pitched yelps of happiness. I picked her up and held her against my shirt. She licked my face flat out, as though I was one big ice cream.

"Punishment's over, Toya," I said. "You've just been invited to a wedding dance."

On the return journey it was easy to see where I was heading. The tent was glowing and bouncing with music. The difficult thing was the dog. She had been shut up for so long that she couldn't keep still in my arms. She was licking, shaking and whimpering, and her tail was beating against me like a whip. As I got near the tent, she barked really loudly. I heard some dogs barking back, a chorus of noise over the top of the music. Toya struggled in my arms, her claws ripping at my T-shirt. Next thing, she was down on the ground, running like greased lightening towards the tent.

What a noise broke out! It sounded as though every dog in the place was barking. People yelled. The music stopped. By the time I got to the opening, the inside of the tent was an incredible mess. The dogs had gone crazy. They were chasing little Toilet Brush around and around. Chairs and tables had been dragged over, spilling coffee and wine. People were whistling and calling, "Come here, boy! Come here at once!" The dogs took no notice. They raced through glasses and bottles and flowers. They skidded on rainbow tablecloths. One dog dragged a chair. Another had its leash caught up with someone's jacket.

"Toya!" I yelled. I couldn't even hear myself for the racket. Uncle Danny dove to grab her but she dodged him and he fell on his face. The other dogs ran right over him and his clown wig and hat came off. Goof chomped on the wig and shook it as though it was some little purple animal.

"Catch her!" yelled Uncle Danny. "Don't let her out of the tent!"

I saw Toilet Brush running my way and I crouched down, my arms held out. As quick as a blink she sidestepped and rushed out into darkness, the other dogs following.

Auntie Ruby and Viv went after them, and Uncle Danny, his clown paint smeared, said, "Who let her out of the house?"

I didn't want to tell him, but I had to. "Ah—I did."

"You?"

I nodded.

"In heaven's name, why?" he said.

I couldn't see the expression behind his messy makeup but he sounded angry. I tried to say something. The words wouldn't come out.

Uncle Danny bent over. "What did you say?"

I looked at the people who were picking up tables and chairs and glasses. Some of the dogs were still in the tent. They seemed bewildered. They sniffed the crumpled tablecloths as though they were wondering what all the fuss was about. "She was so sad," I said. "I didn't want her to miss out on the wedding."

"Wedding is right!" Uncle Danny groaned and felt his head as though he was feeling for his wig. Then he, too, ran after the dogs who were barking somewhere in the parking lot.

# 10.

On the way home, Mom and Dad were shaking with laughter. Dad swerved the car twice, he was laughing so hard. I was amazed that they weren't furious with me. Perhaps Royce was right and Mom had had a few drinks at the barbecue. That had to be it. My parents often smiled but they never laughed out loud like this. Never!

Mom said it was the funniest thing she had seen in a long time and Dad said, too bad, if people invited dogs to a wedding, what did they expect? I couldn't see what was so hilarious. I was worried. All those dogs attacking poor little Toya! Hadn't she been punished enough?

Mom turned in her seat. "Michael dear, they weren't attacking her."

"Yes, they were."

"She was in an interesting state," Dad said.

"Arthur!" said Mom.

Dad glanced at her. "What's the matter, Eileen? Doesn't he know anything? I mean, don't they have sex education at school?"

At the mention of sex, I got an uh-oh feeling in my stomach. I said, "That's about people, not dogs!"

"No need to shout, old boy," said Dad. "There's nothing wrong with my hearing. Let's start at the beginning. There are male dogs and there are female dogs."

"I know that!" I snapped.

Mom put her hand on Dad's arm. Then she said, "Michael, a female dog comes into season twice a year. That means every six months she's fertile and ready to conceive puppies."

"That was why the mutt was kept in the house," said Dad. "Ruby didn't want the other dogs to get to her."

The uh-oh feeling got stronger and I was glad they couldn't see my face. Why, I thought, didn't someone tell me? I wasn't a little kid. I would have understood. I tried to make the best of it. "Do you want to know what I think? I think those dogs *were* attacking her. I saw the way they chased her. They were very aggressive. The dogs that were friendly, they just sat there and didn't do anything."

Mom squealed with laughter and rested her head against Dad's shoulder. He laughed too, his shoulders shaking over the steering wheel.

Now I was really wild. "What's so funny?"

"Oh Michael," gasped Mom. "The dogs that didn't chase her were either neutered or female."

# 11.

As it turned out, no one was permanently upset with me for letting Toilet Brush out of the house. A week later, Auntie Ruby told Royce it was kind of nice that Toilet Brush'd had a wedding too, and when Royce told me that, I felt greatly relieved. Even Uncle Danny joked about it. When he showed Uncle Leo and Auntie Rosie the wedding video, he said what a shame it was they didn't get the dog chase on tape.

I could honestly say that even with the embarrassment over Toilet Brush, it was still the best wedding I'd ever been to. I was sure that one day I'd have a clown wedding. I told Dad. He just laughed and said I wasn't clown material. Well, let him laugh, I thought, and I wondered what Miranda would look like with a red nose and a flower buttonhole that squirted water.

It was Miranda who told me that Toilet Brush had had three pups.

My stomach turned into jelly and custard. Oh, it wasn't fair! Other kids' parents let them have dogs. I tried the next best thing. I said to Miranda, "Why don't you take one?"

"They can't leave their mother until they're weaned," said Miranda. "Anyway, I think Auntie Ruby's already found homes for them all."

The jelly and custard feeling got heavy. I nodded. "I bet they're really awesome pups," I said.

"Why don't you go out and see them?" Miranda said.

I shook my head. "No."

"I thought you liked Toilet Brush."

I didn't answer. It was too hard to explain, all that stuff about Mom and germs and me wanting a dog so badly I could cry.

Miranda understood. She put her hand on top of mine. "You'll have a dog one day," she said.

"I'll have a dozen dogs," I said, and I got brave enough to hold her hand for three whole seconds.

At the beginning of the second term, we had tryouts for the school soccer teams and I couldn't believe my luck. Miranda and I got chosen for the B team which was pretty good considering there were five teams.

I couldn't wait to tell Mom about it. I turned down Royce's invitation to look at an old computer he'd found at the dump and raced home from school. Wings or no wings, I reckon I flew up the drive. I was untying my shoelaces in the porch when Mom opened the door. "I've got a surprise!" she said.

"I made the B team!" I cried. "Miranda and I, we both—"

"Come and see."

I put my shoes side by side on the rack next to the umbrella stand and followed her into the kitchen. There was a cardboard box on the floor.

"You'll never guess what's in it," Mom said.

But I could guess. You bet, I could guess. I knew from the noise—little sniffles and whines! A smell like new hay! I looked in the box and saw the puppy looking right back at me. It had brown wiry hair and a tail that beat the sides of the box.

"One of Toilet Brush's puppies!" I yelled. I wanted to pick it up and hug it, but I knew I couldn't. Mom would never allow me to touch a dog. "Why's it here?"

"Danny West dropped it off," said Mom. "It's from Ruby. A little gift."

I put my hand in the box. The puppy licked my fingers and Mom didn't say anything about germs. "Who does it belong to?" I asked.

"You, Michael," said Mom.

"Me?"

Mom nodded.

I stared at her. I couldn't believe that this person smiling and nodding was actually my mother. "But—but—but—"

"He's a little boy," Mom said. "Don't you like him?"

I picked the puppy up. He had floppy ears and a soft stomach. I held him close to my shirt and felt his warmth. "He's actually mine?"

Mom's smile got a little thin when the puppy licked my face but she didn't say anything, just kept on nodding.

"I can honestly and truly keep him?"

"As long as you are prepared to look after him," Mom said.

"Cool!" I stroked the puppy which was trying to climb around my neck. "Absolutely awesome! But you said—you always said—"

Mom pulled out a chair and sat down. "Michael, Ruby phoned us when her little dog gave birth. She said there was a pup that looked just like its mother and since you were so fond of the mother—don't let him lick near your mouth, dear." Mom folded her hands in her lap. "At first, we said no. To be perfectly honest, I have never wanted a dog. You know that. But your father and I talked about it and we decided it was a little dog, after all, and you were old enough—"

"Mom, you don't know what this means!" I tried to hug her with the puppy between us, but she scraped her chair back across the floor. "Don't push your luck, Michael," she said, waving her hands in front of her face.

"He's amazing!" I cried. "Fantasmo. He's the most gorgeous puppy I've ever seen! Of course, I'll look after him. You won't have to lift a finger, Mom. I'll feed him and clean him and take him for walks and—and—"

"Your father and I decided that a dog is as hygienic as its owners," Mom said. "He'll go to the vet regularly, have all his shots and, of course, we'll have him neutered." She smiled a little as the puppy burrowed into my shirt. "He is quite charming. We finally made up our minds when we saw him, but we decided not to tell you until he was ready to leave his mother."

The puppy was trying to crawl through a gap between my shirt buttons. I said, "This is, by far, the best day of my entire life!"

"The other puppies were sweet too," said Mom. "One was

male and one female. Ruby said they both looked like the father, who was a fox terrier."

"Jacko!" I cried.

"Who?" said Mom.

"That was the name of the fox terrier. He belonged to Marcia." I lifted the puppy out from my shirt and held him in front of my face. "I should call you Jacko Junior," I said.

"Please, no!" cried Mom. "If you're going to have a dog, at least give it a decent name."

"Like what?"

"Something a little more refined," said Mom. "I had thought of Alexander."

"Alexander?"

The little dog wagged its whippy brown tail and gave a tiny yupping bark. Alexander. It liked the name.

"You're a genius, Mom," I said, putting Alexander back in his box. "You're mother of the year!" Then I went to her and gave her a dog-free hug.

She patted me on the back and sniffed at my shirt. "Oh dear! The entire home is going to smell of puppy," she complained.

I grinned to myself. Alexander, I thought, within a month you'll be sleeping on my bed and that's a promise.

# The
# Wild West Gang
# *Go Fishing*

## 1.

The Wests couldn't believe I'd never been on a train.

"You're joking, right?" said Johnny, pushing his suitcase along the platform.

"No, I honestly haven't. We always drive or fly." I put my fingers through the puppy's cage and he licked them. He didn't know why he was locked up in this strange place and he made small squeaky noises. "I hope they look after Alexander."

"He'll be in the luggage van," said Jeannie. "They'll make a fuss of him."

I wasn't so sure. There was a heap of luggage at one end of the station—two big plastic kennels with large dogs, three little cages of cats, and one wooden box of carrier pigeons. The guards would do a lot of fussing if they all got out.

Royce was wandering up and down the station with a ruler, doing his vending machine trick. He lay on his stomach in front of the soda stand and swept the ruler under it, fishing for lost coins. He raked out twenty cents.

Auntie Rosie snorted. "That won't pay for the detergent to wash your shirt. Get up before someone steps on you. Hells bells and buggy wheels. The train'll be here in a minute. Where are they?"

She meant Miranda, Honey, and Uncle Leo who were coming in the second taxi. They were leaving the house after us just as soon as Uncle Leo finished writing a note for the neighbors about feeding the animals.

"Maybe the cab's broken down," Auntie Rosie said.

"Nah, Mom," said Royce. "Taxis don't break down."

I looked along the empty tracks. My first train journey! Wow! I was really pleased that the Wests' old van didn't pass inspection. Riding in that thing was like being in a concrete mixer.

The woman from the ticket office came out to put labels on our bags and cases and on Alexander's cage. "He'll be fine," she said. "We'll give him a pigeon to eat."

I didn't know what to say.

She grinned at me. "Or does he prefer cat?"

I stared at her, and Royce said, "Don't tease him. He hasn't got a sense of humor."

I crouched by Alexander's cage. "I'm sorry. I didn't think it was funny."

"Neither did the pigeon," she said. She took Alexander from under my nose and put him on a cart with the suit-cases. I wished I could have him in the carriage with me.

"Stop worrying," said Royce.

"Sorry."

"And stop apologizing!"

I opened my mouth to say something about Alexander,

and two things happened. The light down the track turned green and a man's voice sang, "When Irish eyes are smiling, sure the world is bright as spring."

At first I thought it was Uncle Leo, then I knew. It's *him*!

"To the lilt of Irish laughter, you can hear the angels sing."

Auntie Rosie's eyes opened wide and she said one of Royce's rude words. I didn't know Uncle Leo's father was coming to the beach with us. Neither, it seemed, did Auntie Rosie.

The old man came onto the platform with his arms out wide, singing and doing a tap-dance with his artificial foot. Clippetty-clip, plonk. Clippetty-clip, plonk. Behind him was Uncle Leo struggling with luggage, followed by Miranda with Honey.

"A fine morning to you all!" said Grandadda West, as Jeannie and Johnny ran to hug him. "Off to the seaside, are we?"

Uncle Leo, red-faced and sweating, dropped the cases. "He arrived at the house just as we were leaving."

"Came for a visit," said Grandadda West, shaking Royce's hand and ruffling my hair. "Time to favor you with me royal presence."

"You—you should have let us know!" cried Auntie Rosie.

"Ah, sure now," he said, "if I'd done that you'd have been leaving sooner. Rosie, Rosie, you're a fine looking flower. How are your thorns?"

"The train!" I yelled.

In the distance the locomotive looked exactly like the HO diesel on my model railway. It came around the curve snaking blue carriages, rapidly growing as it approached the station.

Auntie Rosie and Uncle Leo were still looking at each other with wide stares. Uncle Leo turned away first. "I'll get the extra ticket," he said.

The train swept into the station with a rush of noise that drowned Auntie Rosie's reply. I looked at her and she patted me on the shoulder. "My thorns have never been sharper," she said.

It was Grandadda West who got us kids into the right carriage. Uncle Leo and Auntie Rosie were too busy having a discussion on the platform, Uncle Leo throwing out his arms while Auntie Rosie folded hers. Grandadda found our seats and Miranda tapped on the windows to warn her parents that they might miss the train.

"Now isn't this grand," grinned old man West, grabbing his trousers to lift his artificial foot onto the opposite seat. "We're all as comfy as fleas at a dog show." He turned to the window with a pleased expression. "Faith, we might be leaving those two behind."

The whistle blew. Auntie Rosie unfolded her arms and boarded the train, Uncle Leo close behind her. As they came through the carriage door, the train made a shuddering start and they fell into each other.

"None of that smooching, now!" Grandadda West called to them, and other people in the carriage laughed.

I stood up to see the luggage cart on the platform. It was empty, thank goodness. Alexander was on board.

For a while we traveled between sun dried hills and then we saw a triangle of blue. Within minutes the train was running along the coast, forest on one side and shining sea on the other. My nose was pressed against the window. I was so lucky! Mom and Dad were at a boring old accountancy conference, and here was I on a train with my cousins and my dog, rushing towards a weekend in a beach cottage belonging to Uncle Leo's friend Benny the Canary.

I didn't know why they called him the canary. Royce said it was because he was a fishing inspector but fish had nothing to do with birds. All I knew was that Benny the Canary had a boat and he was going to take us out in it. That was something else I hadn't done. I'd never caught a fish big enough to eat.

All that sand and sea outside the train did something to Auntie Rosie. Her arms came unfolded, she made jokes and she passed around a tin of oatmeal cookies.

"You might have a devilish tongue," said Grandadda West, taking two, "but you can still bake like an angel."

Auntie Rosie just laughed. "You wicked man!" she said. "What'll we do with you?"

Grandadda West winked at her. "I'll be no trouble at all."

# 2.

The train pulled up at the station and in the rush for the door, I was last. By the time I got down to the platform, the luggage had already been unloaded and there was Alexander in his cage, yelping his pleasure at seeing me. I ran to him, crouched beside the cage and let him lick my fingers.

"Beaut pup," said a deep voice. "Yours?"

I looked up. The man beside Uncle Leo didn't look anything like a canary. He was older than my uncle, and most of his hair was on his chin, as gray as a steel pot scraper. He held out a huge hand. "Name's Benny."

I wiped my puppy-licked hand on my shorts then put it in his. "I'm pleased to meet you. I'm Michael."

"Nice manners, eh?" said the man.

Uncle Leo laughed. "I was hoping it'd rub off on my mob. Come on, Mickey. You bring Alexander. I'll get your bag."

Benny had a truck outside the station. Grandadda got in the cab and the rest of us climbed on the back on top of the suitcases. I sat on a big green suitcase and held Alexander's cage on my knees because there was nowhere else to put him. We were all squashed up like pickles in a jar, Miranda said, her arm against me. Her elbow was sharp but I didn't mind. I liked her hair brushing my face. Auntie Rosie settled between the twins and held Honey. "I'm glad this truck's got sides," she said.

"Not far to go," said Uncle Leo. "Just a mile or two."

It may not have been far but it was a rough ride and every time we went over a bump, the green case beneath me rattled and clinked. The others heard it too. "What's that?" asked Miranda.

"Sounds like glass," I said. "I'm sitting on it. The green case."

"Oh, that man!" cried Auntie Rosie.

Uncle Leo laughed. "That's my dadda all over!"

"It's not funny!" yelled Auntie Rosie. "He's diabetic. He's not supposed to drink."

The rattling and clunking went on and I wondered why Auntie Rosie was making a fuss. It could have been bottles of aftershave or medicine.

When we turned off the road and there was a louder clink. I felt something move beneath me and there was a strong smell. Auntie Rosie was right. It was not aftershave. I looked down at a wet stain at the corner of the suitcase, liquid pud-dling out on the truck deck.

"Whiskey!" cried Auntie Rosie. "It'll be all through his clothes."

"His favorite perfume," said Uncle Leo.

"It's not funny!" Auntie Rosie was set to give a lecture, but the truck was lurching over a rough track of grass and sand, to a white painted house wrapped in a driftwood fence. We all fell silent, staring. Curtained windows stared back at us. The backyard was a mess of firewood, fishing floats, an old dinghy, and a clothesline with a vine growing over it. The front yard was the beach.

Wow! I couldn't believe it! We'd be living right against the ocean.

# 3.

Royce, Jeannie, Alexander, and I were off the truck and down to the water before the adults knew it. The beach was all ours, a half moon of gray sand littered with seaweed and shells, waves rolling over at the edge. The air tasted so good, like tears and pickled onions and corned beef. Sniffing it was like eating. Far out, the sea and sky melted together in a blue haze.

Alexander was funny. He'd never been on a beach before. He ran to the water's edge, barked at the waves, then raced away when they came after him. He got sand over his muzzle from biting driftwood and kelp. I threw him a shell. He ran after it but lost interest when he spotted a seagull. He rushed at the bird, ears flying. The gull waited until he was close, then lifted up and landed behind him. Alexander turned and rushed back. Again the gull flew away and dropped a short distance from him. I thought it was playing a game. Even gulls must get bored.

Royce was pulling strands of kelp out of the sand. "See this stuff? It's worth a fortune if we can get it back."

"What for?"

"Gardens. People pay big bucks for a little bottle of liquid kelp manure."

I was not interested in Royce's money-making schemes. I walked along the beach at the front of the cottage. Between the sand and the wood fence there were patches of gray plants with dry leaves and a few spikes of grass. I wondered where I was going to sleep and I imagined a big wave washing up the beach through a window, and breaking over my bed.

Uh-oh. There was a lot of shouting going on. I guessed it was about the broken glass in Grandadda West's suitcase. I walked backwards down the sloping beach, then ran off to play some more with Alexander.

I was sleeping on the other side of the house which meant that someone else would get the tsunami first. Royce and I wanted to share a room, but Grandadda West was in with Royce and I had a creaky bed on the back porch. It was like camping. The porch had some glass but the rest was open and my bed would be almost under the stars. I hoped there were no burglars. At least I'd have Alexander with me.

The bedspread was a faded gray-green color and it smelled like the beach. The pillow had lumps in it and there were dead flies in the corners of the windows. If there was a moon, I'd be able to walk in my pajamas along the beach, when everyone was asleep.

Benny the Canary came out the back door, laughing,

shaking his truck keys like a rattle. "Your grandfather's quite a lad," he said. "Wilder than a wasp's nest."

"He's not my grandfather. He's my cousin's grandfather. And it's not Auntie Rosie's fault. The bottles just broke by themselves." I listened to the voice rumbling in the house. "Anyway, he's not supposed to have whiskey. It's bad for his diabetes."

"It's bad for everything," said Benny the Canary. "But I guess at his age, he can choose his own poison. You going fishing in the morning?"

"Yes, please!"

"Be up bright and early. We leave at dawn."

The fuss about the broken bottles had died down but not the smell. The entire house stank of whiskey although the clothes in Grandadda's suitcase were in a tub full of water and the case itself was outside.

"Breathing in whiskey fumes can make you drunk," said Miranda, who was peeling potatoes.

That was good enough for Johnny and Jeannie who staggered around, talking in loud thick voices. Honey tried to copy them. "I'sh drunk! I'sh drunk!" she said.

I was glad my parents couldn't see them. They'd be so horrified.

Royce was on the beach gathering seaweed, a great waste of time because he had no way of taking it back home. Uncle Leo was preparing chops and sausages for the barbecue and Auntie Rosie sat at the yellow table, chopping salad greens, eating peanuts and saying, "This is the life."

Grandadda West was in an armchair by the window overlooking the sea. He was still grumpy but no longer shouting. I gave him a mug of tea and some chocolate chip cookies.

He took his teeth out, tucked them in his shirt pocket, and dunked the cookies in his tea. He got soggy crumbs around his sucked-in lips and he drank with a loud noise, as though his mouth was a vacuum cleaner, but he had stopped accusing Auntie Rosie of breaking his whiskey bottles accidentally on purpose.

When it was time to eat, everyone went to the back porch where the barbecue was and some of the kids sat on my bed. I saw them wiping tomato sauce and grease off their hands onto the cover, but I didn't complain. They already thought I was too fussy.

This place was Alexander's idea of heaven. Beach, seagulls, and a family throwing him chop bones and bits of sausage. He went from one to another, wagging his little tail and grinning at plates. What a beggar!

Grandadda West ate sausages and mashed potatoes with his bare gums. He looked hard at Auntie Rosie. "Since you destructed me one and only comfort, you'll be buying a new bottle tomorrow in the morning, no doubt."

Uncle Leo answered, "Sorry, Dadda. We're all going fishing with Benny first thing."

Grandadda choked and coughed out a piece of sausage. "You'll not get me on any miserable fishing boat, not with my stomach."

"You can stay here," said Auntie Rosie.

"Truth and all, I'd rather go to Mars in one of them flying things." He glared at Auntie Rosie. "I'll need me bottle before you go."

"No, Dadda!" Auntie Rosie glared back. "That stuff is pure poison!"

"You're not me doctor!"

Uncle Leo put down the lid of the grill. "Tomorrow night," he told his father. "On our way home. I promise."

A new three-way argument began among the adults. Royce and I left to explore the rest of the backyard which had heaps of old fishing gear covered by a tangle of weeds and spear grass. Royce looked at the dented aluminium dinghy. We both decided it could still float. He lifted one end. "What do you think?"

"We'll give it a go."

We carried it through the front gate and down the sand, stopping halfway to catch our breath. "No oars," I said.

"Driftwood," Royce suggested.

"Or maybe he's got an old outboard."

But the bright ideas dimmed when we got to the sea. The waves were strong, lifting the dinghy and throwing it at our legs as we tried to hold it, and water poured through some invisible crack in the bottom.

"Useless," muttered Royce.

We carried it back up the beach and tipped it over on the dry sand. Then we sat on it and practiced throwing shells. If we could find a round cockle shell and fire it dead straight, it would rise up in the air in a long and perfect arc like a flying saucer.

I was getting the hang of it when Miranda called from the house. "Boys do the dishes!"

Royce shut his eyes and made a face.

"At home I do the dishes nearly every night," I told him. "It's not that bad."

"You've got a dishwasher!" Royce said. "Stacking dishes in a machine isn't doing them."

He was right. "Sorry," I mumbled.

"What for? If we had a dishwasher I wouldn't have an atom of sorriness. Come on. I wash, you dry. Race you to the house!"

If I sat up in bed I could see Grandadda West's clothes dripping on the line and, in the distance, the mountains pink with sunset. I could hear the sea like a huge slow heartbeat, and I pretended it was the pulse of a whale. Our teacher Mr. Fromish said a blue whale's heart was as big as a VW beetle car. If that was true, then this was the kind of noise it would make.

Alexander was curled up behind my knees. Every time I sat up, he crawled to my pillow, licking and wagging his tail. I was trying to teach him not to sleep on my pillow. I was sick of getting my face washed in the middle of the night.

The sunset faded and I counted the stars as they came out above the mountains. I guess I fell asleep because the next thing I knew, the house was quiet and dark and the sky was covered with stars like chips of ice. The sea was very loud. I could smell it in my blanket and sheet. I remembered how I had planned to go for a pajama walk on the beach, but I changed my mind. I turned over. "Here boy," I whispered.

Alexander came up to my pillow, his nose against mine, and we both went back to sleep.

# 4.

I heard an engine. Yellow lights ran above my bed and a door slammed. Alexander jumped up and barked yip-yip-yip. His voice wasn't broken and he still did puppy talk.

"Shh!" I put my hand on his quivering back. "It's just Benny the Canary."

The air was cold and damp, the sky a light gray pressing down on the blackness of the hills. The hush-hush of the sea and the idling of the truck filled my head with fishing. I jumped out of bed, rummaged in my bag, found some clothes and pulled them on. In my head I heard my mother's voice saying, what about your shower, what about your teeth, your hair, but the fishing thoughts were much louder. I ran around the outside of the house in the headlights of the truck, and found everyone in the kitchen, yawning, scratching. Miranda was eating cornflakes and cold milk. Royce was looking for his shoes. Uncle Leo had his head in a wool sweater, Jeannie was peeling a banana, and Auntie Rosie had pushed a plate at Grandadda West who was in the same clothes he wore yesterday. He must have slept in them.

"Dadda, we can't leave you here," she said.

When he clamped his mouth shut, his chin almost touched his nose. "That's not what you said."

"Because I was wild with you! You need to come on the boat." She was begging him. "No one can stay back to look after you."

"What do you mean, woman? I was looking after meself before you were ever thought of."

Auntie Rosie waved a finger at him. "I tell you, I won't miss out on this fishing trip!"

The old man waved his spoon back at her. "If you were the last person on earth, I would not be bothering you. I'll stay here on my own and mind the dog."

He meant Alexander. I thought that Alexander was coming on the boat with us. I looked at Benny the Canary who was leaning against the door with a mug of coffee in his hand, but he didn't say anything.

Uncle Leo's head came through the tight neckline of his sweater. "All settled then. Da, you look after the puppy. Help yourself to lunch from the fridge. We'll have fish for tea tonight."

I didn't want to leave Alexander behind. He'd be good on the boat, I knew he would, although I didn't know where he'd go to the bathroom. I was hoping someone would say that I could take him, but no one did. I showed Grandadda West the leash and the water bowl. He didn't seem very interested. "He's just a puppy," I told him.

"Sure now. I thought he was a parakeet," he said.

Alexander was in the house, asleep under the table, when we left. This time, Auntie Rosie was in the truck cab and the rest of us climbed in the back. It was much easier without all the luggage.

There was a pale light over the sea and the rest of the sky was a faraway blue somewhere between night and day. The truck headlights still showed yellow on the road as we headed south of the town. We went down to the harbor where an old launch was tied against the wharf. It was painted white with blue on the deck. The name Lulubelle was in black on the side.

"Oh," I said. "Lulubelle."

"What do you mean by 'oh Lulubelle'?" said Benny.

"I thought it might be called Canary."

He gave me a hard look then wheezed with laughter. "You've got some lip, boy!"

I didn't know what he meant and I had a scratchy feeling that I'd said the wrong thing. I wanted to tell him what a nice boat it was and how glad I was to go fishing, but he had already walked away to help Uncle Leo with boxes of food and drinks and fishing lines.

Jeannie was the one in the family who had motion sickness. She was already pale. "I hope the sea isn't bouncy," she said. "I'd better have a bucket just in case."

"No sweat!" said Royce. "You just lean over the side and do the old heave-ho!"

Jeannie's eyes widened and she put her hand on her stomach. "I might fall overboard."

"Nah. We'll hold onto your ankles," said Royce.

I helped Jeannie down to the boat. "Don't take any notice of him. The sea's as calm as anything. You'll be fine."

Royce grinned wickedly. "But wait till we get out in the waves." He put his finger down his throat and pretended to puke.

"Jumping jelly beans, Royce!" cried Miranda. "Will you leave her alone? Come on, Jeannie. We'll sit over here in the fresh air."

The rest of us went into the cabin to look at the engine. Benny had the hatch up to check the oil. As far as I could see, the oil was not just in the engine but over it as well. Down in the bilge there was a wash of black water with a rainbow of oil on it. It smelled like a dirty drain, but Uncle Leo and Benny the Canary thought the engine was okay so that was the main thing. Benny pushed an old rag back into the oil hole, lowered the hatch, and turned the key. A shrill whistle and the old machinery under our feet roared, rattled, and chugged, shooing the seagulls from the wharf.

I was very worried about Alexander. I wished he were with us. As the launch moved out of the harbor, I asked Auntie

Rosie if we could sail past the cottage. She knew what I was thinking.

She smiled in her kindest way and said, "Dadda's great with dogs. If I was a golden retriever, he and I would get on just fine."

"But what if he goes to town for—you know?"

Auntie Rosie leaned back and her smile grew wider. "He can't. He hasn't got any money. His wallet's sitting on the hot water tank." She winked at me. "Drying out, you understand."

I thought she meant that she hid her father-in-law's money but I was not sure, so I didn't say anything. I went outside and sat with Miranda and Jeannie, watching the white trail of foam behind the boat.

We were going to fish for cod. Benny the Canary said only four people could fish at any one time because lines would get tangled under the boat. We wrote our names on bits of paper, put them in Auntie Rosie's sun hat and drew four out. I was in the first lot. Far out, brussel sprout! Benny gave me a green fishing line with a bit of nylon line at the end, a sinker, and two long hooks already baited with squid.

We were south of the harbor, not far from the shore. The sun was almost clear of the horizon, yellow rays poking through bits of cloud to warm the air. The sea looked flat but with the boat not going, we had turned sideways to the waves and my sinker rolled back and forth on the deck. I looked at Jeannie who held her line over the side, ready to let it drop. Her cheeks were still pink which meant she was okay.

"Down they go!" yelled Benny. "Remember! You can't keep fish smaller than your bait boards."

Jeannie and I unravelled the string lines the way Uncle Leo showed us. Let the sinker and hooks drop into the water, he said, and leave the stick with the line around it, on the deck. As we pulled out the line, the stick bounced around and the fat bundle on it got smaller. This water was deep! I'd only fished once before. That was off a wharf in two yards of sea, and all I caught were baby spotties. Jeannie and I kept putting our lines over until I thought I was going to run out before I got down to the fish. Then I felt some slack. The sinker was on the bottom.

At once, there was a huge jerk on the line. I yelled, "I got a bite. It's big! Man, it's big!" I look down to the bow where Royce was fishing with Uncle Leo. "A huge bite!"

"Mine's biting, too!" yelled Jeannie.

I pull the string a little and felt the vibrations run up it like electricity. "They're still biting!"

"That means the fish is on your hook," Uncle Leo yelled back.

Benny the Canary told us to pull our lines up on the deck. "Just leave it in loops. Next time you put it down, it'll run dead easy."

Hand over hand, I hauled in the green string. Oh! I could feel it bouncing! "It's something enormous!" I yelled at Jeannie.

"Me too!" Jeannie said.

Then I saw it. Below the surface swam a big dark fish with bulgy eyes. It was trying to get away but the nylon line was in its mouth. I hauled it into the boat and it wriggled as Benny took it off the hook and threw it in a plastic bin. "You've still got your bait," he said. "Over you go."

As I put my line back over the side, Jeannie brought her fish on board. It was another big cod, flapping and jumping.

Benny took it off the hook.

Jeannie put her hands up to her face. "Poor fish!" she cried.

The fish fell into the bin and slapped the sides with its tail. "Good one," said Benny. "Nice and fat."

Jeannie looked as though she was going to cry. "It's too beautiful to murder."

"Murder?" Benny stared at her. "You mean you want to let it go?"

Jeannie nodded.

"She likes animals," I explained.

Benny bent over, grabbed the fish, and threw it overboard. For a second it lay just beneath the surface, then it doubled up, flicked its tail, and dove straight down.

Benny shrugged. "They're all beautiful," he said, "and they're all food."

Jeannie nodded again and stepped backwards.

"You want to give your line to someone else?"

"I—I think so." Jeannie turned and called her twin brother. "Johnny?"

She didn't need to say his name twice. Johnny had her line in three seconds and was throwing it over the side, steadying himself as a wave lifted the boat.

My line jumped in my hand before it hit the bottom. "I've got another one!" At once, I started hauling it back up. Wow! I wished someone had a camera so I could show Mom and Dad how big these fish were. I looked up the bow to see what Royce was doing. He was leaning over the rail.

No, he wasn't fishing. Poor Royce! He was busy being sick.

# 5·

Royce caught one fish and then had to go and lie down on the bunk in the cabin, the plastic bucket beside him. His skin was a pale green color under his freckles, his eyes were closed, and he moaned when I talked to him.

"I caught seven and they were huge! Fantasmo!"

He said something that was half mumble and half something rude and leaned over the bucket. I looked the other way.

Benny the Canary offered to teach us how to fillet cod. I left that to Miranda and Johnny. I liked the outsides of fish. I also liked the insides when they were clean white meat. It was the in-between process that put me off. I didn't want to join Royce in the cabin, so I volunteered to put the rinsed fillets in plastic bags. When we finished, Benny the Canary and Uncle Leo hosed down the boat while I helped Auntie Rosie set out the lunch—salad, sandwiches, chocolate cake, plums, and bottles of lemonade. I was quite glad we were not having fish.

The boat was rocking gently from side to side, but Jeannie wasn't sick. She'd been reading. She grabbed a peanut butter sandwich and went back to her book. Royce though, he couldn't get off the bunk. I'd never seen him so pale. I wished I could do something for him, but his temper was as foul as his stomach and we all had to leave him to it.

Over lunch, Benny the Canary talked about his days as a fishing inspector. "A runabout came in with more than a hundred undersized crayfish." He took a bite of chocolate cake. "Those guys weren't pleased to see me, I can tell you. Lost their boat. Hefty fine. Nice cake, Rosie."

"Have you always been a fishing inspector?" Miranda asked.

"Nope. Before that I had a commercial license. Flat fish. Netting for flounder, sole. And before that I was a boat builder."

I asked him, "Why do they call you Benny the Canary?"

"Who calls me that?" he barked.

There was a big silence and I couldn't do anything except shrug.

Benny poked me in the chest with a thick black-nailed finger. "What happened to the nice manners?"

"I'm sorry," I mumbled although I didn't know what I was supposed to be sorry for.

Uncle Leo slapped Benny on the shoulder. "He used to sing."

So that was it. I didn't know why it should be such a big secret. Lots of people sang and were very proud of it.

Benny laughed and pretended to punch Uncle Leo. "Yeah. That's right. I sang for a crust."

"More cake anyone?" said Auntie Rosie. "If you've finished, I'll clean up. We'd better be getting back to Grandadda and the puppy. Wonderful day, it's been. Perfect weather. How many bags of fish do you think?"

When the boat moved further out to sea, we thought Benny was hunting for another fishing spot, but he was not looking at the fish finder. He leaned forward over the wheel, his head turning from side to side, then he picked up his binoculars. "It's your lucky day," he told us.

"Why?" said Jeannie.

"Look! See, over there?" He pointed.

"I can't see anything," said Miranda.

I could see it. There was something in the water like a flat rock—only it wasn't a rock. It was dark, shining where the sun hit it. I lifted my arm and pointed in the same direction as Benny. My hand shook, my voice squeaked. "A whale!"

"Smart kid!" said Benny. "Big sperm whale. Outside, everyone. Get your cameras ready."

As we approached the whale, the boat slowed. Benny didn't want to go too close. He said the whale was resting on the surface, filling up with air for a deep dive.

We held onto the rails and for once the wild Wests were silent. The whale was longer than the boat, and its back was ridged, shining dark in the water. There were crusty things on its skin. Barnacles, said Benny. We could see its blowhole and hear its great huffing breathing. I could even smell its breath—strong and fishy like squid bait.

Uncle Leo turned, put his head in the cabin door and called, "Royce, you have to see this!"

But Royce didn't come out. Minutes passed. I wondered if the whale was staying on the surface because it was curious about us, but Benny said they always rest for a long time. He pointed as the whale's back began to arch. "Watch it! It's going to dive. Here comes the tail!"

The flat black surface curved into a dark hill, sliding into the sea. Behind it a huge tail rose, water streaming off its edges as fine as aircraft wings. For a moment the tail stood straight up, then it too went down, and all that was left was a large patch of sea so flat that it looked like oil.

# 6.

When we arrived back at the wharf it was nearly three o'clock. Royce looked better but he said that even on dry land he could feel the sea moving beneath him.

"I was sorry you missed the whale," I told him.

"I couldn't move!" he said. "Man, that was rough!"

"It wasn't really. Just a little swell."

Royce frowned. "You told me it was your first fishing trip. How come you're such an expert?"

"I was not—" I tried to explain. "I'm sorry, I just pointed out—"

"Don't!" he snarled. "And how many times do I have to tell you? Stop saying you're sorry!"

"Oh. I'm sorry. I mean—I—"

Royce put his hand on the back of my neck and gave me a little push. "You're okay, Mickey. You're odd but you're really okay. You got some choice fish."

I turned to see if he meant it. He did. That was Royce all over. Grumpy one second, happy the next. He looked at the bin half full of white fillets in plastic bags. "Imagine if we could sell that. Say, twenty pounds at eighteen dollars a pound—" He got the blissful expression that came when he was counting money and I knew that he was over his seasickness.

Before we climbed on the truck, Uncle Leo told Benny the Canary that we needed to stop at a liquor store.

"No!" said Auntie Rosie. "Leo? You can't do that! He's diabetic!"

"I promised," said Uncle Leo.

There was going to be another argument and I didn't want to hear it. I got in the back of the truck with Miranda, Royce, Jeannie, Johnny, and Honey and we played played Rock, Paper, Scissors until they sorted it out. I guessed Uncle Leo was the winner because we went back a different way, through the town. There was a huge amount of traffic for such a little town—tourist buses, cars, pedestrians with backpacks. Miranda said that people came here to see whales and dolphins. I was pleased that we'd had our own special whale, just for us.

Benny the Canary parked outside a liquor store and he and Uncle Leo got out. I heard Uncle Leo say to Auntie Rosie. "Just a small bottle! He'll be fine."

We waited in the back of the truck and Miranda put a sack over the fish bin to protect the fillets from the hot afternoon sun. In the nearby parking lot there was a crowd standing around a street performer. We heard the applause and then a clacketty-clack rhythm.

"Someone's got a drum," I said to Royce.

He shook his head. "Not a drum. Spoons."

"Spoons?"

"Yeah. Spoons!"

The West children all looked at each other and Jeannie was giggling, the neck of her T-shirt pulled up over her mouth. Of course! Spoon music! I remembered seeing some-one with big tablespoons, back to back, rattling them over his knee.

"Trouble, trouble, trouble!" said Royce, rubbing his hands together.

A man's voice came over the rattling noise. It sounded hoarse and very loud.

"It's a long way to Tipperary. It's a long way to go. It's a long way to Tipperary, to the sweetest girl I know…"

Auntie Rosie heard it too. The next moment she was out of the truck and across the road to the parking lot, her arms working like pistons. "That terrible man!" she yelled.

We jumped down and followed.

I felt a big lump of ice inside me. If Grandadda West was here in town, where was Alexander?

The crowd was about four people deep and we had to push to get through.

Grandadda West was in the middle of the parking lot and my dog was with him, his leash tied to a post by a trash can. The old man's face was red, shining with heat. He was singing, playing the spoons against his good leg, and tapping the plastic leg to keep time. In front of him upside down on the ground was his cap full of money.

"Grandadda!" yelled Auntie Rosie.

He didn't hear. He wagged his head at the smiling audience and gave an extra rattle of the spoons. "It's a long, long way to Tipperary but my heart's right there."

"You're impossible!" bellowed Auntie Rosie, coming closer.

He stopped singing. Spoons in one hand, he grabbed Auntie Rosie with the other and gave her a smacking big kiss. "Me old Tipperary sweetheart!" he shouted at the audience.

The people laughed and cheered and Auntie Rosie pulled away, looking more embarrassed than angry.

"Ah now, you thought I meant that, didn't you?" Grandadda said to the crowd.

Auntie Rosie started to laugh. She couldn't help it. She tucked her arm through his and said, "What are we going to do with you?"

He smiled close to her face. "I hitchhiked," he said. "Got a ride in a milk truck."

Auntie Rosie waved his breath away. "It's not milk you've been drinking, you wicked man. You'll end up in the hospital again. You know that?"

The crowd realized that the show was over. As they drifted away, I untied Alexander, picked him up and held him close. He licked my face. His tail whipped against my arm.

Royce knelt beside the old cap to count the money that'd been thrown into it. He looked at me with glowing eyes. "Hey cousin! We should go busking."

# 7.

Auntie Rosie got over being annoyed with Grandadda West. She made him a cup of tea, gave him some shortbread, and added his busking money to the wallet she brought out of its hiding place.

"I knew you hid me wallet," he said.

Auntie Rosie looked sideways at him. "It was drying out."

"Pig in your eye!" he said. "You hid it."

"Drying!" she said, and then began to shake with laughter.

"Hid, hid, hid!" he said grinning.

Uncle Leo was stowing away the stuff from the boat. He took two bags of fish for the evening meal, put the other packages into the sack, tied the top of the sack with string and wedged it on a fridge shelf to keep chilled.

"Before we go tomorrow, we'll put the fillets in the cooler," he said. "Mickey, you can take some home. Show them you're a real fisherman."

I went down the beach with my five cousins and Alexander and we played beach volleyball on the sand until it was almost dark. The sea was far out and calm, curling over at the edge with a little hiss. The sky was the color of faded jeans and the hills were black with shadow. It was time to stack driftwood for the bonfire.

The adults came down from the house, all except Grandadda West who was fast asleep in an armchair. Benny the Canary wheeled down a wheelbarrow loaded with drinks and food. Uncle Leo had a tray of fish wrapped in tin foil. Auntie Rosie carried three deck chairs which she set on the sand. "This is the life," she said, for the tenth time.

While Uncle Leo lit the fire, Royce and I sat on the old upturned dinghy and talked about everything except the fishing trip. He was back on the subject of making liquid fertilizer from the kelp on the beach.

"Seaweed's valuable stuff," he said. "You can even make health foods out of it. Good for people. Good for plants. Have you got any space in your bag?"

I looked to see if he was joking. He wasn't. "No!" Then I asked, "What's the point?"

"Experiments," he said. "If I can find a way of making liquid fertilizer, Dad can bring the van down with a trailer."

"It's not my bag, it's my mother's. What'll she say if it goes back smelling of seaweed?"

Royce sighed. "People like your mother get in the way of progress."

Uncle Leo put more wood on the fire. Auntie Rosie passed around ginger ale and a tray of salami, pretzels, chips, and cheese.

"Let's have a concert," said Johnny.

"Great!" said Miranda. "Everyone can do something—song, story, jokes, dance."

Uncle Leo set the foil wrapped potatoes at the edge of the hot ash. "Let me see," he said. "I can recite two hundred pages of politicians' speeches."

Auntie Rosie threw some salami at him.

Royce nudged me. "Mickey'll tell a ghost story."

"I'll do the prince's dance from *Swan Lake*," offered Johnny.

"You can count me out," said Benny the Canary, squashing a beer can.

"Why don't you sing?" I asked him.

It happened again—that funny silence. Benny stared at me, then said to Uncle Leo, "Is this kid for real?"

Uncle Leo laughed so much he sprayed his drink. "He's for real."

My face was hot. I felt Royce's elbow in my side and I shifted away from him on the upturned dinghy. He came after me, and while the others went on talking, he said, "He thinks you're giving him a hard time."

"What?"

"It's not that kind of singing." Royce puts his mouth close to my ear. "Telling tales. Singing to the cops. It's *that* kind of singing. He was a fishing inspector."

"Yeah? Well, why didn't you tell me what it meant?"

"You're supposed to know."

"I didn't know!"

Royce drew back and slowly shook his head at me. Then he got his quick sassy smile. "But you're great at telling ghost stories," he said.

"This is the life, isn't it?" said Auntie Rosie, licking tomato sauce off her fingers.

The stars were out and they seemed to move like blinking eyes above the smoke. We sat in a circle and everyone looked the way I felt, stomachs full, faces half asleep in the orange glow. Uncle Leo did a good job. The potatoes were a bit hard but the fish was extra good and so was the coleslaw and the rest of the chocolate cake. Then Honey was in Royce's lap, her thumb in her mouth, and Alexander lay across my knees, his nose on his paws. I thought he was asleep but when I touched him, his tail wagged.

Jeannie told some neat riddles. What do you call two banana skins in a doorway? A pair of slippers. Who didn't invent the airplane? The Wrong brothers.

Royce started a joke about a man who fell down a sewer but Auntie Rosie, who had heard it before, stopped him and said only clean jokes were allowed.

"If you fell down a sewer, would you be clean?" protested Royce.

Miranda whistled like a thrush, a robin, and a finch. I wished I could whistle like that. I also wanted to dance like Johnny who leapt and spun at the edge of the firelight, perfect steps without music.

My own act wasn't bad, though. I told them a story about a haunted ship that drifted into harbors on foggy nights, and the dripping ghosts that came ashore to glide through the town. "When people looked out their windows, they saw a band of green phantom sailors singing funeral songs."

"One of them playing the spoons," said Auntie Rosie and everyone laughed.

Then Benny jumped up and spread his arms. "Dammit, boy," he said to me. "You want Benny to sing? Benny's going to sing!"

I looked down at Alexander and didn't say anything.

He thumped his chest with both hands, then, grabbing his beard, he yanked his mouth open and began.

*"In the land of Taranaki, when the river froze,*
*a man went out hunting with a speargun up his nose.*
*He accidentally sneezed a sneeze and cut off all his toes.*
*In the land of Taranaki, when the river froze.*
*In a house in Wellington, on a purple mat,*
*a skinny cat got married to a fat little rat.*
*The next day the rat was gone and the cat was fat.*
*In a house in Wellington, on a purple mat."*

Benny sat down. "Your turn," he said to Uncle Leo.

Uncle Leo stood, scratched his head for ages, then sang in his growly voice,

*"On a boat called Lulubelle on the deep blue sea,*
*a gang of kids went fishing with Benny, Rosie and me—"*

He stopped, scratched his head some more, and said, "I can't think of another line."

"I can!" said Royce. "When I began to vomit, the fishes jumped with glee."

"Yuck, Royce!" said Miranda. "What about this? We all had delicious cod for tea."

"Grandadda played the spoons on his knee," suggested Johnny.

The fire had burned down to a heap of orange embers and the night was around us as close as the walls of a house. Wish, wish, wish, whispered the sea. I hadn't had a shower. I hadn't even combed my hair. I dug my toes into the cool sand and wished I could stay forever.

"What about you, boy?" Benny the Canary was pointing at me. "Can you sing?"

I opened my mouth and the words and tune came out all by themselves:

*"The day finished up like a happy memory,*
*on a boat called Lulubelle on the deep blue sea."*

# 8.

The next morning everyone was humming or singing, and Grandadda West was happy, stamping his plastic foot and calling Auntie Rosie his little shamrock. It was a bit cold for swimming. Royce and I took Honey down to the beach to splash at the edge of the surf while the others tidied the house and packed.

"A weekend is far too short," I complained.

"Yeah." Royce ran his toe over scattered bits of charcoal, all that was left of our fire. "But look on the bright side. Benny said we can come down for a whole week in January. Imagine it! We'll bring down the trailer and heap it up with kelp."

I didn't care a peanut about Royce's stupid old kelp. I wanted to know about me. Was I included in the invitation? I waited and when he didn't say, I asked.

Royce looked surprised. "Of course you're included. Benny thinks you're ace. He calls you that funny boy."

"I'm sorry. I didn't mean to be funny."

"He doesn't know that." Royce grinned. "Not many call him the canary to his face."

I shook my head. "No one told me. No one explained. I'm sorry. It was very embarrassing."

Honey laughed and held her hands out to me. "Sorry," she said. "Sorry. Sorry."

Royce groaned. "Now look what you've done! Taught my little sister a new word!"

Uncle Leo was true to his promise to Auntie Rosie. The bottle of whiskey he bought was quite small. It fitted perfectly into his father's jacket pocket and on the way home on the train, Grandadda West snuck it out. We all saw it, but Auntie Rosie was in such a good mood she pretended not to notice. That old tweed jacket had two bulgy pockets. On the other side was a bag of peppermints and a pack of cards. When he wasn't singing or talking about the operation on his foot, Grandadda was stomping around the carriage giving people candy and showing them card tricks. "Did I tell you I won ten thousand dollars with that trick? I didn't? Well, if I did now, you shouldn't believe a word of it."

I sat with Miranda who tried to teach me bird whistles. I got the finch call nearly right. On this return train trip, I wasn't worried about Alexander. I knew he'd be safe in the guard's van along with the luggage and the cooler with the sack of fish. I breathed in deep. I could still smell bonfire smoke on my shirt and my hair was stiff with sea salt. For two days, a whole weekend, I hadn't had a bath or shower. There was sand between my toes and I'd caught not one but seven enormous fish. My life had changed. I was becoming a West.

I'd change back on Tuesday when my parents arrived home. Their plane came in at three in the afternoon, in time for a giant cod dinner. Please, I would ask, could I go fishing again in January?

Alexander loved being back at the Wests' house. He ran around with Goof and they got into trouble when they splashed through Miranda's lily pond, snapping at the goldfish.

Grandadda West had a nap while we helped Auntie Rosie and Uncle Leo unpack. Clothes in the laundry. Food in the kitchen. "Most important, the fish," said Uncle Leo, dragging the sack out of the cooler. "Straight into the freezer."

"It won't fit," said Auntie Rosie as she put the breakfast cereals on the shelf. "Undo it and pack away the separate plastic bags."

Uncle Leo cut the string on the sack, opened it and stopped. "What the blazes?"

Auntie Rosie looked up from the sink. Miranda, who was holding the freezer door open, said, "What's wrong?"

"Royce?" yelled Uncle Leo. "Royce, come here at once!"

He tipped the sack out on the kitchen floor.

It was full of kelp.

It wasn't such a disaster after all, and a phone call put it right. It seemed that Royce filled a sack with kelp and placed it with the luggage. Auntie Rosie, thinking it was the sack of fish, put the kelp in the cooler to keep cool. The sack of cod was still in the cottage fridge. Benny the Canary said he would freeze the fish solid that night and send it by special delivery the next day.

Royce gathered up his experimental kelp and took it to his room. He held up a piece of the dry brown seaweed. "Fishing is greatly overrated," he said, "but this stuff is pure gold."

"Fishing is not overrated," I told him.

"It is for me," he said.

"Oh. Yes, of course. I forgot you were sick. Sorry."

He put his face close to mine. "I told you to stop apologizing all the time!"

"Yeah, yeah. Sorry."

"Mickey?" he bellowed

"Sorry, sorry, sorry!" I yelled back. Then I laughed to show him I was teasing.

He grinned. "Smarty-pants," he said. "Benny's right about you."

I supposed that was a compliment. I ran my fingers through my salt-stiff hair. Royce could be a real pain at times, but if he was my brother instead of my cousin, I wouldn't complain too much.

# The
# Wild West Gang
# *Hullabaloo*

## 1.

"Michael? Michael?"

I recognized that tone. When Mom turned my name into a scream, it meant there was puppy poo or piddle on the kitchen floor. I left the computer and rushed out to rescue him before she started calling him a nasty little animal. Poor Alexander! He was only six months old. I bet I wasn't potty trained when I was his age.

"My-kill? My-kill?"

But it wasn't Alexander. He was outside cutting teeth on a dog bone, and the kitchen floor was clean. Well, nearly clean. There were a few—

It was my turn to yell. "Mom! What have you done?"

Two fat purple earthworms were tying themselves in knots, trying to burrow through Mom's kitchen tiles. Further over, between the counter and the stove, there was an upside-down cookie tin by a pile of dirt and more worms waving their tails in the air.

"My cake tin!" Mom cried.

"My worms!" I knelt on the floor and carefully scooped worms and dirt back into the tin. "Worms are very sensitive, Mom. You could have killed them."

Mom folded her arms. "That's enough, young man. You are beginning to sound like your cousins."

"I'm sorry. I didn't mean to yell." One worm was a bit squashed on its head or tail, I wasn't sure which. I put it in a small hollow of dirt. Maybe it would recover. "I apologize."

"I should think so," said Mom. "My sister may not be able to teach her children manners, but I'll not have you speaking that way. Wash your hands. Those things carry disease."

"They're earthworms, Mom. Clean little creatures."

"They live in dirt!"

"I'm going to start a worm farm."

"Worm farm?" Mom looked at me as though I was from another planet.

I tried to explain. "A farm for cultivating worms. I didn't know that was your good cake tin. It's only temporary. Until I build a proper box." I reached across Mom's feet to pick up the two big worms. They tickled the palm of my hand. "I'll clean up the floor."

"A farm for worms!" Mom shook her head. "The latest wild West scheme."

"No. It's for a school project. Mr. Fromish said we have to do something creative this term. Royce is learning the drums. Miranda's making a movie. I'm making a worm farm." I put the tin back on the counter and looked for a cloth to wipe up the rest of the dirt.

Mom's face changed. She said my teacher has poor dress sense, but she really liked him and her voice became very polite at parent teacher meetings. She put her hand on my arm. "Michael, dear. Worms are not creative."

"Yes, they are. They breed and they're good for gardens. That's creative."

"Darling, it's you who are supposed to be creative. Music, painting, sculpture—" Mom's voice faded and she stared at me. "Surely you can find something."

"Yes, Mom," I said meaning, no, Mom. I didn't tell her that the worm farm was Mr. Fromish's suggestion because I couldn't think of a creative project.

"Those—er—thingies—" She waved her hand at the tin, "—will be much happier in garden. Take them outside, Michael. Now!"

I didn't know how to build a worm farm, anyway. I picked up the tin and carried it to the door, then I looked back, "Do you really think worms aren't creative?"

She looked happy. "Yes, dear, I do."

"Okay. I'll do something else for the project." I gave her my biggest, melt-mother smile. "Can I go and see the Wests this afternoon?"

Her happy look flickered but she had to say yes. "Take the puppy with you and be home before dark, and Michael?"

"Yes?"

"Don't say okay. It's vulgar."

# 2.

"I've got a cool idea for you!" said my cousin Royce. "Finance!"

I thought he was being sarcastic but he meant it. He rattled his drumsticks across two cardboard boxes and the large empty milk powder can at the foot of his bed. "Making money is creative."

I sat on the bed and watched him rattle on the cardboard, top, sides, making different sounds to a fast beat. The West kids were all musical. They could also draw and paint. It wasn't fair. I could tell spooky stories, but that was not Mr. Fromish's idea of a creative project.

"Your father's an accountant," said Royce. "You've got it in your genes."

"No, I haven't."

Royce flicked the drumsticks, whirled them into the air and caught them.

"Yes, you have. I'll help you."

"No thanks." I got off the bed and walked to the window. My puppy was on the lawn playing with their big old dog Goof. Alexander would go home with fleas and I'd have to wash him. I turned to Royce and made my voice severe. "I've had enough of your scams."

He looked hurt. "That's a lousy thing to say after all I've done for you."

"I'm sorry, but you've ripped me off too many times."

"Me? Rip you off?" He jumped up, his face glowing red. "I never did! I gave you fantastic business opportunities, that's what! Just because you're so thick you don't know your butt from your elbow—" He stopped and turned to the door which was ajar and showing a camera lens. His mouth closed, he gave a silly smile and waved.

Miranda waved back over the top of her camera. "Go on fighting," she called. "That's wonderful footage."

I didn't say anything. Royce smiled and waggled his fingers. "My sister Miranda picks her nose," he said pleasantly.

The video camera clicked off and Miranda came into the bedroom, shaking her fluffy red hair and laughing. "I can edit that out." She steadied the camera at eye level. "Please, go on. Please! I need a red-hot argument."

"Don't trust her," Royce warned me.

"Please, Michael?" Her camera turned to me. It was one of those big old-fashioned things that made the arm ache. "Pu-leeese!" she begged over the top of it.

When Miranda looked at me like that, I got a funny feeling and couldn't breathe properly. I'd do anything for Miranda, except make a fool of myself, so I kept my mouth shut.

"We weren't fighting," said Royce. "We were discussing Mickey's creative project which will be bookkeeping and investment."

Miranda switched the camera back to her brother. "What kind of investment?"

"A set of drums," said Royce.

"I knew it'd be a rip-off," I hissed, hoping my voice wouldn't reach the microphone.

Royce didn't look at me. "I need a set of drums for my project. I'll work for them. Mickey won't put in any money. He'll be my accountant, do the books while I raise the funds. That'll be his project. He's a logical choice because he's got a computer and his dad's a number cruncher."

"Accountant," I told the camera.

"Mickey's the obvious man for the job." Royce tossed a smile my way. "It'll be a project partnership. The drums for me, the paper work for my talented cousin." He spread his hands ta-rah for the camera. "Accountancy is creative."

Miranda swung around to me and I heard the camera whirring a waiting noise. I scratched my head and said to

Royce, "You're sure I don't have to put in any money?"

"Not a bent cent," he said.

"Cross your heart and hope to die?"

"Double-cross," he said.

"It's a deal." As I smiled for Miranda, I felt relief. Doing accounts for Royce sure beat worm farming, and it was a project that would please my parents and Mr. Fromish. I went on smiling until the camera clicked off, and wondered why, under the good feeling, there was a little red light flashing danger, danger.

# 3.

Arguments were common in the West house. I wanted to know why Miranda didn't film Auntie Rosie and Uncle Leo having a fight about who put tea leaves down the kitchen sink. Miranda said she'd already shot three fights between her parents and she needed new footage. She swiveled her camera towards the twins who were throwing darts at the back of the old kitchen sofa, then she filmed Honey, the baby of the family, who was in her high chair, having lunch. Honey had bare feet—six perfect toes on each foot. That was proof, Auntie Rosie always said, that she was an angel. All angels had six toes, she said. Honey didn't look too angelic today. She was rubbing peanut butter into her hair.

Miranda lowered her camera. "Sweaty spaghetti! I've run out of film."

I watched her open the back and take out the cartridge. "How many do you need?"

"I've used two. This'll be the third. It's a big project."

"A ten minute movie?"

"To get ten minutes I have to shoot—oh, at least twelve hours. Then I edit to shape the story."

"What story?" I asked.

"I don't know yet."

"I thought it was going to be about a day in the life of your family."

"It is." She put in a new film cartridge. "But it has to have a story line. Holy macaroni! This should be good!" She was talking about her mother who was lying on her back under the kitchen sink with a wrench in her hand.

No one would have guessed that Rose West was my mom's sister. For one thing, Auntie Rosie was twice as big, and she wore bright clothes from the Salvation Army shop. Today it was red shorts with white flowers on them and a yellow T-shirt that wobbled as she tried to undo the blocked pipe.

Uncle Leo knew that Miranda was filming. He tiptoed towards Auntie Rosie, knelt beside her and tickled her under the arms. She squealed and yelled sizzling words that even her children don't say. Would Miranda leave them in the movie? I wondered how our teacher would react when he heard them.

Auntie Rosie slid out and I was sure she'd hit Uncle Leo with the wrench, but all she did was kiss him and call him more of those names.

Honey put the rest of the peanut butter into her pocket. Jeannie and Johnny went on using the sofa as a dart board. Auntie Rosie and Uncle Leo sat on the floor like two fat Russian dolls, hugging and laughing.

Mom was right about the Wests. They could be weird.

Royce came down the stairs, ready for his first fundraising

venture. He wouldn't tell me what it was but said it was important I go with him. As we closed the back door on the noise,
I told him, "Miranda's movie will be very—er—interesting."

"Nah," said Royce. "She's just doing the family."

"That's what I mean."

"Our family?" Royce stared at me. "Boring, Mickey. Dead
boring."

I closed my mouth. If he thought his family was boring, what did he say about mine? Mom? Dad? My tidy room
smelling of plug-in Spring Blossom air freshener?

"What?" said Royce.

"What what?"

"You were shrugging your shoulders."

"Oh," I took Alexander's leash out of my pocket. "Sorry.
Just an itchy back."

Royce didn't want me to take my puppy. He said we'd end
up having to carry him, which was true, but I didn't want to
leave Alexander behind. The Wests spoiled him. They cud-
dled him so much that he'd forget he was my dog, and, even
worse, they'd feed him all sorts of junk that'd make him sick
on Mom's floor. I snapped the leash to his collar. "How far
are we going?"

"Around the corner to Bederman's store." Royce slowed to
match the waddling pace of my puppy. "I'll get you a frozen
chocolate bar."

I shook my head. "Not allowed. Mom said ice cream is
loaded with sugar."

"I'm not buying it for your mother," said Royce. "Man, it's
a hot day. My treat."

I imagined the ice cream coated with chocolate and caramel and my mouth went all juicy. "What's the catch?"

"Catch?" He screwed up his face until his eyes disappeared. "You are so suspicious. You know that? I'm just celebrating my new business manager."

"Accountant," I reminded him.

"Business manager sounds more creative," he said. "Pick up that dog, will you? We'll never get there."

Alexander liked being carried. He went into spasms of licking—my mouth, my nose, my chin—and his fat bottom wiggled as he tried to wag his tail. It was safer to carry him. There was a lot of traffic on the road. On the other side, some little kids played with jump ropes on the pavement. Watching them was a guy about our age in a denim jacket, hat, sunglasses, and a cardboard box on his shoulder.

Royce walked faster and whistled but when we got close to Bederman's store, he stopped and took some money out of his pocket. "I'll hold the dog. You buy them."

I tried to keep a grip on Alexander but he liked Royce a lot and he struggled to get into his arms. He even tried to bite the five dollar bills. "Take it!" Royce pushed the money in my face. "You're the business manager. Get us two chocolate bars."

There had to be a catch. With Royce there always is. "Why don't you get them?"

Royce massaged the floppy skin on Alexander's back. "Mr. Bederman likes you. He plays golf with your father."

"So?"

"He doesn't play golf with my father."

Then I remembered. Last Christmas Royce was supposed to deliver advertising leaflets for Mr. Bederman, one for every mailbox in this part of town. He delivered half and dumped the rest at the recycling center because he reckoned

Mr. Bederman didn't pay him enough.

I took the money. "All right."

"And ask for a box of chocolates that's expiring," Royce said quickly.

"What?"

"Chocolates don't go bad when they're old," he said. "They just get a funny color. He can't sell them."

"I knew it!" I tried to give him back the money but he pulled away, cuddling Alexander with both hands. "Another scam!" I yelled.

"No!" He shook his head. "Definitely not! Mickey, look. I'm going to run a raffle at school."

"That's not legal."

"It's legal for kids. Come on. Just tell the truth. Say you need the chocolates for a school project. He won't refuse his friend's son. Michael! Flipping heck! Bederman can't sell old stock. He'll be more than happy to give away his old out-of-date chewies."

"I'm not doing it!"

"You have to. You agreed to be my business manager!"

I pushed the money at him. "Take your moldy old bribe and give me back my dog!"

Royce opened his mouth and closed it. He looked over my shoulder and got a big stupid grin. "My sister Miranda picks her nose," he said in a loud voice.

I turned around. Behind us was the guy with the sunglasses, long coat and knitted hat, a cardboard box on his shoulder. But there was a strand of fluffy red hair hanging from the hat and the cardboard box had flaps open on a camera lens.

"Don't worry," said Miranda. "I'll edit that out."

# 4.

The chocolate part was easy. Mr. Bederman gave me a huge box. It was the raffle that was hard work. Royce sold a few tickets at school but because I was the business manager, I had to get rid of the rest—one hundred and ninety-two tickets at fifty cents each. The kids at school didn't want them.

"It's a fake raffle," said Jordan Piper examining Royce's penciled ticket. "How do we know you got any chocolates?"

"You can ask Mr. Bederman," I told him.

Jordan sniffed and shoved the ticket back at me. "You probably ate them already."

"I did not. I can't. Mom said sugar's bad for me."

"Yeah, yeah, we know!" Alice Mitchell grabbed the bundle of tickets and tossed them into the air. "Free raffle, everyone."

It was just as well Mr. Fromish was nearby. He strolled over, eating his lunchtime donut. "Having trouble?" he asked me.

Jordan, Alice, and the other kids slid back and I knelt on the concrete to pick up the tickets. "No, Mr. Fromish."

"A worm farm might have been easier," he said and a fine mist of icing sugar sprayed down on me.

I nodded, thinking he was probably right.

He watched me pick up every ticket, then he offered to buy one. "Fifty cents, you say?"

"Yes, Mr. Fromish. Thank you. I hope you win."

He put two sugary coins in my hand and took a ticket. "What are your rates?"

"Huh?"

"A business manager charges for his time," he said,

tucking the ticket in his shirt pocket.

Charges? I hadn't thought about that. "How much?" I asked.

My teacher wiped his mouth with the back of his hand—icing sugar off, smile on. "Be creative, Michael." He turned to walk away, stopped and said, "Oh, hullo, Miranda. Video coming on nicely, eh?"

I looked beyond him to Miranda lounging against the classroom wall, the camera on her shoulder. How long had she been there?

I asked Dad for a few hints on being a successful business manager. He shook his head over the tickets and told me if I was going to run a raffle I'd have to do it properly. Then he sat back, touched the tips of his fingers together and said, "Ah. Now. The terms of your employment. What have you discussed with Royce?"

"Nothing. He thinks he's doing me a big favor."

Dad nodded and smiled. "What would be fair?"

"I—I don't know."

"You can charge by the hour or on a commission basis—ten percent of everything you raise."

"Ten percent!" I sat up straight. "Royce'll go ape!"

"Go what?" Dad adjusted his glasses as though that would help him hear better.

"Sorry. I mean, he'll get upset."

Dad smiled. "Tell Royce you welcome him to the real world."

I designed neat raffle tickets on the computer, printed them and sold them along the streets near home. Mostly, I chose people we knew. One lady from church bought twenty tickets. Another bought one for each of her grandchildren.

In two days, I sold all but five tickets and Royce was as pleased as a dog with two tails. He counted the money on the table in his bedroom.

"Wicked, man! Now we're going to organize a ghost walk."

"I'm charging you commission," I told him.

"Yeah, sure. Now, listen. This is a choice idea. We get a group of kids from school and we take them for a walk after dark. The old parts of town. You know, spooky houses, boarded-up shops. We pretend they're haunted. You make up the stories. I'll be the ghost."

"Commission, Royce. Ten percent. Dad said that's fair. Are you listening?"

"Sure, I'm listening. It's okay." Royce grabbed me by the collar. "Remember those spooky stories you told us?"

"Yeah. Sort of."

"You're awesome at ghost stories." Royce put his arm over my shoulder. "Thirty kids at five dollars each."

Before I could reply, Miranda whirled into the room, turned and positioned her camera. "Parents won't allow children out after dark," she said, her video humming. "Not with you two."

"Hey! Even better," said Royce. "Parents come too. Say, twenty parents and thirty kids—that's two hundred and fifty bucks. Enough for a second hand drum set!"

"You hope," said the voice behind the camera.

Although I liked Miranda a lot, it got up my nose the way she kept following us everywhere. I waved my hand at her. "Buzz off!"

She laughed and said, "Royce's sister Miranda picks her nose but I'll edit that out," and she went off to film Jeannie cleaning out her mouse cages.

"It'll be brilliant!" Royce slapped me so hard on the shoulder that I choked on my own spit. "Parents pay, control the kids, and you scare the sheep out of them all."

Actually, he didn't say sheep, and I'm glad Miranda was no longer filming. I pulled away. "Sorry, Royce. I don't think—"

"You don't have to think, business manager. Just be your genius self. We'll start at school with a haunted classroom, go through town and end up at our place for Mom's lemonade and ginger snaps. All that for only five bucks. It'll be a blast."

"Have you asked your mother?"

"Nope. That's your job." Royce rubbed his hands together. "You can design the fliers tonight. What'll we call it? Ghost Walk?"

In spite of my usual caution, I was interested in the idea. "What about 'The Haunting Hullabaloo'?" I suggested.

Royce was pleased. I could tell by the way he fell back on the bed and kicked his feet in the air. "Cousin, you are seriously brilliant!" he bellowed.

# 5.

An amazing thing happened. Mr. Fromish won the raffle with his crummy ticket. He looked so pleased when Royce gave him the box, you'd have thought it contained a million dollars. "Belgian chocolates! The very best!" he said, making sucking noises, and I wondered if he should talk to my mother about his sugar addiction. Right there, in the almost empty playground, he tore off the wrapping paper. Oh, oh! He was going to open it in front of us. He'd see old chocolates, faded and half-squashed. But the lid came off a tray of perfect chocolate-covered nuts and cherries, caramels, and squares of fudge, glistening chocolates so fresh they filled the air with fragrance. I turned quickly to Royce and saw from his smile that he wasn't surprised. He knew all along that Mr. Bederman wouldn't give me out-of-date chocolates.

I was really wild with him.

Mr. Fromish offered the box to Royce. He took a piece of fudge. When the box came my way, I shook my head even though my tongue was frantic. "I don't eat much sugar," I said.

"I'll have his!" cried Royce and his hand dove back into the box.

As we went out the school gate, I snapped, "You're a user!"

He knew what I was talking about but he pretended he didn't. "Who put a bee in your boxers?" he said.

I shut my mouth tight. In fact, I didn't talk to him all the way to his house. When we got to the back door, I let rip and I didn't care that Miranda was filming every word. I wanted the world to know that Royce West used me and my father's friendship with Mr. Bederman to chisel the storekeeper out of an expensive box of Belgian chocolates.

Auntie Rosie was washing the dishes in a plastic basin because the sink was still blocked with grease and tea leaves. "We can't take out the trap to clear it, Mickey, so everything gets washed in this basin—me, the kids, dog, floor, dishes—in that order."

She caught my look and laughed. "Just kidding. We wash the floor with the hose."

I opened the cupboard door and saw the wrench under the sink. "Can I unscrew the pipe for you?"

She turned, sniffing right and left. "What's that? Do I

smell grease?" Then she winked. "I know when a kid's trying to butter me up."

My face went hot. "I—I just thought—I—to help—"

"No, you can't, Mickey boy, because my pudding-headed husband glued the pipes to stop a leak. They won't budge. And stop sweating. I'll do the lemonade and ginger snaps on your ghost night."

I smiled with relief. "Royce told you!"

"Nope. Miranda did. Dry these dishes, there's a good little toad."

"Oh." I picked up the tea towel. "Miranda."

"Yes indeed!" Auntie Rosie snorted. "I can't cut my toe-nails without that camera aimed over my shoulder. This house has never had much privacy, but now! Saints alive, we might as well be on the TV news."

I nodded in sympathy. So it definitely wasn't just Royce and me. Miranda was filming everybody.

I was late home again which put Mom into one of her moods. I wouldn't have minded if she just told me off but she always got a long face and made out that I went to the Wests just to hurt her.

"I'm Royce's business manager," I reminded her.

"You know what I think of that," she said.

"It's my project. I thought you'd be pleased."

Mom carefully untied her apron and hung it on the back of the pantry door. "Sit down, please, Michael."

I flopped into a kitchen chair. Here we go, I thought, episode number two thousand and fifty three of *Bringing Up Michael*.

"Straight spine, please, dear. You're not the hunchback of Notre Dame and you are not one of my sister's children. I know Rose is very good-hearted, but—" Mom pulled out a chair next to mine and sat with her legs crossed at the ankles. She was wearing high-heeled shoes with gold straps which meant she'd been to town. "We both had a good upbringing, Rose and I. She should know better. The downhill slide began when she married that Leo West—"

"But Mom, you used to date Uncle Leo."

Mom's mouth stayed open. She forgot I knew that. A little shiver ran over her jaw. "I had the sense not to marry him," she said firmly, "but that's not the point. How they bring up their children is their concern. You will be different."

"Don't worry," I said. "I am different."

"Not that I have noticed," she replied. She held her hands out to me. "Michael, dear, it is important to your father and me that your conduct is always gentlemanly."

"I know, Mom."

"I worry about you." She felt in her sleeve for her hand-kerchief. "I don't want to be a nagging mother, but those wild West children—"

I wanted to remind her that she was happy for me to stay at the Wests when she and Dad wanted a weekend of golf, but that would make things worse. I went to her and gave her a hug. "It's okay, Mom. Sorry. I mean, all right. I talked to Dad about it. He's helped me heaps—a lot."

My face was resting on her head. Her hair was stiff with spray-on stuff. She'd been to the beauty salon. "I'm glad of that, Michael." She put her handkerchief to the corner of her eye. "You don't confide in me these days."

"Mom!" I gave her an extra hug and the spiky hair got up my nose. "I didn't think you were interested." I sat down again. "We did a raffle. A box of chocolates. Mr. Fromish won them."

"So the project is over?"

"No. Not yet. That's just the beginning." I hesitated, wondering how I could put it without telling a lie. "You know how you wanted me to do something creative?"

Immediately, she looked interested.

"We're organizing a conducted walk of the old part of town and I'm telling stories."

Mom clasped her hands. "A history tour! Oh Michael, that's wonderful. I might join you."

"Er—no!" I took a deep breath. "It'll be mostly kids—ah—children. Very noisy, Mom. You'd hate it. The walk finishes at the West's house for supper."

"Oh." Mom's interest went flat.

"Your hair's nice," I told her.

She tucked her handkerchief back up her sleeve, and then ran her hand lightly over her hair. "It's not too short, is it?"

"No. It looks great."

"Can you see the gray?"

"Gray what?"

"My hairdresser tells me my hair's going gray," she said. "At my age!"

I made binoculars of my hands and look through them. "I can't see any gray hairs. You look about eighteen."

She smiled then, a real smile. "You're a good boy, Michael. Go and play with Alexander."

# 6.

I was planning ghost stories when Royce came to our back door. I made him take off his shoes on the porch. We went to my room and I put an extra chair in front of the computer. Alexander followed us and fell asleep on my feet, his ears flopping over his face.

Royce, quiet since yesterday, wanted to know if I was still mad at him.

I wasn't but I didn't want to tell him that. "You knew Mr. Bederman wouldn't give me old chocolates. You had it all worked out."

"Sure, I did." said Royce. "What would've happened to us if we'd raffled off a dud box?".

"Mr. Fromish wouldn't have cared."

"We didn't know old Fromish would win, did we? Suppose it'd been Alice Mitchell and her gang of thugs? They'd have ripped us up for toilet paper."

I didn't say anything. Alexander was warm on my toes. I could feel his soft puppy stomach going in and out with his breathing.

"Mickey, don't give me a hard time," said Royce. "It's bad enough with Dad in a lousy mood."

"Uncle Leo?"

"He took the dart board out of the kitchen because we were getting holes in the wall. So Jeannie and Johnny drew a dart board on the back of the couch. He moaned last night, moaned this morning. Holes in the couch! You'd think the twins had burned the house down."

I rubbed my toe up and down the puppy's stomach. "I

can't imagine your father getting grouchy."

"He's a real pain and it's not even about darts. It's because he glued up the drainpipe and the plumber can't come till next week."

I was surprised about Uncle Leo, but I knew what Royce meant. Mom was like that. When one thing went wrong she started complaining.

Royce folded his arms. "The last thing I need right now is a grumpy business manager."

I thought for a moment and then decided that the chocolate business was over. "Okay."

"Friends?" said Royce.

"Friends," I replied.

We drew a map of the Haunting Hullabaloo from the school to the West's house. It was simple: the haunted classroom, then a path along the river with the ghost of a drowned man, three houses, the second hand store, a haunted burger bar, library, more houses, the old movie theater. It was a half hour walk stretched to more than an hour with stories before we finished at the West's house.

"How will your mother—er—wash all those dishes?" I asked.

"Paper cups, paper plates," said Royce. "Have you got your stories worked out?"

"Most of them."

"What are they?"

"Secret!" I breathed in deep and smiled. I was now full of stories and I felt strong with their power. Royce was right about me being a ghost story genius. I was so good at inventing spooky tales that sometimes I even scared myself. Mom didn't know how amazingly creative I could be. If she heard my sagas of eyeballs and dripping blood, her hair would go completely gray.

"Don't be stupid! I've got to know," said Royce. "I'm doing the sound effects. I'll dress in black, see, moaning and shrieking, rattling chains. Tell me!"

I shook my head. "Sorry. For this walk, I need to invent at least—oh—about fifteen ghosts. Don't worry. I'm your business manager. You'll know as soon as I've invented them all. Okay?" I grabbed the computer mouse. "Let's look at this flier."

*The Haunting Hullabaloo*
Saturday, April 30, 7:00 PM
beginning at River Road School
*Dare to be scared as you uncover*
*the ghostly secrets of your town.*
*This haunted walk will give you*
*chills and thrills. It will make*
*your hair stand on end.*
A delicious supper is included.
Price $5.00 per person.
*Kids bring your parents.*

"Cool!" said Royce.

"Do you want me to change it?"

"No, man! That's ace!" Royce's eyes shone like blue marbles. "Print out five hundred copies."

"Ten cents a copy."

Royce blinked. "Okay. Fifty copies. We'll stick them up on the lampposts all over town."

"Is that legal?"

He got his shifty grin, as he punched me on the arm. "It's legal for kids."

# 7.

Dad once said that living at the Wests was like being in a storm at sea. I knew what he meant. It was not a storm exactly, but not calm, either. Mostly it was waves. Sometimes up, sometimes down. The last week at the Wests had been a real dumper with the plumbing problems and then the broken video camera.

Miranda had dropped it. It wasn't her fault. I'd have dropped it too, that camera was so heavy. But Miranda felt awful about it. She slumped over her desk. "It's not insured and Mom said it's too old to fix. They don't make the parts anymore."

For about ten seconds I was pleased, but seeing Miranda's eyes shining with tears really hurt me. I felt that I was going to cry too, which was very embarrassing. I put my hand out to touch her shoulder, then changed my mind. Her hair was shining, red and curly and smelling of lemons. I could see her shoulder blades like wings under her shirt.

"It'll be all right," I told her.

"No. My project's finished. I'll have to think of something else."

"Haven't you shot enough film?"

She wiped her eyes, her nose, and looked at me. "Nowhere near enough. Then there's all the editing. It slipped, Michael. Fell on the step, bounced off, landed on the path in four pieces."

"It was an antique camera."

"It was still good." She wiped her eyes again. "Dad's trying to be nice about it."

"I know what you can do! You can hire a camera! John's Camera Arcade has video cameras—" I lost the words when I saw her hopeless expression. I kept forgetting that Royce was the only West who had money in the bank, and it would be easier for Miranda to fly to the moon than get a loan from her brother. "You'll think of something," I told her.

She picked up a ball point pen and clicked it several times. "I'm happy about your project," she said in a wet voice. "The ghost walk's a cool idea."

I dared to tease her. "Too bad you won't be able to film it."

She didn't smile. "I couldn't anyway. Not enough light." Then slowly, awfully, the tears rolled down her cheeks. She put her hands over her face.

My eyes got prickly. I had to go. "You'll be all right," I said. "Don't worry."

After dinner, I went out to the garden where Dad was planting leeks. He had made grooves in the earth and was putting plants as thin as grass stalks in lines. His feet in old shoes were set wide apart, his body was bent, his head down. As I talked, he said, "Yes, son. Mmm. Yes. That's good, Michael. Yes. Yes."

I asked him, "Can Miranda borrow our video camera?"

"What?" At once he straightened up.

I asked again. "Please, can Miranda borrow—"

"You mean my video camera?"

"Yes."

"My new Sony?"

"Yes."

"Miranda West?"

I nodded.

Dad half-smiled and rolled a leek plant between his

thumb and forefinger. "Michael, are you crazy?"

"So she can finish her project." Then I told Dad the whole story, the big old camera, how heavy it was, how it couldn't be repaired. While I talked, I remembered Miranda at her desk, her hands over eyes, and my voice began to shake.

"Excuse me a minute." Dad waved the leek plant like a miniature flag. "Michael, do I assume from this that you have promised her the use of my new video camera?"

Of course, I hadn't, but I sensed a thin, wild hope and I said, "If it gets damaged, I'll pay. I'll buy you a new one."

"With what, may I ask?"

"My savings."

Dad threw the leek plant over his shoulder and adjusted his glasses with both hands. "You are referring to your college savings?"

I didn't answer.

He looked at me for a moment. "Why on earth would you promise Miranda West the use of my new camera without consulting me?"

I couldn't tell him the truth and half turned to look at Alexander who was scratching in the dirt between the rows of tomatoes.

"Well?" said Dad.

"You and Mom—" I glanced at him and away again. "You tell me I should always be gentlemanly."

Dad let out a long gust of breath. "Get that dog," he said, "before it digs a hole clear through to China."

Miranda hugged me! In front of the whole class, in front of Mr. Fromish, she hugged me and said I was wonderful.

"Ooo-ooo!" the kids called and someone whistled.

My ears got so hot, I knew they were glowing like traffic

lights, and I couldn't stop grinning as I walked back to my desk. I looked at Jordan Piper who always hung around Miranda like a wasp around jam, and my lips got an extra curl.

Mr. Fromish took off one of his shoes and banged it on the desk for silence. "Cut the cackle!" he said. "This is a very noble gesture from Michael's father. Now Miranda will be able to finish her project. What about the rest of you? Mmm? All bursting with creativity?"

The yelling turned to a groaning. As I sat down, Royce leaned across. "Thanks for nothing, friend."

"What?"

He threw a pencil at me. "You ever tried living with a camera up your nose?"

Bang, bang, bang! went Mr. Fromish's brown suede lace-up. "Silence! Do you have something to say to us, West?"

Royce dropped back in his seat and shook his head.

Mr. Fromish frowned. "Well, I have something to say. There has been a complaint from the council about a large number of posters pasted up around town. I have given my word that the offending fliers will be taken down," he looked hard at Royce, "after next Saturday evening."

A wild cheering broke out around the room with some of the wise guys doing moans and clutching at their throats. Fromish banged his shoe again but the noise went on.

Jordan Piper stood up and bellowed in his foghorn voice, "Ain't got nobody to call my own. That's the trouble with being a ghost."

More whistles. More cheers. More groans.

The Haunting Hullabaloo had caused more interest than Royce or I ever imagined and we were not sure how we were going to control it.

343

# 8.

Sick of the stuck drainpipe, Uncle Leo tackled the problem with a hacksaw. He cut the pipe off below the basin and put a bucket underneath to catch the water. The dart board came out of the garage and went back on the kitchen wall.

"All problems solved?" I asked Royce.

He shrugged. "Nope. Mom forgot to empty the bucket so we got a flood in the kitchen, and the kids stuck their darts in the wall like before. Thing is, Dad doesn't care. He's got rid of the glued pipe."

"I don't understand."

"Neither do I," said Royce. "It's one of those parent things."

I nodded in understanding. "Mom's depressed because she's got some gray hair at the back of her head."

"So what?" said Royce. "She's old."

"Thirty-five. She thinks that's young. She's really, really upset."

Royce bent over to scratch Alexander's stomach. The puppy's tail wagged like electric string. "But it's not a glued drainpipe."

"What do you mean?"

"Dad couldn't fix the pipe. Your mother can dye her hair."

"Not likely. She said hair dye is vulgar and it makes people bald."

Royce groaned in the way he usually describes my mother. "Know what I think? Kids should give their parents report cards like at school. For Dad I'd write—is not good at problem solving. Mom is easy. Plays well with others but lacks organizational skills. What about yours?"

I thought for a moment. "Neat and tidy but worries about detail."

"Mother or father?" said Royce.

"Both," I replied.

Royce picked up the puppy and tried to hold him against his shirt, but Alexander wriggled free and jumped onto my knee, eager to lick my face. Why did dogs always go for people's faces?

Royce said, "My sister thinks your father is the kindest guy next to Mr. S. Claus. I tell you, we're in deep sheep, man! Little camera! Big trouble! We can't see her coming. Weapon fits in her hand. What made your Dad do such a stupid thing?"

I put Alexander on the floor and gave him a squeaky rubber ball to play with. "This is supposed to be a business meeting. How did you get on at the old movie theater?"

My mother had been telling her friends that I was doing a school project on local history. I couldn't believe she was saying that. I went back to Royce's idea of a parent's report card and added for Mom—has a vivid imagination.

Perhaps that was where I had inherited mine.

I worked out all the stories while Royce borrowed Miranda's skeleton costume and a tape of Halloween noises. I lent him the boom box I had when I was little. It was red and yellow plastic but it was small and could throw out plenty of noise. We figured a recording would be more scary than Royce's voice and rattled tin cans.

Mom was in her lounge chair on the front deck, talking on her cell phone. Puffs of words came in through my window. "Historical tour—no, for children, my dear—it's to teach children—all by himself—some school project—my uncle was a history teacher at a university, a professor, I believe."

I didn't feel good about this. Surely she had seen our advertising on every lamppost in town. Hadn't she worked it out yet? One part of me wanted to put my head out the window and yell, Mom that's wrong! The other part said, don't upset her while she's depressed.

One thing was certain. The Haunting Hullabaloo was getting a lot of attention. We'd sold forty-seven tickets and people were still asking. Our teacher was coming on the walk. But Royce and I were not sure of his motives. Mr. Fromish asked heaps of questions. He stopped me in the corridor. "How are you going to tell these stories?"

I didn't know what he meant.

"Your voice, Michael." He wagged his finger at me. "Your soft, understated voice."

"Oh. I'll talk really loud, Mr. Fromish."

"Loud enough to be heard by a chattering mob? I don't think so. You need a megaphone."

Royce chipped in. "We haven't got one of those. Please, Mr. Fromish, could we use the school's?"

I lifted my foot to kick Royce but Mr. Fromish scratched his head. He'd recently had a buzz cut and it sounded like sandpaper. "I'll see what I can do," he said.

# 9.

Because it was nearly a full moon, we were hoping for a clear sky. We didn't get it. There were clouds down to the top of the old water tower, but at least it wasn't raining. Auntie Rosie gave me a black cloak to wear. I really needed a top hat to go with it but I had to settle for one of Dad's golf hats. Why was it that golf players always wore baseball caps?

We discovered that we couldn't start the Hullabaloo in the school grounds. Not permitted, said Fromish. The school gates were locked and people had to gather on the pavement by the bus stop, about as far from the haunted classroom as we could get. The only close building was the gardener's shed tucked under the trees. I had to change my story. What could I say about a shed full of rakes and spades? But I had the megaphone. Loud hailer, Royce called it, and it sure was loud. It looked like a sawn off trumpet and it sent out a blast that made me sound like a giant. Cool! I loved it! And Fromish was right. I couldn't have made myself heard without it.

People were still coming and the noise was massive. There were lots of parents and that was good because they'd watch out for their children. But I didn't think little pre-schoolers should be there. Bernie Chan's mother had a stroller with his sister who wasn't walking yet. What if she got terrified and had bad dreams?

Royce told me I worried too much. Okay for him. He wasn't there. I had to do the school part solo while he waited in the trees by the river with the noises for the drowned man.

Stop worrying, I reminded myself. You've got two minutes to think of a story for a garden shed.

An old van pulled in at the curb. Out came Uncle Leo with Jeannie, Johnny, and Miranda. No Auntie Rosie. She and Honey would be home with the lemonade and ginger snaps. Uncle Leo bounced across the pavement to talk to a man he knew, and Miranda gave me a wave. She was standing directly under a street light and her smile was so cool.

Garden shed, Michael, I told myself. Garden shed! Concentrate on the garden shed!

Mr. Fromish walked over and took the megaphone from me, switched it on. "Ladies and gentlemen, boys and girls. As you probably know, this ghost walk is part of a project organized by two students of River Street Intermediate School."

I didn't know Fromish was going to talk. I had my introduction all worked out but he was doing it, telling them to turn on their flashlights, keep together, small children hold their parent's hands, blah, blah.

I made out a mental report card for Mr. Fromish—good teacher, helpful, but a control freak with a sugar addiction.

"Now," said Mr. Fromish, "without further ado, I shall put you in the capable hands of Michael, our tour leader. Let the stories begin!"

My mouth went as dry as dust. My fingers closed around the megaphone and I lifted it up, but I didn't know what to say. I was muddled. Where would I start?

Everyone was quiet, waiting. Somewhere, a little kid said, "Mommy?" and a mother went, "Shh!" Light moved in bands across coats and legs, shoes, pavement.

"Good evening." My voice blasted out such a yell that some kids jumped. I licked my lips and tried a low shivery sound. "Good evening, victims. Welcome to the horrible, terrible, frightening, scary Haunting Hullabaloo!"

A couple of kids squealed and I heard Johnny West laugh in a shaky voice.

I continued. "Be prepared for the worst experience of your entire life beginning with—the haunted garden shed!" As I stretched my arm toward the shed, the story came, all of it jumping into my head with a rush. "This ordinary shed has an extraordinary history. Long ago there was a gardener who was really a mad wizard in disguise. When the kids misbehaved, he turned them into earthworms. One day he went too far. He got annoyed with a teacher." I tried not to look at Mr. Fromish. "What he did to that teacher was really terrible! First, he turned him to wood. Then he used his legs and arms as posts to grow beans. He used his gu—his intestines to tie up the beans."

"Wooden intestines?" said Mr. Fromish.

I definitely didn't look at him. "But the mad wizard couldn't do anything with the teacher's head so he just put it in one of those flower pot things. Every night about now—" I made my voice slow and creepy, "—the teacher's head comes out of the flower pot and bounces around the school looking for its body. If you listen you can sometimes hear it rolling its eyes and calling, 'Where am I? Oh, where am I?'"

Mr. Fromish was laughing. He said in a loud voice, "I can hear my eyes rolling!"

Some people laughed. Others clapped. It seemed everyone liked the story. Uncle Leo called out, "Bravo! More! More!"

I smiled my secret smile. "Come this way, victims. Let's go to the path by the river for another horrifying tale."

There was only one light on the river path. I stood under it, surrounded by flying insects, and everyone gathered around me. They squeezed in close and I thought, good, they're scared. I looked for some sign of Royce but it was impossible to see past the circle of light and the flickering flashlight beams. The trees were solidly black and so was most of the river. He could have been anywhere. I lifted the megaphone and made my voice deep and slow, "Ghost of the river, do you hear me?"

Everyone listened.

I was ready to call again when the air filled with high-pitched laughter. We all jumped with surprise. It was supposed to be a long moan but the tape had started too soon. It didn't matter. The laughter told me that Royce was in the forestes right behind me. Good old Royce.

I began. "Once there was a bank robber who robbed a bank."

"You don't say," said someone, trying to be smart.

I went on. "He filled his pockets with gold bars and ran away but the police chased him. He couldn't run fast. The gold was heavy. He got to the bridge and he jumped over. Down he went, down to the bottom. He could have swum if he got rid of the heavy gold but he was greedy. So he drowned."

"Oo-oo-oo-oo-oo-ooh!"

This time, Royce had got the ghostly moan on the tape. It worked really well. People squealed. They hugged each other. Someone dropped a flashlight and Mrs. Chan's baby laughed.

"Even today, the bank robber's ghost comes out of the river, crying and moaning—"

I waited for the tape but the noise that came was the long creak of a squeaking door.

"—his bones rusty from years in the mud."

"Where's the gold?" yelled the smart voice. It sounded like Alice Mitchell.

"Aw, shut up!" someone else said.

"And that's the story of the ghost of the river. On we go, on, to the house with the ghost in the mirror."

While everyone was clapping, I got nudged in the back, and Royce's voice, smelling of hamburger and onions, hissed, "I told you that you were a genius."

# 10.

We went from River Road to the old houses at the top of Main Street, a different ghost for each. Sometimes I had to change a story to fit the tape, like when a wolf howl came up for the phantom nurse in the Pringle house. The stories got longer and wilder. I heard gasps and little screams when I talked about the wobbly knife sticking out of the head of the old pirate. At the burger bar, the stampede of ghostly cows went so well with the taped thunderstorm that everyone started looking over their shoulders.

Royce was doing a great job. I walked the crowd slowly to each location while he ran ahead. He didn't let himself be seen. We decided to save that for the last.

The rain held off and the night was perfect, mist coming down as low as the street light. But something unexpected happened. The crowd doubled. People who didn't have tickets had added on. By the time we got to the old movie theater, there must have been at least a hundred following me. I didn't know what to do about that.

The movie theater would be our best trick. It closed a year ago but the manager Mr. Pomare was going to open the doors for us. He'd even turn on the lights. When we told him what we wanted to do, he laughed and rubbed his hands together. "Boys, we're going to make this a real *Phantom of the Opera*."

The pavement outside the theater was wide, which was just as well for so many people. I lifted the megaphone. "Gather around, my victims. Closer, closer. We come to the place where all nightmares begin. Why did the old theater close? Was it because of the new cinema in the mall? No, not at all. It closed because of ghastly ghostly murders that happen right here behind these doors." I waved my hand at the double doors and there was a magical click. They opened wide enough to show a thin strip of red light. Blood color! Great!

"A famous Hollywood actor made a movie nobody liked. People hissed and booed. They threw rotten tomatoes at the screen. The Hollywood actor vowed revenge. He hanged himself in a secret room in this theater. When his body was all shrivelled up to a skeleton, he started his ghastly haunting." I turned again to the doors and with exact timing, they swung wide open.

The foyer was the way it used to be. The builders' tools and ladders had gone. The red carpet was clean, the ticket window shining but empty. The dim light put the red and gold walls into shadow and the big curving staircase was so dark I couldn't see the top. As I raised the megaphone, the music started. Wow! This was Mr. Pomare's idea, thundering organ music like they have in horror movies.

I waited until it died down a bit, then I stepped into the foyer. "Come in, oh my victims!"

They didn't come in. Some had their necks forward like chickens, to see into the foyer, others were giggling. It was not only the young kids that were nervous.

Uncle Leo and Mr. Fromish pushed through and stood beside me. Uncle Leo looked up the dark staircase and bellowed, "A perfect night for a murder!"

That got people moving. They laughed and swarmed through the doors, filling all the spaces by the ticket window, the empty refreshment stand, the foot of the staircase. There was a babble of noise. They were talking about the old days and the movies they saw there. The scary atmosphere dissolved in chatter and I felt panic, as I wondered how I'd get their attention. But Mr. Pomare in the projection room did it for me. The red lights faded around us. So did the noise. The glow was so faint that we could hardly see each other's faces. People looked up to see what had happened to the lights. And suddenly, taped laughter rolled down the stairs. It was the same crazy laughter we'd heard at the river but I don't think anyone remembered that. Everyone jumped. Someone screamed.

I went on with the story. "The murders always happen at night. During the movies the skeleton ghost comes down from the ceiling. It carefully chooses its victims and gets behind their seats. Then its bony fingers go around an unsuspecting neck. Listen!"

Half a gurgling scream echoed through the foyer. The tape had started late. Still, half a scream was better than none.

The music started again. This time it was throbbing like a slow heartbeat, sha-boom, sha-boom, sha-boom. It was going to happen. Any second Royce would come down the stairs. The light had almost gone. We were in a red-tinted darkness. People fidgeted and turned on their flashlightes.

"Ai-ee-ee-ee-ee!"

The shriek was above our heads and it was not the tape. It was Royce. He wasn't on the stairs. He was coming down from the ceiling! In that light, I couldn't see his body, just the fluorescent skeleton painted on his suit. It looked the real thing! A mad grinning skeleton coming down to the crowd!

The music was loud, but the yells and screams were louder as everyone rushed out the door and onto the pavement.

Then all the lights went on. The foyer was as bright as

day and above us, on wire ropes and a harness, was Royce in his painted costume, clasping his hands above his head in victory.

"My-kill?"

I nearly dropped the megaphone. I knew that voice.

"My-kill? That's enough!"

I looked through the crowd, trying to see her, but there were too many people, and now everyone was laughing and clapping, so I couldn't hear her, either.

As Royce's feet touched the carpet, Mr. Pomare came out of the projection room and there was a new burst of applause, with some kids whistling and the more daring ones, booing and hissing at Royce.

There was a ripple in the crowd. Mom came through dressed in her black coat with the fur collar and a little black hat. Her white face and bright red lipstick made her look a bit like a vampire. "Oh, Michael!" she said.

"How—how long have you—"

"Since the bank robber ghost," she said.

I looked towards Mr. Fromish's big fat smile. He'd told her. Trust old Fromish to spill the beans.

But Mom wasn't mad with me. She put her hand on her chest and laughed. "You were so convincing, you almost gave me a heart attack. Who said you weren't creative?"

I couldn't believe my ears. If there weren't so many people around, I'd have hugged her. On the mental report card I made a note, my mother is nice but she can be tricky and full of surprises.

# 11.

Mr. Fromish solved the crowd problem by grabbing the megaphone and explaining that this was a ticketed walk. He borrowed my cap and asked the extra people to give a donation. A few walked away but most put in money, some more than five dollars. I got the cap back full to overflowing and we all walked to the Wests' house where Auntie Rosie had party lights on the front lawn. There were tables set with lemonade and ginger snaps shaped like ghosts, enough for everyone. My mother had helped with the baking, said Auntie Rosie. My mother had also lent the Wests our party lights.

I looked at Mom and her sister pouring lemonade. Their heads were together and they were laughing as though they'd never disagreed about anything in their entire lives. Parents are impossible to understand. Royce was much easier. Success fizzed in his head. He jumped up and down, yahooing, because now he had enough money for a drum set.

"Less my ten percent commission," I told him.

He laughed. "Dream on!"

I sprayed ginger snap crumbs at him. "You have to! You promised!"

He stopped laughing and his eyes got that shifty look. "I thought you were joking."

"You did not! Miranda was there. She filmed it." I called "Miranda? Miranda, come here!"

"Okay, okay." He looked sulky. "Tell you what. You can have the extra money from the hat."

"Is that a deal?" I said.

"Deal," he replied and spat on his hand.

I spat on mine and we slapped hands midair to sign and seal the contract. But I didn't tell him the cap collection would be far more than ten percent.

He bought the drum set next morning and my last job as business manager was to peel all those fliers off the lampposts around town. I didn't mind doing it. I was rich. I went home, finished the accounts on the computer, printed them out and put them in a folder to hand in for my project.

The final result of Royce's project was an audio tape of his drumming which, quite frankly, wasn't the best I'd heard.

Mr. Fromish told us, in front of the entire class, that it was a pity we didn't make the Haunting Hullabaloo a joint project since it was by far the most creative entertainment he had experienced in a long time.

"Alas," he said, "some elementary accounting and some equally elementary percussion do not measure up."

The best class project was Miranda's video called "The Project." No, it wasn't about a day in the life of her family. No blocked sink. No fights between her parents. It was exactly as Royce had warned, about him and me and our project, and she had edited out all the boring bits. She had our arguments, me selling raffle tickets and picking up bits of paper from the concrete, Mr. Fromish, the chocolates, more arguments, more planning, all of that very fast.

Then it slowed down for the main story of the Haunting Hullabaloo. I'd forgotten that Dad's new camera could take night pictures. Miranda had filmed the entire walk, my voice booming over frightened or laughing faces, creepy shadows, dimly lit houses. We saw a grinning skeleton descending from the roof of the old movie theater and screaming kids rushing out the doors. Then the lights were on and I was receiving a hat full of money. The end.

Like Royce, I was furious. Miranda had used all our hard work for her own project, and I'd helped her by persuading Dad to lend her his camera.

"Masterly!" Mr. Fromish held up Miranda's video. "Truly professional work."

Yeah. Masterly rip-off. Professional theft. I wasn't sure that I liked Miranda any more. I glared at her as she walked back to her seat but all she did was give me her jazzy smile.

Royce leaned across and tugged at my sleeve. "She didn't make any money, though."

That was a point. Royce had his drum set and I'd just bought a new kennel with a sheepskin blanket for Alexander. Besides, Miranda was mostly nice and she had hair that smelled like lemons.

Maybe I did like her, after all.